CW00541434

The Mercy Chair

Also by M.W. Craven

Washington Poe series
The Puppet Show
Black Summer
The Curator
Dead Ground
The Botanist
Cut Short (short story collection)

Ben Koenig series
Fearless

Avison Fluke series
Born in a Burial Gown
Body Breaker

The Mercy Chair

M.W. Craven

CONSTABLE

CONSTABLE

First published in Great Britain in 2024 by Constable

Copyright © M.W. Craven, 2024

3 5 7 9 10 8 6 4 2

The moral right of the author has been asserted.

All characters and events in this publication, other than those clearly in the public domain, are fictitious and any resemblance to real persons, living or dead, is purely coincidental.

All rights reserved.
No part of this publication may be reproduced, stored in a retrieval system, or transmitted, in any form, or by any means, without the prior permission in writing of the publisher, nor be otherwise circulated in any form of binding or cover other than that in which it is published and without a similar condition including this condition being imposed on the subsequent purchaser.

A CIP catalogue record for this book is available from the British Library.

ISBN: 978-0-34913-556-4 (hardback)
ISBN: 978-0-34913-557-1 (trade paperback)

Typeset in Adobe Caslon Pro by Initial Typesetting Services, Edinburgh
Printed and bound in Great Britain by Clays Ltd, Elcograf S.p.A.

Papers used by Constable are from well-managed forests
and other responsible sources.

Constable
An imprint of
Little, Brown Book Group
Carmelite House
50 Victoria Embankment
London EC4Y 0DZ

An Hachette UK Company
www.hachette.co.uk

www.littlebrown.co.uk

*To Joanne, who either instigated or supported all
the stupid s**t I've done over the years.*

Three may keep a secret, if two of them are dead.

Benjamin Franklin, 1735

It starts with the robber birds.

Black as gunpowder with grievous eyes. Wild and rattling cackles as they mob what has been unearthed. Puffing out ink-stained wings, squabbling for the choicest offerings. Tearing at flesh with cruel, pickaxe beaks, voracious appetites never sated.

Crows.

Nature's clean-up crew.

Dozens of them.

Enough for a murder . . .

Chapter 1

The hospital was old. A cathedral to the sick, built when eight-year-olds crawled up chimneys and a queen's empire was the largest the world had ever known. They called it a lunatic asylum then, now they said psychiatric hospital.

Meet the new boss, same as the old boss.

The man staring out of a high-arched, curtainless window wasn't thinking about the UK's mental health crisis though, he was thinking about the hospital's colour scheme. He was wondering if the paint on the corridor he was standing in had been chosen for its therapeutic qualities. He suspected not. It was institutional green, the type of colour not found anywhere in nature, and still smelled fresh and acrid. He thought it made the hospital seem more like a prison than a place of healing. Perhaps that was the point.

The corridor was empty and echoed as if it were a church. The chemical stink of wall-socket air fresheners soaked the still air; the linoleum floor was buffed to a shine. A fob-controlled navy double door blocked off one entrance, a steel security door the other. The corridor had three rooms and the man was waiting to be called into the middle one. None of the doors had handles.

There were no seats in this corridor, no waiting area with televisions and pot plants and magazines about idyllic lives in the Cotswolds, so the man stood. On the other side of the security door someone screamed and someone else shouted. Before long he could hear accents from all four corners of the country. He didn't turn away from the window. Screaming and shouting and crying and alarms were the hospital's soundtrack, an aria heard all day and all night.

And he knew no one would enter this corridor.

3

Not until it was time.

A crow flew into view. It wheeled overhead and landed on the hospital lawn. Two more joined it. The man watched their strong, scrawny feet scratch at the earth, searching for bugs and beetles and worms. He shuddered in revulsion. He had come to hate crows.

He turned his back on them and glanced at his watch. It was almost time. He removed his phone from his pocket to see if there were any urgent messages. But there was nothing. Not one. Not even a good luck text from his friend. Instead, he saw his face reflected in the black mirror. His eyes were red and gritty and puffed up, as if he'd slept on a plane. The hands holding the phone were heavily calloused, covered in scratches and smelled of the sea. He wondered if they would ever be clean again.

The door to the middle room opened. A shaven-headed man stepped out. He was wearing a royal blue tunic top with black trousers. He had a personal alarm clipped to his belt loop. Pulling the cord or pressing the red button would rush people to his location, like a police officer sending out an urgent assistance request.

A smaller man in a suit joined the shaven-headed man. He had the harried look all doctors seemed to have. 'Doctor Lang is ready to see you now,' he said.

For such a grand building, the room's décor was dreary and flavourless. The walls were cream, not green, but still screamed institution. The carpet tiles were brown and hardwearing; the empty bookcase was cheap with sagging shelves. Thank-you cards and hospital notices were Sellotaped to a red felt noticeboard. Doctor Lang was waiting for the man behind a large desk. A beige file and a box of tissues were the only things in front of her.

She rose to meet him. She was in her early thirties and was wearing a sleeveless, quilted green dress. She wore no makeup, and her long dark hair partly covered her face. The man wondered if she was shy. He then wondered if her shyness had hindered her career. Perhaps not; shy people were often the most empathetic, the easiest to talk to. People opened up to them.

They shook hands and introduced themselves.

'Do sit down,' she said.

'Thank you, Doctor Lang.'

'Please, I'd very much like it if you called me Clara.'

The man was from a generation that stood to shake hands. He wasn't about to call a doctor by their first name. It wouldn't be right. 'I'll do my best,' he said, before sinking into the seat on the opposite side of the desk. It was a heavy armchair and it looked out of place in a doctor's office. Doctor Lang's chair was the same.

'I'm sorry you've had to drag yourself all the way here,' she said. 'I'd have preferred somewhere more suitable, but I have patients to see here today, and it wasn't possible to get away.'

'It was no hardship. It's a nice drive and my boss is happy I'm finally taking the time to do this.'

'Were you waiting long?'

'Twenty minutes, but I was early.'

'And I must apologise for this office,' she said, gesturing around the room. 'It's not mine, I'm just borrowing it for the day. I understand it's about to be decorated, which is why it's almost empty. I see my other patients on the ward but, as you're not a resident here, I thought we might benefit from somewhere less pressurised. It can get a bit lively on the other side of the door.'

'I can imagine,' the man said.

'We'll find somewhere more suitable for our next session. Today is really about getting to know each other.'

'OK.'

Doctor Lang smiled. 'So, like I said, my name's Clara and although I have a PhD, I'm not a medical doctor; I'm a trauma therapist. I'm experienced in CBT, somatic experiencing, sensorimotor psychotherapy, eye-movement desensitisation and reprocessing therapy, sometimes called EMDR, and all the other major disciplines. And, while I don't need you to understand what all that medical gobbledegook means, I *do* need you to understand one thing.'

'What's that?'

'I know what I'm doing.'

She opened the file on the desk. The man could see handwritten and typed notes, held together with plastic-ended treasury tags. He saw photographs of his injuries, particularly his eye socket. He winced at the memory.

'Shall we begin?' Doctor Lang asked.

The man shrugged.

She offered a sympathetic smile. 'As you know, your employer made this referral after some concerning behaviour at work—'

'I made one mistake,' he cut in. '"Concerning behaviour" is a stretch.'

'Nevertheless, they saw fit to pay for three sessions in advance. What does that tell you?'

The man didn't answer. Doctor Lang removed a slim document from the file.

'This is the self-assessment form you completed,' she said. 'I would like to thank you for being so candid. Not everyone is.' She tapped the document with her fingers. Her nails were short and unvarnished. 'This is a good place to start.'

'If I'm doing this, I'm doing it right,' the man said.

'So why don't we dive in at the deep end? I understand you're still having headaches?'

The man touched the thick, lumpy scar tissue around his eye socket. 'I am, although I don't know if that's because of my injury or because I'm not sleeping.'

'Probably a bit of both,' Doctor Lang said. 'But not sleeping will exacerbate the head trauma.' She checked the file. 'It says here you've refused zopiclone.'

'I have.'

'Why is that? It's commonly prescribed for patients with sleeping difficulties.'

The man didn't respond.

'Are you self-medicating? Is that why you refused it?'

'Self-medicating?'

'Excessive alcohol, depressants such as benzodiazepines or bar-biturates. Maybe even heroin. Someone as resourceful as you would have no problem securing something to help him sleep.'

The man smiled. 'I'm not self-medicating, Doctor Lang,' he said.

6

'Then why won't you take zopiclone?'

A knock on the door made the man turn. The shaven-headed man entered the room. He was holding a tray. 'Got tea for you,' he said.

He put two disposable cups and a paper medicine dispenser filled with sugar lumps on the desk. He left the room and shut the door behind him. The man picked up one of the cups and took a sip. He grimaced. The tea was lukewarm. Doctor Lang studied him over the rim of hers. If she'd noticed anything about the tea's temperature, she kept it to herself.

'What happens when you try to sleep?' she asked.

'I lie awake until morning.'

'And yet you still refuse common medications.'

'I do.'

'You don't *want* to go to sleep, do you?' Doctor Lang said.

After a few moments the man shook his head.

'Because when you sleep, you see things you don't like?'

He nodded.

'Nightmares?'

He nodded again.

'What is it you see?'

He didn't answer. He put his hands in his lap and looked at them.

'What is it you see when you close your eyes?' Doctor Lang urged.

The man looked up. His eyes were haunted and wet.

'Crows,' Detective Sergeant Washington Poe whispered. 'When I go to sleep, I see crows.'

Chapter 2

'Crows?' Doctor Lang said. 'You're having nightmares about crows?'

Poe nodded.

'Is this a childhood thing, or something more recent?'

'Recent. Just a few months.'

'You've been through a traumatic experience, Sergeant . . . Look, can I call you Washington? Sergeant Poe is far too formal.'

'Of course.'

'You've been through a traumatic experience, Washington,' she said. 'I've read the case summary and, in my entire career, this is by far the most horrific thing I've read about. People died in front of you. *You* nearly died. Nightmares can be the mind's way of making sense of things and crows have long been associated with loss. In some cultures they are mediator animals between life and death.'

'So I've been told.'

'And some therapists might try to palm you off with a clichéd diagnosis about how the nightmares are your way of coping with what you've been through. They'll tell you that crows are a manifestation of the parts of the case you were unable to control. That your nightmares are little more than an unconscious defence mechanism.'

'If you say so, Doc.'

Doctor Lang smiled. She had a nice smile. It lit up her face. 'But I think you're far too pragmatic to entertain fanciful ideas like Freudian displacement. I don't think you've been redirecting a negative emotion from its original source on to a less threatening recipient.' She put her hand on the file. 'If you've been having nightmares about crows, I think it's likely crows played a significant role in what happened. Literally, not figuratively.'

Poe's spine stiffened as if it had received a blast of electricity.

'And I find this odd, Washington,' she continued.

'You do? Why?'

'Because I've read this file cover to cover and, not only is there no mention of crows, I don't believe you saw anything that might have attracted them. I know crows are attracted to carrion, but by the time you arrived at the Lightning Tree the dead man had been removed. And everything else happened indoors.'

Doctor Lang picked up the file.

'And because the activity log has no gaps, it means if you *did* encounter crows, it must have been before this case started. Am I right?'

Poe said nothing.

'It would have seemed insignificant at the time,' she continued. 'It might not have even registered.'

'Then why do I see them in my dreams?' Poe asked.

'The unconscious mind is a complex beast, Washington. It can make leaps our *conscious* mind doesn't have the bandwidth for. It processes information differently. You can't see it yet, but right now, in your mind, crows are the catalyst for everything that followed.'

'So this is me now, is it?' Poe said. 'Every time I go to sleep, I'm going to wake up terrified and screaming.'

'No, your mind will heal. At the minute the traumatic memory isn't stored properly. It's unprocessed and that means it's easily accessible, easily triggered. We can fix this, but we need to take the first step together.'

'Which is?'

'We need to distinguish between the external threats that demand action and the internal threats that are causing this overwhelming, paralysing fear. In other words, you need to be able to dream of crows without reliving what happened.'

'And how do we do that?'

'Initially, by talking.'

'I'm a man, I'm in my forties and I'm a police officer,' Poe said. 'I don't talk about my feelings.'

'And I don't want you to talk about your feelings. The last thing I want you doing is talking about your feelings. This is about getting to know your history, the kind of difficulties you're experiencing. We'll then target the distressing memories.'

'With what?'

'We'll come to that later, but nothing that will make you uncomfortable.'

Poe wasn't convinced. It must have shown.

'Do you trust me, Washington?'

'You come highly recommended.'

'That's not what I asked.'

'Trust is earned.'

'Spoken like a true police officer. Why don't you let me start earning your trust now?'

'I have to do something,' Poe admitted. 'I can't go on like this.'

'Good man,' Doctor Lang said. She turned to the activity log at the front of the file. 'It says here the case officially began when you were asked to consult on the Lightning Tree murder,' she said. 'But why don't you tell me when it *really* started? Why don't you tell me about the crows?'

Poe looked at his empty cup. He wondered if he could get another tea. His mouth had gone dry. 'It's true that I encountered some crows,' he said. 'But this whole thing began a few hours earlier with another hooligan of the British countryside.'

'Oh?'

'What do you know about badgers, Doctor Lang?'

Chapter 3

Nine months earlier

As a way of getting Poe to stop moping over his lunchtime drink, a well-heeled man holding a posy of flowers marching into the pub and yelling, 'Bloody badgers!' was as good as any. Poe had been about to ask for a second pint of Borrowdale Bitter. Maybe add a Scotch egg to the order. Make it a government-approved substantial meal. Now, he wanted to know what the 'bloody badgers' had been up to.

But the man had slunk to the other end of the Crown Inn's polished mahogany bar. He was now muttering to himself. The landlady, a no-nonsense woman in her mid-forties, winked at Poe before making her way to the man's end of the bar. She planted her elbows on the wood and said, 'You want some water for them flowers, Stephen?'

Instead of answering, Stephen said, 'Bloody badgers' again. Less venomous this time.

'What have you got against badgers?'

'My poor mum. Went to put flowers on her grave. Bastards have only dug her up.'

Poe leaned sideways so he could hear better, all thoughts of Scotch eggs abandoned.

'But she's been dead, what, fifteen years?' the landlady said.

'Seventeen.'

'That's right. I was at her funeral.'

'I remember. Mum liked you.'

'Not as much as she liked a drink though, am I right?'

'She did enjoy the occasional milk stout,' Stephen admitted.

'What's all this nonsense about badgers then?'

Which was when Poe's mobile rang. He frowned. Stephen was about to get to the good bit, and he didn't want to miss anything. He glanced at the screen, readying himself to reject the call.

He stayed his hand.

It was Estelle Doyle.

'You were on your own when this happened?' Doctor Lang asked.

'I was,' Poe replied. 'Why, is it important?'

'Possibly. Why wasn't your partner with you? I thought you lived together?'

'Estelle's my fiancée, actually.'

'She is?'

Poe nodded, a little bit proud, a little bit embarrassed.

'Congratulations are in order then. Is this new? There's nothing in the file.'

'Couple of months now.'

'I'll make a note.' She glanced at the bare desk. 'Darn it, I've forgotten my pen.' She opened the desk drawer and searched inside. 'Would you believe it? A doctor's office without a pen. Could I borrow yours, Washington?'

Poe reached into his pocket. Came out empty. 'I've forgotten mine as well,' he said.

'A police officer without a pen,' Doctor Lang said, her eyes twinkling. 'Isn't that unusual?'

'I'm an unusual police officer.'

She tapped the file. 'Of that I need no convincing. I'll make a note later. Anyway, was it romantic? Where did you propose?'

'I didn't,' Poe said. 'Estelle proposed to me.'

'That's . . . unconventional.'

'You don't know the half of it. She lured me to a post-mortem and when I got there she'd spelled out "Will you marry me?" with finger bones.'

'Finger . . .' Doctor Lang said incredulously. She did some mental calculations. 'But that's forty-three bones.'

'Forty-seven,' Poe said. 'You forgot the question mark. You don't want to know which bone she'd used for the dot.'

'I actually think I do.'

'I've forgotten its name, but it sits at the roof of the nasal cavity.'

'The ethmoid bone,' Doctor Lang said automatically. 'Where on earth did she get it all from?'

'I was too scared to ask.'

'You accepted, obviously?'

'I love her,' Poe said. 'We haven't been together that long, but I think I've loved her for years. I didn't realise on account of her being so terrifying. We toasted it with some beer she'd chilled in one of the mortuary's cadaver fridges.' He paused. Looked at Doctor Lang's incredulous expression. 'Like you said, it was an unconventional proposal.'

'So where was she? Why were you on your own?'

'Estelle was in the States.'

'For work? I understand she's one of the world's foremost forensic pathologists.'

'She is, but she wasn't in America to work. She was there to support Tilly.'

Doctor Lang checked the file. Flicked through to the personal statements Bradshaw, Flynn and a few others had made. The ones he hadn't bothered to read.

'That would be Miss Bradshaw?' she said. 'I have her statement here.' She started to read it. 'Good grief, that's a lot of letters after her name.' She looked up. 'She's a friend?'

'My best friend. She was being presented with a maths breakthrough award at some swanky ceremony in New York. Something to do with the Kissing Number Problem.'

'I'm not familiar with it.'

'Apparently, if a bunch of spheres are packed together, each sphere has a kissing number. That's the number of other spheres it can touch. For example, in a one-dimensional line, the kissing number would be two. Each sphere could kiss the one on its left and the one on its right, like if snooker balls were lined up against the cushion. And in two dimensions it's six.'

'That doesn't seem too complicated.'

'The kissing number for the twenty-fourth dimension is 196,560.'

13

'OK, that sounds a bit more complicated.'

'Indeed. And Tilly's equation was for the twenty-*eighth* dimension,' Poe said. 'I was with her when she wrote it. Took her about half an hour.'

'She's good at maths then?'

'I'm not exaggerating when I say she might be one of the best there's ever been.'

'Did you not fancy going with her?'

'I'd have loved to.'

'Then why—'

'I was giving evidence in a murder trial. Absolutely no way of getting out of it. Neither could the boss.'

'Detective Inspector Flynn?'

'Yes. She was at the same trial so couldn't get away either. Tilly had never been abroad before. Never even been on a plane. She asked Estelle if she wanted to go with her.'

'OK, so you're in the pub and Estelle calls. What happened next?'

Chapter 4

'You at the airport yet?' Poe asked Doyle after they'd caught up with each other's news.

'We checked in a couple of hours ago. Boarding in twenty minutes.'

'How was Tilly's speech?'

'Weird.'

'Thank you, Captain Obvious.'

Doyle laughed. It was throaty and full and genuine and made Poe realise just how much he'd missed her this last week.

'She explained the physics of air travel to a roomful of scientists, then thanked you for five minutes—'

'Me? Why did she thank me?'

'She said she got interested in the equation after she watched you cram four pickled onions into your mouth.'

'But I only did it to make her laugh. She didn't tell them, did she?'

'What do you think?' Doyle said. 'She then told everyone you and I were recently engaged and led the entire audience in three hearty cheers for Estelle Doyle and Washington Poe.'

'She didn't!'

'Again, what do you think?'

'But no one would have had the first clue who we were.'

'There *was* an undercurrent of confusion,' Doyle admitted. 'But because of her infectious enthusiasm, they went with it anyway. Strangest thing I've ever witnessed. That woman could lead armies if she put her mind to it.'

'Oh well, at least she was only talking to a bunch of nerds.'

'And to anyone watching one of the countless news channels

that picked it up. CNN, Sky News, Fox, Al Jazeera and the BBC all had cameras there.'

'You're joking.'

'It's a huge deal, Poe. I don't think we've quite realised how much of a rock star Tilly is in the maths world. After her speech, of which I understood nothing, she received a fifteen-minute standing ovation.'

'Really?'

'And while we were having dinner after the ceremony, representatives from three US agencies came to our table to offer her a job. And I'm sure one of them was the NSA.'

'Blimey. She enjoyed it though?'

'She did. Blundered her way through any number of social faux pas without batting an eyelid. As soon as we arrived, she asked the event organiser, a woman in her fifties, if the dark hairs growing out of her chin were caused by hypertrichosis.'

'Which is?'

'It's more commonly known as werewolf syndrome. A point Tilly was very clear about.'

Poe laughed so hard the men playing pool stopped to watch.

'Laugh all you want; I was standing right next to her. She has no embarrassment threshold at all, does she?'

Poe was about to go toe-to-toe with Doyle on the times Bradshaw had made awkward situations unimaginably worse when the pub's lounge door burst open. A worried-looking man in grass-stained corduroys and a brown felt waistcoat rushed in. His face was ruddy and his hair unkempt, like he'd combed it with his fingers. A man of the soil. Either a gamekeeper or a poacher. He scanned the semi-crowded room until his eyes found Poe's.

'I'd better go, Estelle,' he said. 'I think duty's about to call.'

Chapter 5

'Here, lad,' waistcoat man said to Poe. 'You're that copper, aren't you?'

'When I'm not on holiday.'

'I thought you always had to be on duty?'

Poe drained his pint. 'Tell me what's happened,' he sighed.

'You need to follow me.'

After collecting his wallet and keys from the bar, Poe traipsed after the man. The street was still cold, the frost on the pavement glittering like smashed glass.

'Where are we going?' Poe asked.

'The church.'

'St Michael's?'

'Aye, lad.'

Poe stopped. After a couple of yards, the man turned to see why Poe was no longer biting his heels.

'What's up?' he asked.

'Do you have a name?'

'Anthony Lawson.'

'And what do you do, Anthony?'

'I look after the church grounds.'

'Is this about badgers digging up graves?'

'You already know?'

'A man ran into the bar fifteen minutes before you did. Said he'd been to put flowers on his mum's grave and the badgers had dug her up. It's unpleasant but it's not unheard of for them to burrow under graves and excavate human remains. They're protected, so can't be moved without rarely given permission.'

'But—'

'This isn't a police matter, Anthony,' Poe said firmly. 'If you want a licence to remove them, you'll need to go through the proper channels.'

Anthony waited a moment. 'Are you finished?' he asked.

'I am. And now I'm going back to the Crown for a Scotch egg. I'll buy you a pint if you want me to talk you through your options.'

'It's true, the badgers did tunnel underneath Mrs Hetherington's grave, lad, but that's not why I was sent to get you.'

'No?'

'You say badgers unearthing human remains is a civil matter?'

'I do.'

'But what if the remains they unearthed were never supposed to be there in the first place?'

Chapter 6

There had been a church on the site St Michael's now occupied since 750 AD, predating the nearby, and more famous, Shap Abbey by almost five hundred years. It was in the centre of Shap village and was a cold and stoic Grade II listed building, all ancient stone and stained glass. It had an imposing tower with an embattled parapet. Poe thought it looked more like a fortified house than a church. Maybe a medieval borstal for unruly vicars.

The war memorial at the churchyard entrance, a tall wheel-head cross with a tapering shaft on a four-sided plinth, Poe knew well. He visited it every Remembrance Sunday, although he waited until the crowds had thinned before paying his respects. The memorial was made from Shap granite, the same stone used to build Herdwick Croft, the isolated two-hundred-year-old shepherd's cottage he called home.

'This way, Sergeant Poe,' Anthony said, leading him off the street and into the churchyard. A hushed crowd had gathered at the entrance but, although the wrought-iron gates were open, the grounds remained empty.

The graves at St Michael's were arranged in an ad hoc, scattergun manner, as if no one could agree on the best strategy for planting the dead. The biggest plot pushed up against a clump of gnarled trees, stripped of their greenery, but Poe knew there were graves all over the church grounds.

He cast his eyes around, looking for evidence of badgers: heaps of earth, collapsed headstones, anything that hinted at nocturnal digging. But all he saw was a winter graveyard. It looked like a scene from a Goth Christmas card. Some of the headstones were cracked and crumbling with faded etchings; others hadn't been exposed to the harsh Shap weather long enough. Trinkets and flowers had been left at some graves but, like most old graveyards, the majority were bare and unattended, the deceaseds' relatives long dead too.

'Where is it?' Poe asked Anthony.

'Round the back.'

Anthony stepped off the path and on to the grass. Poe followed suit; the brown frosted leaves crunched under the thick soles of his boots as if he were walking on Pringles. As they neared the north-facing side of the church, the side that got no afternoon sun, the ground changed from mainly grass to mainly moss and creeping ivy. Tree roots crossed each other like pallet straps.

The light was thin and grey. Branches creaked in the breeze. Poe stopped walking. Something felt wrong. He took in a deep breath but all he got in return was damp earth and pine needles. Maybe the suggestion of grave flowers, perhaps some early snowdrops. Nothing funky. He took in another deep breath. Shut his eyes and let his memory do the heavy lifting. There *was* a hint of something else there, he thought. An unwanted seasoning, a smell he knew well. It was sweet and rancid.

Decay.

Poe opened his eyes. In the time it had taken him to stop and smell the flowers, Anthony had disappeared around the back of the tower. Poe followed the footprints he'd left in the frost.

And saw a murder.

Chapter 7

'A murder?' Doctor Lang said.

'Of crows,' Poe explained. 'Technically they were carrion crows. *Corvus corone*. There were some magpies as well, but they're skittish and didn't hang around.'

'But the crows did?'

'They were full of meat and are lazy at the best of times. So, yes, they *did* hang around. Stood around like vultures. A few cocked their heads like they were waiting for me to make a speech, but the rest remained motionless. I think this is the bit I remember most of all – the way they just stared. Watching, waiting, emotionless.'

'This is what you see when you sleep?'

Poe nodded. 'It was like something out of *Hammer House of Horror*, Doctor Lang,' he said. 'There were at least twenty on the ground, more in the trees. Creepy bastards, pardon my French.'

She waved away his apology. 'We're in a psychiatric hospital,' she said. 'This won't be the last expletive I hear today. What happened next?'

'Anthony, the bloke who'd fetched me from the pub, grabbed a fallen branch and started yelling and swinging it about.'

'That scared them away?'

'It did. To the trees at least. They watched us for the rest of the afternoon.'

'And it was badgers?'

'It was. The plot behind the church tower looked like a ploughed field. Clawed mounds of earth, two metres high.'

'I knew badgers ate worms; I didn't realise they also ate corpses.'

'It's not the corpses they like, it's the easy digging.'

'Easy digging?'

'Yep. Although they have powerful forelegs, and long, non-retractable claws, at this time of year the ground is frosty and digging is hard. But, because graveyards are quiet and tend to be on ground that can be dug up with nothing more than a spade, they're attractive to badgers. In other words, the essential characteristics of a graveyard are the same essential characteristics of a badger sett.'

'And this badger was digging a new one?'

'Judging by the amount of spill, it was a medium-sized cete.'

'Cete?'

'A group of badgers. At least four adults, Anthony reckoned.'

'And they'd unearthed the grave of that man's mother?'

'They'd been digging parallel to it, and when they went deeper than six feet, they completely collapsed her grave. The coffin had toppled into the half-constructed sett. And that loosened the earth above. Foxes smelled a cheap meal and dug down for it. And in the morning, after the foxes had slunk back into their holes, the crows began feasting.'

'How disgusting,' Doctor Lang said. 'I assume the coffin had cracked open. That's what the foxes and crows were eating?'

'The coffin was intact,' Poe said.

'Oh? But I thought this man Anthony told you there was a body that wasn't supposed to be in the grave.'

'He did and there was. The corpse he wanted me to see had been hidden *underneath* the coffin.'

'Underneath?'

'The body of a young man, I found out later. And he wasn't fresh. There was barely anything left of him. He had been wrapped in plastic but as soon as the badgers unearthed him, the foxes and crows started picking him clean. That man's mum had been in the ground seventeen years. We assume the young man had been there for as long.'

'But . . . why?'

'Why not?' Poe said. 'I'm surprised it doesn't happen more often to be honest. As a way of getting rid of a corpse, a grave is practically foolproof. They're always dug the night before so it would have been a simple case of digging down a couple more feet and hiding the body. The next morning a bunch of people stand around while a coffin is lowered into it, no one realising that when the vicar does his "I am the resurrection" bit, he's blessing *two* corpses, not one. A headstone is whacked on top like a giant full stop, and the body underneath the coffin is gone, if not forever, then at least until someone gets an exhumation order.'

'That's . . . creative.'

'But, unfortunately for whomever did this, badgers don't bother with exhumation orders.'

'Who was he?'

'My involvement stopped there.'

'It did? But you're a detective and surely this was a murder. Did you not have, what do you call it . . . jurisdiction?'

'I was with the National Crime Agency's Serious Crime Analysis Section, Doctor Lang,' Poe explained. 'My job was to catch serial killers. All I did at St Michael's was call Cumbria Constabulary to tell them they had a deposition site. My role ended there.'

'But you must have wondered?'

'I did,' Poe admitted. 'The senior investigating officer eventually put it down to an undocumented economic migrant dying in an accident at one of the illegal quarries up near the church. The post-mortem had revealed head and upper torso injuries consistent with a bad rock fall. They believe the gangmaster must have panicked and, instead of reporting the death, taken the easy way out and hid the body before fleeing back to mainland Europe. The coroner recorded an open verdict.'

'And you accepted that?'

'Like I said, it wasn't my case. The lead detective handed the whole thing over to the Health and Safety Executive in the end.'

'But something happened to change your mind?'

'Why do you say that?'

'Because, if in your mind the crows are the catalyst for everything that happened in here,' she said, placing the palm of her hand on the file, 'that means the man in the grave is somehow linked to the man at the Lightning Tree.'

Poe took his time, but eventually nodded.

'And the Lightning Tree is where I officially enter this story,' he said.

Chapter 8

The silence of the conference room eventually registered with Poe. He realised it had probably been quiet for a while. He blinked, glanced at the mindless doodling he couldn't remember starting – the margins of his agenda were now almost full; a sure sign he was bored and had been for a while – then looked up. Everyone in the room was waiting for him to respond.

'Sorry, I was miles away,' he admitted.

'I asked you what you thought?' the meeting's chair said.

'About what?'

'Whether the post-Brexit data sharing arrangements we have with the EU will negatively impact on the Serious Crime Analysis Section's ability to do its job? What do you think?'

'I think I must have been annoying DI Flynn recently,' he said. 'It's the only explanation for me being here.'

After the room had stopped laughing, Poe said, 'But I don't think Brexit will hit us in the same way it's hitting other units. Serial killers and serial rapists tend to be shadow men. We rarely know who they are before they start offending.'

'But you do liaise with Europol and our friends across the Channel?'

'We do. But we use back channels when we speak to our counterparts on the continent. It's quicker and you get to speak to the right person straight away.'

The chair frowned. 'Back channels' wasn't something he could put on the report he had been tasked with compiling. The purpose of the meeting was to make a recommendation. Poe didn't care. He went back to his doodling, but this time he left an ear open. His crack about annoying Flynn had been made in jest, of course, but he was now wondering if he *had* done something to upset her. She'd certainly been in a bad mood that morning when she'd packed him off to yet another pointless meeting. He should probably ask if her son was OK.

He turned over his mobile and was surprised to see he had three increasingly irate text messages from her. The last one simply said, 'Call me now!' Poe had ducked out of meetings on flimsier excuses, so he made his apologies and left the room. He tapped out a 'What's up?' She called immediately.

'Where are you?' she said.

'I've just left that meeting.'

'Meet me in the lobby.'

'You're here?'

'All three of us are.'

Chapter 9

'Who were the three?' Doctor Lang asked.

'The boss, of course,' Poe replied.

'How do you get on with her?'

'We've known each other a long time.'

'That's not what I asked.'

'I suppose we're like an old married couple. We get on each other's nerves occasionally, but we both know when to walk away. I used to be her boss, now she's mine.'

'Is that awkward?'

'She's a better detective inspector than I was, and I'm a better sergeant than she was. We work well together.'

'Is she as committed to the job as you are?'

'She is,' Poe said. 'But she has a young son, and a partner who wants her in a less dangerous role.'

'Who else was there?'

'Tilly.'

'She was back from the States?'

'This was five months after the badger incident.'

'Tell me about her.'

Poe smiled. 'Tilly's . . . Tilly,' he said. 'An awkward haircut on top of a brain the size of Wales. Paler than a flour worm, brighter than a thousand suns. She's brilliant, absolutely brilliant, but up until she started working with us, her only experience of life was in academia. She went to Oxford when she was thirteen and stayed there until her early thirties.'

'Doing what?'

'Pure mathematics, I think. I've asked several times, but I never understand her answers. She's a true polymath though; can pretty much turn her hand to anything. Computers, profiling, databases, anything we need to know a lot about, fast.'

'She sounds amazing.'

'She is. But there was a price to taking her out of school at thirteen. She never really mixed with ordinary people and as a result she has a problem integrating. You heard what she said about the hairs on that woman's chin when she was in America for her award?'

Doctor Lang stifled a grin. 'The one she asked if she suffered from werewolf syndrome?'

Poe nodded. 'Well, trust me when I say of all the social hand grenades she's lobbed over the years, that wouldn't even make the top one hundred.'

'Don't people make fun of her?'

'They used to.'

'And now?'

'And now they don't,' Poe said without further explanation.

'You said she's your friend?'

Poe nodded again. 'And I'm the type of person who doesn't have friends. She's loyal, brave and incredibly kind. Probably the nicest person I've ever met. A sort of human mirror, the kind you only see the best version of yourself in.'

'OK, along with Estelle, it sounds like you have decent support networks,' Doctor Lang said. 'Who was the third person?'

'I'm sorry?'

'DI Flynn said there were three people waiting for you in the lobby. She and Tilly are two; who was the third?'

Poe scowled. 'You ever had an intern, Doctor Lang?'

'Trainees occasionally sit in with me.'

'You'll know then.'

'Know what?'

'Just how annoying they are.'

Chapter 10

Flynn was waiting for Poe in the reception area. It was brightly lit with grey pleather seats arranged in horseshoe-shaped booths. Behind the seats was a floor-to-ceiling, wall-to-wall, etched metal print showing the evolution of the National Crime Agency. It officially came into existence in 2013, but subsumed agencies such as the UK Human Trafficking Centre and the National Criminal Intelligence Service, which had much longer histories. Every time Poe saw the print, he was reminded how disparate the NCA's legacy organisations were.

Bradshaw and a man Poe didn't recognise were seated beside Flynn.

'What are you doing this week, Poe?' Flynn asked.

'Depends on the rest of the information you're about to give me, I suppose,' he replied, eyeing the stranger warily. He was wearing a suit. Not the hardwearing suits cops wore, this one looked as though he'd stood on a tailor's box and been asked which way he dressed. His shoes were highly polished and scuff free. He had gel on his hair and his nails were manicured. He looked like the kind of arsehole who modelled designer glasses in airport magazines. Poe took an immediate dislike to him.

'I need you, Tilly and Linus to head up to Cumbria,' Flynn said. 'Detective Superintendent Jo Nightingale is waiting for you. She'll call with directions when you get there.'

'Where's there?'

'Keswick.'

'She can't have another serial, surely?' Poe said.

Cumbria had seen more than its fair share of serial killers recently.

'Not a serial.'

'Then why the referral?'

SCAS only got involved if a territorial police force asked for their assistance. Serial killers were obvious examples, but solving apparently motiveless murders was also a unit speciality. Poe had worked with Nightingale before. She was capable and well respected but, like all cops, she saw calling in outside help as an admission of failure.

'I don't think she wanted to make a referral,' Flynn said. 'I think her hand was forced.'

'I'm not sure—'

'This evening you have a meeting with the Bishop of Carlisle. He'll explain his intervention then.'

'You haven't been told?'

Flynn shook her head. 'Superintendent Nightingale said there might be a religious angle to the case, but other than that neither of us has any idea why the bishop has involved himself.'

Poe sighed. The last time he investigated a crime involving Christians he had walked into a room and they'd all turned their backs on him. One of them had said in a stage whisper, 'The unchurched always look so *miserable*, don't they?' They'd sniggered, right up to the point Poe put his cuffs on one of them and arrested him for rape.

Flynn gestured to the man wearing the inappropriate suit. 'This is Linus Jorgensen. He will be going up with you.'

'Good morning,' Linus said, thrusting out his hand. 'I'm very excited to be working with you, Sergeant Poe.'

Poe ignored him. 'What the fuck is this?' he said to Flynn. 'I work alone.'

Flynn sighed. 'Poe, Tilly's accompanied you on your last eighteen cases,' she said.

'That's right, I work alone with Tilly.'

'Well, not this time. Linus is with the National Audit Office. There's an ongoing value-for-money audit and SCAS has been singled out as it's one of the few NCA units that doesn't directly contribute to the counterterrorism agenda.'

'He's very young,' Poe said. 'Perhaps he's an intern?'

'I'm not an intern,' Linus said.

'And what sort of name is Linus? Wasn't he one of Snoopy's gang?'

'He was Charlie Brown's best friend, Poe,' Bradshaw said. 'He was always sucking his thumb.'

'I'm standing right next to you,' Linus said. 'And Linus is a family name.'

'A cartoon family,' Poe said.

'Grow up, Poe,' Flynn said.

'I am grown up. I couldn't be more grown up if I had a *Saga Magazine* subscription.'

'You might find Linus useful if there *is* a religious angle to the case. He read theology at Durham so he can help you navigate around what can be a habitually irate community.'

'We don't need a chaperone, boss.'

'Poe, last time you met with the bishop, Tilly talked him through constipation in the elderly statistics.'

'It was her first time in the field,' he protested. 'She knows better now.'

'I certainly do,' Bradshaw said. 'Constipation in the over seventies is now at an all-time high. Recent studies suggest that because people are living longer, they are often widowed for longer. And because widowed people often lack interest in eating, they over rely on convenience food, which tends to be low in fibre and high in salt. Do you think the bishop will be interested in this, Poe?'

Flynn looked at Poe. 'See?' she said.

'So, Tilly waits in the car this time,' he said. 'Problem solved.'

'Last year, when that nun's finger had been pickled in vinegar, you referred to that priest's sandals as Nazareth Nikes.'

'And I've already apologised for that.' Poe considered his rapidly shrinking options. 'How about Snoopy stays in London, but I promise to email him a full report every night.'

'Please call him Linus, Poe,' Flynn said. 'And you're going to be emailing a full report every night anyway.'

'I am? Why?'

'Because I'm not coming with you,' Flynn explained. 'Not this time. I have my hands full with this audit.'

Poe walked into the far corner of the reception area. 'Can I have a word in private, boss?' he said.

Flynn followed him. Linus did too.

'Doesn't look like it,' she said.

'Go away, Snoopy,' Poe said.

'For Pete's sake,' Linus said. 'Could you be any ruder?'

'If Tilly will ever let me swear again, yes. Now, fuck off.'

Linus scowled and for a moment Poe thought he wasn't going to back down. But eventually he lowered his eyes and rejoined Bradshaw on the pleather seats.

'I'm sorry, but this is happening, Poe,' Flynn said as soon as Linus was out of earshot. 'This came from the director, and I got the impression he was under orders as well.'

'It wasn't two years ago we broke up that looted antiquities ring,' he said. 'And they were buying directly from Al-Qaeda.'

'What's your point?'

'My point is you don't have to go too far back to find SCAS's contribution to the counterterrorism agenda.'

Flynn didn't answer.

'Which means the counterterrorism budget angle is bullshit,' Poe continued. 'It's a way in, not the end game.'

'The director and I have just had the exact same conversation,' she said.

'I know you have. And that's because neither of you are stupid people. So what's this really about? Who is this guy?'

'We don't know,' she replied. 'And that's what worries us.'

Chapter 11

'Call Superintendent Nightingale for me can you, Tilly?' Poe said, putting his foot down to get past a caravan. The M6 at Birmingham was predictably lively and he wanted to get through it before rush hour started in earnest. It would tighten again around Manchester, but Lancashire and Cumbria would be free and painless.

He had half-heartedly tried pushing back against Linus, but Flynn wasn't having any of it.

'Just pretend I'm not here, Sergeant Poe,' Linus had said from the back of the car.

'That won't be a problem, Snoopy,' Poe had replied, adjusting the rear-view mirror so he couldn't see him.

Bradshaw found Nightingale's number and pressed call. She answered immediately. 'Where are you?'

'Almost through Birmingham, ma'am,' Poe replied.

'About three hours away?'

'Give or take. Traffic should ease up soon and I'll make decent headway. Where do you want us?'

'It's only the two of you this time, I understand. No DI Flynn?'

'Just me and Tilly I'm afraid, ma'am.' Linus cleared his throat. Poe ignored him. 'There's some pain-in-the-arse audit thing going on in the NCA and SCAS has been dragged into it. She's had to stay in London.'

'Do you know what's happening here?'

'Other than there might be a religious angle, we've not been told.'

'Here's the elevator pitch then,' Nightingale said. 'Two nights ago, some Druids found a body tied to the Lightning Tree. Do you know it?'

'I know *of* it.'

'The victim had been dead at least a day when they—'

'You haven't done the post-mortem yet?'

'No, although we're confident we know how he died.'

'Oh?'

'He was stoned to death.'

Which was a new one on Poe. He had investigated men being burned alive, poisoners, contract killers, even murderous chefs, but a stoning wasn't something he'd come across before.

'Have you identified the victim?' he asked.

'A man called Cornelius Green.'

'How very biblical. What do you know so far?'

'Not much. Cornelius ran some sort of religious retreat. One of those places where people study the Bible, discuss what their faith means to them. That type of thing.'

'Is this why I have an appointment with the Bishop of Carlisle tonight?'

'I'll find out why you're seeing the bishop when you tell me.'

'Fair enough,' Poe said. 'What else do you know?'

'Not a huge amount. Poor bastard was tied to the Lightning Tree and had rocks thrown at his head.'

'It's the murder site?'

'The bloodstaining's conclusive and the rocks used were left in situ.'

'How old is the victim?'

'Late fifties, early sixties.'

'Healthy?'

'Nothing to suggest otherwise.'

'So, unless he went to the Lightning Tree willingly, you're looking at more than one offender.'

'That's what we think.'

'Witnesses?'

'Possibly. There's a campsite nearby and someone thought they heard shouting.'

'Meaning you might have the time of death?'

'Maybe. But the witness admits he was high as a kite and it's possible all he actually heard was an argument on the campsite.'

'When's the PM?'

'That depends on you,' Nightingale said. 'I was rather hoping you might ask Estelle. See if she wouldn't mind doing it. The body's at Carlisle now, but we can move it if she needs us to.'

'I'm sure Carlisle will be fine. She's already in Cumbria.'

'She is? Why?'

'Poe and Estelle are engaged to be married, Detective Superintendent Nightingale!' Bradshaw shouted, unable to contain herself. 'When she heard Poe was going to be working in Cumbria, she cancelled some lectures so they could spend some time together.'

'Bloody hell!' Nightingale said. 'The Hermit of Shap and the Pathologist Grim are getting hitched? I'm no expert, but isn't this one of the twelve signs of the Apocalypse?'

'Ho ho ho,' Poe said.

'It's actually one of the seven seals and the seven trumpets of God,' Linus said without looking up from the tablet he'd been typing on since they left London. 'In the Book of Revelation, they're a series of catastrophic events that take place during the End of Days.'

'Who the hell was that, Poe?' Nightingale asked.

'No one,' he replied, adjusting the rear-view mirror so he could glare at Linus.

'I thought it was just you and Tilly.'

'Snoopy's my intern.'

'You've got an intern?'

'I'll explain when I get there.'

'And he's called Snoopy?'

'His real name is Linus, Detective Superintendent Nightingale,' Bradshaw said. 'I don't think Poe likes him very much.'

Poe didn't contradict her.

'Well, this *is* going to be fun,' Nightingale said.

'Where are you?' Poe asked.

'Still processing the murder scene; can you meet me there?'

'Sounds good. Give me the postcode.'

'You've been in London too long, Poe. It's a tree on the side of a hill.'

He smiled, glad to be heading home. 'Directions then,' he said.

'Spoken like a true Cumbrian.'

Chapter 12

From the car, the Lightning Tree looked as if it had been dug up and replanted upside down. That was Poe's first impression. He didn't know how many times the lone oak sentinel had been struck by lightning, but it was leafless, barkless and very, very dead. The skeletal, root-like branches were stark against the clear sky.

Poe didn't need to ask why it was an attractive place to Druids. Even in the low summer sun, the tree looked mystical. He wondered if they would still use it. Surely a man being tied up and stoned to death had to be bad karma, or whatever it was they called it.

Bradshaw said she would stay in the car while Poe met with Nightingale. Linus said he would keep her company. Poe didn't like that idea at all and insisted they all go.

'But I want to start profiling Cornelius Green, Poe,' Tilly said. She looked out of the passenger-side window. 'Plus, it's been raining and my wellington boots are at the bottom of my suitcase.'

'And I only have these,' Linus said, gesturing at his polished shoes.

Which settled it.

'I'll get your wellies, Tilly,' Poe said. 'And Snoopy, you shouldn't have come to Cumbria without outdoor clothing.'

'But you said there wasn't time for me to go home and get—'

'That sounds like a "you" problem.'

Poe's sturdy boots had thick treads, and Bradshaw had bought her wellingtons under his guidance a couple of years earlier. He had insisted she spend decent money, which she had. She was therefore able to stay upright on the wet and slippery slope. Linus, with his smooth-bottomed Italian loafers, fell over twice.

To his credit he didn't complain, even when Poe pointed and laughed.

Nightingale met Poe at the outer cordon. She was wearing the works: white paper barrier suit, forensic gloves, overshoes and a face mask. She ducked under the tape and removed her mask and gloves.

They shook hands. Poe didn't introduce Linus and Nightingale didn't ask.

'Complex scene?' Poe said.

'Not really. Just a lot of it. Whoever did this used whatever rocks were lying around and they all have to be identified. I doubt we'll find the killer's DNA on them, but I'm checking anyway.'

'Any new information?'

'Not since we spoke.' She looked at Linus. 'Can we talk in front of him?'

'Yes,' Linus said.

'Absolutely not,' Poe said.

'The arrangement was—'

'You don't have an arrangement with me, sunshine,' Nightingale cut in. 'If Poe says we don't talk in front of you, then we don't talk in front of you.'

'Wait over there,' Poe said.

Linus folded his arms. 'This is public land and I'm not moving,' he said.

'Can we talk in the outer cordon, ma'am?'

'That'll work,' Nightingale said. 'Mr Intern, if you—'

'I'm not an—'

'—set one foot inside this cordon without my express permission, I'll have you arrested.'

'You might want to write that down in your little tablet,' Poe said.

Chapter 13

'Why don't you like Linus, Poe?' Bradshaw said when they were inside the outer cordon and out of earshot.

'Because I don't trust him, Tilly.'

'I thought you said he was an intern?' Nightingale said. 'What's not to trust? You tell them to fetch your dry cleaning, they fetch your dry cleaning. You want a coffee, they get you a coffee. Unless *The Devil Wears Prada* was total bullshit.'

'What's that?' Poe said.

Nightingale grinned. 'You still don't have a television then?'

Poe told her about the audit and the supposed reasons behind it.

'But the case we had two summers ago was rooted in terrorism, surely?' Nightingale said. 'I remember all the arrests that followed. The main players were all convicted under Terrorism Act offences. And the reason I know this is because I gave evidence at the trial.'

'Which is why we believe the reasons they gave for the audit are horseshit.'

'You don't think it's budgetary?'

'If it was, why not say? I've been a cop long enough to know there isn't a bottomless pot of money.'

'Maybe it's about you two then.'

'What have we done?'

'You get results, Poe. Perhaps they want to see if it can be replicated.'

'I get results because of Tilly,' he said. 'There's no secret to it. If they'd asked me, I'd have told them. Saved ruining that little squirt's shoes.'

'Well, whatever it is . . .' She trailed off when her phone rang. 'Sir?' she said.

The conversation was one-sided and, judging by Nightingale's furrowed brow, it seemed she was being told something she didn't like.

'I'll tell him, sir.' She slipped her phone in her pocket and looked at Poe. 'Who the hell *is* this guy?' she said, nodding at Linus. 'That was the chief constable. He was very clear. Linus Jorgensen is to be given access to all parts of this investigation.'

'That was quick.'

'Extremely.'

'It's your crime scene, ma'am,' Poe said. 'Even the chief constable can't come in without your permission.'

Poe wasn't sure whether that was true or not. It was accepted practice that the senior investigating officer had the final word on who was and who wasn't allowed into a crime scene, although it was unlikely to have been stress-tested when it came to chief constables.

Nightingale sighed. 'There's nothing to see and some battles aren't worth fighting,' she said. She told Linus to suit up. While he was struggling into a barrier suit, she added, 'You got a plan for dealing with this prick, Poe?'

'Working on it.'

'Good. Let me know if you need a hand.'

'We haven't been introduced, Superintendent Nightingale,' Linus said when he was finally allowed into the outer cordon. 'My name is Linus Jorgensen. I'm with the National Audit Office.'

Nightingale patted her pockets theatrically. 'Damn,' she said. 'I thought I'd brought my autograph book to work today.'

Poe sniggered then turned his back on Linus. 'You got a video walkthrough we can watch?'

Nightingale nodded. Her laptop was in her car so she sent one of her cops to bring it up. Staying inside the cordon saved her having to put on fresh barrier clothing.

'And while we wait,' she said to Poe, her eyes twinkling mischievously, 'you can tell me all about your engagement to Estelle. When did it happen? How did you propose? When's the big day? I want to know everything.'

'I might have been down in London for a few days, ma'am, but

I haven't turned into Sharey McOversharer just yet. If you want to know what happened, ask someone else.'

'Tilly, what happened?'

'Except her.'

'Estelle Doyle spelled out "Will You Marry Me?" with finger bones, Detective Superintendent Nightingale,' Bradshaw said immediately. 'It was wonderfully romantic.'

Nightingale let out a deep laugh. 'That sounds about right,' she said.

Behind Poe, Linus Jorgensen began tapping on his tablet again.

Chapter 14

'Your engagement was a joke to Superintendent Nightingale?' Doctor Lang asked.

'Not at all,' Poe replied. 'Cops have a dark sense of humour and taking the piss is how you show trust.'

'It is?'

'Absolutely. I've found the more polite someone is, the more they dislike you.'

'You must have *really* trusted Linus then,' she said with a smile.

Poe didn't respond.

'Tell me about the murder scene.'

'They'd shot two crime scene videos,' Poe said. 'It was still dark when Superintendent Nightingale and her team got there so they set up lights and shot what they could. Took samples in case it rained again, a few other things that couldn't wait. They didn't shoot the main video until first light.'

'I've never seen a crime scene video,' Doctor Lang said. 'Talk me through it.'

'It's sort of like a two-person-crew film shoot. The crime scene manager is the cameraperson, and the senior investigating officer is the director. A good SIO will offer commentary on what's being filmed without second-guessing what has happened. Facts, not opinions.'

'And Superintendent Nightingale is a good SIO?'

'One of the best I've worked with,' Poe said. 'She had the crime scene manager shoot the Lightning Tree, the rocks, potential approaches and the surrounding area from a multitude of angles.'

'And there was a lot to process?'

Poe nodded. 'Superintendent Nightingale had a mass of potential evidence to recover as there was no way of knowing which rocks had been used in the murder, and which were . . . you know, simply rocks.'

'They didn't all have blood on them?'

'Some did. Others had hit the victim without breaking the skin. Some had been thrown but had missed. They all had to be identified, recorded and recovered.'

'That sounds like a thankless task,' Doctor Lang said.

'Good crime scene management *is* a thankless task,' Poe said. 'It was a straightforward video walkthrough at the end of the day though. Cornelius Green had been tied to a tree and stoned to death. The killer hadn't tried to move the body afterwards and there had been no attempt to tidy the crime scene. There was very little room for interpretation.'

'What did Cornelius look like?'

'His own mother wouldn't have recognised him.'

Chapter 15

'Jesus,' Poe muttered.

They had finished watching the videos and were now scrolling through the CSI photographs. The one currently on Nightingale's screen was a close-up of Cornelius Green's head. It was the size of a pumpkin and had swollen so much it looked like it might burst open, like an over-baked potato. It was bruised and cut, with numerous compression fractures. The eye sockets and nose were so badly damaged that shards of needle-sharp bone had jutted through the skin like sawgrass. The blood was thick and crusty and black.

'How did you identify him so quickly?' Poe asked.

Nightingale scrolled through to the next photograph. This one was of Cornelius's torso. It had been battered with rocks, but nowhere near as badly as his face. Probably where the killers' aim hadn't been 100 per cent. Or maybe they had wanted to start somewhere that wouldn't be fatal. That keeping him alive and conscious, prolonging his horrific death, had been part of whatever the hell this was.

Cornelius's skin was pale and hairless, and his muscles were well defined. Like he worked out, but always in a dark room. It would have taken a big, burly man to drag him to the Lightning Tree unwillingly. His hair was grey and shorn. Not the uniform buzzcut of the electric clipper, this was lumpy and irregular, like he'd done it himself with scissors. Poe reversed his opinion that Cornelius had worked out. Hair like this didn't belong to a vain man. More likely he had a manual job.

But, as strange as the pale skin and the weird haircut were, there was something far stranger about Cornelius's torso. Something Poe hadn't seen since his time with the Russian organised crime unit.

'Holy mackerel,' Bradshaw said. 'That's a lot of tattoos.'

Which was the understatement of the day. Apart from his head, neck, hands and groin area, every inch of Cornelius's body was covered in religious iconography. Big crosses and little crosses; single words and complete Bible passages. Angels and demons. Moses holding the Ten Commandments. Candles and doves. Jesus wearing his crown of thorns; Jesus walking on water. Praying hands and the Virgin Mary. Dozens more Poe didn't recognise. There were so many tattoos they had merged with each other. It made him look as though he didn't have lots, he just had one.

'Finding something to put in the "did the deceased have any distinguishing features" box wasn't a problem then, ma'am,' Poe said. 'But unless someone on your team knew him, I'm still not seeing how you identified him so quickly.'

Nightingale pointed into the distance, towards the outskirts of Keswick.

'What's there that isn't usually there?' she said.

Poe strained his eyes. 'Ah,' he said.

Chapter 16

'What was Superintendent Nightingale pointing at?' Doctor Lang asked.

'Tents,' Poe said. 'And not the two-person tents you find wedged next to the trombones in the middle aisle at Aldi, these were revival-style tents. If they'd been painted red and yellow, they'd have been full of clowns and acrobats.'

'Your use of "revival" is no accident, I think?'

'It wasn't. The tents were part of a large religious convention.'

Doctor Lang frowned. 'I didn't know they had things like that in the Lake District.'

'Unless you're serious about being a Christian there's no reason you would,' Poe said. 'But for three weeks every summer, fifteen thousand evangelicals descend on Keswick for readings, seminars and celebrations.'

'You don't approve of Christians?'

'I have nothing at all against Christians,' Poe replied. 'Although I suppose I'm more Clement Atlee than Spencer Perceval.'

'Believe in the ethics, don't believe in the mumbo-jumbo?'

'That's the quote.'

'So it's the convention you don't approve of?'

'In things like this,' Poe said, 'I always listen to the locals.'

'The locals don't approve? Why not? I thought they'd be glad of the extra footfall.'

'It lasts half the summer holidays, and they mob the town but don't spend any money. You speak to business owners and they'll tell you: Keswick essentially shuts its doors to the outside world when the convention is on. There's nowhere for tourists to stay and nowhere for them to park. Everywhere is booked up a year in advance. The conventioneers demand special treatment in restaurants and do things like bring their own teabags into cafés.'

'It's that bad?'

Poe shrugged. 'The *Church Times* featured an article in 2017 that acknowledged businesses such as pubs and other licensed premises suffer due to attendees not using them the same way regular tourists do. And I've personally been harangued by someone telling me I had to repent my sins.'

'How did you deal with that?'

'I asked him how long he had,' Poe said. 'The point is, the convention and a victim covered in religious tattoos gave Superintendent Nightingale's team somewhere to start. They asked around the tents and churches and other meeting places, and it wasn't long before they had his name.'

'What else did they find out?'

'Not much. Although Cornelius was well known in Keswick, other than some vague notion of him running a religious retreat, no one really knew anything about him.'

Doctor Lang checked her file. 'But that all changed when you, Tilly and Linus met with the Bishop of Carlisle?'

'It was just me and Tilly.'

'Oh? I thought Linus was supposed to be shadowing you?'

'There was a . . . misunderstanding.'

Chapter 17

'We're going to need a specialist in religious iconography,' Nightingale said. 'Is there anyone in the NCA who might be able to help?'

Linus cleared his throat.

'I'll make some calls,' Poe said. 'Someone on the Russian desk will be able to help. The Russians love their Jesus tattoos.'

Linus cleared his throat, louder this time.

'Will you stop that?' Poe snapped. 'Either suck a Locket or piss off somewhere we can't hear you.'

'I think Linus wants to say something, Poe,' Bradshaw said.

'Tough luck. This isn't playschool; not everyone gets to have a go.'

'This man had a deep understanding of Christianity,' Linus said, ignoring him. 'There are no conflicting images here.'

'I told you—'

'Let him speak, Poe,' Nightingale cut in. Then to Linus, 'What do you mean, "this man had a deep understanding of Christianity"?'

'There's no fluff,' Linus replied. 'Nothing superficial. All these tattoos are deeply significant.' He pointed at the laptop. 'May I?'

Nightingale handed it over without a word. Linus clearly knew his way around computers and it wasn't long before he had blown up some of the dead man's tattoos.

'There are a lot of crosses and crucifixes, right?' he continued.

'What's the difference?' Nightingale asked.

'A crucifix is a cross with Jesus on it, a cross is symbol free.'

'I didn't know that,' she said. 'Please, go on.'

'This one here' – Linus tapped a solid black tattoo: three crosses, all different sizes, all touching each other – 'has a dual meaning. It represents the three aspects of God: the Father, the Son and the Holy Spirit, but it also symbolises Christ and the two others

48

crucified with him at Golgotha.'

Linus expanded another cross. This one was upside down.

'This is the Petrine Cross, and it doesn't, as many people assume, represent anti-Christian sentiment or Satanism. It's associated with Peter the Apostle who, after being sentenced to death, requested the cross was put in the ground upside down as he didn't feel worthy of being crucified the same way as Jesus. It's come to mean humility before God.'

Linus swiped to a new photograph.

'The one on his elbow, the eye enclosed in a triangle surrounded by rays of light, is the Eye of Providence,' he continued. 'It signifies how God watches over humanity. The Greek letters on his left shoulder come from Revelations: "I am Alpha, and I am Omega, the First and the Last, the Beginning and the End". There's even a peacock.'

'Peacocks are Christian symbols?' Nightingale said.

'They are. You really have to know your stuff, but Ancient Greeks believed peacock flesh didn't decay after death. Early Christians adopted it as a symbol of immortality.'

Poe looked at him shrewdly. He wondered if Linus was giving away more than he intended. Flynn said he'd read theology at Durham. But, instead of using it as a stepping stone to become ordained, or a chaplain, a teacher or youth worker, he'd found a job with the National Audit Office. That didn't make sense. But listening to Linus reminded Poe there was another career choice for bright people with an in-depth knowledge of Christianity. He wondered if he would be able to prove it. His phone rang, an unrecognised number. He answered it.

'Sergeant Poe?'

'Speaking.'

'My name is Peter Overton and I'm calling on behalf of the Bishop of Carlisle. He was wondering if you could do him a huge favour?'

'I'm listening.'

Overton explained what the favour was. Poe smiled, the seeds of a plan already starting to take root. 'That's fine,' he said.

'Who was that, Poe?' Bradshaw asked, when he'd ended the call.

'Tell you later.'

'OK,' Nightingale said. 'It seems this man was serious about being a Christian. Was it why he was killed? Is the convention a coincidence?'

'Should we focus on the victim this time, ma'am?' Poe said. 'I know we usually profile the perpetrator, but in this case finding the killer might be easier once we've identified a motive.'

'And we'll hammer the forensics and the witness statements,' she agreed. 'Meet you in the middle somewhere.'

'Sounds good.'

'What time are you seeing the bishop?'

Poe checked his watch. 'Soon.'

'Will you be asking him about this?'

'Oh, I have *lots* of questions for the Bishop of Carlisle,' he said.

And I might be able to get answers to something else at the same time, he thought.

Chapter 18

Presumably to make it easier for the Royal Mail, the Bishop of Carlisle's official residence was called Bishop's House. It was on Ambleside Road in Keswick and Poe was soon prowling for a parking space. There were so many bed-and-breakfast signs, the residential streets looked more like Blackpool than rural Cumbria. None of them had vacancies, he noticed. The streets were nose-to-tail with cars and before long Poe was cursing the convention like an angry local. After fifteen fruitless minutes, he gave up and drove to the town centre. He pulled up outside Greggs then turned in his seat.

'Make yourself useful, Snoopy,' he said, passing him a ten-pound note. 'We might not get another chance for a brew tonight. I'll have a black coffee, Tilly will have a green tea, and you'll probably want a fizzy pop. I'll park in the Theatre by the Lake's grounds, and we'll meet you back here. The bishop's is only a five-minute walk and it's a nice evening.'

'But—'

'But what? You wanted to be involved – *this* is being involved. And trust me, if I run out of caffeine I become sarcastic and judgemental.'

'Why can't Tilly—'

'Because Tilly's useful and you're an intern.'

Poe waited for Linus to get out before putting the car into gear and navigating out of Keswick. Instead of turning left towards Derwentwater and the Theatre by the Lake, he turned right on to the A66 and headed towards the motorway.

'Poe! Poe!' Bradshaw yelled. 'You've forgotten Linus!'

'Didn't he say we should pretend he wasn't there?'

'He did, Poe.'

'Well, that's much easier to do when he isn't in the car.'

'But where are we going?'

'Carlisle Cathedral.'

'Why?'

'That was the bishop's office on the phone earlier,' he said. 'The meeting's been moved there.'

'But what about Linus? He won't know where we are.'

Poe said nothing. He didn't think it would take Linus long to find them. And if he did, the first piece of the puzzle would slot into place.

Chapter 19

Although Carlisle Cathedral was colossal by Cumbrian standards, it is actually the second smallest of England's ancient cathedrals. It started life as a Norman priory church in 1122, and due to Carlisle's proximity to the Scottish border, and the city's consistently shifting allegiances, it still bore the scars of its long and bloody history.

Lying within the Abbey precinct, a gated area of Castle Street, the cathedral was constructed from red sandstone, discoloured to black on parts of the exterior, and was typical of the Norman architectural style: large round piers, round arches, and small round-headed windows. Like most cathedrals, the architectural floor plan of the building was in the form of a cross.

As he always did when he was in Carlisle's historic quarter, Poe ignored the East Window, the largest Flowing Decorated Gothic window in England, and instead stopped underneath the south-facing outer wall. He looked up. Nestled high in among the stone faces of the traditional medieval gargoyles and grotesques was a policeman. A twentieth-century addition to the fabric of the cathedral, the grotesque had a policeman's helmet, complete with star badge. It was a monument to PC George Russell, a Lake District cop, who was shot and killed after a skirmish with an armed thief at Oxenholme railway station. He gave the copper a nod and silently wished him well as he stood guard over the citizens of Carlisle.

Poe checked his watch. They were a bit early. He was about to suggest they go inside anyway when a small cheer from behind made him pause. He turned, squinted then smiled.

'You haven't been introduced to Bugger Rumble yet, have you, Tilly?'

'I don't know what those words mean, Poe.'

Like Type 2 diabetes, part-time street entertainer/full-time lunatic, Bugger Rumble was a Carlisle staple. A man unfamiliar with subtlety, he was snaggle toothed, had hair like over-sugared candyfloss and a beard down to his belly. The suit he was wearing looked like it had been stolen from a vampire. He completed his look with a top hat, fingerless gloves and the kind of black plimsolls only ever seen in a 1970s school gymnasium. He looked like Bob Geldof during a laundry workers' strike. The council occasionally tried to move him on but, like ringworm, he returned, stronger and even more irritating. And, like ringworm, you felt itchy just looking at him.

But, because Bugger had always had his finger on the pulse of the city's sketchier areas, he'd been Poe's best snout during his time as a Cumbrian detective. Bugger was so obviously batshit crazy, people who really should have known better talked openly in front of him. But just because you didn't notice Bugger, didn't mean Bugger didn't notice you. He saw everything, he *heard* everything, and he forgot nothing. Underneath the grime and the outlandish clothes and the ridiculous street entertainment, was a sharp and insightful mind, a mind Poe had been happy to press for the occasional nugget of intelligence.

Poe reckoned Bugger Rumble had once been involved in the world of antiquarianism, as his knowledge of old books was unparalleled. How he had ended up in Carlisle, living the way he did, was anyone's guess. Poe had occasionally considered making discreet enquiries with Oxford and Cambridge to see if they were missing a professor or knew of a visiting fellow who no longer visited. But he never did – Bugger was happy, and Poe reckoned that was pretty much life's Holy Grail. Who was he to interfere?

The last time Poe saw Bugger, his act, and that was using the loosest possible definition of the word, was to draw a chalk line on the pavement then wobble his way along as if it were a tightrope. The world's only low-rise walker, he called himself. But it seemed he had moved on. Instead of a simple narrative – that he was perilously crossing a canyon and stepping off the chalk line would mean instant death – his act had morphed into something that combined mime with interpretive dance.

Poe watched in amazement.

Silently, and with an expression of absolute concentration, Bugger started putting himself into all sorts of weird and wonderful positions. Sometimes he would throw up his hands and kick the air; sometimes he would strut in a circle like a gimpy chicken. He got on the ground and did what looked like yoga; he stood up and changed an imaginary light bulb. He jumped in the air and kicked his heels.

Bradshaw was mesmerised. Poe imagined this was a new experience for her. To be fair, it looked like this was a new experience for everyone. And judging by the way the crowd was drifting away, maybe not a welcome one.

Bugger finished with a leap in the air, a shout of 'Hey, hoopla!' and a theatrical bow. He then held out his grubby top hat.

Bradshaw clapped enthusiastically. 'Bravo!' she cried.

Reluctantly Poe joined in. 'Yes, very good, Bugger. Not at all weird.'

Bugger waited until the crowd had dispersed before saying, 'Who's the specky lass, Sergeant Poe?'

Which was quite polite for Bugger.

'Tilly, this is Bugger Rumble – no, don't shake his hand! As you can see, he's monetised arsing about.'

Bugger cackled. He was the only person Poe had met who could.

'Arsing . . . I wasn't "arsing about", Sergeant Poe,' he protested. 'This is a series of non-narrative shows about important historical texts.'

'Get stuffed, Bugger. You were dicking about and hoping to earn enough for a pint in the Kings Head.' Poe reached into his pocket and removed his wallet. 'And it just so happens, today's your lucky—'

'That was *fascinating*, Mr Rumble,' Bradshaw interrupted. 'When I was twelve, I wrote a paper on whether visual thinking in mathematics might have an epistemically significant role. Unless my eyes were deceived, that was a one-man play depicting the geometric diagrams contained in Euclid's *Elements*.'

Bugger stared at Bradshaw in astonishment. He tilted his head

55

to one side and started whacking it, like he had a pebble in his ear. 'Begone, pink elephant!' he shouted.

'Tilly's not a figment of your imagination, Bugger,' Poe sighed. 'I can assure you, she's very real.'

Bugger stopped hitting himself. 'She is?'

Poe paused. 'Almost certainly,' he said.

'Stop being cruel, Poe!' Bradshaw said. 'Yes, I am real, Mr Rumble.'

'You've read Euclid's *Elements*?' Bugger asked.

'All thirteen volumes,' Bradshaw confirmed.

His eyes narrowed. 'What's your major criticism?'

Bradshaw frowned. 'Probably when he moved two triangles on top of each other to prove that if two sides and their angles are equal, then they must be congruent.'

'Ah, the third construction.'

'Fourth,' Bradshaw corrected.

Bugger laughed delightedly.

'Wait,' Poe said to Bradshaw, 'you understood all that?'

'You *didn't*?'

He turned to Bugger. 'And you, you mad bastard, that wasn't a load of bollocks? That actually was *something*?'

'Of course, Sergeant Poe. Euclid was an Ancient Greek and considered by many to be the father of geometry. What better way to celebrate his life than with a solo performance in Carlisle's pedestrianised city centre?'

Poe shook his head. 'You've got me there, Bugger.' He pulled a twenty-pound note from his wallet. 'Anyway, I need a favour.'

He told Bugger Rumble what it was. When he'd finished, Bugger nodded.

'Keep your money, Sergeant Poe.' Bugger pointed at Bradshaw and said, 'If I do what you ask, she has to have tea and cakes with me for an hour.'

'I think I'd enjoy—' Bradshaw said.

'Fifteen minutes and not tonight,' Poe said.

'Forty-five.'

'Thirty and don't push your luck.' He checked his watch and glanced at the cathedral. It was time. 'Ready?' he said to Bradshaw.

'I am, Poe.'

He turned to Bugger Rumble. The street entertainer was star-ing at Bradshaw like a dog stares at cheese. This must have been what it was like when Doyle had accompanied Bradshaw to that maths award in the States. Even the Fields Medal winners there had been so awed by her intellect they'd become star struck. And now she was having the same effect on a bark-at-the-moon nutjob. Sometimes Poe wished he were intelligent enough to really appre-ciate the once-in-a-generation mind of his friend.

'Don't let me down, Bugger,' he said.

Bugger's eyes didn't leave Bradshaw.

'Scratch that,' Poe continued, 'don't let *Tilly* down.'

'I won't,' Bugger said.

Chapter 20

The inside of Carlisle Cathedral was smaller than the outside suggested, sort of like a reverse TARDIS. Bradshaw said this was because part of the nave was destroyed during the English Civil War so the stone could be used to reinforce Carlisle Castle. Poe wondered how long it had taken her to become an expert on the cathedral's history. The time it had taken to drive from Keswick to Carlisle, he suspected, minus the five minutes she'd lectured him on the folly of ditching Linus outside Greggs.

The service hadn't quite finished, so they took a seat on one of the carved, black oak choir stalls. The cathedral had forty-six and they were at a ninety-degree angle to the East Window and the High Altar; twenty-three on each side. They were tiered and faced each other, kind of like a basketball court if the bleachers behind the nets were removed. Seats for the congregation were to the left and right of the stalls, although only the seats near the front were currently occupied.

'There's the Bishop of Carlisle, Poe,' Bradshaw said, pointing at the pulpit.

'Yeah, thank you, Tilly. As he's fifteen feet up in the air and the only person talking, he's really difficult to see.'

'You're welcome, Poe.'

The goblet-shaped pulpit was made of the same black oak as the choir stalls, and was tall, freestanding and ornately carved. The Bishop of Carlisle fitted it like Humpty Dumpty fits an eggcup. He was wearing a purple cassock with big cuffs. A large metal cross hung from his neck. Other members of the clergy, lesser in rank and seniority, stood on the flagged floor, looking up. If their mouths had been open, they'd have looked like a nest of chicks waiting for worms. Clearly the bishop conducting a service was a big deal.

He was called Nicholas Oldwater and they had crossed paths on a previous case. He had been helpful and Poe liked him. He was keen to protect the Church, but not at the expense of covering up a crime. Poe hoped he was about to be as helpful now.

But whatever it was he wanted from them, it would have to wait. Right now, the bishop had his hands full. The service he was conducting wasn't straightforward. It seemed to be a cross between Gregorian chanting and a carefully orchestrated theological debate between the bishop and the congregation. There were no hymns, no sermons, and definitely no smiling. This was a serious service.

After five fruitless minutes of trying to figure out what was happening, Poe gave up. He gazed at the barrel-vaulted ceiling – royal blue with gold stars – and let his mind wander. He didn't bother trying to second guess why the bishop had summoned them; they'd find out soon enough. Instead, he reviewed what he knew so far. A man had been murdered. No, that wasn't right. A man had been *stoned to death.*

Christianity had a complex history with stoning and the victim was covered in religious tattoos. Poe was familiar with most religious dogma and he knew the Old Testament in particular prescribed capital punishment for a variety of sins, and the most commonly used method was death by stoning. Some of these sins – murder and rape, for example – were still classed as serious crimes but others like disobedience to parents and homosexuality were spectacularly outdated. According to the Bible, even gathering firewood on a Saturday was enough to be put to death. So, Christianity and death by stoning had a bloody past, and now the Bishop of Carlisle had asked to see him. Poe doubted this was a coincidence.

Poe turned his thoughts to Linus Jorgensen. If Linus *was* a trainee in the National Audit Office, Poe hated sausages. He had strong suspicions about who Linus really worked for and, if the trap he had set with Bugger was sprung tonight, he would be able to confirm it. He could then turn his mind to the 'why'.

Bradshaw nudged him. 'The service has finished, Poe,' she said.

She was right. The chanting had stopped, the small congregation was breaking up. The bishop had climbed down from the pulpit and was chatting to some of the clergy.

'Let's go and see what he wants,' Poe said.

Chapter 21

The Bishop of Carlisle was in his sixties. It was five years since Poe had seen him, and it looked like he'd lost a bit of weight. Probably cut down on the biscuits. Poe seemed to remember he had a fondness for Rich Tea; a wan, flavourless biscuit the nation should be ashamed of. Poe had seen the bishop in an ill-fitting cardigan before, and he'd seen him in a suit, but he'd never seen him wearing his religious fripperies. Perhaps it was because of where they were, but they conveyed an air of authority Poe hadn't noticed before. The bespectacled man he was talking to certainly thought so – he could only have been more deferential if he'd been lying on the floor kissing the bishop's feet.

'Thank you, Peter,' the bishop said. 'Can you make sure we aren't disturbed?'

'Certainly, Bishop.'

'And perhaps some tea?'

Peter nodded and left. Oldwater guided them towards the seats near the pulpit. 'Sorry you had to wait,' he said. 'That went on a tad longer than I anticipated. It was good of you to come.'

'I didn't feel as though I had a choice,' Poe said.

'Sorry. But, in my defence, I think you might find what I have to say quite useful.'

'That was a pretty hardcore service.'

'Evensong? Yes, I suppose it is one for the purists. It's taken from the Book of Common Prayer and dates back to the Reformation. It went out of fashion for a while, but for some reason it's going through a bit of a revival at the moment. Anyway, enough about my day job – how are you both?'

After they'd caught up, Poe said, 'You asked to see me, Nicholas?'

'Both of you actually.'

'Oh?'

'But before we get to the nub of the matter, I would like to ask you something. Something personal.'

'OK,' Poe said cautiously. 'Go for it. Can't promise I'll answer.'

'Do you believe in God, Washington?'

Poe didn't think he'd ever been asked that before. Not in a serious way.

'Well, someone's out to get me,' he replied, to buy time more than anything else.

'Given where we are, it's not an unreasonable question,' the bishop said.

Poe stopped to give it some thought. His answer was obviously important to the bishop, and he wasn't a monster – he wasn't going to lie to him in his own church.

'I know the words to the Lord's Prayer,' he said eventually.

'But do you *believe*, Washington?'

'Do I think that two penguins walked all the way from Antarctica to the Middle East simply to get on a big wooden boat?' he said. 'Or that you can live forever by symbolically eating the flesh and drinking the blood of Jesus, or that a talking snake grifted a woman made from a man's rib into eating a Granny Smith?'

'The Bible isn't meant to be taken literally, Washington,' Oldwater laughed. 'Nowhere in its thirty-odd thousand verses does it claim to be inerrant. It was never an accurate account of the history of that time and place. And it wasn't until the middle of the nineteenth century that scholars stopped examining it as they would any other historical document. And if it *were* meant to be taken literally, it would actually undermine, rather than reinforce, the word of God. Moses is a murderer, David slept around, and Abraham pretended his wife was his sister. If it's read in context, the sole purpose of the Bible is to reveal God to us. It tells us who we are. Where we've come from and where we're going. The Bible isn't the ancient predecessor of your Police and Criminal Evidence Act.'

'That's good, Nicholas,' Bradshaw said. 'Because Poe doesn't believe in that, either.'

Oldwater laughed again. 'I imagine if I asked you the same question, Matilda, I might get a similar answer?'

'Genome studies have shown that modern humans cannot possibly have descended from a single pair of individuals. There is far too much genetic diversity.'

'Like I said to Sergeant Poe, the Bible cannot be taken literally. It's metanarrative, a blueprint to living a good life. But I take it this means you don't believe in a higher power at all, Matilda?'

'I believe we are all star dust, Nicholas,' Bradshaw said.

Oldwater's eyes widened, but not as much as Poe's.

'What a beautiful way of putting it,' Oldwater said, recovering quickly.

'You believe in God, Tilly?' Poe said, astonished.

'Genesis 2:7, Sergeant Poe,' Oldwater smiled. '"Then the Lord God formed man from the dust of the ground and breathed into his nostrils the breath of life, and the man became a living being." Matilda believes that God is all around us, and if you open your mind, you will find the meaning of true peace. That we are Him and He is us. At least I think that's what Matilda's trying to say.'

Bradshaw snorted. 'Don't be ridiculous, Nicholas,' she said. 'I was talking about astrophysics.'

'You were?' Oldwater replied, his eyes twinkling.

'Of course,' she sighed. 'Let me explain.'

'Oh great, you've put a coin in her,' Poe groaned. 'I hope you haven't got any pressing business, Nicholas; this might take a while.'

'The Big Bang took just a billionth of a trillionth of a trillionth of a second,' Bradshaw said, 'but it kick-started the whole universe . . .'

Chapter 22

'Tilly thinks we're made from space dust?' Doctor Lang asked.

'According to her, after the Big Bang there were only light elements like hydrogen and helium,' Poe said. 'Over billions of years, like cosmic lint, they clumped together into ever-denser masses. Some of these masses formed stars, and apparently converting light elements into heavy elements is what stars do.'

'She explained all this to the bishop?'

'And more. She said stars are essentially giant hydrogen furnaces and the intense heat causes atoms to collide, creating new elements like iron and gold and oxygen. After billions of years, tens of billions sometimes, most stars have used up all their hydrogen fuel and they collapse. The outer layers explode, and this fires the elements they forged into the universe. Earth started with hydrogen and helium but now has ninety-two elements, all of which have landed as cosmic dust. Tilly says forty-thousand tons of this space dust still falls to Earth every year.'

'And these star-forged elements are the building blocks of life,' Doctor Lang said. 'I think I remember this stuff from university.'

'Not only life,' Poe said, 'they're the building blocks of everything. My phone, my cottage on Shap Fell, Tilly's Harry Potter glasses, *everything.*'

They were an hour into their session and Poe had been talking for most of it. His throat was beginning to dry up and he looked longingly at the empty plastic cup. Another lukewarm tea would have been welcome.

'How did he take the cornerstone of his religion being challenged?'

Poe put his dry throat aside and said, 'He took it in his stride. He's forward-thinking enough to publicly state that science and religion aren't diametrically opposed positions. He believes they can and should coexist.'

'Which makes me wonder why he bothered asking about your beliefs at all.'

'I think he wanted help fixing the church roof.'

Doctor Lang peered over the file. 'You do this a lot, don't you?'

'What?'

'Use humour to deflect things you aren't comfortable talking about.'

Poe shrugged. 'I hadn't realised.'

'You make light of things you shouldn't and you dismiss emotion as weakness.'

'It's what we do in District Twelve.'

Doctor Lang frowned. 'I don't understand the reference?'

'It's what Tilly calls Cumbria. Usually when there's a bad internet connection or she hasn't been able to buy the right kind of lentils. It's got something to do with a book called *The Hungry Games*. I think that's what it's called.'

'I haven't read it.'

'I haven't either,' Poe admitted. 'But my point is this: I'm a cop in my forties and I'm from the north of England; pushing down emotions is what we do.'

'That doesn't sound healthy, Washington.'

'Oh, it's not healthy at all. But it doesn't last long; eventually we keel over from heart attacks.'

'If I had a pen I'd underline something at this point,' Doctor Lang said.

Poe grinned. 'Now who's making jokes?'

'Anyway, we've got off topic. Why *did* the bishop ask about your religious beliefs?'

'He had his reasons,' Poe said.

Chapter 23

'I think some of the Church's younger, more militant members could do with a shot of what you've told me, Matilda,' Oldwater said when Bradshaw had finally finished. 'Hearing the other side of the argument so cogently explained would do them good. Might take them down a peg or two. Could I interest you in guest speaking at one of our conferences?'

'No thank you, Nicholas,' Bradshaw replied. 'That would bore me foolish.'

'A refreshingly honest answer. Now, to business. You must be wondering why I've asked the National Crime Agency's most stubborn detective and the world's most eminent mathematician if they believe in the same things I do.'

'I assumed it was ill-advised small talk,' Poe said.

'Goodness no, that would be a dreadful waste of your time.'

'You really needed to know?'

Oldwater looked over Poe's shoulder. 'Ah, here's the tea,' he said.

Peter, the bespectacled vicar Oldwater had been talking to earlier, was walking down the nave. He had a tray in one hand and a leather document holder in the other. He set everything down on a couple of spare seats and left without speaking.

'May I?' Oldwater said. 'Yorkshire Tea for me and Washington; peppermint for Tilly. Is that OK?'

They confirmed it was. After they'd all had a drink, the bishop picked up the leather document holder. He left it zipped. 'Before I open this, we need to agree some ground rules,' he said. 'The first is that this file doesn't exist. If it ever gets into the public domain you will confirm you haven't seen it before. Is this acceptable to you both?'

'Fine by me,' Poe said.

'If it is with Poe, then it is with me, Nicholas,' Bradshaw added.

'The second thing we need to agree is the reason for this evening's meeting,' Oldwater said. 'Loose lips sink ships and the three of us sitting together will not have gone unnoticed. And while I trust Peter implicitly, I cannot say the same for everyone else here tonight. I simply do not know them well enough.'

'How about we were just catching up?' Poe suggested. 'You heard through the grapevine that we were working up here and it's been a while.'

'The simplest solutions are often the best,' Oldwater agreed. 'And technically I'm not bearing a false witness under God's roof. We *did* have a catch up.'

'You OK with that, Tilly?'

'We don't know why we're here, Poe,' Bradshaw said. 'I would ordinarily say we'd be ill-advised to agree to anything until we know what's in the file, but I trust Nicholas.'

'I do too. But if he's about to admit to embezzlement or something, we'll just say we had our fingers crossed. I have no problem whatsoever bearing a false witness under God's roof.'

'What about Linus, Poe?'

'Damn, I forgot about that twerp.'

'Who's Linus?' Oldwater asked.

'He's either a trainee with the National Audit Office, here to see how SCAS contributes to the national security agenda . . .'

'Or?'

'Or he's something else. I think we'll find out one way or another very soon.'

'Can you trust him?'

'Not even a tiny bit,' Poe said. 'That's not an insurmountable problem, however, as I have no intention of telling him what we're doing.'

Oldwater looked at his document holder.

'Maybe it's best if—'

'Nicholas,' Poe cut in, 'if there's something sensitive in there, the best thing you can do is let Tilly scan it to her tablet, then shred it. I can assure you, once it's in one of her devices, not even R2-D2 could get it out.'

'Who?'

'It's a robot dustbin that Tilly likes,' Poe said. 'But, my point is, it's as safe in Tilly's tablet as anywhere on earth.'

'Please pass me the file, Nicholas,' Bradshaw said. 'You can trust Poe to do what is right, and you can trust me to keep this information safe.'

'And it was you who asked for this meeting,' Poe reminded him.

The bishop nodded decisively and passed Bradshaw his file.

Chapter 24

'During the course of your investigation you're going to come up against a group called the Children of Job,' Oldwater said. His pronunciation of Job rhymed with globe. He gestured towards the file that Bradshaw was scanning. 'This is everything we know about them, and everything we know about their founding member, Cornelius Green – your victim.'

'Job? The man whose family were killed after God made a bet with Satan?' Poe said.

'That's right. God was demonstrating that true believers hold fast whatever their personal hardships. You've read the Book of Job?'

'I hunt serial killers, Nicholas. I'm up to date with *all* religious dogma.'

'Of course,' he said. 'Anyway, wiser men than me have tried to understand the lessons we were meant to learn from Job's suffering. Some believe it's meant to demonstrate that suffering isn't a punishment; others believe mortal men are not meant to understand God's motivations.'

'And what do you think?'

'I think we need to stop looking for easy answers to hard questions. Life isn't a meritocracy – we don't always get what we deserve,' Oldwater replied. 'And like I said: the Old Testament isn't meant to be taken literally.'

Poe patted the thick file. 'Would it be fair to say the Children of Job are of interest to the Church?'

'They are,' Oldwater agreed. 'As was Cornelius.'

'Why?'

'Initially it was because my office was asked to provide background information on their first application to become registered with the Charity Commission.'

'Their *first* application?'

'They've applied several times. And each time they fall down at the final hurdle.'

'Which is?' Poe asked.

'For a religious organisation to be recognised and registered as a charity, there are four characteristics the Charity Commission must consider. Belief in a supreme being, a relationship between the believer and the supreme being, and a degree of cogency, seriousness and importance.'

'And the Children of Job were able to demonstrate this?'

'They were. Technically they're a Christian organisation, so the first two characteristics were easy boxes to tick. And they're certainly serious in what they believe so they were able to demonstrate adherence to the third characteristic.'

'But not the fourth? What is it?'

'An identifiable positive framework. In other words, to obtain charitable status, a religious organisation must demonstrate they are working from a moral and ethical framework.'

'And they weren't?'

'Not by today's standards.'

'Anything illegal?'

'Not that I uncovered.'

'But you did uncover something?'

Oldwater leaned across and grabbed the pages Bradshaw had finished scanning. He flicked through them until he found what he wanted.

'The Children of Job describe their mission as providing theological training, seminaries and biblical study groups to equip the Christian leaders of tomorrow.' Oldwater handed Poe a flyer. 'As you can gather, their ultimate goal is to see the cross of Christ reigning over these green and pleasant lands again.'

'They're advocating the UK becomes a theocracy?'

'Officially, yes, that *is* what they want.'

'Never gonna happen,' Poe said. 'When it comes to religion, the UK is near the bottom when it comes to believing in God and near the top when it comes to atheism. And that's now – the future's even bleaker for you guys. Only one per cent of people between the age of eighteen and twenty-four say they identify as Christian.'

'I agree, the Church has to redefine its role in the twenty-first century, but you're missing the point.'

'I am?'

'The Children of Job state the UK must become a theocracy *because* of declining religious beliefs, not in spite of it.'

'This is how people think, how can we change them; rather than this is how people think, how can *we* change?'

'Exactly. They believe it's the only way that the soul of the nation can be reclaimed. And they're playing the long game.'

'How?' Poe asked.

Oldwater searched through the file again. He found two documents and passed one of them to Poe. It was a residential study group schedule. Poe ran his eyes down the list. It was packed with religious-sounding subjects like 'An Introduction to the Old Testament', 'Dynamics of Spiritual Growth', 'The Christian Role Model' and 'Scripture in the Contemporary World'. The rest of the sheet was filled with dates, fees and joining instructions.

'The Children of Job work from the Chapel Wood Institute. It's a converted boarding school on the southern slopes of Sale Fell, near Bassenthwaite Lake. Do you know the area?'

'Sort of,' Poe said. 'It's near the Pheasant Inn.'

'That's right,' Oldwater said. 'The institute is only accessible via a single-track dirt road, and they've been there for years. They don't bother anyone and they rarely venture into the community. The paper in your hand is the children and youth curriculum for last year. It's for kids who haven't had any formal theological training. They get the occasional self-referral, but usually it's their families who send them.'

'And would these kids be at risk of straying from the flock?' Poe said.

Oldwater nodded. 'Not necessarily the kind of behavioural problems that might bring them to your attention but, in the context of deeply religious families, behaviour that *is* at odds with the

Bible. Tell me, Washington, what do you notice about the children and youth curriculum?'

'There's no context,' Poe said. 'There are fancy-sounding topics, but no details. Take this one,' – he pointed at one of the residential courses – '"The Christian Role Model"; it could mean absolutely anything. It might be two weeks of singing hymns, it might be lance and shield training ahead of the next Crusade.'

Oldwater handed Poe the second sheet. It was a companion piece to the one in Poe's hands, but instead of administrative details next to each of the study groups, there was something else.

Something bad.

'Ah,' Poe said.

Chapter 25

'What was on the second sheet, Washington?' Doctor Lang asked.

'The Children of Job's *real* agenda,' Poe replied.

'Which was?'

'Opposition to same-sex marriage and infidelity. Reclaiming the traditional male role as head of the household. The teaching of Creationism in schools. The passive dependency of women. The Christian right claim their loss of dominance in UK culture is due to a sustained attack on their faith. They take extreme measures to cling on to their relevance, and groups like the Children of Job do that by vigorously fighting for these outdated issues. Issues that exclude almost everyone in the country.'

'Is that even legal?'

'They had professional help in drawing up their itinerary,' Poe said. 'There was nothing that would have put them at risk of being classified as a hate group.'

'What about the courses?'

'More of the same. Extreme religious instruction with the sole purpose of correcting undesirable character traits. Nothing that would have drawn the attention of children's services.'

'I see,' Doctor Lang said. 'It was like a Chinese re-education camp then?'

'That's a fair analogy.'

'And who decided what was an undesirable character trait?'

'The Children of Job did. The parents did. The kids *themselves* did. The annual curriculum was essentially a programme of religious brainwashing. Have a daughter who's flirting with boys or wearing red lipstick? If she's at risk of becoming what they call a "licked lollipop" her parents might put her on the Children of Job's

"Christian Role Model" course. A Children of Job ex-nurse will do a virginity test, then she'll go through two weeks of indoctrination on why a chaste life is the *right* life. Give her a purity ring at the end so she's got something to show for it. Have a son who believes dinosaurs lived millions of years ago? "An Introduction to the Old Testament" will sort out that nonsense.'

'What's next? Having ginger hair? Being left-handed? Listening to rock music?' Doctor Lang shook her head in frustration. 'Half of what I do is unpicking childhood trauma and most of that goes back to overzealous parenting. Anything else?'

'Yes,' Poe said grimly. 'A course they ran intermittently. They called it "Restored Faith".'

'Oh, I don't like the sound of that at all,' Doctor Lang said. 'Is it what I think it is?'

'It is. They dressed it up with therapeutic language to give themselves legal cover, but to all intents and purposes, "Restored Faith" was conversion therapy. They were trying to pray away the gay.'

Chapter 26

'This is barbaric,' Poe said to Oldwater. 'You can't forcibly change someone's sexuality. All you end up with is a gay person with psychological scars.'

'You understand why they can never become a charity?' Oldwater said. 'You've heard of that infamous Baptist Church?'

'Those dickheads who picket soldiers' funerals in the States? They were banned from entering the UK a few years back for inciting hatred. Shame really; I'd have enjoyed watching what would happen if they tried that shit at a British squaddie's funeral.'

Oldwater nodded. 'That's them. Well, in my opinion, the Children of Job are the UK's equivalent. They aren't so overt, which is why they aren't on anyone's radar, but by whatever definition you care to use, they are a virulently anti-LGBTQIA+ organisation.'

'You seem remarkably well informed, Nicholas,' Poe said. 'Might this explain your reticence in showing me your file? I don't imagine you found all this out by reading the parish newsletter.'

'I have a discretionary fund and a congregation with an *olla podrida* of skills, experiences and contacts.'

'*Olla podrida* is a Spanish stew, Poe,' Bradshaw said without looking up from her scanning. 'The phrase has been appropriated to mean . . . I guess hodgepodge would be the closest English definition.'

'You have a bunch of ex-spies and ex-cops to call on?' Poe said.

'And business leaders and politicians and diplomats, Washington. The Church is a . . . well, broad church.' Oldwater reached into his pocket and pulled out a business card. He passed it to Poe. 'Speaking of which. This is my private number; I can be contacted on it at all times. If you run into difficulties with some of my more mulish members, please do not hesitate to call. Maybe I can open doors that might otherwise remain closed to you.'

Poe tucked it into his wallet. He tapped the top sheet in his hand. 'And what about this guy?'

'Cornelius Green?'

'Yes.'

'Born in Ohio to biblical literalist parents, hence the name. According to the New Testament, Cornelius was a Roman centurion who converted to Christianity. He's widely regarded as the first gentile convert. *Our* Cornelius was active in his local church from an early age and, from what we can gather, on the periphery of unsavoury activities in his teens and early twenties.'

'Such as?'

'Firebombing abortion clinics. Threatening to kill doctors. Daubing homophobic slurs on HIV healthcare centres. Nothing that could be proven but he was a person of interest to the FBI. He called himself a Christian soldier.'

'Are his parents still alive?'

'They're in their eighties, but yes.'

'What did they think of all this?'

'Pride, I imagine,' Oldwater said. 'They're currently in prison for sending letter bombs to a COVID-19 vaccine production plant in California. They called the virus God's Judgement and anyone interfering in the cull of the fallen had to be held to account.'

'Well, don't they just sound delightful?'

'When he was twenty-two, Cornelius must have got involved in something he didn't want to face up to as he fled the States. Ended up in Cumbria. He's been here for almost forty years.'

'You said he was a founding member of the Children of Job?'

'*The* founding member. It was basically his.'

Poe read the top paragraph of Cornelius Green's biography. 'He owned the land and the old school buildings outright?'

'That's correct.'

'How did he fund it? If he was twenty-two and fresh from the States, I don't imagine banks were falling over themselves to lend him money.'

'An American benefactor bankrolled him. One of those revivalist preachers with a mega church and an even more mega bank account. Probably a friend of his parents. Cornelius bought what was then Chapel Wood School, changed the name to the Chapel Wood *Institute*, and founded his organisation.'

'Who inherits it, now he's dead?'

Oldwater pointed at the file. 'It's all in there. There's a robust continuity plan.'

'He planned for his death?'

'Seems so. Don't assume too much from that though – most big organisations have plans for the death of their founder.'

'Is it possible he had a falling out with his benefactor? Rich men can reach all the way around the world without leaving their bed.'

'Perhaps,' Oldwater said.

'But you don't think so?'

He shook his head. 'In my world, as in yours, Washington, a zealot is just another word for an extremist. I think it's there you need to start.'

'And sometimes religious group is just another name for a cult.'

'If the toe tag fits,' Oldwater said.

Chapter 27

'The bishop took quite a risk sharing that file with you, Washington,' Doctor Lang said. 'Did you ever doubt his motivations?'

'Oh, I knew what his motivations were,' Poe said. 'He wanted the Children of Job discredited beyond repair.'

'He told you this?'

'He didn't have to; he knows how I work. Knew that if something the Children of Job were doing had led to Cornelius Green's murder, I would find it. He also knew I wouldn't be intimidated by threats of going above my head.'

'Did you trust his information?'

'I treated it as I would any other unverified source of intelligence. It was robustly checked.'

'And?'

'It was accurate. The Children of Job were a cult in all but name. Their aim of establishing a theocracy in the UK was insane, of course, but it was an aim they pursued vigorously.'

'By indoctrinating their students in biblical literalism?'

Poe nodded. 'As the bishop said, they were playing the long game. Putting Children of Job alumni into as many influential positions as possible, in the hope that someday they would be able to effect national policy.'

'Reverse same-sex marriage laws, stop a woman's right to choose, ban gay men and women from serving in the military?'

'All of that, yes.'

'I imagine not everything in the file Tilly scanned had been obtained legally?'

'Is this a privileged meeting?'

'It is. You can speak freely.'

'Then no, I suspect not everything *was* obtained legally. It wasn't exactly Watergate, but I wouldn't be surprised if someone had broken into the Children of Job's offices at some point. Someone took that stuff about conversion therapy from a locked filing cabinet.'

'What else was there?'

'The file was over an inch thick, Doctor Lang. There were financial records, previous applications to the Charity Commission, non-disclosure agreements, employment records. Details on the seminars they ran. Contracts with outside catering and laundry services. Lots of information on Cornelius Green. They even knew about his tattoos. A gold mine, basically.'

'Details of the students attending their courses?'

'No,' Poe said. 'That bit was missing. I think the bishop saw them as victims.'

'OK. You had your file; you had your marching orders, and you had the bishop's card should you run into difficulties. What did you do next?'

'I went to see if my Bugger Rumble trap had been sprung.'

'And had it?'

'Oh yes,' Poe said.

Chapter 28

They left the cathedral to find Linus leaning against the bonnet of Poe's car. In his tailored suit, he stood out like a pube on an egg. Poe sighed. This was one of those occasions when he'd hoped he was going to be wrong. 'Where's my coffee, Snoopy?' he said.

'You *ditched* me?' Linus said. 'What are you, ten years old?'

'How'd you find us?'

Linus ignored him. Instead, he gazed at the cathedral and said, 'I kind of feel this is wasted here. That it should be in London where it can be properly appreciated.'

Poe, who was rude about Carlisle on an almost daily basis, bridled anyway. 'I asked how you found us.'

Linus shrugged. 'Where else could you be? After I'd checked you hadn't simply gone to the bishop's house without me, this was the obvious choice.'

'Really?' Poe said. 'There are two hundred and forty parishes across Cumbria, the diocesan office is in Penrith and there are hundreds of pubs and restaurants we could have been meeting in. Yet you came straight to the cathedral. So, I'll ask again: how did you know where we were?'

'Lucky guess,' Linus said. 'Perhaps I should buy a scratchcard.'

'How long have you been here?'

'Taxi dropped me off five minutes ago.'

'Let's see about that, shall we?' Poe raised his hand. Bugger Rumble came running. For a man of advancing years, he was surprisingly spry.

'I did what you asked, Sergeant Poe,' he said when he reached them. 'Can I speak to the specky lass now?'

'I told you, Bugger; not today.'

80

Linus narrowed his eyes. 'Who's this?' he said.

'Bugger, meet Snoopy; Snoopy, meet Bugger Rumble: Carlisle's most original street entertainer.'

Bugger removed his top hat and bowed. 'At your service, sir.'

'Okaaay,' Linus said. 'And this . . . person is here why?'

'Bugger, what time did Snoopy get here?'

'About three minutes after you went into the cathedral, Sergeant Poe.'

'Not five minutes ago then?'

'He's been leaning against the bonnet of your car for an hour.'

'And did he arrive in a taxi, Bugger?'

Bugger shook his head. 'A black Range Rover dropped him off. It's waiting for him around the corner on Fisher Street. He's parked outside that music venue.'

'The Brickyard?'

'That's the place.'

'This man is what? An informant?' Linus said.

'Informants report back on illegal activities,' Poe said. 'You're not doing anything illegal are you, Snoopy?'

Linus didn't answer.

'No,' Poe continued, 'Bugger is . . . how can I phrase this in terminology you might understand?' He paused as he pretended to consider it. 'I know,' he said after a beat, 'Bugger Rumble is HUMINT.'

'What does HUMINT mean, Poe?' Bradshaw asked.

'Human intelligence, Tilly,' Poe said. 'Linus is a spy.'

Chapter 29

'Are you stark raving mad, Poe?!' Linus snapped. 'I don't know how many times I have to say this: I work for the National Audit Office!'

'Of course you do,' Poe said. He turned his back on him and faced Bradshaw. 'It's why he knew so much about Cornelius Green's tattoos. The biggest threat to Western democracy right now isn't Islamic fundamentalism, it's the far right. And they love hiding behind crosses and Bibles. In the old days, it was speaking Russian and Farsi that got you through MI5's door. Now it's a theology degree.'

'Golly,' Bradshaw said. 'What a sneak.'

'This is absurd,' Linus said. 'Do you want to ring head office? Confirm it with them?'

'Oh shut up,' Poe said. 'The National Audit Office doesn't have the capabilities to track a mobile phone and that's the only way you could have found us. Hell, the National Crime Agency barely has it. Not in real time anyway.'

'Can I go now, Sergeant Poe?' Bugger Rumble asked. 'It's about to rain.'

'Yeah, you get away, Bugger. I'll bring Tilly for a chat when all this has finished. You have my word.'

After the happy tramp had disappeared, Linus said, 'I'm not your enemy, Sergeant Poe.'

'But you're not my friend either, are you?'

'It seems we might have got off on the wrong foot.'

'And I suppose now that you and the other covert bellend have had your trousers pulled down by a man so conspicuous he wears a top hat, you want to do what – pool resources?'

'I was going to suggest mutual cooperation.'

'And why should we do that?'

'Because it's the right thing to do.'

Poe considered that for a moment. 'OK then, you can start this mutual cooperation by answering this question: what exactly is MI5's interest in Cornelius Green?'

Chapter 30

'What *was* their interest?' Doctor Lang asked.

'I've worked with the security services before,' Poe explained. 'Their definition of cooperation isn't found in any dictionary you or I have on our bookshelves. You've heard the phrase "Eat like a bird, shit like an elephant"?'

She smiled. 'I have. It means spreading knowledge liberally.'

'Well, MI5's phrase might as well be, "Eat like an elephant, shit like an egg-bound ant". As far as information goes, they're a black hole – they consume everything in their gravity well and don't let anything out.'

'Linus didn't cooperate?'

'To be honest, I don't think he knew *why* he'd been asked to monitor the investigation.'

'He didn't?'

'That's the impression he gave anyway. As soon as he realised his cover story had sprung a leak, he was able to disclose who he really worked for. He told us he had only been with the security services for a couple of years and was relatively junior.'

'Maybe their interest was in the Children of Job. If they were as extreme as the bishop painted them, they're bound to be on a list somewhere.'

'Which is exactly what Tilly and I thought,' Poe said. 'We assumed they'd taken the opportunity to piggyback on a legitimate police investigation. Have a root around and see if there was anything they needed to be concerned about.'

'But that's *not* why he was there?'

Poe shook his head. He waited before he replied. The pain was still too raw. 'No, Linus was there for something else entirely.'

'Oh?'

'We'll get to it later, if you don't mind, Doctor Lang. If I tell you now, it won't make sense.'

'I'm a passenger on this story, Washington. You tell it any way you want.'

'Thank you,' Poe said. 'Anyhow, I called Detective Superintendent Nightingale and updated her. I couldn't share the contents of the file, obviously, but I told her what I could. I then rang DI Flynn and told her about Linus and asked her to do some digging.'

'And then what?'

'It was raining. I went home.'

Chapter 31

Herdwick Croft, the remote, once dilapidated shepherd's cottage Poe called home, had stood unoccupied for a week. Poe had been in London and Doyle had been staying at her ancestral home in Northumberland. It would need a bit of work before it became habitable. The generator would need to be filled and serviced; fuel would have to be cut. The wood burner wasn't going to fire up itself.

Poe had dropped off Bradshaw at the Shap Wells Hotel. The ex-prisoner-of-war camp was usually where she stayed when they were working in Cumbria. It was the closest occupied building to Herdwick Croft and she was well liked there. The staff knew which room she preferred. Unsurprisingly, it was the one with the strongest wi-fi signal. Linus had sloped off to find the black Range Rover that had dropped him off. Poe had told him to be at Shap Wells, outside the main entrance, at 7 a.m. the next day. He'd then driven into Kendal and bought some food and a few beers. He wasn't sure how long he was going to be up in Cumbria, but a bacon sandwich and a Spun Gold at the end of a long day never went amiss. Doyle was joining him the following day, so he reluctantly bought some fruit and vegetables as well. Some of that bread she liked, the brown stuff covered in seeds with a crust so hard it made your gums bleed.

Herdwick Croft was inaccessible by car, so Poe rode a quad bike to travel between Shap Wells and his home. Usually he would have collected Edgar, his springer spaniel, from Victoria, his neighbour, but the combination of a late finish and an early start meant there was little point.

The dry stone walls that bordered his land were as twisty and undulating as Shap Fell itself. The coping stones, the upright, tightly packed stones sitting on top of the walls that the vast flocks of hardy Herdwick sheep were unable to reach, sported delicate wigs of yellow and green lichen. Walls such as these had been used to demarcate land in Cumbria for hundreds of years and Poe knew his own like the back of his hand. Cumbria was essentially a tiny country between England and Scotland. It had its own customs, its own language and, although millions of tourists descended upon it every year, it had never lost its identity.

Poe had always accepted that the moment he purchased a part of Cumbria, he'd become a custodian of it. One of the first things he did was learn the skills needed to maintain his walls. He attended a course and found out how to prepare the land and dig a trench. How to use layers to form an A-shaped wall and how to fit locking stones and through stones. But ultimately he learned that repairing two-hundred-year-old dry stone walls was essentially a 3D jigsaw puzzle – complex if you didn't know which piece went where, but once you understood the wall, it was straightforward. And therapeutic. When a case was getting in his head, and he was unable to sleep or focus, he would often grab his trimming hammer and his pry-bar and go looking for something to repair. Sometimes the simple act of looking for a section of wall in need of attention was all it took for his mind to reboot.

It had stopped raining and the fell steamed like a damp dog. The earth smelled of sheep and heather and a hundred other things. Poe breathed in deeply and felt his muscles soften. That business with Linus had got to him. MI5 was looking over his shoulder and he didn't know why. It would be something to think about when he stripped and serviced his generator.

Shap Fell was usually so isolated that Poe felt like an astronaut, abandoned on a distant planet, but when the quad crested the final peak, Poe saw something unexpected. Instead of the shepherd's cottage being dark and gloomy, his home had light pouring from the windows, smoke spiralling from the chimney and the barking of a happy spaniel who knew what the sound of a quad bike meant.

It could only mean one thing: Estelle Doyle was a day early.

Chapter 32

Doyle had guessed Poe's meeting with the bishop might go on longer than expected, so had made the decision to travel across from Northumberland early and get Herdwick Croft ready. She owned a temperamental 1974 MGB Roadster so servicing and booting up a modern generator presented no difficulties. Poe had somehow missed her car at Shap Wells. Doyle had even collected Edgar from Victoria. The two women got on well, far too well for Poe's liking. Whenever they were laughing and giggling together, he suspected it was at his expense.

She was wearing one of his old Ferocious Dog tour T-shirts, a pair of faded jeans and no makeup. Poe thought she was the most beautiful woman in the world.

'Have a beer and catch up with Edgar,' she said. 'I have a stew in the oven. It'll be ready in half an hour.'

After they'd eaten Poe said, 'The bishop asked if I believed in God today.'

Doyle burst out laughing. 'How on earth did you answer that? I hope you were tactful.'

Poe considered it. 'I was certainly more tactful than Tilly's science answer,' he said eventually. 'By the time she'd finished explaining how we were all born in the heart of a star, I think he was ready to throw in the towel and open a payday loans company.'

Doyle laughed even harder. 'She didn't?'

'This is the same woman who asked someone if they had were-wolf syndrome – of course she did.'

'But now you've had time to think about it?'

Poe shrugged. 'I don't know. Life is decay. We're all going to die and at some point we'll be forgotten.'

Doyle smiled. 'Tough day?'

Poe told her about Cornelius Green and the Children of Job's not-so-secret agenda. 'They call girls who are at risk of, you know, being girls, "licked lollipops". That if they don't comply with their rigid views of purity no decent man will want them. It's abhorrent. So no, right now I don't believe in a higher power, certainly not the same one they believe in.'

'I wouldn't worry about it, Poe,' Doyle said. 'You're the most spiritual man I know. I've seen you sit on the fell and stare into nothing for hours at a time. Just you, Edgar, and a flask of tea.'

'You say spiritual, *I* say hungover,' he said.

'Anyway,' she said, standing up, 'forget about answering to a higher power – tonight you're answering to me.'

Which shunted the Children of Job out of Poe's mind immediately. He smiled happily.

'Oh, before I forget, Jo Nightingale wants you to do Cornelius Green's post-mortem. I told her it would probably be OK.'

'I'm not your personal pathologist, Poe,' Doyle said. 'If you want to schedule a PM, call the office like everyone else.'

Poe checked his watch. 'I'll call first thing in the morning.'

'Ring them now, Poe. We operate an out-of-hours system for emergencies.'

He scrolled through his phone until he found the number for Doyle's office. He pressed call. The ringing tone hiccupped slightly. 'I think it's being redirected,' he said.

Doyle's mobile began to ring. She answered it. 'Hello?'

'Ha ha,' Poe said, throwing his phone on the couch.

'I'm on call this week,' she said.

'Can I schedule a post-mortem, please, Professor Doyle?'

'Of course you can, Poe.'

Chapter 33

Poe arrived at Shap Wells at 7.30 a.m., half an hour later than he'd arranged to meet Linus, but at the *exact* time he'd arranged to meet Bradshaw. He swapped his quad for his car and drove to the front of the hotel. Bradshaw and Linus were waiting for him under the covered entrance. Wordlessly, Linus got in the back.

'Good morning, Poe,' Bradshaw said, climbing into the passenger seat and buckling up. She jerked the seatbelt twice to make sure the locking mechanism was working. 'How is Estelle Doyle and how is Edgar?'

'Both fine, Tilly.'

'Linus tells me you said to be outside at seven a.m., but you told me seven-thirty, Poe.'

'I didn't want him missing his ride again.'

'But you drove off on purpose yesterday.'

'That's not how I remember it, Tilly.'

Linus rolled his eyes. 'Where are we going, Sergeant Poe?'

'Didn't I tell you last night? How forgetful of me.'

'No, you didn't. Your last words to me were, "If you use my phone to track my whereabouts again, I'll remove the SIM card and stick it up your fucking arse." It seemed like a suitable way to end the evening.'

Poe grunted. He'd made a conscious decision last night to not let Linus's presence bother him. Doyle had said if there were national security concerns with the Children of Job, he should let Linus do his job. He'd called Flynn but she seemed less bothered about Linus's motives and more bothered about whether Poe would lose his temper and do something stupid. It seemed the universe was telling him to calm down and accept it.

'Tell Snoopy where we're going, Tilly,' he said.

'The Chapel Wood Institute, Linus,' Bradshaw said. 'We're going to see the Children of Job.'

Chapter 34

The Chapel Wood Institute estate was on the southern slope of Sale Fell, on the A66 side of Bassenthwaite Lake. It was three hundred yards from the *actual* Chapel Wood and half a mile from Barf, a steep, rocky fell internationally known for the whitewashed pillar of rock on its lower slopes. According to local legend, the rock marked the exact spot where, in 1783, Frederick Augustus Hervey, the Bishop of Derry, was killed falling from his horse after a foolish – and no doubt drunken – wager he could ride all the way up to the top. Poe had mentioned this to Bradshaw a couple of years earlier, thinking she'd be impressed he knew something she didn't. She'd responded by telling him that Frederick Augustus Hervey had actually died twenty years later in the Italian peninsula. When he'd asked her why the mountain rescue team still whitewashed the rock every year if it hadn't happened, she'd replied that tradition was just peer pressure from dead people. This time when they passed Barf, Poe refused to look at it.

As soon as he turned off the A66 he hit a series of smaller and smaller roads. Poe's satnav gave up but Bradshaw was able to direct him via the GPS on her mobile.

'Turn left in thirty metres, Poe,' she said.

'There *isn't* anywhere to turn, Tilly. It's . . . oh, hang on, here it is.'

He stopped the car and the three of them stared at the track leading to the Chapel Wood Institute.

'Not exactly welcoming, is it?' Linus said.

Linus had a point, but Poe wasn't going to admit it. He put the car back in gear and began inching along what was little more than a sun-baked dirt track, broken up by clumps of dandelions, their petals the colour of egg yolk.

The Bishop of Carlisle had told them that when it had been a private boarding school, the access road to Chapel Wood had been well maintained, but it seemed the Children of Job had allowed it to fall into disrepair. It had so many craters it looked like the satellite image of a bombed runway, and the vegetation either side was so overgrown it was scratching Poe's car. In the rare gaps between the dense brush, Poe caught glimpses of barbed wire fences, and beyond them fields and grazing cattle. The grass here was valley grass and it was lush and green. The exact opposite of the short, dry stuff on the fells that the Herdwick sheep eked out a living on.

'Superintendent Nightingale says they have a modern minibus,' Poe said, his eyes back on the road. 'They use it for supply runs and for picking up students.'

'She knows more than she did yesterday afternoon then,' Linus said.

'Her guys were here yesterday. They took a load of things from Cornelius's office. Spoke to a few key people.'

'Cornelius Green lived here?'

'A lot of them do, apparently. Superintendent Nightingale said it's weird and insular, but not in a *Wicker Man* kind of way. And while they weren't obstructive, the group didn't offer anything unless asked directly about it.'

'Who's in charge now?'

'*Pro tem*, a man called Joshua Meade,' Poe said, 'but I'm told the board will make a permanent appointment in the next three weeks.'

The road turned a hard left, the bend half-hidden by two giant rhododendron bushes. Poe slowed and squeezed between them like he was driving through an automatic car wash machine. He winced as one of his wing mirrors got caught on a branch.

'I can understand them not wanting to spend money on maintaining a road,' Linus said, 'but why the heck wouldn't they keep on top of these branches? It makes no sense. Not if they have a nice shiny minibus.'

Poe rounded the corner. He blinked in surprise. 'That's why,' he said.

Chapter 35

The moment they turned the corner, the road changed from dirt track to tarmac. The difference was stark, like the rhododendron bushes were Checkpoint Charlie and they'd just left Soviet-controlled East Berlin and entered the more vibrant West.

Poe thought back to what Linus had said: that it wasn't exactly welcoming. He thought the spook was probably right. The first one hundred yards of access road were deliberately in disrepair to discourage nosey tourists. Cumbria hosted twenty million a year and, like a flea infestation, they got everywhere. The potholes and the overgrown vegetation would be enough to deter even the most inquisitive weekend camper. Anyone who persevered down the track had legitimate business with the Children of Job. It was a bit like Herdwick Croft in that regard. In all his time there, Poe had not once had a casual visitor.

'Blimey,' Poe said. 'I wasn't expecting this.'

The Children of Job's estate was sprawling and impressive. Poe had assumed there'd be the old boarding school and maybe one or two outbuildings, all sagging roofs and black mould.

He was wrong.

The old school was the centrepiece of the estate, a beautiful three-storey building of pink granite and creeping ivy. The roof was slate and immaculate, the windows were highly polished and reflected the flinty sky and the quince-yellow sun. The main entrance was an imposing double door of oak and brass, although Poe noticed people going in and out of a smaller side door. And instead of the 'one or two outbuildings' he'd expected, there was at least a dozen. Some were as old as the school, some were new.

Poe pulled up in the small car park. There was one other car there. A flock of house sparrows roosting in the ivy on the old school were startled by the growl of Poe's diesel engine and took to the sky in a flutter of small wings. He turned off his engine and took in the rest of the estate.

It appeared that as well as providing conversion therapy, virginity tests and hosting 'Why Jesus Was White' seminars, the Children of Job also ran a farm. In addition to the cattle Poe had noticed earlier, there were goats, sheep and chickens. In a meadow a hundred yards from the buildings was an apiary, a series of white beehives. A woman wearing a suit, gloves and fencing hood fussed around them with a stainless-steel smoker. Poe could hear the angry buzz of displaced bees.

In front of the school was an expansive lawn dotted liberally with tables and chairs. The eastern edge had a slight slope and a small stage had been positioned at the bottom. Wooden benches were arranged on the slope in tiers like an amphitheatre.

'They have ducks as well, Poe,' Bradshaw said, touching his shoulder and pointing at a pond in the half-shade of a willow tree. A score of Aylesbury ducks rested on the grassy banks and the ramp of the pond's duck house, their plumage thick and white, their bills as pink as a kitten's tongue.

'What now, Poe?' Linus asked.

'We wait.'

'For what?'

'Him,' Poe said, nodding towards the prissy-looking man marching towards them like he was wearing someone else's underpants. 'I want to ruffle some feathers.'

Chapter 36

The man approaching the car was five-and-a-half-foot tall, finger-nail-thin with neatly trimmed silver hair that matched his piercing grey eyes. He was wearing a tan safari jacket, one of those numbers with pleated breast pockets and a cotton belt. He looked like an extra from *It Ain't Half Hot Mum*, which Poe reckoned was probably the exact opposite of what he'd intended. He was probably the kind of man who'd brag about once owning a wheelie-bin cleaning busi-ness. His face was set to 'hostile and suspicious' as he glared at them through the car window. He gestured for Poe to wind it down.

Poe did as he was asked. 'What?' he said.

'This is private property,' the man said. His voice was pinched and officious. 'Unless you have business here, please leave immediately.'

Poe reached into his pocket and opened his ID. Bradshaw did the same. Linus didn't bother. The man leaned in to examine them.

'And you are?' Poe said.

'Joshua Meade,' he said, straightening up. 'I'm the chief instruc-tor here.'

'Ah, just the man we're looking for. I understand you're in charge, Josh?'

'I would appreciate it if you could make the effort to use *all* of my christened name, Sergeant Poe, not just the bits you can be bothered with.'

'Fair enough,' Poe said. 'What was it again?'

'Joshua. And the local constabulary was here yesterday. May I ask why the National Crime Agency is now involved?'

'No, you may not,' Poe said.

'Then might I ask what you are here for?'

'I haven't decided yet.'

Joshua folded his arms and pressed his thin lips together. 'This is a place of worship, study and meditation; I hope you're not here simply to be disruptive.'

Poe turned to Bradshaw. 'Are you feeling disruptive, Tilly?'

'I'm never disruptive, Poe.'

'How about you, Snoopy?'

Linus shook his head.

'Seems none of us is in a disruptive mood today, Joshua,' Poe said, opening the car door and climbing out. He arched his back and removed the cricks. 'But we would like a look around.'

'But—'

'We'll be as quiet as church mice.'

'I'm afraid that won't be possible.'

'No?'

'No.'

'Why not?' Poe asked.

'Half the staff are in Keswick for the convention and the rest are either teaching or getting ready for tonight.'

'What are they doing in Keswick?'

'The convention is on,' Joshua said, holding his gaze. 'They're spreading the word.'

'Jolly good,' Poe said. 'And what's happening tonight?'

'A ceremony for graduating students. A small presentation followed by a chance to relax and socialise.'

'Guess we're stuck with you then.'

'I'm sorry, Sergeant Poe,' Joshua said. 'I'd like to help, but Cornelius's death has hit us all hard. It wasn't just a terrible tragedy; given his founder-member status, it was also a huge blow to the organisation. The board is meeting soon to discuss his replacement and there is much to do.'

'Murder,' Poe said.

'I'm sorry?'

'You said "Cornelius's death". Did you not mean Cornelius's *murder*?'

'Slip of the tongue, Sergeant Poe,' Joshua said. 'Now, I'm sorry this has been a wasted journey for you all, but I really must be getting on.'

'Am I right in thinking that the Children of Job still has aspirations of getting charitable status, Joshua? In fact, don't you have another application pending right now?'

Joshua's eyes narrowed. 'How could you possibly know that?'

'I think you'd be surprised at what I know,' Poe said. 'And I imagine a positive word from the Church would go some way to help you achieve that goal?'

'That goes without saying, Sergeant Poe. However, many of us feel that the modern church is now too liberal for our organisation, and I'm sure they feel the Children of Job is too conservative for theirs. I fear a positive reference might be too much to ask.'

Poe found the most recently entered number on his phone. He pressed call and when it was answered he spoke quietly. He then passed his phone to Joshua. 'The Bishop of Carlisle would like to speak to you, Joshua.'

'Excuse me?'

'He said the Bishop of Carlisle would like to speak to you, Joshua,' Bradshaw chipped in. 'He's called Nicholas Oldwater and he's our friend, isn't he, Poe?'

'He certainly is, Tilly.'

Joshua took Poe's phone. 'Hello?' he said uncertainly. It was clear he thought he was being pranked.

'Oh, and don't forget to tell the bishop how the Children of Job is spreading the word in Keswick,' Poe said. 'I think he'll find that particularly funny.'

Joshua scowled and stepped away to take the call. He returned two minutes later. 'Very well,' he said. 'Let's get this over with.'

'Splendid,' Poe said.

Chapter 37

'We aren't completely self-sustained yet,' Joshua explained, 'but we're not far off.'

He had started their tour of the Children of Job by taking them around the working farm. They grew crops and raised livestock, most of which Poe had already seen. At the back of the main building was a walled kitchen garden, lush and bountiful underneath the warm summer sun. It looked like Mr McGregor's garden, the one Peter Rabbit raided for lettuce, French beans and radishes. There were raised beds packed full of vegetables, fruit and herbs. Rhubarb forcers lined the north-facing wall and fruit trees were trained against the south-facing one. Half-a-dozen men and women tended the crops. Some had trowels, others held watering cans. All of them worked in silence.

'I thought you said all your staff were in Keswick,' Poe said.

'No, I said around half of them were,' Joshua said. 'The rest are teaching or helping set up the graduation ceremony.'

Poe gestured to the people tending the walled garden. 'So who are they?'

'Volunteers.'

'Singing for their supper?'

'We do farm therapy here, Sergeant Poe. Some of our members struggle in the outside world. They can't understand why politicians mock their faith and why atheism is at an all-time high.'

'I didn't realise politicians *did* mock their faith.'

'Really?' Joshua said. He seemed genuinely surprised. 'You don't think same-sex marriage laws mock our faith? You don't think teaching our children about evolution mocks our faith? You think undermining the fundamental right to life isn't mocking our faith?'

'No, no and I don't know what that last one is,' Poe said.

'He means abortion,' Linus said.

'Ah. Then that's another no from me, I'm afraid.'

'Are you married, Sergeant Poe?' Joshua asked.

'I'm not.'

'And why is that?'

'Guess I haven't found the right man yet.'

'Yes, very funny,' Joshua said. 'But the more you liberals sneer, the more determined we are to become authentically Christian. And I asked if you were married because this is exactly the kind of thing our members struggle with.'

'And what's that?'

'Family is a biblical and fundamental institution. Being looked down on, even pitied, by people with . . . different, sometimes morally repugnant values is confusing. The farm and the garden allow our members to reconnect with their faith through nature. It acts like the reset button on those smartphones of yours.'

'Poe's engaged to be married to Estelle Doyle,' Bradshaw said. 'She's a woman. Also, he doesn't know how to use the reset button on his smartphone. I have to do all the updates for him.'

'Thanks for that, Tilly,' Poe said.

'You're very welcome, Poe.'

'You say you're opposed to same-sex marriage, Joshua,' Poe said.

'We opposed the Same Sex Couples Act in 2013. I know it's not fashionable, but our consciences couldn't allow us to adopt any other position.'

'And what about gay people in general? Do you oppose them too?'

Joshua's spine stiffened. He pushed his neck into the back of his collar. 'The Bible says it's an abomination.'

'And what do *you* say?'

'It's divine law, Sergeant Poe,' he said with cold superiority. 'Who am I to go against the will of God?'

'What would you do if a member approached you about a child who was . . . how can I put this without sounding ridiculous . . . at risk of *breaking* divine law?'

'I would pray with them.'

'That's all?'

'What else is there?'

'You don't have a course you can put them on? One that might cure them?' Poe wrapped 'cure' in air quotes. 'Nothing like that here?'

'Of course not.'

'Are you positive?'

Joshua avoided eye contact. 'I am.'

Poe let his answer hang for a few moments. 'OK,' he said eventually. 'Where to next?'

Chapter 38

Joshua took them to Cornelius Green's rooms. He had lived on the grounds, in the old headmaster's residence. It was tucked into a grassy embankment and was a traditional Lake District cottage, all coarse, unevenly sized stones. Superintendent Nightingale's team had already been through it, and she'd OK'd them to go in and have a root around.

'It's not locked,' Joshua said.

'Bloody hell, how much stuff did they take?' were Poe's first words when he stepped inside Cornelius's cottage. It was usually murder suspects, not murder victims who had their homes raided by the cops. All Nightingale had left was a cot, a small table and a single chair. There was a Bible on the table and a wooden cross fixed to the wall.

'I don't think they took anything, Sergeant Poe,' Joshua said. 'Cornelius preferred his quarters sparse and functional. He took all his meals in the main building.'

'What did he do in his spare time?'

'He read his Bible and he prayed.'

'Nothing else?'

'What else is there?'

'I don't know,' Poe said. 'Friendship? Intimate relationships? Beer? The usual stuff.'

'Cornelius *was* in an intimate relationship.'

'Who with? And you'd better not say God.'

'Does our faith frighten you, Sergeant Poe?'

'*Zealots* frighten me, Joshua,' Poe said. 'Zealots fly planes into buildings. Zealots make pipe bombs. Zealots kill doctors.'

'The Children of Job is a peaceful organisation.'

102

'Some people say it's a cult.'

'Is that what you think?'

'I haven't made up my mind yet.'

Joshua had no answer to that.

'Who gets the top job now?' Poe asked.

'As I told you, the board will meet soon.'

'You after it?'

'I won't be applying.'

'Why not?'

'I don't have the seniority.'

'Who has?'

'Why do you want to know?'

'*Cui bono*, Joshua?'

'Who benefits?'

'You know your Latin.'

'I used to be a barrister. You want to know who would benefit from Cornelius Green's death?'

'I do,' Poe said.

Joshua sighed. 'Cornelius was an easy man to admire, but a hard man to like, Sergeant Poe.'

'Why was that?'

'His piety. Some of our members found it hard to live up to.'

'His faith was too extreme?'

Joshua shook his head. 'That's not what I'm saying. We're all devout here, but sometimes Cornelius's commitment could be . . . overwhelming.'

Poe nodded. Human behaviour crept into every aspect of life. It didn't matter if it was investment banking or religious extremism – there was always a never-acknowledged but sharply observed hierarchy. And the people at the bottom of the ladder were always eyeing the rung above. He'd make sure Superintendent Nightingale was aware of this; he had neither the time nor the authority to bring in every member of the Children of Job for questioning.

'I understand Cornelius had an office,' he said.

'Of course,' Joshua replied. 'He was the founder.'

'Let's see it then.'

Chapter 39

Cornelius Green's office in the old school building *had* been emptied by Superintendent Nightingale's detectives. Finding out how the victim lived was often the key to finding out how they died, and as Cornelius's work *was* his life it made sense to do a deep dive. Poe spent less than thirty seconds in there.

'Show me the rest of the building,' he said to Joshua. He wasn't expecting to see anything, but sometimes, as Bradshaw said it was in science, unguided research resulted in unintended discoveries. And anyway, the more he poked his nose in, the more irate Joshua became. Irate people slipped up.

The first floor used to be the old school's dormitories, and the Children of Job had seen no reason to change it. Where once the sons of wealthy Cumbrians had masturbated in rows, a generation of confused young adults now prayed and slept. And secretly masturbated, no doubt. There was nothing to see. Attendees of the residential courses the Children of Job offered had either been told not to bring any personal possessions with them, or, like Cornelius, they didn't have any.

They walked down the grand central staircase to the ground floor. The rooms on this floor were of more generous proportions. The old classrooms were the same size as the ones Poe had been taught in, although he suspected there would have been fewer pupils back in Chapel Wood's day. There were storerooms, a well-equipped staffroom and two changing rooms – one for men, one for women. The gender-neutral movement clearly hadn't reached the Children of Job.

'What's through there?' Poe said, pointing at a doublewide door. He could hear the thump of a bass guitar.

'It used to be the school gymnasium,' Joshua said. 'It's where the graduation ceremony is being held tonight. We'd better not go in; it sounds like the band is rehearsing.'

'Yeah, we'd better leave them alone,' Poe said, pushing open the doors and stepping inside.

Joshua sighed and followed him. Bradshaw and Linus brought up the rear. As she always did when Poe was being deliberately antagonistic, Bradshaw looked worried about self-inflicted wounds. Linus on the other hand seemed to be enjoying himself. Poe was wondering why that might be when, out of nowhere, something happened that Poe was sure he'd remember for the rest of his life.

Chapter 40

As the only large indoor communal space on the estate, the Children of Job used the old school gym as a multipurpose room, Joshua explained. Poe asked for examples.

'Morning and evening prayers, obviously,' Joshua replied. 'Harvest festivals, a few of the other traditions we celebrate. Anything too large for one of the classrooms basically. It's used every day and it has to be booked in advance. Any diary clashes were mediated by Cornelius.' He paused. 'I imagine that will fall to me now.' It didn't look as though it were something he would relish.

Despite the unexpected turn the gym had taken, echoes of its past were there if you knew what you were looking for. Scars on the polished maple floor where badminton and basketball court markings had been scraped off. Walls that still bore evidence of climbing frames, hooks for the ropes that remained in the ceiling. He could almost hear the slap-slap of kids in plimsolls as they ran and jumped and yelled in excitement.

It was currently being dressed for that evening's graduation ceremony. Half-a-dozen men and women were hanging up banners and putting out chairs; another two were setting up what looked like a dry bar in the corner. One end of the gymnasium was wall-to-wall stage. Poe couldn't tell if it was new, or whether this was where the headmaster had stood during assembly. Probably the latter. It was made from the same wood as the floor. The wall behind the stage was bare brick. On it hung a large crucifix, at least ten feet tall. It was a simple design, two bits of oak and a wooden Jesus. No colour. Given how frippery-free Cornelius Green's life had been, Poe wouldn't have been surprised to learn that the Children of Job's founder had personally chosen it. On the stage underneath the crucifix the band rehearsed. They watched for a while.

Poe had always thought Christian rock was to music what Michael McIntyre was to stand-up comedy – cosy, clean-cut, with no personality. Nothing to dislike, but nothing to admire either. It had none of the Sex Pistols' disenfranchisement or the Clash's politics, the Ramones' humour or the raw sexuality of Led Zeppelin. It was music without danger, and it therefore had no value.

Poe listened for a while and decided that the rosy-cheeked musicians on stage, two boys and two girls, weren't actually that bad. They finished a song he didn't recognise and moved straight into a punchy, guitar and drum-heavy cover of 'Kumbaya'. When they got to the bit about 'Someone's singing, Lord, kumbaya', a voice behind them started chanting in time with the beat.

'I cast thee out, serpents, I cast thee out! Oh serpents, I cast thee out!'

Bradshaw frowned. 'Those aren't the right words,' she said.

They all turned. A wild-looking woman shuffled towards them. She continued chanting, getting louder and louder, until it was little more than unhinged ranting. When she was twenty yards away, she stopped. Her ranting did not. She was younger than Poe had imagined. Mid-thirties if he were forced to guess. Her back was stooped, and it was this that caused the shuffling gait. She had Edward Scissorhands's hair and wore a chewed up old cardigan that was grey rather than the white it had once been. The buttons were in the wrong holes, adding to her lopsided look. Her eyes were manic and unfocused; her face mottled with rage.

One of the men who had been quietly putting up a 'Congratulations!' banner climbed down from his ladder. He approached the woman cautiously but made no move to intervene.

Poe faced Joshua. 'Well, she's not with me.'

'That's enough, Alice,' Joshua said kindly. 'These people are our guests.'

'Sinners!' she shrieked.

She began tugging at her hair. No wonder it was wild, Poe thought. She probably pulled it out in clumps.

'That may be the case,' Joshua said, 'but the heart of the Gospel is rooted in hospitality, is it not?'

'Hey,' Poe said. 'Tilly isn't a sinner.'

'Hello, Alice,' Bradshaw said. 'My name is Matilda, but you can call me Tilly if you want. I am very pleased to meet you. I like your jumper – is it wool?'

'I cast thee out, serpent!'

'Oh my.'

'I think they need some help in the greenhouse, Alice,' Joshua said. 'The tomatoes will go soft if we don't get them picked. You like working in the greenhouse, don't you?'

'I do,' she mumbled.

'Why don't you let Mark take you there?'

'OK.'

'And I'll see you at evening prayers.'

As Alice was gently led away, Joshua said, 'This is what happens when a devout woman can no longer cope in a society that mocks her faith.'

'She'll be OK?' Poe asked, ignoring the dig.

'She will. The greenhouse will calm her and we'll have a chat later. See if she needs some extra support.'

'Who is she?'

'Alice is part of the furniture, Sergeant Poe. She's been here fifteen years and I doubt she'll ever leave.'

'And why's that?'

'The locals call her Mad Alice, which is why she's so wary of strangers. This is the only place she feels accepted. And yes, she occasionally has her little episodes, but she's never violent and an hour in the chapel or the garden always calms her.'

'Does she work here?'

Joshua shrugged. 'She doesn't get paid, if that's what you mean. But she's here almost every day of the week and she takes her meals with the permanent staff whenever she wants. If she wanted a job, we'd give her one, but every time we broach it, she says no. She says she's just happy to be here.' He sighed. 'And I suppose this is what the people who mock us don't realise. The Children of Job isn't only a religious organisation or a pressure group or a training company; it's also a place for the people who don't quite fit in. A sanctuary for the forgotten. No one will ever be turned away from here, Sergeant Poe.'

Unless they happen to be gay, Poe thought but didn't say. The band started playing again and he watched as Alice reached the gym door. Just as she was about to step through it, she turned and caught Poe's eye. It might have been his imagination, but he was sure she winked.

After Alice had left for the greenhouse, Poe said, quietly and without looking at Joshua, 'I want to know why you won't tell me about the conversion therapy groups you run.'

'I told you; we don't do that kind of thing here, Sergeant Poe,' he replied. 'It's been proven to be ineffective.'

'OK,' Poe said. 'Now I want to know why you're lying to me.'

'I'm not—'

'Tilly, show Joshua the scanned conversion therapy programme you have on your tablet. The one that's on this year's curriculum.'

Bradshaw found it quickly. She passed Joshua her tablet. He paled as he read what was on the screen. For a moment he seemed lost for words. His Adam's apple bounced up and down. 'I think I would like to discuss this somewhere a little more private,' he said eventually.

Chapter 41

The somewhere 'a little more private' was the old school basement. It was directly underneath the gymnasium and appeared to mirror the dimensions above, albeit with a claustrophobically low ceiling. It looked like school basements did the world over. Tables and chairs stacked high. Old chalkboards pushed against the wall. A storeroom for anything too big to go in a storeroom. At the far end, a table and chairs were set up conference style.

Poe cocked an eyebrow.

'Sometimes we have to discuss things of a . . . sensitive nature,' Joshua explained. When they were seated, he said, 'I would like to know how you came to be in possession of this information.'

'Not gonna happen,' Poe said.

'I will discuss what was on Miss Bradshaw's tablet momentarily, Sergeant Poe, but first I must know where your information came from. Our course members expect . . . no, *demand* confidentiality, and if there has been a data breach then there are actions I must take immediately.'

'Your information is secure, Joshua. Tilly didn't find this in a dumpster.'

'Then where?'

'I won't be revealing my source, but I can assure you I am unaware of anything in the public domain.'

'I have your word?'

'Is my word worth anything to you?' Poe said. 'If it is, then you have it; if it isn't, then rest assured, I don't imagine anyone else is looking for it.'

Joshua breathed a sigh of relief. 'I know your opinion of us is very low, Sergeant Poe, and to be honest I don't care. I've dealt with this my entire adult life and I am used to it.'

'You have no idea what my opinion is, Joshua.'

'Your mind was made up the moment you read what was on Miss Bradshaw's iPad.'

'Time and time again conversion therapy has been discredited as ineffective, and worse, deeply damaging,' Poe said. 'The fact the Children of Job persist with it is a damning indictment of what you stand for. What you might be capable of.'

'I completely agree,' Joshua said.

'You do?'

'Of course. You can't stop someone being who they are in here,' – he pressed his hand against his chest – 'any more than you can stop the wind. And although I believe homosexuality is a mortal sin, it is not my role to judge. That is God's privilege alone.'

'So why do you run them?' Poe asked.

Joshua hesitated before answering. It looked as if he was deciding the best way to frame his response. 'I've already told you Cornelius was an easy man to admire, but a hard man to like,' he said eventually.

'You have.'

'And you've referred to him as a zealot.'

'I said zealots frighten me, Joshua. I don't think I attributed the term to Cornelius Green.'

'But that's what you think?'

Poe shrugged then nodded. 'I've read his file. If I were asked, I would say he *does* fit the Home Office definition of an extremist.'

'Although I'm a relative newcomer here, I'm told conversion therapy was entirely Cornelius's idea,' Joshua said. 'He believed it worked and developed the programme accordingly. Other than a few tweaks to keep up with technology, the core programme has stayed the same for thirty-five years.'

'Talk me through it.'

'I can't.'

'A man is dead, Joshua. Now is not the time to be coy.'

'I can't because I don't know.'

'It was running for thirty-five years,' Poe said. 'How can you not know?'

'Because I wasn't told.'

'You weren't told, or you didn't ask?'

'I agreed with Cornelius Green on almost everything. His position on abortion, the sanctity of marriage, how our children should be raised, his belief that Christian values should form the central tenet of government.'

'But not conversion therapy.'

'I'm an intelligent man, Sergeant Poe. I read law at Corpus Christi. I was a practising barrister. I've reviewed many papers on the subject, and a man with half my intellect would come to the same conclusion I did. Conversion therapy is futile, counterproductive and the psychological impact has the potential to be catastrophic. Ultimately, there are only three ways to achieve aims such as ours: we win the argument, we win the election, or we put judges in the right places.'

'But?'

'But for Cornelius it was a burning belief, almost a crusade. He couldn't be talked down and there was no point trying. Over the years there have been three or four other members who believed in the efficacy of conversion therapy, and they were the only ones Cornelius allowed to assist with the programme. The rest of us remained unaware of what went on in that classroom.'

'It must be written down somewhere though.'

'I'm told it isn't.'

'I want to speak to the ones who *do* believe in conversion therapy then. The ones who helped him run it.'

'I wish you luck. One died of liver cancer in 2016; the others ventured to pastures new many years ago. The only man currently running conversion therapy was Cornelius Green.'

'The course died with him?'

'And maybe that's a good thing,' Joshua said. 'I believe the Children of Job deserve a voice in discussions about faith – and that wasn't going to happen while we ran that course. Perhaps this is a chance for us to take a step towards palatability as far as mainstream Christianity is concerned. To redirect the narrative. That's certainly the position I'll be urging the board to adopt.'

'Is there anything you *can* tell us about Cornelius Green?' Poe said, checking his watch. They'd been there for almost two hours now. 'Something we might find helpful in tracking down the person who killed him?'

Joshua considered the question carefully. 'Whatever you might hear, Sergeant Poe, whatever impression I might have given you, know this: Cornelius Green was a good man. Some of his ideas were misguided but his faith never wavered. I am profoundly sorry that he never managed to find the peace he deserved, and I can only hope the rest of us can live up to his exacting standards.'

As they left the basement Poe hummed 'Always Look on the Bright Side of Life', partly to annoy Joshua, although he doubted the starchy bigot had ever seen *Monty Python's Life of Brian*, and partly to keep up his spirits. It had been a disturbing interview in a weird, dank location.

They walked back through the rapidly filling gymnasium and out into the fresh air. Poe took in a lungful, glad to be above ground again. The sun was now high in the sky and he wished he'd had the foresight to park in the shade. His car was going to be like an oven. He squinted at his windscreen. There was something off with the glare. It wasn't uniform. He shaded his eyes and realised what it was.

'We'll see ourselves out from here, Joshua,' Poe said.

'I'll walk you to your car, Sergeant Poe. I'm going to check on Alice anyway and the greenhouse is on the way.'

Poe stopped. 'I'm afraid I must insist. There's something I need to talk to my colleagues about and it's confidential. Don't worry, it's nothing to do with you or your organisation.'

They shook hands outside the old school's front entrance.

'Why didn't you want Joshua to walk back to the car with us, Poe?' Bradshaw asked.

'Have a look at the windscreen, Tilly.'

Bradshaw's eyesight wasn't as good as his, but they were now close enough for her to see it. 'There's a bit of paper tucked under one of the windscreen wipers,' she said. 'What do you think it is?'

113

'I have no idea, but the fact it wasn't hand-delivered must mean something. As Joshua's probably watching us, I'm going to leave it where it is until we're out of sight.'

Which was what they did. The moment Poe drove around the guardian rhododendron bushes he stopped the car, nipped out and collected the piece of paper. It was a folded page torn from an A5 notebook. He climbed back in the car and read the neat, cursive writing.

If you really want to understand cornelius green, seek out israel cobb. They had a massive falling out – ask him what it was about. Ask him why the courses stopped. This is where your answers will be found.

Linus reached forward and took the note from Poe. After a moment he said, 'Who the hell is Israel Cobb?'

'He sounds like a salad,' Poe replied, frowning. Israel Cobb was an unusual name. He would have remembered if it had been in the bishop's dossier. He retrieved the note from Linus and read it again. Who the hell had written this? And what courses were they referring to?

He passed the note to Bradshaw. She glanced at it then opened her laptop.

Chapter 42

'You ain't with that lot, are ya?' the heavily tanned barman asked with an even heavier London accent. He pointed at the table next to the window overlooking Keswick's Main Street. Three men and three women, quietly chatting.

'Who's "that lot"?' Poe replied, surprised to be talking to a cockney in a Cumbrian pub.

'Them seat-blocking conventioneers. Been here three hours already and they ain't spent a tenner between 'em. They ain't even ordered meals; just six orange cordials, two decaf green teas and a packet of salted nuts.'

It was lunchtime and although the pub was full, the bar staff were standing idle. Poe had some sympathy for the barman. They had tried to find a table but had given up. Instead, they were perched on barstools, facing the guy like he was a blackjack dealer.

'What can I get you, miss?' he asked Bradshaw.

'A decaffeinated green tea, please.'

'Oh, for fu—'

'And I'll have a pint of Sneck Lifter,' Poe cut in. 'Snoopy will have the same and we'll all need menus.'

'Steak and kidney pudding's the special today if you're interested?' the barman said, mollified he was finally getting to pull some pints.

'*Very* interested,' Poe said. 'Snoopy?'

'Same, please.'

'Can I tell the kitchen we want three, miss?' the barman asked.

'Don't be absurd,' Bradshaw replied, looking at the specials board. 'I'll have the watercress soup.'

'But that's a starter.'

115

'And a heavy meal during the day makes me feel sluggish and dull-witted.'

'You're the boss,' he said, tapping the order into the till.

'I'm not the boss,' Bradshaw said, frowning. 'I've never worked in a pub in my life. And while I'm out in the field, Poe's my boss.'

'Who's Poe?'

Poe reached across and shook his hand. 'I am.'

'Mike,' the barman said.

'You the landlord?'

'How can you tell?'

'You're the only one with a tan.'

Mike laughed. 'You saying I should pay this lot more?' He gestured to the other bar staff. Two of them were on their phones and another was staring, dead-eyed, into space.

'You been here long?'

'Ten years now,' Mike said, putting Poe's pint on the drip tray.

'Not a fan of the convention, I take it?'

'I don't mind 'em really. I mean, I wish they'd spend some money, but they're polite enough and they seem like decent people. It's just I had to turn down two groups of eight yesterday. Fresh off the fells and thirsty as hell. Wanted lunch and afternoon drinks. Between 'em they'd have spent four 'undred quid. Instead, I had sixteen conventioneers sharing four plates of chips.'

'You get any of that Children of Job lot in here?'

'The cult? They have that compound on the dark side of Barf?'

Poe was surprised to hear the term being used so openly. Then again, perhaps he wasn't. Bar staff were constantly taking the pulse of the local zeitgeist. And what else could you call a group who lived as the Children of Job did? Their hair was too short to mistake them for a hippy commune. In the vernacular of the straight-talking local, that only really left cult. 'Yep, them,' he said.

'Nah. They don't come in 'ere. You see them outside sometimes, haranguing the punters about the demon drink. But they're harmless. Locals ignore 'em and tourists film 'em for Twitter and Facebook.'

Poe knew what he meant. On the walk from the car to the pub they'd passed a trio of wild-eyed men badgering people about how

116

it wasn't too late to renounce something Poe didn't catch and accept something else he didn't catch. He had been more interested in the crowd's reaction. Most were giving them a wide berth but a few had their smartphones out. Although they didn't have identity cards clipped to their pockets, once you knew what you were looking for, they were clearly Children of Job. He had surreptitiously taken a photo. The more of them he could recognise, the better.

Poe's phone buzzed in his pocket. The dark side of Barf, as landlord Mike had called it, had been a reception dead spot and Keswick, surrounded by some of the steepest fells in the Lake District, wasn't much better. It seemed to have picked up the pub's wi-fi rather than a mast signal. Bradshaw must have logged him in the last time they were there and the password hadn't been changed.

He had messages and calls from both Doyle and Superintendent Nightingale. He used WhatsApp, another of Bradshaw's additions to his phone, to call Doyle. She didn't answer. He called Nightingale and she did.

'Where are you, Poe?' she said. 'Estelle and I have been trying to get hold of you for ages.'

Poe told her about his visit to the Children of Job, his meeting with Joshua Meade and the strange note that had been left under his windscreen wiper.

'You can brief me when you get here,' Nightingale said.

'Where's "here"?'

'The RVI. Your missus had a sudden gap in her schedule and she was able to get Cornelius Green on the slab today. The body's arrived from Carlisle. How long will it take you to get to Newcastle?'

'Couple of hours,' Poe said, ignoring the 'missus' comment. He'd get this a lot now, he suspected. Cops loved things like that.

'You OK if we make a start?'

'It's your case, ma'am. And we're not expecting anything helpful. I'm sure Estelle will have a medical way of saying this, but he died because his head was bashed in with rocks.'

'See you soon.' She rang off.

While Poe had been on the phone, their meals had arrived. Poe's plate was as big as a wheel cap and overloaded with thick-cut chips and honey-glazed parsnips. The steam rising from the steak and kidney pudding smelled of beef and gravy and childhood.

'We'd better get these to go,' he sighed.

Chapter 43

The journey from Keswick was a caravan of caravans. They were mainly heading *into* Cumbria, but there were so many of the bloated white carbuncles it had made overtaking impossible. It wasn't until Poe reached the dual carriageway section of the A69 that he'd been able to put his foot down and get above fifty miles an hour. It was close to two and a half hours before they finally pulled into the car park at Newcastle's Royal Victoria Infirmary.

He found a parking space and they hurried to the mortuary and Estelle Doyle's new post-mortem suite. An attendant was waiting to take them straight through. A few years ago, they would have had to suit up and get in the same room as the pathologist; now they had a suite with negative air pressure and a purpose-built viewing area. Superintendent Nightingale was sitting down, a notebook on her lap and a phone glued to her ear. She gave them a reverse head nod and the two-minute sign, then went back to her call.

'Ah, you're here,' Doyle said. 'Living together doesn't mean you get special treatment, Poe.' She winked at Bradshaw. 'Not unless he's been extra naughty, Tilly. Please try to be punctual next time.'

Poe could see Doyle's lips moving, although her voice came through the speakers in the suite. Some posh new microphone system. Previously she'd had to stand on a pedal when she wanted to be recorded; now it picked her up wherever she was in the room. Cornelius Green's cadaver was on an inspection table, naked and, apart from his tattoos, colourless under the harsh halogen lights. The Y-shaped incision had been made and closed with the usual 'baseball stitch'. The top of his skull had been sawn off and sewn back on. Standard post-mortem cuts. Doyle had finished the internal examination. Poe glanced at Linus. The spook had turned green.

119

'First dead body, Snoopy?' Poe asked.

Linus nodded but said nothing. Poe figured his mouth was flooded with saliva and any attempt to speak would result in vomiting. That was how he'd felt at his first PM.

'Have a seat next to Tilly,' Poe continued. 'And if you're going to spew, go outside. The viewing room's negative air pressure means that while we might not smell it, Estelle certainly will. And you really don't want that to happen.'

'That counts for you too, Poe,' Doyle said without looking up.

'Why would I be sick? I've been to hundreds of these things.'

'I'm talking about your dinner – you're not eating it here.'

'I wasn't going to.'

'He's fibbing, Estelle,' Bradshaw said. 'He asked the man who showed us in if he could bring in some knives and forks.'

'Take your food outside please,' Doyle said.

Poe rolled his eyes but did as he was asked. While he was in her post-mortem suite, he wasn't the man she lived with; he was just another idiot cop. He either did what he was told or he waited in reception. There was no third option. So instead of protesting, he said, 'Snoopy, make yourself useful and find somewhere safe for all this.'

Linus looked at him gratefully. Any excuse to leave the viewing area.

'Still picking on your intern, Poe?' Nightingale said, putting her phone in her pocket.

'He shouldn't have lied to me.'

'I don't imagine he was given any choice.'

'Not my problem.'

'Have you figured out what their interest is yet?'

Poe shook his head.

'How did you find the Children of Job?'

'Intense. And their views are outdated and abhorrent by today's standards. Saying that, I got the feeling some of them are relieved Cornelius Green is dead. It seems he was the driving force behind the more extreme programmes.'

'Do you think someone killed him to make them appear more progressive?'

'Can't rule it out.'

'Speaking of Cornelius Green,' Doyle said. 'As clinically suspected, he died from blunt force trauma. Any number of the blows he took to the head could have proved fatal.'

'There were no other injuries?' Poe asked.

'Did I say that?'

'You didn't. Sorry.'

Doyle smiled. 'Still can't help butting in, can you, Poe? Cornelius Green did in fact have other injuries. Quite interesting ones.' She tilted her head towards her assistant. 'Can we move the body on to its side, please? I want his back facing the viewing area.'

In a well-practised move, they manoeuvred the cadaver until Cornelius's back was facing them. Like his chest, it was covered with religious tattoos. Crosses, crucifixes, the Virgin Mary, more obscure religious iconography.

Doyle pointed the inspection camera – one of those with a semi-rigid cable – at the base of Cornelius's spine. The monitor in the viewing room flickered into life. Nightingale glanced at it and went back to her notebook. It seemed this was only for Poe's benefit.

'You can't see these clearly because of his tattoos,' Doyle said, 'but there are recent histological changes to the skin. If you look here, here, here and here,' – she tapped Cornelius's back with a pen – 'there are two pairs of dot-like lesions. There's a third pair higher up, just under the shoulder blade.'

'Three pairs?' Poe said. 'Not six separate ones?'

'Each pair is exactly thirty-five millimetres apart, Poe.'

'What are they?'

'Burns.'

Poe frowned. 'They can't be from a cigarette, not if they're so precisely spaced.'

'They were caused by a stun gun,' Doyle said. 'The marks are quite specific, and once you know what they look like, they're not difficult to identify. The lowest pair is the deepest. The other two pairs are relatively superficial.'

Poe ran through the most likely sequence of events. 'The first was to debilitate him, the rest were unfriendly reminders,' he said.

Nightingale looked up from her notebook. 'That's my line of thinking as well, Poe,' she said. 'The killer makes Cornelius wobbly with the first jolt then threatens him with more if he doesn't comply. He has to be reminded of this twice. It explains how he was taken to the Lightning Tree without a noticeable struggle.'

'We may not be looking for a big burly killer after all then.'

'Nope,' Nightingale agreed. '*Anyone* could have killed Cornelius Green.'

Chapter 44

'Was this the first time you'd worked with Professor Doyle since your engagement?' Doctor Lang asked.

'I think it probably was,' Poe replied. 'Why do you ask?'

'Because she seemed unusually harsh on you. I'm wondering if in her desire to be seen as impartial, she overcompensated.'

'You're talking about when I asked if there were any other injuries on Cornelius Green?'

'I am.'

'Then I haven't described Estelle properly. She doesn't suffer fools at the best of times and cutting into the body of a murder victim is not the best of times. If you don't respect the science, she doesn't respect you. I've seen her reduce her assistants to tears and I've seen her ban senior investigating officers from her post-mortems.'

'But she *was* harsh on you.'

'I'd asked a question.'

'Surely asking questions is a step towards finding answers?'

Poe nodded. 'Estelle encourages questions, but only when she's finished her briefing. She talks police officers through her findings in a logical, linear manner. She uses accessible language and, because she needs you to understand the scientific sequence of events, she doesn't like to be interrupted. I knew this and I asked a question anyway. If anything, she went easy on me.'

'OK,' Doctor Lang said. 'I think I'm beginning to get a grip on her. Is she like this with you when she isn't working?'

'Absolutely not. The moment she steps out of the mortuary, the cold, logical scientist is put into a locked drawer. It's me who can't get my work/life balance right. When I'm working a murder, I'm *always* working it. Even when I'm not, if that makes sense.'

'You think about it when you should be thinking about your friends and family.'

'I do. Always have.'

'Everyone needs downtime, Washington. Taking a break isn't a sign of weakness; it's a sign of strength. It's an acknowledgement that the most powerful tool at your disposal,' – she touched herself on the temple – 'needs to be recharged. If it runs flat, it doesn't work properly. Mood, cognitive functioning, even memory begins to suffer. And because of your nightmares, you're not even getting the restorative power of sleep. I think you're now operating on sheer willpower, and although this case is over, there'll be others that require your undivided attention. There will be times when you have to work for thirty-six hours straight, and the only way you can do what you need to do, is to *not* do it when you don't need to.' She gestured at where they were and added, 'Otherwise you might find yourself in a place like this. Estelle's a doctor; I'm sure she'll agree.'

'Oh, I *know* she agrees,' he said.

'We have something we can work on then. Now, where were we?'

'Estelle had finished telling us the killer had probably used a stun gun to get Cornelius Green up to the Lightning Tree.'

'Was there anything else?'

'Oh yes. She'd noticed something about Cornelius's tattoos.'

'Something important?'

'It didn't seem so at the time.'

'And later?'

'Everything, Doctor Lang,' Poe said. 'The tattoos were the key to *everything*.'

Chapter 45

'I have one last thing to show you,' Doyle said. 'You too, Superintendent Nightingale.'

Nightingale frowned. 'You've kept something back?'

Poe winced, but Doyle took it in her stride.

'No, I was waiting for a confirmatory email. It has only just arrived. I saw no reason to burden you with my suspicions until then. I report facts, it's you who interprets those facts.'

'And you have a new fact?' Nightingale asked.

'Show slides twenty-three to twenty-eight on the monitor, please, Carlos.'

Doyle's assistant fiddled with the computer. The screen in the viewing room changed from the stun-gun marks to six close-ups of Cornelius's lower torso and upper thighs. They were just as heavily tattooed.

'I understand an expert in religious iconography will go through the victim's tattoos with you,' Doyle said, 'but I wanted to show you something that is more my field of expertise. Now, as you can see there are hundreds of tattoos on the victim's body, and because he's used every available bit of skin, it does appear they're a bit rough and ready.'

'They're not?' Nightingale asked.

'No. Most are exceptionally well done. The new ones are sharp with clear lines and the older ones haven't bled into the epidermis as much as you might expect. Probably because he's had a consistent body mass over the years.'

'You said "most" were exceptionally well done,' Poe said. 'I take it some weren't?'

'No. Six alphanumeric strings stood out. I'll highlight them on the screen now.' Doyle walked over to her computer. She drew on a tablet with a stylus-type pen. Red circles appeared on the slides in the viewing area. 'They're not easy to see so I've put them in a spread-sheet for you.' She tapped her tablet and a seventh slide appeared.

CC.58.R4.HI
SM.15.NP
AS.104X.GO
CSM.12.R2.CL
SB.47.R9.SG
SJE.77.PC

Now he knew what he was looking for, Poe could make out the corresponding letters and numbers on Cornelius Green's skin. There was something a bit off with them, something he couldn't quite put his finger on. Maybe a stylistic thing.

'They're old tattoos,' Doyle said, 'but I don't think they were done at the same time – the ink colour is inconsistent and I'm fairly sure different needles were used. At least two of the needles were blunt-judging by the scarred letters and numbers.'

'Do you know what they mean?' Poe said.

'I assumed they were Bible verses,' Doyle said. 'But when I typed them into a reference site none got a hit. Your victim *does* have Bible verses tattooed on his torso, but these alphanumeric strings repre-sent something else entirely.'

'Any idea what?' Poe asked.

'Even checking if they were Bible verses was stepping out of my remit and into yours.'

'They aren't dark web URLs, they aren't lines of code, and I don't think they're passwords,' Bradshaw said. She was already on her computer. 'Airline seat maps are alphanumeric, the seats are lettered but the rows are numbered, as are vehicle identification numbers.'

'Can we try them?'

'No point, Poe. VINs are seventeen characters long and air-line seat maps follow a standard format. Seats start at A and go up to K on planes with four aisle seats and two lots of three window seats. And there's an I, and I isn't used as it can be mistaken for the number one. I'll try computer and mobile phone serial numbers, but I don't think that's what they are.'

'Why not?'

Bradshaw shrugged. 'What possible reason could there be? I suppose they could be numbered bank accounts, but I think that's unlikely.'

'Why is that, Tilly?' Linus asked.

'The numbers and letters don't work.'

'They don't?' Linus leaned in to see what was on Bradshaw's screen.

'Am I allowed to tell him, Poe?'

'Go ahead, Tilly. He'll only snitch if you don't.'

Nightingale and Doyle smirked.

'The alphanumeric strings don't work because if they were accounts from the same bank they would have the same number of letters and numbers. They don't. And if they were from different banks, we would not see R repeated the way it is. It's on three of the strings and always in the same place, four from the end. Statistically, that's so improbable I was able to discount it.'

Linus looked at Poe. 'She's good,' he said.

Poe ignored him. 'What else, Tilly?'

'Usernames or passwords would be my next guess, although I doubt it. If something were so secret it had to be tattooed on his body, I would expect a more complex password chain. None of the alphanumeric strings contain special characters like an exclamation point or a hashtag. The strings also fit Benford's Law of naturally occurring collections of numbers, which suggests these are real-life sets of data.'

'What's Benford's Law, Tilly?' Linus asked.

'Benford's Law makes predictions about the frequency distribution of the first digit in large numerical data. If the first numbers were distributed uniformly, numbers one to nine would appear approximately eleven per cent of the time. But Benford's Law proves that number one appears first thirty per cent of the time, while number nine is first less than five per cent of the time. The number two is less likely to appear first than the number one, but more likely than three. This pattern continues all the way to nine. It's often used to detect fraud. Obviously, you and Poe are too dumb to understand the maths, so I won't bother explaining it.'

'Aw,' Poe said.

'So if Cornelius had chosen those numbers himself, he'd have selected more random numbers?' Linus said.

'Exactly. But in these alphanumeric strings, the number one appears first fifty per cent of the time. They therefore comply with Benford's Law of real-life sets of data. That means they are real alpha-numeric strings, not invented ones.'

'I doubt it was anything like passwords anyway,' Poe said. 'We've seen his room. There was nothing electronic in it. *I* probably know more about computers than Cornelius Green did.'

Bradshaw frowned. 'Or at least the same.'

Nightingale hid a smile. Doyle openly guffawed.

'Best guess as to what they are then?' Poe said, ignoring them.

'I think this is a locally developed categorisation system, Poe,' Bradshaw said. 'Without more data there is no way to decode it.'

'Something to ponder,' Poe said. He faced Doyle. 'They look homemade; was this what made them stand out?'

'It wasn't,' Doyle replied. 'Look again. And think about where they are on the body.'

He did. One was on Green's left thigh, two were on his right and the remaining three were on his lower torso, just above the groin area. All six were oblique rather than parallel. Poe frowned. He tilted his head and looked at them from a different angle. 'They're upside down,' he said eventually.

'Because?'

Poe paused, but only for a second. 'Because he tattooed himself.'

Doyle winked. 'I knew there was a reason I'm marrying you.' She faced Nightingale and said, 'I took the liberty of sending the pho-tographs to a forensic handwriting expert I know. It was his email I was waiting for. He confirmed that the formatting and the line and letter forms is the same on all six exemplars—'

'Exemplars?'

'What he calls samples. He confirmed that the same person wrote all six samples. That they are upside down, and on parts of the body Green could easily reach, supports our hypothesis.'

Poe nodded. He didn't doubt for a moment that Cornelius Green had tattooed himself and he could think of only one reason to do that. 'He didn't want a record of them anywhere. Didn't want a tattooist remembering them. Tattoos like this stick in the memory.'

'They must be there to remind him of something,' Nightingale said. 'Something he couldn't risk forgetting.'

Poe considered that. Decided there was a more probable explanation. 'Or they're a memento.'

'A memento of what though?'

'Nothing good,' he replied.

Chapter 46

With the post-mortem over, they had said goodbye to Doyle over the Perspex barrier that separated the viewing area from the post-mortem room. Doyle was still wearing full barrier PPE, so Poe was at least spared having to kiss her goodbye in front of a grinning Nightingale.

'See you for tea?' Doyle asked.

'If I can,' Poe replied. 'I'll text you.'

Nightingale was needed back in Cumbria. She took the note that had been left under Poe's windscreen wiper. 'I'll arrange for this to be forensically examined,' she said. 'What are your thoughts on it, Poe?'

Poe shrugged. 'Although they weren't as batshit crazy as I'd been led to believe, a close-knit community like the Children of Job is the perfect breeding ground for resentment to build up. It's possible someone saw we were cops—'

'Linus isn't a police officer, Poe,' Bradshaw nipped in.

'Great point, Tilly. It's possible someone saw *some* cops and decided to get even on a long-held grudge.'

'You'll look into it?' Nightingale asked.

'If that's what you want us to do, ma'am?'

Nightingale didn't immediately answer. 'The note was left for you, not me,' she said after a while. 'It makes sense if you stay on it for now.'

'Then I have my instructions.'

'Where will you start? Israel Cobb isn't on any local or national databases we can access.'

'Same place I always do when I'm searching for someone who doesn't want to be found,' he said. He turned to Bradshaw. 'Tilly, find me Israel Cobb, please.'

***

'Shall I keep working on the alphanumerical tattoos as well, Poe?' Bradshaw asked when they were back in the car.

'No, you were right, Tilly,' Poe replied. 'Without more information we run the risk of wasting hundreds of hours decoding what might end up being something as stupid as his crop rotation policy.'

'OK, Poe.'

Bradshaw removed two computers from her bag and connected them with a cable. She fiddled with her phone and began typing. Poe knew she was doing something she called 'tethering' although he didn't have a clue what that meant. As far as he was concerned, 'tether' was almost tethera, number 'three' in the ancient Cumbrian sheep-counting system. The rhythmic yan, tan, tethera and so on had been used by shepherds up until the Industrial Revolution. He had yan, tan, tethera on one of his mugs at home.

'How will you find Israel Cobb, Tilly?' Linus asked.

Bradshaw glanced at Poe. He nodded his permission.

'First of all, I will confirm that he exists,' she said, continuing to type. 'Once I have done that—'

'What if he *doesn't* exist?'

She paused. 'He does.'

'You can't possibly know that. Israel Cobb could be someone's nickname. It could be the name mothers use to make children eat their vegetables. If you don't finish your green beans Israel Cobb will come for you. It could—'

'He exists.'

'How can you be so sure though? Just because Poe thinks he exists doesn't mean—'

'I know he exists because I've already found him.'

Linus went quiet. Poe smiled to himself.

'You've found him?' Linus said.

'I have.'

'In less than a minute you've found someone Superintendent Nightingale couldn't find in' – he checked his watch – 'three hours?'

Bradshaw shrugged.

'But . . . but how? Which databases did you search?'

131

Bradshaw didn't answer. She was wearing a look Poe had come to know well. It was the look that said she'd been accessing databases she had no legal right to.

Poe came to her rescue. 'Trade secrets, Snoopy.'

'But—'

'But nothing. What did you find, Tilly?'

'Israel Cobb was born in 1964 in Suffolk. He moved to Cumbria twenty years later and I don't think he ever left.'

'He isn't in any of the Children of Job records though,' Poe said. He added, 'Nightingale would have found something by now if he were,' to give the bishop some cover. Linus didn't need to know what they knew.

'He isn't, Poe. If he was ever there, his records were expunged.'

'Which would fit with him falling out with Cornelius Green,' Poe said, remembering what the note had said. 'It must have been a full-on row if Cornelius had Israel's life deleted. Perhaps we have our first suspect. Maybe Israel Cobb thought it was time he reclaimed whatever position he had previously held at the Children of Job.'

'Then why didn't the note just say, "Israel Cobb did it",' Linus said. 'Why be so cryptic?'

'Tilly?' Poe said. 'You want to remind Snoopy what my motto is?'

'Which one, Poe? You have lots of mottos.'

'The one about stupid questions.'

'Ah, that one.' She turned in her seat to face Linus. 'Poe says that the person who said there are no F-word stupid questions had never had to listen to the F-word idiots he has had to listen to.'

'I hardly—'

'He also says why can't people F-word think for themselves every now and then? Or at least look on F-word Google before they start F-word bothering him. I think he means we have no way of knowing why the person who wrote the note said what they did. That's what we'll be trying to find out next, I imagine. Isn't that right, Poe?'

'It is, Tilly,' Poe said. He glanced at Linus in the rear-view mirror. His face was beetroot-red. Good, Poe thought. He knew the bloke was a spook, but he was too interested in their methods as far as Poe was concerned. He'd have a word with Bradshaw later.

Make sure she didn't drop herself in it. 'Where does Israel Cobb live now, Tilly?'

'Just outside Skelton. It's near Penrith, Poe.'

'I know Skelton, Tilly. Small village. Has a pub that does nice food.' He checked the clock on the dashboard. 'It's coming up to six now and we still have an hour before we get to the M6.'

'We'll be standing down then?' Linus said. 'It'll be nearly eight o'clock before we get there.'

'Tilly and me aren't paid to stand down, Snoopy. We're paid to stand up.'

'It's too late to interview witnesses, Poe. Eight o'clock is an intrusion.'

'You got somewhere else you need to be?' Poe said. 'This is a murder investigation and Israel Cobb isn't a witness, he's a suspect. That means he keeps our hours; we don't keep his.'

Chapter 47

They arrived in Skelton a little after 8 p.m. Bradshaw directed Poe to Israel Cobb's house. It was a mile out of the village, at the dead end of a single-lane track where the weeds had punched through the tarmac and tyre-piercing stones lay like spilled marbles. The house was almost derelict. It was in the shade of three tall oaks and Poe doubted it had ever seen sustained sunlight. The low, misshapen roof sagged, and the walls were wet with algae. If it hadn't been for the light coming from the partially drawn curtains, it would have looked abandoned.

Poe rapped his knuckles against the thin door and winced when the wood splintered. He waited twenty seconds then knocked again, harder. He was about to knock for a third time when he heard a shuffling noise from behind the door.

'Who's there?'

'National Crime Agency, Mr Cobb,' Poe said. 'We need to talk.'

'Talk to each other then; I'm busy.'

Poe knocked again. The door opened.

Israel Cobb was as thin as garlic skin and twice as pale. He had hair like an unshorn sheep, and the physique of someone who drank his meals. His back was banana-curved. Given his background, Poe had been expecting an older version of Joshua Meade. Prim and prissy with a distasteful look, as if he had something smelly on his upper lip. But, in his ratty dressing gown and even rattier sandals, Israel Cobb looked like a featherweight Merlin. His toenails were jagged and yellow and dirtier than a dustbin lid.

'May we come in, Mr Cobb?' Poe said, stepping past him before he'd finished asking.

'Apparently you may,' Cobb replied in a voice sculpted by filterless cigarettes. He had teeth like baked beans.

Bradshaw stepped inside too. She said, 'Good evening, Mr Cobb. My name is Matilda Bradshaw and I work with Poe at the Serious Crime Analysis Section.'

'Is that right?'

'Yes, it is. And you should see your GP about your onychomycosis.'

'What's that, miss?'

'The fungal infection on your toenails. It's why they are yellow and smell like strong cheese. Your GP will prescribe antifungal cream and it will take six-to-nine months to clear up.'

Cobb shrugged. 'Do I look like I have a GP?'

'I know that you do,' Bradshaw replied.

She blinked as she realised what she had said. Poe rolled his eyes. So, *that* was how she'd found Cobb. She'd been rooting around in NHS databases again. Luckily Linus had stayed outside so he hadn't heard. MI5 must have different rules to Poe on entering private residences without permission, he thought. Poe's rule was if he wanted to go into someone's house, he'd go in and make up the reason why afterwards.

'You've been looking through my medical—' Cobb started to say.

'Cornelius Green is dead, Mr Cobb,' Poe cut in. 'Did you kill him?'

Cobb staggered like he'd taken a crossbow bolt to the chest. He collapsed into a greasy, but comfortable-looking, stuffed armchair. 'How?' he wheezed, reaching for his cigarettes. His hands shook as he lit up.

'He was tied to a tree near Keswick and stoned to death. Where were you the night before last, Mr Cobb?'

'Cornelius was stoned to death?'

Poe nodded as Linus finally decided to enter the cottage. 'He was.'

'Who did it?'

'That's why I'm here.'

Cobb didn't immediately respond. It looked like he was struggling to understand what Poe was saying. 'Cornelius is dead,' he said. Poe thought he needed to hear himself say the words. See if it sounded more believable that way. 'And he was definitely stoned to death?'

Poe nodded again.

A low, rattling noise started in Cobb's bony chest. It sounded like the build-up to a wet cough, but when it finally reached his throat it was laughter that erupted. Not the mean-spirited laughter of someone enjoying a colleague's misfortune, this laughter was free and pure. Tears of joy streamed down his face. This continued for a full minute. When the laughter eventually subsided, he gasped, 'Tell me everything.'

'A stun gun was used to get him to the place he was murdered.'

'One of those electric burny things?'

'Yes.'

The intensity of his laughter trebled. He was now laughing so hard Poe was worried it would turn into a fit. 'You're killing me, Sergeant Poe!' he gasped.

Poe looked at Bradshaw. She shrugged. Linus did too.

'There was no love lost between you two then,' Poe said. At least it confirmed part of the note was accurate. You didn't take so much delight in someone's death unless something had happened. Hate like this wasn't organic; it didn't build up naturally. If someone rubbed you up the wrong way, you avoided them. This was the hate of two people who were close and now weren't. The note had told them to find out what had caused their rift and Poe intended to.

It was five minutes before Cobb was composed enough to talk to them. 'That's that then,' he said. He lit another cigarette from the embers of the previous one.

'What's what?' Poe said.

'Nothing. Now, how can I help you, Sergeant Poe?'

'You can start by answering my first question: where were you two nights ago?'

'Two nights, two nights,' Cobb muttered. He wasn't even trying to hide his grin. 'Ah, yes. Two nights ago, I was helping out at the community allotment.'

'What as, a scarecrow?' Poe muttered.

136

'What's that?'

'Nothing. Where did you go after the allotment?'

'I walked to the Dog and Gun and had the ox-cheek ragu. They will be able to vouch for me.'

'That's very specific.'

'I've had ox-cheek ragu every night this week.'

'What time did you leave?'

'Kicking out time. I don't wear a watch any more, but I think it will have been around half eleven.'

It wasn't a cast-iron alibi, but it didn't seem manufactured either. Poe was always suspicious when suspects had alibis that covered the entire crime window. The all-night poker game, the party with shady guests; they stank of deception. A night in the pub two nights ago would be easy to check.

'I understand you and Cornelius had a big falling out?'

'Did we?'

'Your records at the Children of Job have been expunged. We were there this morning and no one mentioned you. And while living there is hardly the lap of luxury, it has to be better than this . . .' – Poe wanted to say hovel but didn't – '. . . place.'

'And from that you got there was a falling out?'

'If you were there for as long as we think you were, your faith must have been very strong,' Poe said. 'And yet, here we are in your home, and there isn't a cross on the wall or a Bible on your coffee table. And though you might look like a hobo-Jesus, I don't believe that's intentional. I think you look the way you do because of neglect.'

'No offence taken.'

'I'm investigating a murder; I don't care if I offend you.' Poe sighed, aware he wasn't getting anywhere. 'Tell me what happened, Mr Cobb. You didn't only lose a friendship; you lost your faith as well. What did you and Cornelius Green fall out over?'

'I don't know what you're talking about,' Cobb said. 'I was friends with Cornelius, but we grew apart. I left the Children of Job fifteen or so years ago because it was the right time for me to do so. There *was* no falling out, Sergeant Poe. And I didn't lose my faith, I just practise it differently now.'

'People aren't expunged from existence simply because they grew apart, Mr Cobb. What is it you aren't telling me? And what were these courses that stopped?'

Cobb's eyes, dead until now, sparked into life. 'Unless you're here to arrest me, please leave my house,' he said, his voice suddenly cold and hard. He spun and left the room, his dressing gown flaring up like he was Marilyn Monroe standing over a New York air vent. He slammed the door behind him, leaving them alone in his front room.

'The truth's a swamp bubble, Mr Cobb,' Poe called out after him. 'It doesn't matter how thick the mud is; eventually it'll work its way to the top.'

Judging by the clang of pots and pans, Cobb had stomped off into his kitchen.

'Did you see that when he turned round?' Poe said.

Bradshaw nodded. 'He wasn't wearing any underpants.'

'Also, his lower back was covered in alphanumeric tattoos.'

Chapter 48

'We have course records going back twenty years,' Poe said, as soon as they were back on the road, 'and there's nothing that was running then that isn't running now. But the note under the windscreen wiper was clear: we were to ask Cobb why the courses stopped. What are we missing?'

'Perhaps the person who left the note was wrong, Poe,' Bradshaw said. 'Perhaps there was a course they only *thought* had stopped.'

Poe considered that carefully. 'I don't think so, Tilly. We were annoying him with all those questions about Cornelius, but he didn't boot us out until I asked about the cancelled courses. And Cobb was obviously lying when he said he and Cornelius Green hadn't fallen out; no one can fake hate like that. Everything in the note has been accurate so far, so we have to assume the Children of Job were running courses we don't know about.'

'Perhaps the answer is in Cornelius's tattoos, Poe,' Bradshaw said.

'Perhaps,' Poe agreed.

'I can try to decipher them if you want. I don't think I have anywhere near enough data though. They could be the equivalent of a one-time pad and they're theoretically secure. With a pre-shared key that is only used once, the alphanumerical tattoos cannot be cracked, even with unlimited computing power.'

'What if you had Israel Cobb's tattoos as well, Tilly?' Linus asked. 'Assuming it's not a one-time pad, would you have enough data?'

Bradshaw shrugged. 'More data is always better than less data, Linus.'

'Did you see what his tattoos were, Poe?'

'I only saw them for a second, Snoopy,' Poe replied. 'They were underneath his dressing gown the rest of the time and I don't have 3D vision.'

'Yes, you do, Poe,' Bradshaw sighed. 'Everyone does.'

Poe paused. Realised he'd meant to say *X-ray* vision, not 3D vision. 'Steeleye Stan doesn't,' he said eventually. 'He's only got one eye.'

'Who?' Linus asked.

'A bouncer in Carlisle. Lost an eye in a bar fight and he uses a ball bearing as a prosthetic now.'

'Bloody northerners,' Linus muttered, before adding, 'OK, because you *don't* have X-ray vision; why not apply for a warrant instead?'

'To examine his tattoos?' Poe replied.

Linus nodded.

'On what grounds? I've sent Superintendent Nightingale a text and she's agreed to chase down Cobb's alibi for the night of the murder. Unless it's full of holes all we have is a man with possibly similar tattoos who knew the victim fifteen years ago. Not only would we not get a warrant, it would be an abuse of police powers to even apply for one. For all we know, all the Children of Job old-timers have these tattoos.'

'We're ignoring them?'

'For now,' Poe said. 'We need to chase down everything that was in that note first. We need to know about these missing courses.'

'But they weren't on any of their curriculums, Poe,' Bradshaw said.

Poe considered what he knew about the courses they *did* have on their curriculum. They were well attended. Some were rooted in rigid interpretations of the Old Testament. Some, like the thinly disguised conversion therapy, were repugnant. Others, such as the Christian and spiritual leadership courses, were more positive. But they all had one thing in common: none of them were free.

'Start with their bank records, Tilly,' he said. 'Even if Cornelius Green didn't record the courses anywhere, you can be damn sure he charged money for them.'

Chapter 49

Poe didn't sleep well. Doyle had picked up a summer cold and snored the whole night, although he would rather have pickled his own tongue than tell her that. And at 3 a.m. Edgar had started barking at what Poe assumed to be rabbits. Possibly a fox. Whatever it was, they were long gone by the time he'd put on some clothes to let the excited spaniel out. At five he gave up on sleep and crept downstairs to read the bishop's file again. Bradshaw had downloaded it to his phone, and although the text was too small for his unaided eyes, he'd found a magnifying glass that made it bearable.

Usually he would have asked Bradshaw to print off everything and they would spend a couple of hours Blu Tacking it to the wall he kept free for exactly that purpose. The murder wall, they called it, and they'd spent many an hour in front of it, rocking back and forth on their heels as they stared at an unbound case file. Poe found it easier to make links this way. Murder files were arranged in a necessarily predetermined order but being able to see everything at once was how he liked to review the information. In this case, though, with him having sworn secrecy to the bishop, he didn't feel he had the right to print off anything.

So Poe made coffee and bent over his phone with his little magnifying glass until his back was crooked and he looked like Sherlock Holmes examining cigar ash. By the time Doyle came down he was no further forward. He got up, stretched, and poured her a cup of the rich dark roast he was drinking. Doyle said the smell of coffee was part of her day's rhythm and she drank it black and intense.

'Couldn't sleep?' she said after she'd taken a sip. 'I wasn't snoring, was I?'

'Absolutely not,' Poe said.

'Who were you referring to when you told Edgar, "She sounds like an asthmatic bulldog"?'

'You heard that?'

She shrugged. 'You woke me when you got up.'

'Sorry.'

'Don't be. I had another two hours uninterrupted sleep. Have you been staring at your phone all this time?'

'I need to absorb what's in the bishop's file and I can't do that in front of Snoopy.'

'As a medical doctor, you know what I'm going to say next, don't you?' she said.

Luckily Poe was spared another lecture on digital eyestrain as his phone jauntily chirped out the opening lyrics to 'YMCA' by the Village People. Doyle raised a perfectly sculpted eyebrow. 'How did you upset her this time?'

Bradshaw responded to Poe's numerous transgressions by changing his ringtone to songs she knew he'd hate, safe in the knowledge he wouldn't know how to change it back. Poe had said this was passive-aggressive behaviour. She had responded by making his ringtone Terry Wogan's 'Floral Dance'. She hadn't changed it back until he had apologised.

'I asked her why Obi-Wan Kenobi didn't recognise R2-D2 in *A New Hope*, when they'd been in the three prequels together.'

'Ouch,' Doyle said. 'She wouldn't have liked that. And when did you watch *Star Wars*? I can't even get you to watch *The Wire*.'

'She made me watch them on the Spring-heeled Jack stakeout last year.'

'Aren't you going to answer your phone?'

'Not yet. I'm pretending the ringtone doesn't work so she'll change it to something less embarrassing.'

Doyle stared at him. 'You're a peculiar adult, Poe,' she said eventually.

Poe stuck out his tongue. He reached for his phone and showed Doyle the screen. A photograph of a grinning Bradshaw was flashing on and off.

'Told you,' he said. He pressed receive. 'Tilly, this is early, even for you.'

'I've found something you need to see, Poe,' she replied.

She told him what it was.

'I'm on my way,' he said.

Chapter 50

Bradshaw said that when she cross-referenced the Children of Job's bank records against the register of course attendees, she had uncovered six payments made between 2001 and 2007 that hadn't corresponded to anything on the curriculums provided by the Bishop of Carlisle. There was a gap in 2002, otherwise there had been one a year for six years. Four of those payments appeared to have been made in cash, and that was where the trail ended, but the remaining two had been made by credit card. Working on the hypothesis that the payments might have been for more intensive versions of the routine conversion therapy courses the Children of Job ran, she checked whether either of the credit cards belonged to families who, between 2001 and 2007, had sons in their teens or early twenties. They both had. In 2004, Nathan Rose was twenty, and in 2007, Aaron Bowman was fifteen. Their families had both paid the Children of Job one thousand pounds.

But it wasn't until she had fed the name Aaron Bowman into the National Crime Agency database that she reached for her phone to call Poe.

'How did Tilly find this so quickly?' Nightingale asked.

Poe had called Nightingale immediately after Bradshaw had called him.

'Cornelius wasn't just a zealot, ma'am, he was also a shrewd businessman,' Poe replied. 'Even if he was running courses he wasn't prepared to put on paper, I figured he'd still be charging for them. Money always leaves an auditable trail, so I asked Tilly to look for any unreconciled deposits. She was supposed to be doing this today, but you know what she's like. I don't think she sleeps at night; she simply plugs herself into the mainframe.'

'What did she find?'

'Six large bank deposits that didn't correlate with any course on the curriculum. There was no trail at all for four of them, so we're assuming they were cash payments, but the other two were paid with credit cards.'

'And one of those payments was made by Aaron Bowman?'

'His parents, yes.'

'Just when I thought this case couldn't get any bloody weirder,' she said. 'OK, can you follow this up? I have a manhunt to arrange.'

'Who's Aaron Bowman?' Linus said.

Poe had picked them both up at Shap Wells and they were now on their way to Underbarrow, a small but geographically dispersed village on the outskirts of Kendal. Poe hadn't been there in years. It was a beautiful village, full of charm and largely unspoiled, but if you were driving to Underbarrow it was because you wanted to be in Underbarrow – the road didn't lead anywhere else.

'He's a kid Tilly thinks might have attended one of these secret courses,' Poe explained. 'The courses the note said had stopped when Israel Cobb left the Children of Job.'

'Is Aaron Bowman a suspect?'

'I doubt it, Snoopy; he's dead.'

'Dead? How?'

'He was murdered in 2012. I'm surprised you didn't recognise his name; he was killed at the same time as his mother and father.'

Understanding slid across his face. 'Wait, he's *that* Aaron? The one from the Keswick massacre? He was killed by his own sister?'

Poe nodded. 'Bethany Bowman. She'd been estranged for four or five years by then, but for reasons that were never established, she broke into the family home and murdered Grace and Noah Bowman while they slept. Used a clasp knife to slit their throats from ear to ear. She left it on the kitchen table as if it were a trophy. Covered in blood and her fingerprints. I was a detective constable up here then and I've seen the crime scene photographs. The sheets from her parents' bed looked like they'd been used to clean an abattoir floor. The senior investigating officer thought killing Aaron had never been part of Bethany's plan. He was supposed to be with his other sister Eve at a Children of Job Bible study group, but he'd been ill and had stayed at home. The SIO believed Aaron had got up for a drink of water in the middle of the night and stumbled into what Bethany was doing. She murdered him where he stood – right outside his parents' bedroom door. The SIO believed Bethany only killed Aaron so she could get away. Eve Bowman found the murder scene when she returned the next afternoon.'

'I remember watching the documentary,' Linus said. 'Bethany stole a boat and dumped all three bodies in the sea, didn't she?'

'She did,' Poe confirmed. 'Bloodstains showed that she used a wheelbarrow to take the bodies to her dad's old Range Rover. Drove them to St Bees and stole an inflatable dinghy. Wrapped them in chains and threw them overboard. She hadn't counted on the strong riptides, and Grace and Noah washed up a couple of days later. That's what the SIO concluded anyway.'

'But Aaron *didn't* wash up?'

'His body was never recovered. It seems while the tide sent Grace and Noah to the beach at Seascale, it had different plans for Aaron.'

'The documentary I watched will be a few years old now,' Linus said. 'Was Bethany ever caught?'

Poe shook his head. It was one of Cumbria Constabulary's burning failures. Bethany Bowman had disappeared like morning mist. 'The case is reviewed every year as it's technically still open,' he said, 'but between you and me, they aren't actively pursuing her any more.'

'Why not?'

'Because, although she was nineteen when she murdered her family, she was fourteen when she ran away from home – no one has a clue what she looks like now. Their best hope is that she'll be arrested for something minor and get fingerprinted. There's an INTERPOL red notice out on her so if she ever pops up in any one of the one hundred and ninety-four member countries, Cumbria will extradite her to the UK for trial. I don't think Bethany makes those kinds of mistakes though.'

'What do you think happened? As in *really* happened?'

Poe turned on to a road so twisty and narrow it was like a theme park water chute. He tapped his brakes and slowed down. If he met a car coming the other way he would have to stop to avoid a head-on collision; the road was too narrow to pass each other. The two drivers would stare at each other for a moment, before one of them buckled under the pressure and reversed to one of the rare passing spaces. 'I think fourteen-year-old girls don't run away from home without a reason. And, if they do, they certainly don't return five years later to slaughter their own family.'

'Maybe she'd been abused?'

'There's certainly something we don't know. Whatever her reasons, now we've established a link between her brother, Aaron, and Cornelius Green, Bethany Bowman is a suspect. She has to be.'

'I thought the Bowman family lived in Keswick – why aren't we heading there?'

'They did live in Keswick, Snoopy, but they owned two houses; the Underbarrow property belonged to her mother's parents. After the massacre Eve moved away. She must have missed Cumbria though, as three years ago she moved to the house in Underbarrow. I imagine the house in Keswick held too many dark memories for her. She rents it out now.'

'Why bother coming back?'

'Tilly says she's recently married,' Poe said. 'Probably wants to raise a family and there really isn't a better place. The village is safe and the schools are excellent. She works part-time for an estate agent in Kendal so hopefully she'll be in.'

'And we're here to question her?'

'No, Snoopy, we're here to *warn* her.'

Chapter 51

Eve Bowman lived in an old farmhouse, all whitewashed walls and traditional slate roof, same as all the other houses in the area. Underbarrow fell within the Lake District National Park boundary so she was limited in what she could do to the exterior of the house. 'Restrict unwelcome change' was what the National Park Authority called it, which Poe believed was just an excuse to make everything look like a Beatrix Potter film set. Tradition was OK, but not at the expense of the people who lived there.

A tumble of outbuildings and a bunch of chickens roaming in the old farmyard completed what was a lovely, isolated property. Poe imagined coming back to Cumbria had been a big deal for Eve. She'd probably yearned to return but hadn't wanted to cope with being a curiosity. The sole survivor of an infamous massacre. Someone to point at and whisper about. Underbarrow was far enough away from Keswick for her to start again, while still having the fells and lakes that she'd have fallen in love with as a child.

Eve Bowman was thirty-two years old but looked younger. She had watched them walk up the long and winding garden path from her front room, where she had been halfway through a strenuous yoga workout. She beat them to the front door and opened it as Poe was reaching for the bell. She wore black leggings, jade-green trainers and a matching vest. She was slightly out of breath. She was a tall, rangy woman and the muscle definition on her arms was perfect, suggesting she had played sport in her youth. A university sport, such as rowing or fencing. The kind you only ever saw during the opening week of the Olympics. Her face was free of makeup and her hair was pageboy short.

Poe hadn't done the death knock since he was in uniform, and although he wasn't there to tell Eve that someone she loved was dead, he had the same sense of unease. How did you tell someone the person who'd butchered her entire family might be back? During death notification training, it had been drummed into Poe that, apart from checking you were delivering the bad news to the right person, the most important thing to do was use plain language. Phrases like 'I am very sorry to tell you that such-and-such is dead', rather than phrases that could be misinterpreted like 'passed away' or 'gone to a better place'. Although the reality was that you just had to find a way that worked, Poe had always tried to do as he'd been trained. So, after he had shown her his identification he said, 'May I come in, Ms Bowman? I'm afraid I have some bad news.'

She clamped a hand over her mouth and Poe realised his mistake at once.

'It's not about your husband,' he said quickly. 'I'm sorry, I should have led with that.'

'Thomas is OK?'

'As far as I'm aware,' Poe said. 'He's not here? I was hoping to speak to him too.'

'He's at work.' She stared at Poe; her relief at her husband not being dead tempering what would have been wholly justified anger. 'You'd better come in.'

She led them through the hall and into the kitchen. The south-facing window overlooked a field full of freshly shorn sheep. She flicked a switch on a stainless-steel bean-to-cup coffee machine and for a moment they listened to automated grinding and tamping. Poe had a headache, and he hadn't planned on having any more coffee, but the smell coming from the machine was intoxicating.

'Coffee?' she said.

'Please,' Poe said.

'This wasn't cheap,' Eve said, gesturing at the machine, 'but there are some things you don't scrimp on. Coffee is one of them.'

'Smells lovely.'

'Apologies for the way I'm dressed; I try to do a workout before I leave for the office.'

'It's us who should apologise, Ms Bowman,' Poe said.

'Eve, please.'

'Apologies, Eve. It's very early and we didn't call ahead.'

She waved away his apology. 'Now, what's this bad news?' she said. 'If it's about one of my ex-renters, the agent handles it all. I have nothing to do with any of it.'

'We think Bethany might be back,' Poe said.

Which sort of killed the conversation.

Chapter 52

'Bethany can't be back, Sergeant Poe,' Eve said. 'She just can't.'

Poe drained his espresso before responding. Eve had served the coffee in small white cups, the kind used in coffee shops and restaurants. Poe had never learned how to make espressos last. He felt uncultured when he was served one. To him, espressos felt like coffee chasers, there to be gulped down in one and the cup slammed upside down on the counter. Linus was sipping his like a pro and Bradshaw had hot water with a slice of lemon in a normal-sized mug. They were seated at Eve's kitchen table, a sturdy oak thing with matching high-backed stools.

'This isn't the only line of enquiry we have, but we think she might be back. And if she is, it's possible she's already killed someone.'

Eve put down her cup and wiped her lips with a cotton napkin. 'Who?'

'Cornelius Green,' Poe said. 'He was murdered three nights ago.'

'Cornelius is dead?'

'He is.'

'I don't know whether to clap or cry,' she said.

'You knew him then?'

'From years ago. Mum and Dad were heavily involved in that bloody place they have near Keswick. Believed Cornelius Green was some sort of Messiah. They were there every weekend and most evenings. You say he was murdered three nights ago; I say I'm surprised it took so long.' She stood and refilled their cups. Put them back on little cork coasters. She retook her seat and said, 'I hope this isn't a shock, Sergeant Poe, but Cornelius Green wasn't a pleasant man. In fact, I would go as far to say he was a monster. Some of the things he put those poor children through—'

'What things?'

'He ran courses, Sergeant Poe. Horrible, horrible courses.'

Poe nodded. 'We know about the courses, Eve. They're what brought us here.'

'Oh?'

'We believe your brother Aaron attended one in 2007.'

'Are you asking me or telling me?'

'Like I said, we believe he did. We were hoping you might be able to confirm it.'

'He did,' Eve said.

'You seem very sure.'

She sighed. 'It's not something I'm likely to forget, Sergeant Poe.'

'And why is that?'

'Because when he got back, he and Bethany had a blazing row. I have no idea what the fight was about, and Aaron never spoke of it, but that night Bethany packed her bags and ran away. Again. Only this time she never returned.' She smiled sadly. 'Not until . . . well, you're a police officer, you *know* when she returned.'

Poe wasn't there to get bogged down in the Bowman family massacre – Cumbria would merge it into the Cornelius Green murder, and he didn't want to interfere with their witnesses any more than he had to.

'This is going to seem like an odd question, Eve, but was your brother gay?'

'I don't know,' she replied. 'You'd have to ask him. Oh, that's right, you can't, my psycho sister murdered him.' She closed her eyes briefly. 'Sorry. Even now it still hurts. Why do you ask?'

'It's possible Cornelius Green was running some of his conversion therapy courses off the books. It wasn't a tax fiddle so we're working on the presumption he was doing something he shouldn't have been. I'm wondering if they were maybe more extreme versions of the courses on the regular curriculum.'

'A course for super-gays, you mean?'

'I mean a course misguided parents might send their sons on, maybe if they were at their wits' end and didn't know any better. I don't pretend to understand why someone might think they can forcibly change someone's sexuality, but I accept it happens, the same way I accept that the Metropolitan Police need a unit dedicated to protecting children accused of witchcraft.'

'Fair enough,' Eve said. 'And Mum and Dad *were* the type of people to believe in that stuff. Whether or not Aaron was gay?' She shrugged. 'I'd be surprised. Not because a boy from an ultra-conservative Christian family can't be gay, but because, even if he *was* feeling sexually attracted to someone of his own sex, he certainly wasn't doing anything about it.'

'I'm not sure I—'

'We were rarely allowed out unsupervised, Sergeant Poe. All our social interactions were at the Children of Job. We were dropped off at school in the morning and collected in the afternoon. We weren't allowed to join clubs or play sports. There is no way he had a boyfriend, not without me knowing anyway.'

'Being gay isn't simply about sex,' Poe said. 'It's about who you are.'

'I know that,' Eve said. 'But if Aaron *were* having feelings like that, given what I've just told you, do you really think he'd have confided in Mum and Dad?'

'I suppose not.'

'There's no suppose about it, Sergeant Poe. If he were going to confide in anyone, it would have been me.'

'Not Bethany?'

'No. Bethany was . . . troubled. Even from an early age she was in a constant state of war with Mum and Dad. They did the best they could, of course, but I don't think they were equipped to handle someone so rebellious. Perhaps if a less Christian-centric family had raised her she might have turned out OK, but whenever she was bad, my parents' response was either to consult Cornelius Green or seek solace in the Bible. I still believe in God, Sergeant Poe, but sometimes the answers to life's problems are found in the real world, not in the pages of texts written thousands of years ago. And I'm not saying Bethany and me didn't get on, because we did. I'm not even saying that some of her tantrums didn't break up what was at times quite a monotonous childhood, but there was an edge to her. And while it was occasionally entertaining, it was always unpredictable.'

'Aaron wouldn't have confided in her?'

'No, if he'd told her a secret like that, she'd have told Mum and Dad just to spite them. She wouldn't have meant to hurt Aaron, but he would have ended up as collateral damage.'

Poe considered this. Decided that the more he knew about Bethany Bowman, the more she scared him. 'Do you have a photograph of her?' he asked.

'From when she was fourteen?'

'If it's not too much trouble. Tilly's a bit of a whizz on the old computer. She'll be able to put it through some age-progression software the Cumbrian cops don't have access to.'

'Why don't they have access to it?'

'I only wrote it a month ago,' Bradshaw said. 'It's still at the beta-testing stage.'

'There'll be some photographs in the filing cabinet,' Eve nodded. 'I'll go and get one.' She left the kitchen and walked through a door to what Poe had assumed was a larder, but it turned out to be the door to the basement. A lot of the old farmhouses had basements – a pre-fridge legacy, when root cellars were the only way to keep food fresh.

'"A whizz on the old computer"?' Bradshaw said. 'You really are a twit, Poe.'

Eve returned a few minutes later with a handful of Polaroids. 'I'm sorry they're not digital; our parents wouldn't let us have mobile telephones.'

She handed Poe half-a-dozen photographs of a spiky, sullen teenager. She had a ferocious stare, like she was trying to kill the photographer with the power of her mind. In all the pictures she wore scruffy jeans and ripped T-shirts.

'As you can see,' Eve said, 'she hacked off her own hair. She did it to annoy Mum and show her up in front of her church friends.'

'Thank you,' Poe said. 'I'll get these back to you as soon as I can.' He tucked them into his top pocket. He opened his notebook and checked he hadn't missed anything. He had. Something important. The reason they were there. 'Is your husband from Cumbria, Eve?'

'Thomas? Good grief, no. Thomas is a valley boy.'

'He's Welsh?'

She nodded. 'Pontypool.'

'And does he still have family down there?'

She narrowed her eyes. 'Why do you ask?'

'Because if he does, now might be a sensible time to visit them.'

'Even if Bethany *is* back, I'm in no danger, Sergeant Poe.'

'How can you be so sure?'

'Because she didn't hate me.'

'From what you've told us, she didn't hate Aaron either.'

'He got in her way. Maybe he tried to stop her. I wasn't there that night, but killing Aaron was never part of her plan. I'm convinced of that. And if she wanted to kill me I'd already be dead, Sergeant Poe. I haven't been hiding. I even kept my maiden name.'

'Yes, why is that?'

'It was all Bethany left me. It didn't seem right to let it go. My husband understood.'

'What does he do for a living?'

'Graphic design. When we moved up here, he got a job with a company in Preston.'

'That's a bit of a journey,' Poe said.

'There isn't a specialist company in Cumbria like the one he works for so he had no choice.' She smiled. 'I actually think he enjoys the time on his own. He says the commute helps keep his creative edge sharp.'

Poe could relate to that. Decluttering his mind on long journeys, or on extended walks with Edgar, was often when he made breakthroughs in cases. Not looking at something was often the clearest way to see it. He checked his watch. They'd already been there an hour and it was now bordering on being intrusive. 'One last question,' he said. 'If it *is* Bethany who has killed Cornelius Green, why do you think she's returned after all these years?'

Eve considered this for several moments. 'Because she's insane,' she said eventually.

'There must be more to it than that.'

'I don't care.'

'But—'

'I loved my sister, Sergeant Poe, but she murdered my little brother. As far as I'm concerned, she can rot in hell.'

'Where to now, Poe?' Bradshaw asked when they were back in the car and Poe had three-point-turned his way on to the Kendal road.

'I have a case progression meeting with Superintendent Nightingale this afternoon. I'll drop you off at Shap Wells, Tilly. I want you to start profiling Bethany Bowman. If she's up here again, we need to know who we're dealing with. I'll get Cumbria to send you everything they have on her.'

'OK. I'll have a look at the alphanumeric tattoos while I wait.'

'And Superintendent Nightingale has sent me a text confirming our meeting with Nathan Rose this evening.'

'Nathan's the other guy Tilly identified?' Linus said. 'One of the six who attended the secret courses?'

'He is,' Poe confirmed. 'Superintendent Nightingale spoke to his wife while we were with Eve Bowman. Nathan will be home by six o'clock. He has a job with the council and he's on site somewhere until then. Snoopy, I assume you want to come to this meeting at police headquarters?'

'I'll observe Tilly if you don't mind.'

'I do mind.'

'Why?'

'Because Tilly doesn't have an agenda; you do.'

'I don't know how many times I need to tell you this, Poe. I do not have an agenda. My role is to observe the unit.'

Poe stared at him in the rear-view mirror. 'You *do* have an agenda, Snoopy. I just haven't figured out what it is yet.'

'Watch out!' Linus yelled.

Poe whipped his head back. A woman was standing in the middle of the road. He slammed on his brakes and the car skidded to a stop inches from her legs. She made no attempt to get out of the way. Although he'd only been going thirty miles an hour, it had been fast enough to engage everyone's seatbelt locking mechanisms.

'Bloody hell, that was close,' Poe said, breathing a sigh of relief.
They stared at the woman in the road.
Mad Alice stared back.

Chapter 53

'It was Alice who stepped in front of your car?' Doctor Lang said. 'The woman who shouted at you when you visited the Children of Job?'

'Yep, the one who called us sinners,' Poe confirmed. 'Even Tilly.'

'Was she trying to kill herself?'

'Far from it. She figured it was the only way to make me stop.'

'And you did?'

'Of course.'

'What did she want?'

'To talk.'

'She was lucid?'

'Very much so,' Poe said. 'The wild hair was gone, as was her stooped back. It was like the end of that film Tilly made me watch. This master criminal, the one the cops weren't even sure existed, had been in their office all day long and as he's leaving the station the limp gradually disappears and the arthritis in his hands clears up.'

'*The Usual Suspects.*'

'What is?'

'The name of the film.'

'OK. Anyway, she was like that. Turns out she adopted the guise of "Mad Alice" to ingratiate herself with the Children of Job. She'd been creeping around their compound for fifteen years like a world champion undercover cop.'

'Which she wasn't?'

Poe shook his head. 'She wasn't a cop.'

'What was she?'

'She was Bethany Bowman's best friend. And from the age of fourteen she'd been trying to find out why Bethany ran away from home, only to return five years later to butcher her family. She was convinced the answers were with the Children of Job.'

'Oh, the poor thing,' Doctor Lang said. 'Friendships at that age, particularly among vulnerable girls, which Bethany certainly appears to have been, can be all-consuming. Betrayals can be devastating. It usually manifests as over-the-top rage towards the betrayer, or complete denial.'

'It was the latter with Alice. Even when we talked her through the evidence, she wouldn't accept Bethany was capable of murdering her parents and brother.'

'And she only wanted to talk?'

'She had something to give me,' Poe said. 'Something she'd been guarding for sixteen years.'

Chapter 54

'Bloody hell, that was close,' Poe said. He was relieved and then he was angry. He unlocked his seatbelt and jumped out of the car. 'What the hell do you think you're doing? I could have sent you flying over my windshield!'

Alice looked over his shoulder. 'Not here,' she said.

She walked past him and climbed into the back. Linus bunched up to make room. Bradshaw turned in her seat to look at her, then turned back to Poe. She shrugged.

'Fine,' Poe said to himself. He got back in the driver's seat and said, 'Where to?'

'Anywhere.'

Until they were out of the village, Alice's eyes were skittish, darting around as if she were a tweaker. Poe took the time to compose the first of what he was sure would be many questions. He adjusted the rear-view until he could see her clearly. Alice didn't appear to be mad any more. She wore standard fell-walking garb – light fleece, cotton trousers and walking boots. Her hair was tucked under a long-billed baseball cap. When she glanced down her face was completely hidden. She looked like a primary-school teacher on a long weekend. She could have walked into any shop or pub in Keswick and no one would have given her a second look.

She saw him watching her. 'I wear two skins,' she explained. 'Mad Alice gets me into the Children of Job and Tourist Alice' – she gestured at her outfit – 'gets me everywhere else.'

'It was you who left the note under my windscreen wiper,' Poe said.

'It was.'

'Who *are* you? And more importantly, why are you cowering in the back of my car like we're smuggling you out of North Korea?'

'I'm Alice Symonds,' she said.

She said her name like Poe should recognise it, and the weird thing was he did. It was a name from his past. He got the feeling the name was a test, one he had to pass before he could advance to the next level. He thought it through logically. He'd never met Alice before, so she hadn't been a witness or a suspect in one of his cases. But she thought he should know her name and she'd been hanging around Eve Bowman's house. Had she been waiting for them or watching Eve? It didn't matter if it was A or B; both answers led back to Bethany Bowman and Cornelius Green. And although he hadn't been part of the original investigation, he *had* read the file. He glanced in the mirror again. Tried to put an age on her. Bethany had been fourteen when she ran away from home and if Poe were any judge, sixteen years ago Alice would have been roughly the same age. Poe remembered from where he knew the name Alice Symonds.

'You were Bethany's best friend,' he said.

'Yes, I was,' Alice replied. 'And we need to talk.'

Chapter 55

As long as it wasn't anywhere near the Children of Job, Alice didn't care where they went, and as Poe needed to be at police headquarters for his meeting, he headed towards Penrith. The North Lakes Hotel and Spa had a cosy bar with plenty of secretive nooks and crannies. It also had free wi-fi, which meant Bradshaw wouldn't have to break the law hacking into it, something Poe was keen to avoid with Linus constantly looking over her shoulder.

Now he'd passed Alice's test, Poe expected her to open up, but for some reason she didn't want to talk. He asked her why.

'You're Detective Sergeant Washington Poe,' she said. She switched her attention to the passenger seat. 'And you're Tilly Bradshaw.'

'I am,' Bradshaw said.

'How did you know?' Poe asked.

'Like I said, I go where I want in the Children of Job's compound. No one pays me any attention and they talk freely in front of me. You caused quite a stir yesterday.'

After a short delay, Poe said, 'Good.'

'You work for the Serious Crime Analysis Section, and you're supposed to be very good. You in particular, Sergeant Poe, have a reputation for following the evidence, not the story.'

'That's not what DI Stephanie Flynn says,' Bradshaw said. 'She says Poe is the end of a bell. Although she won't tell me what that means and she says I'm not allowed to google it.'

Alice didn't crack a smile. 'But you have caught a lot of killers.'

'Oh yes, lots.'

Alice turned in her seat and faced Linus. 'But I don't know who you are,' she said.

'My name's Linus Jorgensen and I work for the National Audit Office. I'm shadowing Sergeant Poe and Tilly, but I'm not part of their investigation.'

'Can I trust him?' she asked Poe.

Poe studied her face in the rear-view mirror. 'No,' he said.

'I'm sorry, Snoopy, but she doesn't trust you,' Poe said.

'That's because you told her not to!' Linus snapped.

They were in the lobby of the North Lakes Hotel and Spa. Poe had asked Linus to make himself scarce while he and Bradshaw talked to Alice. Linus had refused. Bradshaw and Alice were already ensconced in a dark corner. Bradshaw was making notes on her laptop.

'And that's because *I* don't trust you,' Poe said.

'Do I need to remind you I am to be given full access?'

'And do I need to remind you that I'm triple-warranted and you're not.'

'Meaning?'

'Meaning if you try to interfere in my investigation, I *will* arrest you.'

Linus's lips flattened. He reached for his phone.

'I don't care if you go above my head,' Poe said. 'Not this time, Snoopy. I have a jittery witness who will have more insight into what's going on at the Children of Job than anyone else we can speak to.'

'So—'

'So here's what's going to happen – you're going to sit over there,' Poe pointed towards an armchair in front of an unlit fire, 'and I'm going to speak to my witness.'

'And what do I get?'

'Nothing, you little twerp. This is a murder investigation, not a game of Top Trumps.'

Poe left him standing and went to join Alice and Bradshaw.

163

Chapter 56

'If anyone had a reason to kill Noah and Grace Bowman, it was Bethany,' Alice said. 'She had a deep hatred for them.'

'I sense a "but" coming,' Poe said.

'But I don't think she did it.'

'I've read the original file. The evidence is compelling.'

'It is,' Alice agreed. 'Her fingerprints were all over the clasp knife used to kill Noah and Grace and Aaron, the same knife she used to cut herself sometimes. And, as it was well known she hated her parents, she was the logical suspect. She was rebellious, had a history of violent behaviour and was known to self-harm. If I were a police officer, I might also have been tempted to think that the inevitable had happened.'

'Which was?'

'That a deeply damaged teenage girl, almost certainly suffering from an undiagnosed mental illness, had suffered a psychotic episode. She had fixated on a family that to the outside world had only ever had her best interests at heart, and acted upon some long-held grudge.'

Poe looked over her shoulder. He could see Linus sitting at the bar, sulking. He had his phone to his ear and every so often he glanced at Poe. 'And yet you don't think that's what happened?'

'If she had snapped, then yes, I could have believed it,' Alice said. 'It had happened before, both at home and at school, and it was never pretty. If she'd had an episode while she'd been holding her clasp knife, again, yes, she certainly hated them enough to do something horrible. But to come back five years after she'd left, to murder them in that cold, premeditated way, made no sense. Not to me. And it shouldn't have to the police officers running the investigation either.'

'What makes you say that?'

'Because as troubled as Bethany was, she was also the most honest person I've ever met. If she'd killed her parents she would have owned it. She wouldn't have tried to hide the bodies; she would have called the police herself then waited for them to arrive. She'd have wanted to tell her story in court.'

'Maybe,' Poe said. 'Or maybe she panicked after she killed Aaron. The senior investigating officer never thought his murder had been part of her plan.'

'And that's the other thing, Sergeant Poe,' Alice said. 'She would *never* have killed her brother. She loved Aaron. Ask her teachers. Ask anyone who knew her. The Bowmans were the religious freaks at school and that should have made them bully magnets. But while Aaron was quite timid, Bethany was fierce and fearless. She was a year younger than Aaron, so he had to fend for himself when he was in secondary school and she was still in primary school. But a year later, when Bethany started secondary school as well, the kids soon learned that if they bullied Aaron they might as well have bullied Bethany. And *no one* bullied Bethany. She didn't care about consequences and she didn't care if she bled. She would fight until she dropped from exhaustion, then she'd get up and keep fighting. You can't beat someone like that. Aaron survived school because of Bethany and if it had come down to a choice between killing him and getting away, or letting him live and getting caught, well, that wouldn't have been a choice at all.'

'You admit she hated her parents?'

'She did,' Alice said.

'But?'

'But only because they hated her first.'

Chapter 57

'Noah and Grace Bowman were evil, evil people,' Alice said. 'And for reasons neither of us understood, they hated Bethany.'

Poe frowned. 'I didn't know that,' he said. 'There's certainly nothing to suggest it in the file.'

'When I'm not Mad Alice or Tourist Alice, I work for a domestic abuse charity, and one of the first things we're taught is that perpetrators become extremely skilled at hiding their abuse. They don't just control their victim; they also control the narrative.'

'She was abused?'

Alice nodded.

'Sexually?' Poe asked.

'No.'

'She was beaten then?'

'Nothing like that either.'

'Then—'

'Emotional abuse, Sergeant Poe,' Alice said. 'In the very purest sense, she was being emotionally tortured.'

'Do you believe me, Sergeant Poe?' Alice asked.

'I don't *not* believe you.'

'Even though me telling you this makes Bethany appear more guilty?'

'I'm a detective, Alice, and that means I'm a cynic,' Poe said. 'You tell me you're Bethany's friend and that you don't think she killed her brother and her parents. Yet you're also painting a picture of someone who had every reason to do exactly what she stands accused of. Let's just say you haven't convinced me of your true motivation yet.'

Alice nodded in satisfaction.

'What?' Poe asked.

'You're following the evidence, not the story,' she replied.

'You've already said that.'

'But now you're demonstrating it. I have something to give you, Sergeant Poe, something I maybe should have given the police in 2012.'

'But I can have it?'

'You can.'

'Why me?'

'I've been waiting for you.'

'Me?'

'Someone *like* you.'

'What is it you want to give me?'

'Not yet.'

'OK,' Poe said. 'Whatever it is, why didn't you give it to the police in 2012?'

'Because, taken superficially, it's damning evidence against my friend.'

'Then why risk giving it to me?'

'I left you the note as a test, Sergeant Poe. If you were interested enough for it to lead you to Eve, I figured you might be worth my time. None of the police officers I spoke to back then were. They thought Bethany butchered her family and they weren't considering other ideas.'

'Have you spoken to Eve?'

'Not since she came back to Cumbria.'

'Why not?'

Alice shrugged. 'She partly blames me for what happened. She thinks Bethany killed her entire family and, because I was her friend, I must have known what she was planning.'

She paused to sip her green tea. Bradshaw, who hadn't yet spoken, had finished hers fifteen minutes ago. Poe drained his cold coffee.

'How do I know you're not spinning me a yarn?' Poe said. 'You claimed back in 2012 that Bethany was your friend, but we have only your word for that. There's no one left to confirm it; they're either dead or in the wind.'

She eyed him over the rim of her mug. 'You could always go back to Underbarrow and ask Eve,' she said. 'But you're missing the point.'

'Then what *is* the point?'

'That if you took everything at face value then you'd be of no use to me. The very fact you're doubting me makes you the right person.'

'For what?'

'Did you know Bethany wasn't allowed any possessions, Sergeant Poe?' Alice said, switching lanes without indicating.

'From what I gather, none of the Bowman kids were allowed possessions. Eve said they didn't even have mobile phones. She gave us some photographs of Bethany and they were those old Polaroids. The ones that whirred out of the bottom of the camera. You had to waft them about until they were dry.'

'That's true.'

'Well then, was it not just a case of unconventional parenting? Three children have an extremely religious upbringing – two of them accept it, one of them doesn't. I'm from the generation that played outside, Alice – if I were a parent, and I appreciate I'm not so my view isn't born from experience, I wouldn't want my kids to have mobile phones and Ataris and—'

'Ataris? You really are a buffoon, Poe,' Bradshaw said.

'Eh?'

'Tilly thinks you're a dinosaur, Sergeant Poe,' Alice said, smiling for the first time.

'She does,' Poe agreed. 'And she tells me at least five or six times a day. My point is not only are these gadgets recruiting grounds for paedophiles and stalkers, they stunt childhoods. I'm not suggesting parents go back to handing out hoops and sticks, but the odd Space Hopper wouldn't go amiss.'

Bradshaw and Alice shrugged at each other. 'See?' Bradshaw said. 'Dinosaur.'

'Bethany had no toys whatsoever, Sergeant Poe,' Alice said. 'While Eve and Aaron were given things to play with, and occasionally they'd be allowed what Grace and Noah Bowman thought were suitable books to read, Bethany wasn't allowed anything, not even a Bible. When they were older, Eve and Aaron wore new clothes;

Bethany wore only what Eve had outgrown. She wasn't allowed to eat with the family. They basically did the bare minimum to keep her alive. Other than how it reflected on them, they had no interest in her welfare at all. Bethany said to me once that it wasn't that they were indifferent to her, they actually went out of their way to make her feel unwelcome. Which of course made her behaviour even worse.'

'She was the youngest of the three, right?' Poe said.

'She was.'

Poe thought this through. It wasn't unheard of for parents to favour one child over another, but outside of *Cinderella* it was rarely so blatant. If Alice was telling the truth, Grace and Noah Bowman deserved to be in prison.

If Alice was telling the truth.

Chapter 58

Poe ordered more hot drinks. He did this at the bar rather than at their table. Not because the hovering waiter was incompetent, but because he needed time to think.

'What's happening?' Linus asked.

'Hard to tell,' Poe admitted. 'According to Alice, Noah and Grace Bowman were emotionally abusing Bethany.'

'And it wasn't just an ultra-strict upbringing?'

'Alice believes Bethany was unfairly singled out. According to her, the root cause of all Bethany's behavioural problems was the way she was treated by her parents.'

'What's the problem then? Doesn't this provide the motivation the case was lacking all those years ago?'

'The problem, Snoopy, is that Alice is supposed to be Bethany's friend,' Poe said. 'And if this was the sentencing part of a court case, I'd say she was doing a superb job of offering mitigation.'

'It doesn't add up?'

'There's a contradiction I'm not seeing yet. Why vehemently deny Bethany was capable of doing something while simultaneously providing the missing motivation?'

'Maybe they aren't friends.'

'Maybe,' Poe conceded. The barman brought a tray over. Fresh coffee for him, green teas for Bradshaw and Alice. Poe picked it up and began walking back to the table. He stopped and returned to Linus. 'If you want to make yourself useful, Snoopy, you can start by abusing the powers of the state.'

'What do you want?'

'Dig out everything you can on Alice Symonds. I want to know if she's the real deal or if she's rat poison squared.'

Poe didn't wait for an answer. Linus either would or he wouldn't. And even if he refused, an hour of Bradshaw rooting through the life of Alice Symonds was worth a week of the security services doing it anyway. He got back to the table, passed Alice her drink and said, 'What aren't you telling me, Alice?'

She blew on her tea and studied his face. 'The more important question is why are you still focusing on what happened in 2012?'

'You think Grace, Noah and Aaron Bowman being butchered like pigs isn't worth focusing on?'

She shook her head. 'No, I don't.'

In anyone else that would have been an outrageous statement, but he sensed he was being tested again. 'Then what is?'

'The catalyst, Sergeant Poe,' she said. 'You say the murders are the most important thing, I say they're the end result of something that started five years earlier.'

Poe worked backwards. The Bowmans were murdered in 2012. Five years earlier was 2007, the year Aaron attended one of Cornelius Green's secret courses. But Alice was interested in Bethany, not Aaron.

'Bethany ran away from home in 2007,' he said eventually. 'Although she returned in 2012 to murder her family, 2007 was the last time she was seen. You think the catalyst for what happened in 2012, and for what's happening now, was what caused Bethany to run away from home in the first place?'

Alice nodded her encouragement.

Poe frowned. 'But you've told us what the catalyst was: she had a horrific childhood and she hated her parents.'

'Then why am I here?' Alice said. 'Why have I spent years shuffling around the Children of Job? Why am I Mad Alice?'

'You don't think she *did* run away?'

'No, I believe she did.'

'Then what?'

'She'd run away before, Sergeant Poe. More than a few times actually. She would stay at my house, her refuge she called it, or she would hide out in the woods. Never for more than a day. Attention-seeking behaviour really.'

'But it was different in 2007?'

'Something happened, Sergeant Poe,' she said. 'And it must have been awful because she didn't stop at mine to collect her things; she just stuffed some clothes in her schoolbag and disappeared. Some people think she got on a bus in Keswick; others that she hitchhiked to the M6 and got a lift with a lorry driver.'

'What do you think?'

'That unless she'd had no choice, Bethany wouldn't have left like that. Not without saying goodbye to me.'

'You were that close?'

Alice's face coloured. 'We were.'

'Maybe you were *more* than close?'

'We were.'

'She was your girlfriend?'

'Neither of us was gay, Sergeant Poe. We kissed once. I suppose we were experimenting. Certainly nothing more.'

'Did Noah and Grace Bowman know about the kiss, or any other experimenting Bethany might have done? Was that why they hated Bethany?'

'They didn't know. I'm sure of it.'

'But if they did, would they have tried to stop her?'

Alice shrugged. 'I doubt they'd have cared enough. Not unless she'd flaunted it in front of their friends.'

Poe wasn't convinced. Young love was a weird and powerful thing, and it wasn't easily hidden. And if Noah and Grace Bowman had found out and tried to stop the relationship, Bethany could have reacted violently. It didn't explain the five-year gap between her running away from home and returning to murder her parents, but it did explain some of the animosity they had towards her. The more Poe thought about it, the more he thought Alice was right: the answer wouldn't be found in the present, it would be found in 2007, the year Bethany ran away from home and the year Aaron attended his course.

'I'm told Bethany and Aaron had a blazing row immediately after he got back from the course he attended,' Poe said. 'Do you think that was why she ran away?'

Alice nodded. 'And in all the time I've spent there, I've never heard a whisper about what went on,' she said. 'If anyone knows, they aren't talking.'

'Yet *you* knew enough to leave me that note.'

'That was years of putting two and two together. The existence of courses came from me pestering Eve about what Bethany and Aaron had rowed about. That the courses had stopped after Israel Cobb was banished from the Children of Job, I picked up by paying attention to Cornelius when he flew into one of his rages.'

'Did you speak to Aaron Bowman about what he'd been through?'

'He refused to talk about it. In fact, Aaron didn't speak to me again after Bethany ran away. He withdrew into himself. It wasn't long after that his parents began home-schooling him.'

Poe sighed. 'We're speaking to another witness tonight, some-one else who might also have attended one of these courses. Perhaps he'll be prepared to talk.'

'Good luck with that.'

'You don't think he will?'

'I think there's an impenetrable fog of secrecy around those courses, Sergeant Poe. No one talks about them. And I mean *no one*. Cornelius Green and Israel Cobb ruled the Children of Job with a rod of iron and even now, with Cornelius dead and Israel in the wind, I don't think anyone will speak out. Something happened on those courses and I think everyone now wishes it hadn't.'

Which sort of fitted with what Joshua had said about now being the time to redirect the narrative. He had clearly wanted to move on from the Children of Job's Cornelius Green era. But Poe hadn't been exaggerating when he'd told Israel Cobb the truth was like a swamp bubble. In his experience, particularly when Bradshaw was on the case, it always rose to the top. And the longer it had been under the mud, the smellier it often was. Poe wondered if that would be the case this time. He suspected it would.

'You say Bethany couldn't have killed her parents because she wasn't capable of killing her brother,' Poe said. 'But, given what you know, do you think she would be capable of killing Cornelius Green?'

Alice considered the question carefully. Eventually she said, 'If she held him responsible for Aaron's death, then yes, I think she would.'

'But do you think she *did* kill him?'

'On my lighter days, when the sun is shining and the lambs are gambolling about the fells, I sometimes imagine the life Bethany made for herself. I like to think she found her peace, somewhere far away from here. She's with people who love her and she has a job she enjoys. Maybe she even has children of her own.'

'And on your darker days?'

'The same, but it's cloudy,' Alice said. 'You have to understand, Sergeant Poe: Bethany is a survivor. She experienced something neither of us can truly comprehend and yet, despite her problems, she never stopped smiling. You ask if she was capable of killing Cornelius Green – absolutely. Do I think she did? Absolutely not. I have no doubt Cornelius Green's death was a long time overdue – the man was monstrous – but I don't think for a second Bethany returned to the life she left to do it. Why on earth would she?'

'Maybe she wanted to pop a swamp bubble,' Poe replied. He swigged down the last of his coffee. It was muddy and bitter, and like a shot of adrenaline to the heart. 'What things?' he said.

'Excuse me?'

'You said Bethany wouldn't have left without stopping at yours to collect her things.'

'And *you* said how would you know if I was spinning you a yarn? That it's possible I'm making this whole thing up.'

'Poe says until he's hit a witness at least three times with his interrogation truncheon, whatever comes out of their mouths is as much use as white dog . . . dirt,' Bradshaw explained. 'Except he doesn't say dirt. And his interrogation truncheon is a metaphor for shouting at someone.'

Poe shrugged. 'I'm a police officer,' he said. 'Not trusting people is my default position.'

'I just want to know what happened to my . . . friend,' Alice said. 'That is my only concern. It's why I've spent so long as Mad Alice and it's why I left that note under your windscreen wiper.' She reached into her tote bag. She removed something bulky and placed it on the table. It was a book; thick, tatty and leatherbound. 'And luckily, you don't need to take my word for it.'

'What's this?'

'The inside of Bethany's mind, Sergeant Poe.'

Chapter 59

'What was it?' Doctor Lang asked.

'It was Bethany's journal,' Poe replied. 'Alice had kept hold of it all those years. The pages were stiff with age and the ink had faded a little, but it was perfectly readable.'

'At that point you didn't fully trust Alice, did you?'

'I still had concerns about her motivation.'

'Is trusting people a problem for you, Washington? It seems to be a recurring feature in this case.'

'It does?'

She nodded. 'You thought the Bishop of Carlisle had ulterior motives for sharing his information on the Children of Job.'

'Yeah, but—'

'And you never trusted Linus.'

Poe showed Doctor Lang his oil-stained, scarred hands. 'With good cause,' he said after a short delay.

'And yet you trusted the journal's provenance. Why was that?'

'I didn't trust it. Not immediately.'

'What changed?'

'Tilly is an expert in forensic handwriting analysis,' he said. 'After she'd scanned the journal's contents into her tablet, I dropped off Alice in Penrith then went to police HQ. I handed the journal to Superintendent Nightingale and while I was there I collected some samples of Bethany's schoolwork, so Tilly had some of her writing to compare the journal against. I then went back to the North Lakes Hotel.'

'The police had kept samples of Bethany's handwriting?'

'They'd kept *everything* from the Bowman massacre. Although it wasn't being actively investigated, it was still an open case.'

'So Tilly matched the handwriting in the journal to Bethany's schoolwork?'

'She did and it didn't take her long. Even I could see it had been written by the same person.'

'What did you do then?'

'We still had some time before meeting with Nathan Rose—'

'The man who had been on another of Cornelius Green's secret courses?'

'That's right. Anyway, we had some time, so we spent it reading what Bethany had recorded in her journal.'

'It was bad?'

Poe nodded slowly. 'Very.' On the front page she'd written 'Welcome to my wonderful life', although if Frank Capra had used Bethany Bowman as the inspiration for his film, George Bailey wouldn't have been the only one contemplating suicide that night – the entire cast would have been on that bridge.

Chapter 60

Poe swiped to the first page of Bethany's journal. 'Welcome to my wonderful life by Bethany Bowman, aged 12 years old' was written on it. He was using one of Bradshaw's tablets. Bradshaw was on some sort of e-reader Poe hadn't seen before, and Linus had been afforded the rare privilege of being allowed to touch her laptop.

'I have disabled the internet and Bluetooth connections, so you won't be able to email yourself a copy,' she told him. 'You don't have the skills to reconnect them and if you try I'll know.'

'And why would you do that?' Linus asked.

Poe put his hands to his face and formed a loudspeaker. 'Because we don't trust you, Snoopy.'

They didn't have time to read everything, so Poe decided to choose pages at random. See if he could get a quick flavour. He would read it cover-to-cover in the order it had been written when he got home. Bethany wrote using curved, bubbly letters. Neater than his untidy scrawl, but easily identifiable as a teenage girl's. Extravagant doodles filled the margins. Whole pages were dedicated to drawings of flowers and butterflies and small dogs and anything else that looked like it had caught her attention that day. All harmless stuff. He swiped a few more pages until he came across one that was different in scale to the others. Up until then, Bradshaw had scanned one page per file. This one was two pages. It was why it had stood out. They were the centre pages, where the photograph of the main footballer would have been in *Shoot* magazine, the one you pinned to your wall after carefully removing the staples. Bethany had used the bigger canvas to draw a much more detailed picture. Poe zoomed in. 'Ah, shit,' he said.

'What is it, Poe?' Bradshaw asked.

'You seen file . . .' – he checked the number – '124?'

Bradshaw found the right page. 'Crikey,' she said.

'That settles it,' Linus said.

Bethany's masterpiece was a full-colour, crude rendition of what Poe could only assume was Noah and Grace Bowman. They were bound to a tree, heads at an angle, necks cut almost through, obviously dead. Bethany must have used all of her red felt-tip pen colouring in the blood. Next to the corpses of her parents was a young girl. She appeared to be holding a knife. She was smiling.

Poe's phone rang. It was Superintendent Nightingale.

'Have you seen—'

'The centre pages?' Poe finished for her. 'Just now.'

'Seems young Bethany wants an encore. I know we've just had a meeting, but we're regrouping in Conference Room B in fifteen minutes. Any chance you can pop your head in? We've upgraded Bethany Bowman to our number-one suspect. This is now a nation-wide manhunt.'

Poe was about to say of course, but the drawing stayed his hand. In 2012 Bethany's rage had been focused on her parents; now it was Cornelius Green. 'I'll keep my meeting with Nathan Rose, if you don't mind, ma'am?' he said. 'Perhaps I can get a steer on who else she might have in her sights.'

'I'll put an alert on Eve Bowman's house. Underbarrow is so isolated that even if she called nine-nine-nine, it could be forty minutes before we get to her. I'll make sure the area patrols get cosy.'

'Yep. Eve doesn't think Bethany is a risk to her, but better safe than sorry. Maybe keep a close eye on Alice Symonds as well? They were in a developing relationship when Bethany disappeared. I doubt she'll try to make contact but we'd be fools to ignore the possibility.'

'I'll keep Alice at HQ for a while. Even if I have to arrest her.'

'And you'd better have someone swing by Israel Cobb's as well. He knows more than he's letting on.'

'Will do,' she said. 'And Poe, I don't care how late it is, I want you to call me after your meeting with Nathan Rose.'

After Nightingale had hung up Poe checked the time. They

still had an hour before they needed to leave. Poe swiped to another page and lived a little longer in the nightmare that had been Bethany Bowman's childhood. This time he ignored the drawings and focused on her written entries.

If anything, they were worse.

Chapter 61

Aaron tried to sneak me some honey tonight. He'd made a small pot from some folded cardboard and Sellotaped it together, as he didn't think it was fair I had nothing to go on my bread. The honey had made the Sellotape come away and it had leaked in his pocket. Of course that was my fault! Grace said I must have threatened Aaron. She tore my bread in half, so that's another night without any supper!

I asked Grace why all our pictures of Jesus show him as a white man, when he was actually a first-century Palestinian Jew. I told her that at RE today Mr Kelly said it was to subliminally engrain white superiority into the minds of people of colour. She called me an unclean spirit and went to bed early with a headache. Noah came into my room later and took my pillows and blankets. He didn't even look at me. I had to wear my school uniform just to stay warm and in the morning I had pins and needles. I won't be asking about white Jesus again!

I finished top in cross-country today. Sometimes I feel I should keep running and never come back! Mrs Jenkins presented me with my certificate in front of the whole class. She said it was a school record and I should be very proud. Alice treated me to a milkshake on the way home. I like Alice. Today was a good day!

I showed Noah my certificate when I got back. He tore it in half and handed it back without saying anything. Why do they hate me!!!??? Later Aaron sneaked some tape into my room so I could fix it. I'll take it to school so Alice can keep it safe for me.

'Jesus,' Poe muttered.

Aaron wet the bed again last night. Grace said it was my fault for being evil. Typical. It's not Aaron's fault, but tonight I pinched his arm when I went to brush my teeth. I said sorry straight away but he started crying. He didn't tell Grace though, which was cool of him. I must make it up to him tomorrow.

Poe's phone rang. It was Flynn. 'Boss?' he said.

'How's it going up there?'

Poe spent ten minutes bringing Flynn up to speed. Told her about the note that had been left under his windscreen wiper at the Children of Job compound, and how that had led them to Eve Bowman and the subsequent ambush by Alice Symonds.

'You *have* handed the journal in to Jo Nightingale, Poe?' she said when he was finished. 'Tell me you're not sitting on what might be key evidence?'

'I handed it to her personally,' Poe confirmed.

'Tilly took a digital copy first?'

'Of course. How's the audit going?'

Flynn paused.

'What's up, boss?' he said.

'They're saying the right things. They're *looking* at the right things . . .'

'But?'

'But it's superficial, Poe. I spoke to the director last night and we're in agreement.'

'About what?'

'We think this is about you, Poe.'

'Me? What have I done?'

'I haven't got a spare six months, but it's the only thing that makes sense. They certainly aren't interested in anything we're doing down here.'

Poe glanced at Linus. He was reading Bethany's journal, the same as he and Bradshaw. If the young spook was spying on him, he was doing a good job of hiding it. But, if Poe *were* the subject of a secret investigation, they would hardly send someone incompetent. And yes, Poe, with the help of Bugger Rumble, *had* tricked him into

182

revealing who he really worked for, but that type of thing only ever worked once. The truth was, he had no idea what Linus wanted. He told Flynn as much.

'Just be careful, Poe,' she said. 'Do everything by the book and try not to piss him off too much. I'm too old to break in a new sergeant.'

'When do I *not* do things by the book?'

'I'm not dignifying that with a response,' she said, ending the call.

'Everything OK?' Linus asked.

Poe ignored him and went back to reading Bethany's journal.

Chapter 62

'You come across the phrase "bad biscuit" yet?' Poe said, glancing up from the journal entry he was reading.

Linus and Bradshaw both nodded.

'If you give me ten seconds,' Bradshaw said, grabbing her laptop from Linus and typing something so fast her fingers went blurry, 'I can tell you how many times.' Her laptop beeped. 'The phrase "bad biscuit" is used twenty-seven times, Poe.'

Poe reread his entry.

Grace is a bad biscuit! She took the bulb out of my lamp tonight as she said I'd been reading when I should have been sleeping. I'm not even allowed books! I said I would tell my teacher what she'd done and she said that no one would believe me and even if they did, they would take me away and put me in a horrible orphanage and I'd never see Eve or Aaron again.

'What do you think it means?' Poe said. 'I've never heard that phrase before.'

'I think it's an insult, Poe,' Bradshaw said. 'I've scanned the whole document for swear words and there aren't any.'

'Maybe some of that strict religious upbringing rubbed off on her,' Linus said. 'Some of the worst killers in history were prudish when it came to curse words.'

'Yes, thank you, Snoopy,' Poe said. 'As Tilly and I both work for the unit responsible for studying serial killers, we were, of course, completely unaware of this.'

'I was just saying.'

'Well don't.'

Poe swiped right and read an earlier entry.

Grace and Noah call me Bethany at church and when they are forced to meet my teachers, but at home they call me 'It'. 'It' was talking to Aaron last night. 'It' didn't come straight home from school today. We'd better give 'It' some food, people will notice if 'It's underweight. I borrowed Stephen King's It from the school library and read it at Alice's house. Maybe if I were a killer clown instead of a thirteen-year-old girl they wouldn't pick on me so much. I wish they were dead!

She wasn't a killer clown, Poe thought, but had she turned into a murderer, nonetheless? Everything pointed to this. Alice might be viewing Bethany through love-tinted glasses, but Poe wasn't. Alice had asked why Bethany had waited five years to take her revenge, but Poe thought she was missing the point. If the journal was an accurate reflection of Bethany's childhood, the real question was why had it taken her so long?

He opened the index of the scanned journal and selected the final entry. He read it twice then checked the date. Bethany had written it two weeks before Aaron attended his course.

Something has happened! Grace was shouting at Aaron when he got back from school, REALLY shouting at him. She called him a bad biscuit and threatened to cut it off, although I couldn't hear what the 'it' was. Aaron was crying and so was Eve. We all got sent to our rooms and for once it wasn't just me going without tea. Eve sneaked me in some cheese just before she went to bed, but she wouldn't tell me what had happened. She looked scared. I crept outside when the house was quiet, as I wanted to make sure Aaron was OK. I over-heard Grace and Noah whispering. I couldn't make out what they were saying, but when they finished, Noah said, 'OK, I'll go and see Cornelius.' I hope Aaron doesn't have to go to that horrible place. He's not strong enough. I wonder what he's done.

'It all comes down to that course,' Poe said, turning off Bradshaw's tablet. 'If that last entry is to be believed, Aaron did something, something that upset his parents. His father went to see Cornelius and two weeks later he was on one of those undocumented courses. Maybe Noah and Grace discovered Aaron was gay, maybe it was something else. Whatever it was, he went on that course and, when he got back, he and Bethany rowed. Bethany ran away immediately afterwards.'

'Do you believe her, Poe?' Bradshaw asked. 'If it's deception, it's very clever deception.'

'My gut feeling says this isn't the bug-eyed ranting of a psychopath, Tilly; this is the real deal. I don't think a teenage girl would have the nuance or subtlety to make up something like this. Bethany *did* hate her parents, but I think Alice was right – they hated her first. And I don't think it was because she was getting close to another girl.'

'But why, Poe? She was only a little girl. And why didn't they do those terrible things to Eve and Aaron as well? Why did they single out Bethany so much?'

'I don't know,' he said, his eyes monstrous in North Lakes's dimly lit bar. 'But I'll tell you one thing, Tilly – I *will* find out.'

Chapter 63

'Bad biscuit?' Doctor Lang said, frowning. 'She used the phrase bad biscuit to describe someone she didn't like?'

Poe nodded. 'According to Tilly she used it twenty-seven times in her journal but never swore once, and believe me, Doctor Lang, she had every reason to.'

'For someone like her, that's . . . unusual. Language is one of the few things the powerless have at their disposal.'

'I called Alice about it and she said Bethany never swore as she hadn't wanted Aaron to copy her. And Snoopy said that whether they liked it or not, some of Grace and Noah's values had imprinted on their daughter.'

'Had she been writing daily entries?'

'No. Which isn't surprising considering she had to keep her journal at Alice's house. Sometimes there were one or two a week; sometimes there was a month-long gap.'

'What did Cumbria Police make of this new evidence?'

'The cop in charge of the original investigation was called Ian Gamble and he's long retired. Superintendent Nightingale is in charge now and she thought the same as me.'

'Which was?'

'That they'd finally found their missing motivation.'

'For the Bowman family massacre?'

'And Cornelius Green's murder. We didn't know what the link was at that point, but everything seemed to start with Noah Bowman contacting Cornelius Green about whatever it was that Aaron had done.'

'We have a young girl undoubtedly suffering from rejected child syndrome and her brother, the only person in the family she has any real attachment to, is forced to go away for some real or imagined transgression. She must have been terrified.'

'Why?'

'Children are tough and adaptable, Washington. In situations like Bethany's, they develop coping mechanisms. Bethany had Alice and her temper and her rebellious nature. I would imagine it's why she was never physically beaten. I suspect her parents knew there was a line they couldn't cross with her. But if they had threatened her brother with something, well, that could have been a psychological tipping point.'

'It was threatening Aaron that sent her over the edge, not the abuse she suffered. That seems . . . counterintuitive.'

'That's because you're thinking like an adult male, not a fourteen-year-old girl. You said she saw her role as Aaron's protector. That she defended him from bullies at school and she bore the brunt of her parents' ill behaviour at home. If something horrible happened to Aaron, in her eyes, she had failed him completely. And when she tried to internalise that, it could easily have manifested as violence towards him. She might have blamed him for putting himself in a situation in which she was unable to protect him. That might have been why they rowed.'

'You said she would have suffered from rejected child syndrome?'

'Almost certainly.'

'What is it?'

'It's where children are rejected by the very people who are sup-posed to love and care for them. And it goes beyond favouritism, it feels like parents actively dislike a child. Biologically, as vertebrates, the mother's bond with the child is supposed to become unbreakable within the first three years of life. It used to be essential for sur-vival. If that bond *isn't* established, the rejection can continue well into adolescence. The child will never feel like part of the family and, as feelings of security and stability are fundamental to emo-tional development, getting through adolescence without making unfortunate decisions will take a great deal of luck. And, as it was in Bethany's case, when the child has siblings, the emotional trauma can be even more profound. It will feel like their brothers and sisters can do no wrong, while they're punished for minor infractions.'

'Bethany wasn't even allowed to eat with the family,' Poe said. 'I suppose if she'd been an only child she might have been able to rationalise what was happening as the norm, but when her rejection was so blatant, so *cruel*, it was perhaps inevitable she became who she did?'

'And recent studies have confirmed what we therapists have always known – that the anterior cingulate cortex, the cortical area of the brain that registers physical pain, is also involved in the detection and monitoring of social and emotional pain. An Australian study even showed that remembering physically painful events is less traumatic than remembering emotionally painful events.'

'Meaning?'

'Meaning, if a child was physically tortured for fourteen years no one would be surprised if they subsequently developed behavioural problems. Now we understand emotional trauma a little better, we should not be surprised to learn that things such as rejected child syndrome lead to similar problems.'

'Tell me what the long-term effects might be.' He already knew some, of course, but it was interesting to hear a professional's opinion.

Doctor Lang considered this carefully. 'In cases like Bethany's, I would expect the child to suffer from type-two post-traumatic stress disorder,' she said. 'And, as the reason *you're* sitting in this makeshift office is trauma related, you'll know that comes with a whole range of symptoms.'

'I suffer from nightmares,' he said. 'I assume that's one of the milder ones?'

'The long-term effects have primarily been studied in the US.'

'Why's that?'

'Because of their mass shootings. Although lots of countries have what we would consider lax gun laws, the US is the only country to regularly suffer from this phenomenon.'

'Extreme violence is one of the long-term effects?'

'A rare one, but yes.'

'What would be more usual?'

'Alcoholism and drug abuse. Postures that show self-protection, like slouching or haircuts that hide most of the face. Membership of a gang isn't uncommon and paradoxically neither is the desire for extreme solitude.'

Poe sucked air through his teeth. His mother had abandoned him when he was a toddler, and although he had subsequently discovered she'd had reasons he could understand, he had always been a bit of a loner. Herdwick Croft was in the middle of nowhere and until Estelle Doyle had entered his life, he had never had a relationship that had lasted more than a few weeks. He could count on one hand the number of people he trusted. He wondered if it all stemmed from his childhood.

'Alice said if Bethany was going to murder her family she would have just snapped, she wouldn't have waited five years,' he said. 'Does that bear out with the studies into mass shootings in the US?'

'No,' Doctor Lang replied. 'That's not what the studies found. The evidence suggests that mass shooters enter into a long-term plan. Their anger builds up over a significant period of time, often since childhood. They rarely snap.'

'So a five-year gap between running away and returning to murder her family . . . ?'

'Is entirely consistent with the US studies, yes.' Doctor Lang tapped the file on the table. 'Can I remind you, Washington, that I haven't read this part yet as I want to hear your version first? Other than knowing the guilty parties are either dead or behind bars, I have no idea who did what to whom.'

'We're getting there, Doctor Lang,' Poe said. 'In fact, we're now getting to the stage where things started to go wrong, both in the case and for me personally.'

'What happened?'

'You remember the alphanumeric tattoos I told you about?'

'The ones Cornelius Green had on his body? You said Israel Cobb might have had them too.'

'You have to understand that at this stage of the investigation our priority was finding out what had happened on those secret courses.

We believed that once we knew, we would be one step closer to finding out who else Bethany Bowman might target. We'd sort of put the tattoos on the backburner. Tilly was spending a little bit of time on them when she could, but they weren't our priority.'

'And they should have been.'

'Like I said before, the tattoos were the key to everything. Something we were left in no doubt of after our visit to Nathan Rose.'

'And this was where things started to go wrong?'

Poe looked at the cuts and scars on his hands. Some had healed; some were fresh. Some were little more than scratches; others were deep and had needed stitches. None of them were older than six months. 'It was,' he said.

'What happened?'

'I'd been reading Bethany's journal on the way there and by the time I got to the Roses' I guess I was looking for a fight. Mrs Rose and I took an instant dislike to each other.'

'Why?'

'I suppose it saved time.'

'Washington,' Doctor Lang warned, 'we've talked about your use of humour as a deflection technique.'

'Sorry,' Poe said.

'What happened?'

'Something horrible. And later on it gave certain people everything they needed.'

Chapter 64

Nathan Rose lived in Portinscale, a small but typical Lake District village within walking distance of Keswick. With white-washed houses and ancient pubs, it had once been picturesque and unspoiled, but when tourists found it they infected the village like a fungal rash. It now had as many B & B signs as Keswick. Bradshaw told them Portinscale meant 'harlot's hut' in Old English. Poe said she'd better not tell the deeply conservative Roses that. 'I don't imagine they'll have a sense of humour, Tilly,' he'd added.

Poe had made Linus drive so he could finish Bethany's journal. Nothing he read improved his mood. Unless she was a skilled fanta-sist, Bethany had suffered an appalling childhood.

'Where am I going?' Linus said.

'Second left after the Farmers Arms,' Poe said.

'House number?' Linus said.

'Park behind that Audi,' Poe said, pointing at a gap in the on-street parking. He checked the Audi's registration with what he had in his notebook. 'That's their car, so this must be it.'

Linus was a city driver and squeezing into tight parking spaces was second nature. They were soon on the street, arching their backs and rotating their necks. It had been a long day.

Poe stopped at the back of the Roses' Audi. He pointed at the bumper sticker: a cross with the words 'Unashamed' underneath. For some reason it annoyed him.

'We'd better go in, Poe,' Bradshaw said. 'I think Mrs Rose is wondering why you're scowling at her car.'

Poe looked up. Sure enough, a woman was glaring at them through the lace curtains behind a bow-fronted window. Poe smiled.

Mrs Rose didn't return it. She moved away and a moment later the front door opened.

Poe held up his ID card. She examined it carefully then said, 'You had better come in.'

Virginia Rose was thinner than a lolly stick and meaner than skimmed milk. Her words were precise, her vowels trimmed. She spoke as if it was a necessary but unpleasant chore. Poe reckoned that five hundred years earlier she would have been a witchfinder's assistant, gleefully passing them the heretic's fork. Some people just gave off that vibe. She was wearing a pantsuit Hillary Clinton would have been proud of, a dark, funereal number. Poe thought it looked like the death of spirit.

She led them through the hall into a living room that was almost as austere as Cornelius Green's. No television, no radio, not even a turntable, only two uncomfortable-looking chairs and a bare coffee table. An IKEA lamp in the corner and a crucifix on the wall. Some religious paintings. The wallpaper was straight out of the seventies, a trippy, shimmering design that looked chic and retro now, although it was almost certainly the original décor.

She took one of the two seats and Poe, aware that talking to witnesses was best done when one person didn't tower over the other, took the other. It was as uncomfortable as it looked. Bradshaw and Linus stood behind him.

'What do you want?' Virginia Rose said.

'We were told your husband would be here, Mrs Rose,' Poe said.

'He is.'

'Could I speak with him, please?'

'Not until I know what this is about,' she said. 'I assure you we have broken none of His laws or yours.'

'His?'

She gestured towards the mantelpiece. A tablet leaned against the wall, where other people might have put a mirror. It was white marble with blue veins, like cheese. Poe squinted and read the first line of engraved writing. It said, 'I am the Lord your God: you shall have no other gods but me.'

'Yes, we live by the Ten Commandments, Sergeant Poe,' she said.

'Who doesn't?' Poe replied.

'You don't, Poe,' Bradshaw said. 'You're always working on the Sabbath, even after DI Stephanie Flynn told you to take at least one day off a month.'

'She told *us* to take at least one day off a month, Tilly. It wasn't just me in that HR meeting.'

'Yes, but—'

'We don't work on the Sabbath,' Virginia Rose cut in. 'Nor do we break the law of the land. So, I'll ask you again, Sergeant Poe, why do you need to speak to my husband?'

'I'm not suggesting your husband *has* broken the law, Mrs Rose,' Poe said. 'I want to speak to him about a course he attended almost twenty years ago. It was run by a man called Cornelius Green.'

Her eyes narrowed and her lips thinned. 'That was simply a silly phase Nathan was going through.'

'What was?'

She didn't immediately respond. She seemed to be choosing her next words carefully. 'We are pro life and anti same-sex marriage in this house, Sergeant Poe,' she said. 'When my husband was a young man he was confused. Luckily his parents were good Christians, and they were able to get him off the path of destruction and back on the path to heaven.'

'And Cornelius Green helped with this?'

She nodded. 'Through a highly personalised regime of therapy and prayer, he was able to show Nathan that living as a sinner was not who he really was.'

Her words sounded second-hand, as if she'd rehearsed them. Nathan Rose was thirty-nine years old and Virginia was at least ten years older. He wondered if theirs was a lavender marriage – a marriage of convenience to conceal the sexual orientation of one or both partners. If Nathan had been gay when he was a young man, he was probably gay now. Virginia had to know conversion therapy didn't work, yet she'd married him anyway. Poe could see what Nathan got out of it. In a deeply religious community, marriage might give everyone the cover they needed to accept that Nathan being gay had been, as Virginia had stated, simply a 'silly phase'. But, unless she was also gay, Poe couldn't see what she was getting out of it. He put it to the back of his mind. He wasn't interested in Nathan Rose's sexuality, and he certainly hadn't come for a fight about the efficacy of conversion therapy.

'Are you aware Cornelius Green was recently murdered?'

'I am. Awful news. All deaths are awful, of course, but that man was a great help to my husband. Is that why you're here?'

'Can I speak to Nathan now?' Poe said, ignoring her question.

'I've told you everything I know, Sergeant Poe.'

'But you haven't told me everything *he* knows.'

'I can assure you we have no secrets.'

'Mrs Rose,' Poe sighed, 'this is a murder enquiry. It's possible Cornelius Green's death is linked to the Bowman family massacre in 2012. Aaron Bowman also attended one of Cornelius's courses and we need to know what went on.'

'Fine,' she sighed. 'Wait here and I'll go and get him. He's in the shed tinkering with something.'

Chapter 65

'What do we think?' Poe said, standing up. He had pins and needles in his feet and he looked accusingly at the chair. Why would anyone design something so uncomfortable? The Geneva Conventions banned sitting in the stress position, but apparently this didn't apply to chairs for the puritanical.

'About what?' Linus asked.

'Her. Virginia Rose. What's she getting out of this marriage?'

'In some countries secular conservatives stigmatise older, single women, Poe,' Linus said. 'Marriage is put on a pedestal. It's described in elevated terms and legislation that strengthens it is aggressively supported. Given she just told us she's anti same-sex marriage, it's reasonable to assume she's very much *pro* opposite-sex marriage. I doubt it's anything more complicated than that.'

'Or perhaps she loves Nathan Rose because his genitals are like those of a donkey,' Bradshaw added.

Poe was glad Virginia Rose hadn't offered them tea; he'd have spat it all over the Ten Commandments tablet. He stared at Bradshaw in astonishment then glanced at the door to make sure Virginia Rose hadn't returned yet. That would have been all they needed. 'Why on earth would you say that, Tilly?'

'It's in the Bible.'

'Don't be ridiculous,' Poe said, ignoring his golden rule of never, under any circumstance, arguing with Bradshaw about matters of fact.

'She's right, Poe,' Linus said. 'Ezekiel 23:20 says that Oholibah, "lusted after her lovers, whose genitals were like those of donkeys and whose emission was like that of horses". If I remember correctly, Oholibah was a metaphor for Jerusalem and the unfaithful and ungodly behaviour of the Israelites.'

Poe considered this. 'It's not an *obvious* metaphor,' he said after a beat. 'And Tilly?'

'Yes, Poe?'

'Please don't ask Mrs Rose if her husband has a donkey dick.'

'I won't, Poe. I promise.'

Linus was studying the paintings on the wall. He pointed at one and said, 'Bethany Bowman was right, wasn't she? Christians in the West *always* depict Jesus as being a white European with blond hair and blue eyes, instead of a first-century Judean with dark skin, dark hair and brown eyes.'

'That's supposed to be Jesus?' Poe said. 'I thought it was Björn Borg.'

Bradshaw looked over Poe's shoulder and bit her bottom lip. He turned. Silently, Virginia Rose had re-entered the living room. She had been standing in the doorway, listening to them. She barked a short, humourless laugh. It was brittle and sharp, like breaking glass. 'Our lives must seem very small to you, Sergeant Poe.'

'Mrs Rose, I didn't mean—'

'Nathan is on his way. I would appreciate it if you could keep that tack-sharp wit to yourself. He's a man of delicate disposition.'

Chapter 66

Nathan Rose was in his late thirties and paunchy. He had wet lips and a smile that didn't connect with his eyes. Slightly shorter than his wife, he was timid looking and seemed overwhelmed by having police officers in his house. He was also the most miserable-looking man Poe had ever seen.

Poe offered his hand and Nathan touched it the same way someone might touch a plate the waiter had just said was extremely hot. He stood beside his wife and Virginia Rose immediately took a step forwards. Her body language was clear: if you want to hurt my husband, you have to go through me first.

'Has your wife told you why we're here, Mr Rose?' Poe said.

Nathan nodded. 'You think Cornelius's death might be connected to what happened to the Bowman family.'

Poe gave his one-minute elevator pitch: that a visit to the Children of Job had led them to Israel Cobb and the discovery of some off-the-books courses Cornelius Green had been running. That two of the six attendees had been identified through their parents' credit-card payments: Aaron Bowman and Nathan Rose.

'What does Cornelius's murder have to do with the course I attended?' Nathan asked.

'That's what we're here to find out,' Poe said. 'We believe that when Aaron Bowman returned from his course, he and Bethany had a serious falling-out. She ran away from home that night and as far as we know, didn't return until—'

'She killed her parents and her brother,' Nathan finished for him. 'I've lived in this area all my life, Sergeant Poe; I'm aware of what happened.'

'We think she's back, Mr Rose,' Poe said. 'And we need to

198

understand why. If we can find out what happened during those courses, not only might it help us find Bethany, it might also give us a steer on anyone else who could be at risk.'

'We prayed and we talked.'

'That's all?'

'I was having . . . horrible thoughts and Cornelius helped me sort through them. It took three days and I had to fast and pray and read the Bible. He was able to show that my attraction to men was a projection. That really, I wanted to *be* like them, to be more masculine, and I had mistaken the longing to be accepted for attraction.'

'Nothing more extreme?'

'Like what?'

'I don't know,' Poe admitted. 'But if it *were* just talking and praying, why the big need for secrecy? Why not simply schedule them with the rest of the courses they ran? He recorded the payments so he wasn't trying to hide income.'

'Did it occur to you that my husband's parents didn't just require treatment for his . . . confusion; they also required confidentiality?' Virginia Rose said.

'I doubt that was it, Mrs Rose,' Poe said. 'Half the young men who attended Cornelius's regularly scheduled conversion courses didn't have names ascribed to their places, and for those who did it was first names only. If confidentiality really was the issue, it could have been managed within the Children of Job's existing policies.'

'Then I'm afraid my husband can't help you, Sergeant Poe.'

Poe pushed past Virginia Rose. She was about to kick them out and Nathan Rose was hiding something. Poe grasped his arm. 'Think!' he urged. 'There *must* be something you're not telling me, something that's slipped your mind. It doesn't matter how insignificant you think it is.'

'I'm sorry, Sergeant—'

'Do you know how Cornelius Green died, Mr Rose?'

'I . . . I don't think it's been in the newspapers yet.'

'He had rocks thrown at his head until he was dead. If we don't—'

'Cornelius was stoned to death?' Nathan Rose said, paling.

'He was.'

Nathan's eyes flickered briefly as if the channel in his head had just changed. He closed them. For a few seconds he said nothing. A brief, localised sweat dotted his brow. He rubbed the back of his neck and sighed. When his eyes opened they were brimming with anguish. He nodded once, as if he'd made a difficult decision.

'I'll help you, Sergeant Poe,' he said eventually.

'How?'

'I still have some course material. It's in the loft.'

'What material?' Virginia said.

'Just leaflets and worksheets, my dear,' he said. 'Harmless stuff, but if it helps Sergeant Poe catch whoever killed Cornelius, he should have it. Don't you agree?'

'I suppose he must,' his wife said. 'Although I don't see how dredging up your past is relevant to anything that has happened more recently.'

Poe frowned. 'Why the change of heart, Mr Rose?'

Nathan smiled weakly. 'I'll get it for you,' he said.

He turned on his heel and, before his wife could object, he left the room.

Chapter 67

While they waited for Nathan to return with his course material, Poe tried to make small talk with Virginia, aware he had been unnecessarily rude earlier. And he'd make sure she understood the NCA complaints procedure before they left.

'Where did you meet Nathan?' he asked.

'At church,' she replied. 'We've been married eight years now, and I think it's been a successful union. We haven't been blessed with children, but that's OK, the Lord has a different path for us.'

'You sound like an intelligent woman, Mrs Rose,' Poe said, 'so I won't insult you by telling you what you undoubtedly already know – conversion therapy has been widely discredited. It's been condemned by the medical profession and even the Church says it's unethical, harmful and not supported by evidence.'

'I'm aware it is intrinsically flawed.'

'So why—?'

'Nathan's family were on the verge of disowning him, Sergeant Poe,' she said. 'I know his therapy didn't work, his *family* knows it didn't work and he knows it didn't work. But because Cornelius provided him with a plausible explanation: that he wasn't gay, he had simply been projecting his feelings, it gave everyone the chance to step back from the edge. To pretend it had all been a misunderstanding. So Nathan still sees his parents and he's still welcome at church. His therapy might not have worked, but it gave him back what was most important to him.'

'Marriage was a way of emphasising this?' he said.

'It was.'

Poe didn't know how to respond. 'I suppose sometimes there are no good options,' he said eventually.

'Ask your question, Sergeant Poe.'

'What question?'

'You want to know what I get out of a mixed-orientation marriage,' she said.

Poe shrugged. 'I suppose I do.'

'You aren't the first person to ask, and you won't be the last. The answer is straightforward – Nathan and I had been going to the same church for a long time. I could see how unhappy he was, how people he had grown up with avoided his handshake when we passed the Peace. I was unmarried, lonely, and lived in this big house. I had little chance of marrying for love, so I did the next best thing.'

'Which was?'

'Have you read the "Parable of the Lost Sheep", Sergeant Poe?'

'Not recently,' Poe admitted.

'It's about a shepherd who leaves his flock of ninety-nine sheep to find the one that has strayed. It's been interpreted as meaning the recovery of sinners, but I've always thought that was a bit too . . . exact. I prefer the wider interpretation that it refers to *any* lost human.'

'Nathan was a lost human?'

'And a good one. I love my husband, Sergeant Poe, and he loves me. Yes, it's a sexless marriage, but according to the research I've read, a lot of traditional marriages are too.'

Poe studied her again. This time he looked beyond the puritanical, wannabe witchfinder facade and saw a good woman who just wanted what was best for her husband. And while their life was undoubtedly a struggle at times, at least they were struggling through it together. Which reminded him: Estelle Doyle was at Herdwick Croft waiting for him. He would see what Nathan had stored in the loft and then he'd leave the Roses alone. If there was something to follow up, he'd get one of Superintendent Nightingale's cops to do it. He'd done enough damage for one night.

'Your husband's taking a long time, Mrs Rose,' he said.

She glanced at the stairs. 'Yes, he is. I'd better go and check he's—'

A sudden, ear-splitting bang stopped her mid-sentence. It

sounded like a car had crashed through the roof and landed on a drum kit. Poe and Virginia Rose looked at each other, then looked up. Flakes of paint floated down from the ceiling. There were a few seconds of residual clattering then nothing but ominous creaking.

'Oh shit,' Poe said, racing for the stairs.

Chapter 68

Nathan Rose had fastened an old tow rope to a roof beam, looped the other end around his neck, and stepped through the open loft hatch. He wasn't kicking and jerking; the drop had been long enough to snap his neck. Poe held up his legs anyway.

Virginia Rose started to scream.

'Get her out of here, Snoopy!' Poe yelled. 'Tilly, dial nine-nine-nine. We need fire and rescue, we need an ambulance and we need the police! When you've done that, call Superintendent Nightingale – she needs to get here now!'

Linus dragged Virginia away from her husband and back down the stairs. Poe knew he would never forget the cries of anguish he'd somehow caused. Bradshaw darted into a bedroom to make her calls, her eyes wide and wet. Poe took a deep breath and tried to hold Nathan Rose up, tried to relieve the pressure on his neck. He knew it was futile, but he wasn't letting go until Nathan had been cut down.

For some reason Nathan had decided to remove his shoe and sock from his right foot. His hairless shin was rubbing against the side of Poe's face.

Still Poe didn't let go.

Fire and rescue arrived first. Keswick Fire Station was staffed by on-call firefighters and they only had a mile to travel. It wasn't the crew commander's first hanging. It wasn't even the first that week. With Nathan Rose's suspended body preventing access to the loft through the hatch, the commander, a burly Scot called Donald, took one look at Nathan and told Poe to let go.

Poe refused. 'Is there an aerial ladder on your engine?' he grunted.

'Aye.'

'Go through the roof and cut him down. The beam he used has splintered and I don't think I'll be able to hold him if it snaps.'

'But why—'

'Just do it!'

Donald held his hands up in supplication. 'You're the boss,' he said. He turned to his crew. 'Right, lads, you heard him; we're going through the roof. Tim, take a hammer up there and remove the slates. Try not to damage anything but don't hang aro . . . don't dawdle.'

Five minutes later, Nathan Rose's corpse was lying on the landing carpet. He had pinned a note to his shirt.

It said:

I'm sorry, Virgy, the time has come for me to sit on the mercy chair.

Poe stepped back so Bradshaw could take a photograph. He would get the crime-scene copy off Nightingale later, but he wanted one for the file now. What the hell was the mercy chair? Was it real or was it a metaphor? If it was a biblical term, it was one Poe hadn't heard of. He glanced at Bradshaw. She hadn't moved yet. He hoped she was OK. She'd seen dead bodies before, more than a civilian analyst really should have. But she looked as she always did in situations like this – upset but determined. For some reason she was ignoring the suicide note and concentrating on the sole of Nathan Rose's bare foot.

Poe looked too.

And saw the alphanumeric tattoo.

Chapter 69

'Is it a new tattoo or is it one of Cornelius Green's, Tilly?' Poe asked. He had Cornelius's tattoos in his notebook, but Bradshaw retained information like a NASA computer.

'CSM.12.R2.CL is one of Cornelius's six tattoos, Poe,' she replied.

'I doubt Nathan did this to himself, not on the sole of his foot. When we check the writing against Cornelius's, I'd be very surprised if it isn't the same.'

'It *is* the same writing, Poe. The angle-step, size and spacing are identical. I would need to examine both samples side-by-side, of course, but my field analysis is that they're a match.'

Poe nodded. 'And when Estelle strips him for the post-mortem, what's the betting we'll find the other five tattoos?'

'I don't imagine we will, Poe.'

'You don't? What makes you say that?'

'Because there were six self-penned tattoos on Cornelius Green's body and we uncovered six undocumented conversion therapy courses. I believe the tattoo on Nathan Rose's foot relates to the specific course he attended.'

'Like a course code?'

'Yes, Poe.'

Poe glanced down at Nathan Rose's corpse. 'Maybe it's a reminder of what he went through,' he said. 'A permanent elastic band.'

'I don't understand that reference, Poe.'

'Neither do I,' Linus said from behind him.

Linus had sat with Virginia Rose until the police arrived. Now specialist officers were with her, he had nothing left to do. Poe wanted to get away but Superintendent Nightingale had asked him to wait until she arrived.

'It's sometimes used with addictive behaviour,' Poe said. 'The user wears an elastic band on their wrist and when they have a craving, they stretch it and let it snap back. It's a distraction technique for intrusive thoughts.'

'What good's a distraction technique on the sole of the foot though?' Linus asked. 'He wouldn't have been able to see it.'

'You make a good point,' Poe admitted. 'But once you have a tattoo, you *always* have a tattoo. It's part of you.' He slapped his right bicep. 'I have a tattoo here and even though I can't see it, I know it's there. Perhaps that was enough.'

'I don't think that's it, Poe,' Bradshaw said. 'If it *was* a distraction tattoo, why is it a seemingly random collection of numbers and letters? Why is it not something motivational? Or, given the rich pickings in the Old Testament, why not have a Bible passage like Leviticus 18:22, which says homosexuality is a "detestable sin"? We know from Cornelius Green's profile that he held these extreme views.'

'You make a good point as well,' Poe said. 'So why *are* the tattoos so ambiguous?'

A high-pitched wailing noise cut through their whispered conversation. Poe wondered if Superintendent Nightingale was downstairs now. Under circumstances like this it was procedure for the senior investigating officer to inform the next of kin that the paramedics had confirmed death.

'Poor woman,' Poe said. 'She was quietly leading her life the best way she knew how, and we turn up and smash her world to pieces.'

'You had to ask those questions,' Linus said.

'I didn't have to ask them the way I did though, Snoopy. I shouldn't have read Bethany's journal on the way here. I wasn't in the right frame of mind for an interview like this. I should have postponed it.'

'I agree with Linus, Poe,' Bradshaw said. 'We couldn't possibly have known something like this would happen.'

'But—'

'How many times have you told me that investigating murder isn't a nine-to-five job?'

'I don't know. Twice maybe?'

'Twenty-six times.'

'That many?'

Bradshaw nodded.

'I need a new saying then,' Poe said.

'At least it's better than your black pudding saying,' she said. 'That makes no sense and it's kinda gross. No wonder your doctor—'

'That's enough, Tilly,' Poe said, clipping her sentence. Superintendent Nightingale had joined them on the landing.

'Poe, can I have a word?' she said. She walked into the bedroom from which Bradshaw had called the emergency services. Poe followed her.

'You need to leave,' she said.

He didn't need to ask why. 'Mrs Rose is blaming me?' he said.

'She is. She said you were antagonistic towards her and her husband from the moment you arrived. Your interview was aggressive and it brought up too many painful memories for her husband to cope with. That it should have been done more sensitively. She claims he hanged himself as a direct result of how you spoke to him.'

'He also took off a shoe and one of his socks so we wouldn't miss that he had one of those alphanumeric tattoos.'

Nightingale's eyes widened. 'He has one as well?'

Poe nodded. 'And it matches one of Cornelius's.'

'What the hell's going on?' she whispered.

'Tilly has a theory,' he said quietly. 'She thinks the six tattoos on Cornelius were bespoke codes for the six courses. We know Nathan Rose's course was one-to-one conversion therapy because he told us before he hanged himself, so it's safe to assume the other five were as well. Tilly thinks, after each course had finished, the course code was tattooed on both Cornelius and the attendee. If the post-mortem shows Nathan has just the one tattoo, I think she's probably right.'

Nightingale considered it carefully. After a few moments she said, 'What possible reason could there be for that?'

Poe shrugged. 'No idea, but decoding those tattoos is what I'm working on from now on.'

'And when you say you—'

'I mean Tilly, yes.'

'Good,' she nodded. 'Didn't you say Israel Cobb had those tattoos?'

'I only saw them briefly, but I think they were the same.'

'And you don't want to re-interview him?'

'I don't think I'll get anything more from him,' Poe said. 'He stormed off last time.'

'I'll send one of my guys round tomorrow. We can't not try.'

Poe nodded. 'We'll get away,' he said. 'All I'm doing here is causing Mrs Rose distress.'

Nightingale moved aside to let him pass. As he did, she said, 'She says you made a joke about Jesus?'

Poe said nothing.

'I told her she must have been mistaken.'

'She wasn't,' Poe said. 'She overheard me talking to Linus.'

'Shit, Poe,' Nightingale said. 'She said it was a sign of deliberate disrespect and indicative of how you conducted yourself this evening. I can't protect you if she wants to take it further.'

'Nor would I ask you to, ma'am.'

Nightingale sighed. 'What a bloody mess.'

Poe glanced at Nathan Rose's corpse then across at Linus. The man from London was furiously typing into his tablet. 'In more ways than one, I suspect,' he replied.

Chapter 70

'Did Mrs Rose complain, Washington?' Doctor Lang asked.

'Eventually,' Poe confirmed.

'I'm not surprised.'

Poe raised an eyebrow.

'No, not because you'd done anything terribly wrong,' she said. 'But the newly widowed often lash out. Usually, it's close relatives who bear the brunt, but in this case Mrs Rose had someone to focus her anger on. I'm not surprised she made a complaint.'

'And she did overhear me make an insensitive joke about Björn Borg.'

'And if her husband hadn't killed himself, you'd have heard nothing more on the subject. But marriage, even a mixed-orientation marriage such as theirs, doesn't only mean sharing your life with someone; it means *changing* your life for someone. You'd be amazed at how entwined two lives can become. It's a big investment and it ended that night.'

Poe thought about his life with Estelle Doyle. An outsider might think it hadn't changed too much, but that would be a superficial view. When Poe dug down, he knew his life was very different now. Not permanently living at Herdwick Croft was an obvious change, but there were other, subtler changes as well. He always called to say he was leaving work. He no longer hung around the incident room if he had no reason to be there. He thought about *her* needs, not just his own. So yes, Poe understood why Mrs Rose had sought someone to blame – if the roles were reversed, he'd probably have done the same.

'Did it ever get to the formal disciplinary stage?' Doctor Lang asked. 'There's nothing in the file to suggest it did.'

Poe shook his head. 'It didn't,' he said.

'Why not?'

'That depends on who you ask.'

'Which sounds . . . complicated.'

'It was,' Poe said. 'The official reason Mrs Rose withdrew her complaint was because of what we discovered about her husband.'

'And the unofficial reason?'

Poe held up his hands for her to see. 'You see these scars? There are what, seven or eight that are visible now? Maybe another twelve or thirteen that have healed and gone away. Loads more that are too small to make out.'

Doctor Lang frowned. 'I don't understand,' she said.

'You will.'

'But not yet?'

Poe shook his head again. 'It'll make more sense later. You don't have the context yet.'

'OK, it's your story,' she said. 'What happened next?'

Poe smiled. 'Tilly tried to do the impossible.'

'And did she?'

Poe offered a grim smile. 'Of course she did.'

'You don't look happy about it, Washington. Surely progressing the case was a good thing?'

'It was.' Poe nodded. 'But also, it wasn't.'

Chapter 71

Poe assumed Bradshaw would want to start immediately. That she would put her computers next to the strongest wi-fi signal she could find and stay there until her cargo pants were enmeshed with the chair cushion. Or at least until she had an answer for him. His role now was to stay out of her way. Do the occasional fruit-tea run.

But Bradshaw didn't want to start immediately. She wanted to go shopping.

'Why's that, Tilly?' Linus had asked.

'Can I tell him, Poe?'

'As long as it's boring.'

'Ha ha,' she said. She faced Linus and continued. 'CSM.12. R2.CL was tattooed on both Cornelius Green *and* Nathan Rose.'

'It was.'

'And handwriting analysis has now confirmed Cornelius Green didn't just tattoo himself, he also tattooed Nathan Rose.'

'It has.'

'Well, I think Poe was right earlier when he said the tattoo would be like the elastic band addiction trick, a reminder of a shared experience.'

'Really? Why?'

'Because CSM.12.R2.CL means something, Linus. It isn't a random mishmash of letters and numbers and full stops; there's human intelligence behind this alphanumeric string. It's code for something. And because the purpose of codes isn't mathematics, it's about messages being safely passed between individuals, even countries, the sooner we understand what these messages might be about, the sooner we have somewhere to start.'

'The courses,' Linus said.

'The courses,' Bradshaw agreed. 'Because we now know the course was a shared experience between Nathan Rose and Cornelius Green, we can use CSM.12.R2.CL as the basis for a metadata search. I can use it as my frame of reference. Something I can test certain words against.'

'What words?'

'I don't know yet. That's why we need to go shopping.'

'What do you need, Tilly?' Poe asked.

'Religious books and pamphlets, Poe. Lots of them, the more obscure, the more extreme the better. Old Testament rather than New Testament. Cornelius Green didn't own a computer so CSM.12.R2.CL will be a reference from a book, not a web article.'

'And if it was online, you'd have found it,' Poe said, not completely covering a yawn. He checked his watch. It was getting late, too late for the bookshops to be open. 'OK, here's what we'll do. We'll get some rest and, in the morning, Tilly can make a start with what she already has while me and Snoopy hit the bookshops. That way we can cover twice as many—'

'I'll observe Tilly, if that's OK?' Linus cut in.

'No, it's not OK, Snoopy.'

'Nevertheless.'

'"Nevertheless"? What the hell does that mean?'

'It means I can call my director and order your director to order you if necessary.'

'I don't give a shit who you call, you little knob, it's not—'

'It's OK, Poe,' Bradshaw said. 'Linus can watch me tomorrow if he wants. What's the worst that could happen?'

Poe really wished she wouldn't say things like that.

Chapter 72

Poe walked into the room Bradshaw had taken at the North Lakes Hotel and Spa without knocking. The bed had been pushed up against the wall, the TV was on the floor, and the dressing table, coffee table and TV cabinet had been joined together to form a workstation. Bradshaw was going back and forth between some open textbooks and her computer screen, her grey eyes sparkling, her chin jutting out in concentration. She was in full Bradshaw mode.

Poe dumped the latest pile of books by her computer. She didn't look up; said 'thanks' and passed him a note with a new book to hunt down: *Seductive Poison* by Deborah Layton.

'Never heard of it,' Poe said.

'It's about the Jim Jones Peoples Temple mass suicide event, Poe,' Bradshaw said. 'Nine hundred and thirteen cult members died by cyanide-poisoned Flavor Aid; three hundred and four of them were children. *Seductive Poison* was written by one of the few survivors.'

'And why do you want to read it?'

'Jim Jones was a charismatic leader; Cornelius Green was a charismatic leader. With the help of a very small inner circle, they both ruled their respective cults like a demagogue. It's possible there was something in Jim Jones's life that Cornelius Green was trying to emulate.'

'And if there was?'

'Then I have another frame of reference when it comes to deciphering these,' Bradshaw said, tapping photographs of the alphanumeric tattoos.

'You coming, Snoopy?'

'I'm fine here, thanks, Poe,' Linus replied.

And he was. Poe had been a spare wheel on these Tillyathons

many times and they all ended the same way – after twenty minutes he got bored and fidgety. Bradshaw barely spoke, she hummed and tutted, she blew hair out of her eyes, and she never stopped, not even for a toilet break. There was only so much sitting around Poe could handle before he got restless-leg syndrome.

But Linus didn't look bored; Bradshaw's process seemed to fascinate him. He was making notes; he was standing over her shoulder and watching her work. He was interested in the uninteresting. He wasn't stupid enough to interrupt and ask questions, but Poe could see he had a load lined up for later.

Poe had arrived home shortly before midnight the day before. Doyle was waiting with a bottle of cold beer and a shepherd's pie in the oven. Poe had called Flynn to let her know a witness had committed suicide in front of them. Flynn had immediately called Doyle – knowing Poe wouldn't – so she was aware he might be upset. Doyle didn't say anything, just wrapped her arms around him and hugged until she felt him relax.

She had led him to the sofa and handed him his beer before opening one for herself. She patted the cushion in the middle and Edgar hopped up. The spaniel turned around five times before slumping down in a heap, his head resting on Poe's leg. Poe idly fondled his ears.

'Tell me what happened,' Doyle said.

'I don't think I'm ready . . .'

'Tell me what happened,' she repeated.

So Poe had. He told her how he had been reading Bethany's journal before his interview with Nathan Rose and how he now knew that was a mistake. He told her that the shared antagonism between him and Virginia Rose was entirely his fault. He told her about the Björn Borg remark Virginia Rose had overheard. Doyle had groaned at that bit. She hadn't chastised him, however; it was obvious there was nothing she could say that he hadn't already said to himself.

They stopped to eat and to refresh their drinks.

'It was definitely a suicide?' Doyle asked during their late supper.

Poe nodded. 'No doubt about it; I saw the change in his eyes when he decided to do it. Something I'd said made him believe being dead was better than being alive, and that's a big call for a Christian to make. I'm told God decides when they die; not them.'

Doyle waited until she had finished chewing. She'd looked thoughtful when she put down her fork and picked up her frosted bottle of beer. She took a deep draught then said, 'Suicide's been called a permanent solution to a temporary problem. There are really only two reasons someone like the man you've described would make such a sudden and drastic decision.'

'Go on.'

Doyle held up a long, slim finger. 'Something terrible happened to him, something he simply couldn't bear revisiting. And he knew it would come out as a result of your investigation.'

'Something like sexual abuse?'

She nodded.

'What's the other thing?'

'He'd *done* something terrible, something he didn't want to face the consequences for.'

Poe considered that carefully, as he did everything Doyle said.

'What if it was both?' he'd said eventually.

Poe tracked down *Seductive Poison* in Fred's, a small bookshop in Ambleside, in the heart of the Lake District. It was only accessible via twisting, dangerous roads. They were fun to navigate in winter, when you had the freedom to pretend it was the final lap at the Nürburgring, but awful in summer, when you were reduced to twenty miles an hour as dawdling tourists stopped in the middle of the road to take photographs of lakes and mountains and sheep.

He parked on the double yellows outside the shop, ignored the outraged honking horns, and dived inside. Within two minutes he had paid for the book – a tatty, dog-eared second-hand paperback – and was back on the road, cursing as he got wedged between a camper van and an elderly tractor.

Chapter 73

When Poe slipped back into the room it was as if nothing had changed. Bradshaw's eyes were still glowing, still darting between her computer and the books he'd brought her. And Linus was still hovering over her shoulder, still interested in what she was doing. He looked up guiltily when he saw Poe watching him.

Poe handed Bradshaw the copy of *Seductive Poison*. She turned to the back and ran her finger down the index.

'No,' she said, throwing it on to a pile of discarded books by her feet. She reached to her side and handed Poe a piece of paper. 'I have a new list, Poe.'

'Do you actually need these, Tilly, or is this just your way of getting rid of me?'

'If I wanted you to leave, Poe, I would tell you.'

'Yes, you would,' he agreed. 'How are you getting on?'

'I've discovered several things that the alphanumeric tattoos are not, so that's good.'

Poe nodded. Bradshaw said there was value in scientific failure, in the cul-de-sacs, in the dead ends. Failure was the necessary and positive characteristic of science; without it there could be no discovery. He wondered if Linus understood this. The spook was a millennial; a generation that had grown used to instant gratification. Watching Bradshaw methodically check and recheck data, only for it to be another dead end, must have been maddening for him.

The new list only had two books on it. Poe tucked it into his wallet.

'Both are at Withnail Books in Penrith, Poe,' Bradshaw said. 'Make sure you get the editions I've specified.'

'Yes, boss.'

'I'm not your—'

'It's just an expression, Tilly,' Poe said. 'I'll grab us something to eat while I'm out. What do you fancy?'

'There's a smoothie bar not far from the bookshop, Poe. I'd like a spinach and kiwi fruit blend, please.'

'That sounds awesome,' Poe said. 'Snoopy, what do you want?'

'Same, please.'

'Get your coat then.'

'I'm staying here.'

'You're coming with me.'

'Why?'

'Because the way you're staring at Tilly is making me uncomfortable,' Poe said. 'It's creepy. Also, I'm not trying to carry three smoothies with two hands.'

Bradshaw looked up. 'You? You're having a smoothie, Poe?'

Poe shrugged. 'I'll have an ice-cream milkshake. I might even go to the Chopping Block and get one of their meat and potato pies. Been ages since I've had one of them.'

'Poe, you have a Chopping Block meat and potato pie *every single time* we're in Penrith. And every single time you say it's ages since you've had one.' She shook her head in disgust. 'Honestly, your epitaph is going to read "Washington Poe: Died of a Saturated Fat Overdose. What An Idiot". Would a salad kill . . .'

She trailed off and frowned. Her face went momentarily blank.

'What is it, Tilly?'

'What is what, Poe?' she said, distracted.

'You stopped talking.'

'I did?'

'You did.'

'I'm probably hungrier than I thought,' she said. She turned back to her makeshift desk and opened a new window on her laptop and began typing. 'I'll need those books now please, Poe. And Linus, please go with him and make sure he only buys *one* pie. Thank you.'

Chapter 74

One of the problems with juice and smoothie bars was that however much they dressed it up, they really only served fruit and vegetables. It didn't matter that the ingredients had been blended, put in a cup and served with a soggy cardboard straw, it was still a gunky mess of unpalatable leafy greens and unbearably sour or sickeningly sweet fruits. Ingredients supermarkets wouldn't put on the same aisles were forced together then given misleading names such as Liquid Sunshine and Endless Summer.

But the main problem was that for a supposedly fast and conven-ient food, smoothie and juice bars were slow and *in*convenient. Poe reckoned he and Linus had been waiting for fifteen minutes. And, to make matters worse, the place Bradshaw had sent them no longer did milkshakes. The teenager behind the counter had offered Poe frozen yoghurt instead, to which Poe had replied, 'I'd rather piss in my shoes.'

While they waited Linus said, 'You seem to have a lot of these little "life battles", Poe.'

'What battles?'

'Well, this one for a start. All you had to do was say no thanks to the frozen yoghurt. Instead, it became a whole big thing. I'd be surprised if they don't spit in our smoothies.'

'And I'd be surprised if you noticed,' Poe said.

Linus smiled. 'She's like a machine, isn't she?' he said.

'Who, Tilly?'

'Yes.'

'Only in that she won't get bored,' Poe replied. 'By every other metric Tilly's far superior. She'll think her way around problems, spot patterns and make connections that even the most advanced computer never could.'

'But you don't think she'll crack this one, do you?' Linus said. He looked disappointed.

'The problem is, it'll be something low-tech,' Poe replied. 'Cornelius Green tattooed himself and he tattooed Nathan Rose and that means it's likely the alphanumeric string is something he came up with. He didn't own a computer and he lived a simple life. That means if it *is* his code, he came up with it using a pencil and a piece of paper. And as Tilly says, human brains aren't capable of generating random numbers. If he *had* tried to come up with a secret squirrel code, she'd have figured it out within minutes.'

'Which is why she's been sending you all over Cumbria tracking down random books.'

'Exactly. Because if it *isn't* random, those alphanumeric strings meant something to Cornelius. Therefore, the more information she has – or frames of reference, or metadata, or whatever the hell else she calls it – the more likely it is that Cornelius's beliefs will align with her notes.'

'So you think she *will* crack his code?'

'I think she got rid of us both earlier because she had a theory she wanted to test.'

'What? Why didn't she tell us?'

'Because if she had, she'd have got bogged down explaining every little thing. We'd have asked endless questions, we'd have made suggestions, all of which she would have already considered, and all of which would slow her down.'

Linus checked his watch. He craned his neck to check the status of their smoothie order. 'I assume we're heading straight back?'

'Why would we? I haven't got my pie yet.'

'But if Tilly—'

'She'll call if she has something.'

The teenager plonked Poe's order down on the counter. The smoothies were in tall, clear plastic cups and were a sort of olive-green colour. Flea-sized black seeds, the kind you were still finding in your teeth three months later, were suspended in the thick gloopy mixture. Poe took a ten-pound note from his wallet and placed it on the counter. 'Sorry about earlier,' he said. 'Keep the change.'

'That will be sixteen pounds, sir,' the young woman said.

'Jesus,' Poe muttered. He put the tenner back in his wallet and put a twenty down. 'OK, keep the change now then.'

'Ooh, now I can afford that new iPhone.'

Linus sniggered. 'Serves you right,' he said to Poe on the way out.

Chapter 75

The reference books were closed when they got back to Bradshaw's hotel room. She was leaning into her laptop, muttering, while making notes on the hotel stationery pad.

'I need you to get me something, Poe,' she said as soon as he'd grabbed a coaster and carefully placed her smoothie on the desk.

'Another book?'

'Not this time. I need you to go to the All Saints Church on the outskirts of Kendal and get me their records.'

'The birth, marriages and deaths register? What the hell do you want that for?'

'No. That's just a list of events they have a statutory obligation to record. I need the church records. That's where everything else that happens is written down. Minutes of meetings, architect's plans, maps, drawings, anything at all that affects the church that isn't required to go in the BMD register.'

'And they're kept in the church?'

'Until they're deposited in the archive office, yes. They have to; they're working documents.'

'OK,' Poe said. 'But what's this about? The Children of Job aren't affiliated to any church. They don't even have charitable status.'

She turned her back and said, 'And I don't need anything before 1985 or after 2007.'

Poe had been dismissed again.

'How the hell are you going to get something like that?' Linus asked the moment they were outside Bradshaw's room. 'And that's twenty-odd years' worth of records Tilly has asked for. There'll be lever-arch file after lever-arch file of the stuff. Imagine wading through years and years of the stuff they talked about on *The Vicar of Dibley*.'

'Where's his parish?'

'You really don't have a TV, do you?'

By the time he had finished speaking, Poe already had his phone to his ear. The Bishop of Carlisle answered on the first ring.

'Washington?'

'I need something, sir.'

Poe told him what it was.

'I'll make a call,' the bishop said. 'You make your way to the church and I'll have someone meet you there. What's this about, Washington? What's in those records?'

'Tilly wants them, sir. That's all I know.'

'I'll get back to you within twenty minutes.'

'The Bishop of Carlisle is being extraordinarily helpful,' Linus said when Poe finished his call. 'What was it he wanted to see you and Tilly about again?'

'Nice try, Snoopy.'

'Fine, don't tell me.'

'Oh, shut up,' Poe said.

Chapter 76

Poe was fifteen minutes away from All Saints Church when the bishop called. He pressed the accept button on his steering wheel but before the bishop could speak, Poe said, 'You're on speakerphone, sir, and I'm not on my own.'

'I don't have any state secrets to share, Washington,' the bishop replied. 'At least not today.'

'Are we good?'

'We are. The warden of All Saints will meet you at the church in ninety minutes.'

'Why so long?'

'It's going to take a bit of time to put everything together, I'm afraid. There are computer records to print, old ledgers to dust off. Believe me, ninety minutes is quick for what Tilly has asked for. I hope you have a strong-backed young man with you.'

'Just my intern,' Poe said.

Linus rolled his eyes.

'Ah, hence the warning about the speakerphone. Anyway, I have things to be getting on with, Washington – let me know if I can be of further assistance.'

'It seems we have an hour to kill,' Linus said, after Poe had ended the call.

'We do,' Poe agreed. He glanced at the dashboard clock. 'Eve Bowman doesn't live that far away. If we hurry we can drop in on her and still keep our meeting with the church warden.'

'Why do you want to see her again?'

'I want to know why she didn't tell me about her sister's journal.'

Chapter 77

Eve Bowman was making summer jam when Poe knocked on the door. Strawberry, apricot and plum by the smell. She was wearing jeans, a 1 of 100 Rebus T-shirt and a fruit-smeared apron. Her hands looked sticky, as if she'd been raiding Hundred Acre Wood's honey tree.

'Come in,' she said. 'And please do forgive the mess.'

'Nothing to forgive,' Poe said. 'And I'm sorry for the unannounced visit; we were in the area with a bit of time to kill.'

'And you could smell the warm jam?'

Poe laughed. 'It does look good.'

Eve washed her hands then dipped a foot-long wooden spoon into a pot of bubbling yellow liquid. 'Taste this,' she said, holding out the spoon. 'It's vanilla peach with whisky. Careful, it's hot.'

When they were seated around the kitchen table, Eve said, 'Although my jam is award-winning, Sergeant Poe, I doubt it's why you're here.'

'We're now in possession of your sister's journal, Eve,' Poe said. 'I wanted to talk to you about it.'

'Her journal? How on earth did you get that? I assumed she'd taken it with her.'

'It seems she kept it at her friend's house. That friend recently handed it in to the police.'

'You don't mean Alice, do you? Alice Symonds?'

Poe nodded. Although it was technically a breach of confidentiality, Bethany had only had one friend and Eve didn't need the brains of Bradshaw to work out where the journal had been stashed. He would have liked to mention Nathan Rose as well. See if Eve knew him, see if she had any insight into his suicide, but that would have been a breach too far. Nightingale would have had him strung up.

'Gosh, I haven't seen Alice for years. I haven't even *thought* about her for years, truth be told.'

'How well did you know her?'

Eve shrugged. 'As well as any sister knows her younger sister's friends, I suppose. Mum and Dad didn't allow us to have visitors, so we only ever really interacted with other children when we were at school or church. But I knew her well enough to know she was a nice girl. Bethany used to go round to hers after school. She would pretend she was doing extra lessons or had to help the teacher or something. Mum and Dad rarely took an interest in what she was doing so they never thought to check, and Aaron and I weren't going to tell them she was lying.'

Poe nodded. That fitted with what was in the journal.

'Have you read it?' Poe said. 'She makes some extraordinary claims.'

'I saw it every now and then,' Eve admitted. 'Bethany kept it well hidden most of the time, but I'd occasionally stumble across it; usually when I was trying to find her cigarettes.'

'She smoked?'

'Of course, she was a rebel. She smoked, she drank, she fooled around with boys. I never told her this, but I thought she was about the coolest person in the world. The way she stood up to Mum and Dad. I know I couldn't have done it. So, if she smoked, I wanted to smoke.'

'And the journal entries?'

'Some were exaggerated, but not much.'

'It was an accurate account of her childhood?' Poe said. 'You didn't mention she was being abused.'

'I didn't realise it *was* abuse,' Eve said. 'Not back then. It wasn't until I was older that I began to question whether Bethany caused my parents to treat her the way they did, or if it was the other way round; that she behaved that way as a result of what they did to her.'

'And what did you decide?'

'That Bethany had a spark of life that Mum and Dad couldn't stamp out. There was just something about her that they didn't like. They said she was a bad biscuit; pretty much their worst name for someone.'

'I'm familiar with the phrase,' Poe said. 'It's peppered through-out her journal entries. They thought she was a bad biscuit and Bethany thought *they* were bad biscuits.'

Eve nodded. 'I don't know what their problem was, Sergeant Poe, but when I view things through my older, and hopefully wiser, eyes, I see that although none of us had happy childhoods, Bethany's was dreadful.'

'Yet you didn't mention this when I spoke to you earlier in the week?'

'It's . . . hard to talk about your parents like that, Sergeant Poe. Were they monsters? No, I don't think they were. Did they *behave* monstrously? Yes, occasionally, they absolutely did.'

'I sense an unsaid "but",' Poe said.

Eve shrugged. 'But she killed Aaron, Sergeant Poe. I don't care what grievances she had with Mum and Dad, Aaron was a sweet, gentle boy. He worshipped the ground Bethany stood on and he didn't deserve to die. He didn't deserve any—'

A banging noise made her stop. It came from Eve's basement and sounded like something hard and hollow had fallen on to some-thing harder and hollower.

'That's Thomas,' Eve explained. 'We have a short break coming up and he's sorting through our camping equipment.'

'He's not working today?'

'He *never* works on jam day. He claims it's in case I burn myself, but really it's an excuse to taste everything while it's warm.' She frowned. 'I'd better go and make sure he's OK.'

She disappeared, returning less than a minute later.

'He's fine,' she said. 'He'll be up in a bit. Says he wants to meet you. I suspect he also wants to try the vanilla peach and whisky. I'll get us all a coffee.'

'Not for us, Eve,' Poe said. 'We'll say hello to your husband but we need to get away. We have a meeting nearby and we don't want to keep anyone waiting.'

'Of course.'

Eve's husband was wearing a cardigan with mismatched buttons and a pair of faded green corduroys. Reading glasses hung from a chain around his neck. He had a sharp nose and full lips. His hair was combed and parted to the side. He was around the same age as his wife.

'I'm Thomas Gruffud,' he said, reaching across the kitchen table to shake their hands.

'Everything OK down there?' Poe said, pointing to the basement entrance. 'We heard a bang.'

'Ah, yes. I'm afraid that was just me dropping the tent pegs. Made quite the din.'

'Eve tells me you're a graphic designer in Preston?'

'For a few years now.'

'Anything I might have seen?'

'Not unless you're familiar with French banking law, Sergeant Poe. I lead the team that designs websites, logos and marketing materials for the Bank of France. Last year I redesigned the font they use on their stationery. I'm afraid that must seem rather dull compared to what you do.'

'Not at all,' Poe lied.

Eve walked up behind her husband and threw her arms around his neck. She kissed the side of his head and said, 'Thomas is being predictably modest, Sergeant Poe. He's been heading up the company's most important accounts for years now. Without him there *is* no company.'

Thomas reddened but didn't contradict his wife.

'Have you always enjoyed camping?' Poe asked.

'No, not always,' he replied. 'But as I get older, I find that a digital detox does wonders for my work. It reboots my mind. Reminds me why I got into graphic design in the first place.'

'You and Eve have talked about my previous visit?'

He nodded. 'We have. You believe her sister might be up to her old tricks.'

'It's one of a number of lines of enquiry. I don't suppose I can convince you both to leave the county for a while?'

'Well, we *are* heading into the Lakes for a small break, but that's been planned for a couple of months,' Thomas said. 'My wife doesn't believe she's in any danger from Bethany, Sergeant Poe.'

'And what do you believe?'

'I believe my wife.' He glanced over Poe's shoulder at the pots bubbling on the large range. 'Anyway,' he added, standing up, 'we can't leave now; it's summer jam week.'

Chapter 78

All Saints Church was a Grade I Listed building on the outskirts of Kendal. It had a tower, a long nave and a large, well-maintained graveyard. Poe had passed it many times but never had any reason to visit. A hard-boiled woman waited for them by the wooden lychgate.

'She looks like she's just eaten a warm oyster,' Poe said, parking at the side of the road.

'Are you Sergeant Poe?' she snapped before he'd had a chance to undo his seatbelt.

Poe got out of the car. 'I am.' He showed her his ID.

'What's this about then? Why do you want to look at my records?'

'And you are?'

'I'm Alana Williams, the senior churchwarden. And you can tell the bishop we have nothing to fear from an audit.'

'The National Crime Agency doesn't do church audits, Mrs Williams,' Poe said. 'And even if we did, *I* wouldn't.'

'What do you want then?'

'I honestly have no idea,' Poe admitted. 'I've just been told to grab your records between 1985 and 2007. This is a murder investigation.'

'A murder? Who's been murdered?'

Poe didn't answer. Instead, he said, 'Do you have everything ready?'

Alana nodded. 'Follow me,' she said.

She led them to the back of the church. One of the transepts, the parts of the church that form the arms of a cross-shaped floor plan, had been turned into office space for the clergy. There were two desks. Both were piled high with files, printouts and ledgers.

Alana opened a drawer and handed Poe half a dozen CD-ROMs.

'I've put all our digital records on these,' she explained. 'I wasn't sure what you wanted so you've got everything.'

'That's OK,' Poe said. 'The person who requested this loves data, the more the better.'

'When can I have this back?'

'I haven't taken it yet.'

Alana folded her arms.

'As soon as possible,' Poe relented.

'Tomorrow?'

'Maybe next week.'

That seemed to be too long for Alana. Poe was wondering if he would need the bishop to intervene when a large book caught his eye. It was open and on a pedestal. It was A3 in size and thicker than his foot. It wasn't a Bible, as Poe could see handwritten entries.

'What's this?' Poe said.

'That's the log,' she replied.

'And what's "the log"?'

'Every time something happens in the church, it goes in here.'

'What things?'

'Weddings, funerals, repairs, extraordinary services. That type of thing.'

'How far does it go back?'

'A long time,' Alana said. 'We'll start a new one when this is full, but as it only gets line entries, they last for years. I've included the previous log in the records you can take with you.'

'How far back does this one go?' Poe asked.

'I think it's coming up to twenty years now.'

'We'll take this as well then.'

'You can't; it's a working docu—'

'Thanks,' Poe said, picking it up and handing it to Linus. 'Take this to the car, Snoopy.'

Linus grabbed the logbook and a couple of lever-arch files.

'I need that!' Alana said.

'So do I,' Poe said. He grabbed a pile of records and followed Linus out of the church office and down the nave.

'I really don't know how you get away with being so rude to people, Poe,' Linus said, shaking his head.

'The secret is not to care,' Poe replied.

Chapter 79

All the books and papers and documents Bradshaw had been using had been pushed into one untidy corner. She waved Poe and Linus in.

'Did you get it?' she said without preamble.

'I don't know what "it" is,' Poe said, 'but we have the All Saints Church records for the time period you wanted.'

'You've been ages, Poe.'

'There's a lot of stuff and it had to be collated. The churchwarden didn't want to hand over everything, but my charm won through in the end.'

'What did Poe do, Linus?'

'He stole it.'

Bradshaw nodded. 'Good,' she said.

'We popped in to see Eve Bowman while we were waiting,' Poe said. 'She was making jam.'

'Oh, why did you do that?' Bradshaw said. She frowned and added, 'And how much jam did you eat?'

'I wanted to ask her about Bethany's journal.'

'And?'

'She sort of admitted knowing Bethany was being abused, but claims she didn't realise at the time. Oh, and we met her husband, Thomas. Bit of a geek but he seemed nice enough. They're off camping and he was sorting through their equipment.'

Bradshaw leaned into her laptop. 'It's teatime now, so if you want to go and get something to eat, I think I may have something in an hour.'

'OK,' Poe said. He pointed at the stolen logbook. 'But if you can start there, I can maybe return it tomorrow. The rest we can have as long as we want.'

'I'll do that, Poe,' Bradshaw said.

Poe ordered the slow-braised lamb and a pint of Citadel, an easy-drinking beer from the Carlisle Brewing Company. He scanned the menu for something Bradshaw might find palatable, eventually settling on the pumpkin, sage and honey tortellini.

'Is honey vegan?' Poe asked Linus.

'Why would I know?'

'You're an intern; go and intern me the answer.'

Linus rolled his eyes. 'That little "VE" beside it doesn't stand for Victory in Europe, Poe. It's a vegan dish so it must have vegan-friendly ingredients.'

'I'll take the pasta to go,' Poe told the waiter. 'Everything else we'll eat here.'

'The restaurant is dine-in only, sir. If you want takeaway food, you'll need to order from the bar menu.'

'Does the bar food come in takeaway boxes or tubs?'

'Cardboard boxes, sir.'

'OK then,' Poe said. 'Bring our order to the table along with one empty takeaway box.'

The waiter obviously didn't get paid enough for an argument like this. 'Very good, sir,' he said. 'I'll be along shortly with your drinks.'

Linus shook his head after the waiter had left. 'So much hostility,' he said.

'Why should Tilly eat from a different menu because she's still working?'

'Fair enough.' He looked at Poe shrewdly. 'You're very protective of her, aren't you?'

'She's my friend.'

'It goes deeper than that.'

'What can I tell you, Snoopy? She dragged me out of a burning building, she stopped me being charged with murder, and because of the work she does – is doing *now*, in fact – countless potential victims have been spared. So yes, if I feel protective, it's because I owe her.'

'And you think she still needs you?'

234

'Needs me?' Poe said. 'I don't think she's *ever* needed me, Snoopy. Even when we first met, she was stubbornly independent. What you won't know is that, because Tilly didn't have friends growing up, she'll do anything for the ones she has now. Her friendship is absolute. There is not a thing she wouldn't do for me or Estelle or the boss, and there is not a thing we wouldn't do for her. And because I'm the one who tends to walk into things with one eye closed, she's got used to watching my back.'

'Meaning?'

'Meaning that you have it back to front, Snoopy. She doesn't need my protection; I need hers.'

Poe's phone rang. He glanced at the screen and said, 'Speak of the vegan.'

'What's up? I've ordered you a pumpkin pasta thing. Sounds disgusting, which means you'll love it.'

She told him.

The waiter came back with their drinks.

'You'd better make that three takeaway boxes,' Poe said.

'What's happened?' Linus said.

'Tilly knows what those tattoos mean,' he replied.

Chapter 80

'I am now convinced each of Cornelius Green's tattoos match one of the courses he ran,' Bradshaw said. 'We suspected as much, obviously, but until you brought that information back from All Saints Church there was still one thing that didn't make sense. And in breaking codes like this, if one thing doesn't work, none of it works.'

Poe was perched on the edge of the bed. Linus was standing next to the desk. He was peering over Bradshaw's shoulder.

'What do you mean, they match?' Poe said.

'There were six self-penned alphanumerical tattoos on the thighs and torso of Cornelius Green.'

'There were.'

'And we think there were six courses that hadn't been recorded anywhere.'

Poe nodded. 'We do.'

'This is where things get slightly more complex,' Bradshaw continued. 'When we discovered that Nathan Rose, one of the course attendees, had CSM.12.R2.CL tattooed on his foot, we suspected there was a link between the courses and Cornelius Green's tattoos.'

'That was the logical leap.'

'And it was the correct one. However, we were mistaken when we thought the tattoos were some sort of obscure course code or a type of one-time-pad.'

'What are they then?'

'They're locations, Poe,' Bradshaw said.

'Locations? Like a grid reference?' Poe's brow furrowed. He had been taught to read maps in the army and he still preferred using Ordnance Survey to GPS. Maps could be trusted; GPS relied on batteries – which could run out – and hackable satellites. Not that he'd ever tell Bradshaw that, of course. If Cornelius Green's tattoos were grid references, he'd been using a system with which Poe was unfamiliar. Admittedly, grid references varied, but they all tended to work on intersecting lines, and they all had an even number of digits – half denoted the vertical axis and half denoted the horizontal. Ordnance Survey divided the UK into 100-kilometre squares and assigned a two-letter code to each one. Within each square, the standard numerical grid reference was used.

'They're sort of like grid references, Poe,' Bradshaw said. 'But only in the sense that each tattoo denotes something specific on the ground.'

'Maybe it was where each course took place?'

'No, that's not it.'

'What then?'

'They're graves, Poe.'

Chapter 81

'Graves?' Poe said. 'Does this mean Cornelius Green isn't our only victim? There might be six more bodies out there?'

'I don't know what's out there, Poe,' Bradshaw replied. 'I *do* know that each one of those tattoos represents the location of an officially registered grave.'

'But we could have a serial killer?'

Bradshaw shook her head. 'Not unless he's been active since the Second World War.'

'I think you'd better explain, Tilly.'

She pulled a sheet of paper from the portable printer she carried everywhere.

'This is the tattoo found on both Cornelius Green and Nathan Rose,' she said.

She placed the sheet on the desk.

CSM.12.R2.CL

She circled 'CSM' with a red pen.

'CSM stands for Christ and Saint Mary,' she said. 'It's a church near Ulverston.'

'There's more than one Christ and Saint Mary in Cumbria, Tilly,' Poe said. 'How do you know it's that one?'

'I'll get to that, Poe.' She circled '12' and 'R2'. 'Their graveyard is set up in rows. Therefore, the middle section of the tattoo refers to grave number twelve on row two.'

Poe nodded. 'And CL?'

'According to the cemetery map CL stands for "Circle Lawn". It's the name of that part of the graveyard. I assume it's circular and grassy.'

'But how do you know you have the right church?'

'Apart from the fact there is only one Christ and Saint Mary with a Circle Lawn in the north of England, the dates line up.'

'What dates?'

'The grave belongs to a woman called Hazel Rampling. She was sixty-three years old when she died.'

'She was murdered?'

'No, Poe. She died in a car crash in 2004.'

Poe made the link. 'Nathan Rose attended his course at the Children of Job in 2004. How close do the dates match?'

'Hazel Rampling was buried on the fourth of June, Poe. Nathan attended his course on the second of June.'

'I'm not following this at all,' Linus said. 'Nathan Rose attends a course at the start of June and two days later Hazel Rampling is buried in a Cumbrian graveyard at the other end of the county. For some reason both Cornelius Green and Nathan Rose feel the need to tattoo themselves with the location of Hazel's grave. Is that about it?'

'It is, Linus.'

'What links a car-crash victim to a man who attended a conversion therapy course? A man who later kills himself when he's asked about it?'

'I have no idea,' Bradshaw admitted.

'There was definitely nothing suspicious about Hazel Rampling's death?' Poe asked.

'Nothing I could find, Poe. But you're missing the wider point, I think.'

'Which is?'

'Hazel Rampling wasn't an isolated incident.'

'She wasn't?'

'No, Poe.'

'I think you'd better talk me through the others, Tilly,' Poe said. 'There has to be an explanation for this. Let's see if we can figure it out.'

Bradshaw began talking them through the remaining five tattoos.

'CC.58.R4.HI is Christ Church in Barrow. Grave fifty-eight, row four in the Holy Innocent plot, belongs to Alex Stanton. He was twelve years old when he died of leukaemia. He was buried in 2001, a week after one of Cornelius Green's undisclosed courses.'

Bradshaw raced through the rest. SJE.77.PC was Saint John the Evangelist in Maryport. The church graveyard didn't have rows, simply numbers, and a thirty-six-year-old called Aleksy Nowak was buried in PC, the Polish community plot.

SB.47.R9.SG was grave forty-seven, row nine in Saint Bega in Appleby. SG was the Saint George plot.

'AS.104X.GO was the tricky one, Poe,' Bradshaw explained. 'There are four All Saints churches in the north of England and the south of Scotland, but only one with a grave that matched Cornelius Green's AS.104X.GO tattoo.'

'The church we've just been to?'

'Yes, Poe.'

'Why did we need to go to that one and not any of the others?'

Bradshaw pointed at AS.104X.GO and said, 'As you've no doubt worked out, AS stands for the All Saints. One hundred and four is the grave number and X means there is an extra grave there, almost certainly to do with lack of space. Instead of renumbering all the graves, they simply add an X to denote the extra one. The grave belongs to a man called Erich Brandt.'

'Fewer and fewer people can get buried these days,' Poe said. 'The graveyards are all full. What does the GO stand for, Tilly?'

'It stands for German Officer, Poe.'

She waited for the significance of what she'd said to register.

'German Officer?' Poe said. 'Hence the Second World War reference.'

'I don't get it,' Linus said. 'Why would a German officer be buried in a graveyard in Kendal?'

'Shap Wells, the hotel you and Tilly stayed at, used to be prisoner-of-war camp number fifteen, Snoopy. It was mainly used for German officers. Presumably when they died, they were buried in local graveyards.'

'That's right, Poe,' Bradshaw confirmed.

'But this doesn't fit with the pattern, does it?' Poe said. 'You said all the graves tattooed on Cornelius Green were of people buried between 2001 and 2007. I failed O-level history, but even I know the Second World War ended in 1945.'

'Which was why I needed the church records, Poe. Everything fit, but not the AS.104X.GO tattoo. Erich Brandt was buried in 1943 after a brief bout of pneumonia.'

Poe shrugged. 'I wouldn't worry about it, Tilly. The one thing I've learned on this case is that Cornelius Green was a nutter. Trying to second guess the meaning behind his tattoos is the quickest way to a padded cell.'

'But I *do* worry about it, Poe. Cornelius didn't invent the grave location system; it was well-established and in use long before he was born. Each grave's location is correctly identified by his tattoos, and five of them were of people who were interred within days of one of those six secret courses. I needed to know why one grave was different. If I couldn't answer that, none of it made sense. Like I said, when it comes to deciphering codes it all works or none of it works.'

Poe looked at the masses of church records he and Linus had brought back from All Saints. They had only been at the restaurant fifteen minutes; no way had Bradshaw had the time to go through it all. But she'd called them back anyway.

'You know why Cornelius had the location of the German officer's grave tattooed on his torso, don't you?'

'I do, Poe. In 2007 some of the German graves were vandalised. The headstones were knocked over and smashed and chemical waste was poured on the ground. The church moved them all.'

'And when was Erich Brandt's grave moved, Tilly?' Poe asked, already knowing the answer.

'Four days after Aaron Bowman's course ended, Poe.'

'OK, I think I need to call Superintendent Nightingale now. She needs to know that Cornelius Green had the location of six random graves tattooed on his body.' He selected her number. 'This was an odd dot to connect, Tilly,' he said while he waited for Nightingale to answer her phone.

'It was your diet, Poe,' Bradshaw said. 'When I said your epitaph would read "Washington Poe: Died of a Saturated Fat Overdose. What an Idiot", it reminded me that grave location systems use letters and numbers. I thought it was worth checking out.'

'Poe?' Nightingale said. 'Is this urgent? I'm about to chair a meeting.'

Poe told her what Bradshaw had discovered. She asked a few questions but there really wasn't much to misunderstand: Cornelius Green's tattoos were the locations of graves.

'There's definitely no link between the people buried?' Nightingale asked.

'One of them was a German prisoner of war. He died in 1943.'

'But there's a connection to the courses Cornelius ran?'

'Tilly thinks there is.'

'Good enough for me,' Nightingale said. 'I'll work on an exhumation order. We'll get one out of the ground and see what we find. That work for you, Poe?'

But Poe didn't answer. He had just noticed Bradshaw's handwritten notes next to the last grave on the list. The one they hadn't discussed yet. He swallowed hard and bit down the urge to vomit.

'What is it, Poe?' Nightingale said.

'I know what we're going to find, ma'am.'

Bradshaw and Linus stared at him in astonishment.

'You do?' Nightingale said. 'How?'

'A badger told me,' he said.

Chapter 82

'I don't understand,' Doctor Lang said.

'It's simple,' Poe said. 'For reasons we didn't yet know, Cornelius Green had tattooed the locations of graves on himself. One of those tattoos was SM.15.NP. Tilly had narrowed it down to grave fifteen, north plot, St Michael's Church in Shap. That was the grave I was called to months before I'd even heard of Cornelius Green. The one the badgers dug up.'

'No, not that. I mean I don't understand why this is the straw that broke the camel's back. Nightmares are an entirely rational psychological response to traumatic experiences, but I've read your file, Washington, so I know you've seen worse than a grave with an extra body in it. I don't know, maybe there's only so much death one man can see before he starts to see it everywhere, but, from a clinical perspective, that being the root cause of your nightmares surprises me.'

Poe offered a wry smile. 'You're wondering why I still see crows when I sleep?'

'To be frank, yes,' she said. 'And don't think I'm suggesting weakness on your part. Although the brain is robust, it's also surprisingly fragile. The Cornelius Green case being linked to the earlier one must have been quite a shock.'

'Two things, Doctor Lang,' Poe said. He held up a finger. 'The badger exhumation case was never mine; I was just the unlucky sap with a warrant card who happened to be having a pint nearby. Cumbria picked up the investigation and, mistakenly as it turned out, classed it as a fatal quarry accident among the black labour market.'

'And the second thing?'

'You're looking for the catalyst to my nightmares?'

'I am.'

'This wasn't it.'

She frowned. 'You said at the start of this session you were having nightmares about crows.'

'I did.'

'And there were crows pecking at the body the badgers unearthed.'

'There were.'

'And we've agreed that, in your mind, you associate crows with the events surrounding the murder of Cornelius Green.'

'I do.'

'What am I missing? Why are you so convinced this isn't the cause of your nightmares?'

'Do you think what I've told you is disturbing, Doctor Lang?'

She nodded. 'I would say so. Your victim was stoned to death. A witness hanged himself in front of you. Everything is linked to a massacred family and a body dug up by badgers. In all my time as a trauma therapist, I've never had a patient disclose anything so disturbing.'

'Well, believe me when I say that compared to what came next, what I've told you so far is about as disturbing as those Japanese cartoons Tilly watches.'

'What happened?'

'I visited Israel Cobb again.'

Chapter 83

Nightingale arrived, panting, within minutes. She had blown off the meeting she was due to chair and by the looks of it had run most of the way. She didn't even try to catch her breath. Just stormed into the hotel room and growled, 'What the hell's going on, Poe? Every time I let you loose, another fucking body turns up.'

'Honestly, ma'am, I have no idea,' he replied. 'The whole thing's bonkers, absolutely bonkers. I don't think I've ever been involved in something with so many moving parts.'

Nightingale slumped on the bed beside him. She looked exhausted. Poe was in this up to his ears, was barely sleeping himself, and he didn't have a tenth of the responsibilities she did. He wouldn't be the SIO on a complex murder investigation for a giant black pudding. Everyone second-guessed your decisions, everyone knew better than you, and you were the only one without an umbrella when the brown rain started.

'This is a nightmare,' she said. 'I'm getting grief for Nathan Rose's suicide. We'll have to reopen the accidental death for the body the badgers dug up, which, at best, will make us look incompetent. And the chief constable's now getting calls from the religious community.'

'Why?'

'They're claiming we aren't taking Cornelius Green's murder seriously.'

'They're ignoring the Children of Job's agenda to score cheap political points?' Poe said. He wondered what the bishop thought of that.

'They are. And rather than placating them with case progression, the chief's now going to have to tell them we'll be exhuming graves up and down the county.'

Anything Poe could say would be trite, and Nightingale was a rugged enough cop to get by without platitudes, so he kept his mouth shut. She was expressing her frustrations now so she wouldn't later when she was briefing the troops. Other than Flynn, Nightingale was the best senior officer he'd worked with and if she wanted to blow off steam in a safe environment that was fine with him.

'Honestly, Poe,' she continued, 'if someone had sat me down years ago and told me to list the worst things I'd ever have to do in this job, informing an almost certainly still grieving family that I have to dig up their twelve-year-old son to see if some bastard's hidden a body under his coffin, would be number one.'

'I don't actually know what would be worse,' Poe said. 'Finding an extra body or digging up his grave for nothing.'

'Finding a body,' Nightingale said immediately. 'Definitely finding an extra body. Think about it – you've been putting flowers on your son's grave every other Sunday and suddenly you find out he's been sharing his eternal resting place with a stranger. How's that going to make you feel?'

'Not great,' Poe admitted.

'You'd better tell me everything. I'm going to have to brief the chief constable and I'll need to answer her questions. And believe me, she *will* have questions.'

'Tilly can take you through it, ma'am. She made the connection.'

Nightingale stood and stretched. She crossed the room and took a seat beside Bradshaw. 'I hate to ask this, Poe, but could you get me a coffee? I'm dead on my feet here.'

'Of course,' Poe replied. 'Snoopy, go and get the superintendent a black coffee.'

'But she said you . . .'

Poe stopped him with a look. 'Why have an intern and bark yourself?' he said after Linus had grumbled his way out of the room.

While Bradshaw took Nightingale from A to B, 'A' being Cornelius Green's post-mortem and 'B' being a corpse dug up by badgers, Poe considered what the latest bombshell meant. Up until Bradshaw's discovery, they had assumed Cornelius Green was the victim and Bethany Bowman was the most likely perpetrator. But, if

Bradshaw was right, and Poe knew she was, these new bodies had been dumped between 2001 and 2007. Bethany Bowman was eight in 2001. Poe didn't care how psychotic she was, she wasn't killing people when she was little more than a toddler. He had the feeling they'd got things the wrong way around. That despite being dead, Cornelius Green should be their primary suspect. He strongly suspected Bethany Bowman was a killer, but was she a victim as well?

A noise returned Poe to the present. Linus was back. He used his hip to open the door and edged into the hotel room like a crab. He was carrying a tray full of drinks. He handed Nightingale her coffee and Bradshaw a cup of something funky.

'I've got you a coffee too, Poe,' he said, passing him a mug. 'You know, because that's what us interns do. We get coffees and we bark.'

'You heard that?'

'I did.'

Poe considered this. Realised he didn't care. 'Eavesdroppers never hear good of themselves, Snoopy,' he said after a couple of beats. He inhaled the steam, enjoyed the rich smell. Bradshaw's room had a kettle and some of those little sachets of crumbly, freeze-dried stuff, but at the front end of a long night you needed the real deal.

'This is so messed up,' Nightingale said.

'Agreed,' Poe said.

'Theories?'

'Some people had corpses that needed to disappear – and given his tattoos, Cornelius Green has to be at the centre of it – and the same people knew when and where these poor sods were due to be planted. Tilly says the graves for morning interments are dug the night before, so I suspect it was simply a case of going to the graveyard in the early hours and digging down a bit further. Throw in the corpse and cover it with six inches of loose earth. Stamp it down so it looks like it did before they arrived. Who's going to notice? And as soon as the grave's rightful inhabitant is in the ground, you need a coroner's order to get it back up.'

'You've given this some thought.'

'It was either that or talk to Snoopy.'

'But who are they?' Nightingale said.

'Cult members who crossed Cornelius, maybe? He was charismatic but he also had a cruel side. Lots of people admired him, but no one liked him.'

'Tilly says his grave tattoos represent roughly a burial a year over a six-to-seven-year period. We'd have noticed a pattern of missing people like that.'

Poe agreed. There were computer programs these days and police intelligence systems were all linked. 'And even if you had somehow missed it, someone would have talked by now. No way a group that size keeps a secret like this. You'd have known if Cornelius was murdering members of his own cult.'

'And you said Alice Symonds has taken it upon herself to work undercover there. Even if they *had* managed to stop any external leaks, there's no way it could have been kept a secret internally. She'd have heard something.'

'People gossip,' Poe said, nodding. 'We're social animals and we like to share stuff.'

'You're not a social animal, Poe,' Bradshaw said. 'The other day you said you wanted to move to that remote Scottish island you'd read about. The one with all the seals.'

Nightingale laughed, the first time she had for days, Poe suspected.

'OK,' he said. 'Maybe they're cult members who died of natural causes then. No one knows how many of them there are up there – perhaps one way of keeping their numbers hidden is to hide the dead as well as the living.'

'Possible, I suppose,' Nightingale said. 'Some are registered with GPs, and some have jobs in the community, but you're right; we don't really know how many live at the compound. Children's Services go in occasionally, but they always come away with the suspicion that they haven't been given full access.'

'The problem with that theory is that the poor sod the badger unearthed doesn't fit the profile of a Children of Job member.'

'No. The post-mortem found evidence of long-term intravenous drug use. He was a heroin addict basically.'

'He was never identified, was he?'

She shook her head. 'No, he's still a John Doe. His DNA wasn't on the system and foxes had eaten his fingers. We've ordered another post-mortem and I was wondering if Estelle might do it? To see if her opinion matches the original pathologist's? I somehow doubt it will.'

'You think Cornelius wasn't the only person stoned to death, don't you?'

'It's hard *not* to think that,' she admitted. 'Which means, if there are extra bodies in these graves, we're back to asking who they were. And if they were also stoned to death, why? And what the hell's the connection to Cornelius Green's murder?'

'I don't know,' Poe said. 'But I know a man who might.'

'Who?'

'Israel Cobb,' he said. 'I think it's about time we had a chat without coffee.'

Chapter 84

Poe used the flat of his fist to hammer on Israel Cobb's door. He waited five seconds then did it again. He was on his own. Nightingale was arranging ground-penetrating radar and making sure she had everything she needed to apply for the five exhumation orders. Bradshaw was trawling through the badger case file to see if anything had been missed, and Linus had wanted to shadow her rather than drive out to Skelton with him. For once, Poe was happy to acquiesce. What he was hoping to achieve now was best done on his own.

Before he'd left, Bradshaw had handed him the age-progressed photograph of Bethany Bowman, the one she'd got from the Polaroids Eve had given them. Bradshaw had explained that at fourteen years old the shape of Bethany's face was unlikely to have changed, although the nose would be longer and there would be some vertical stretching. A few other variables. Poe had only asked one question: does this look like her? Bradshaw said that unless she'd had cosmetic surgery to alter her appearance, it was accurate.

Nightingale agreed that Poe's visit to Cobb should be done under the guise of an Osman warning; used when there is police intelligence of a threat to life but not enough evidence to arrest or locate the potential offender. Poe would deliver it verbally tonight and she'd follow it up the next day with the paperwork.

Poe put his ear to the door and listened. If Cobb was in, he was passed out drunk, dead or keeping very still. Poe checked his watch. It was coming up to 10 p.m., an hour or so before chucking out time at the Dog and Gun. Poe got back in his car and drove it a couple of hundred yards down the road. After reversing into a dark verge, he got out and checked Cobb wouldn't be able to see it when he staggered home from the pub.

Because if he wasn't home, the pub was the only other place Cobb could be. He had reeked of booze last time, he had been in the pub the night Cornelius Green had died, and he looked like a functioning alcoholic. He might not drink every day, but when he *did* drink, he drank a lot. They were called binge drinkers when Poe was in the army, and if they weren't in the pub they were sleeping off a hangover. Anyway, Cobb didn't own a car and Skelton was miles from anywhere – the pub was the only place open.

Poe was thinking this as he made his way down the narrow road to the Dog and Gun. The sun had dipped below the horizon, leaving pink clouds and a warm glow in the air, like a hearth the morning after a fire. The air was drenched with the fragrance of summer flowers: the pungent, thick perfume of honeysuckle and the coconut scent of gorse bushes. Shap Fell only ever smelled of heather and stunted grass and sheep, but the hedges around Skelton were a bouquet for the soul. Poe breathed in deeply. If he'd been with Bradshaw she would have been complaining about her hay fever and reaching for her allergy tablets. He smiled for the first time that day.

Light spilled out of the Dog and Gun's windows. Men and women, forced outside because of the smoking laws, laughed and drank in the evening air. There were beer tables and umbrellas, but it was that time of night when people wanted to stand and mingle. If this had been a TV commercial, they'd have been drinking peach cider with great big chunks of ice.

To Poe's sober ears their voices were shrill and loud, but good-natured nonetheless. He stopped a hundred yards from the pub. He didn't want to speak to Israel Cobb there. This was reconnaissance. If Cobb was inside Poe would go back to his car and wait for him at his home. If he wasn't inside, he'd call Nightingale and see if she would authorise a welfare check. So far, this case had thrown up a victim of stoning, a probable victim of stoning, a suicide and a massacred family. A welfare check would be fully justified.

Poe briefly considered finding a local and asking them if Cobb was inside. In a village this small, everyone knew everyone. He quickly discounted it. Poe was a cop and he asked questions like a cop. If Cobb were blameless in all this, then telling the village boozer the police still wanted to talk to him was verging on harassment. Virginia Rose's complaint was in the pipeline and he didn't want another. And if Cobb *was* up to his ears in all this, advance warning of yet another police visit might be enough to convince him it was time to bug out. Far better he didn't find out Poe was back in his life until he was standing right next to him.

In the end, he didn't have to do anything because Israel Cobb stepped outside. For a moment, Poe thought he would have to hide in someone's garden, but Cobb wasn't leaving the pub. Instead, he let out a great hacking cough and rolled a cigarette. He stood on his own while he smoked it. He ignored the scattered groups of chatting drinkers and they ignored him. There didn't appear to be any animosity, but it was clear he wasn't part of anyone's social circle.

That was good enough for Poe. Cobb was obviously staying until last orders; if he wasn't, he would have rolled his cigarette and smoked it on the walk home. Poe waited until Cobb had gone back inside before he made his way to his car. He reckoned he had another hour before Cobb would be home. He sent Bradshaw a text telling her what he was doing – and got one back within seconds saying she and Nightingale were still working on the exhumation orders – then switched on the overhead light and took his copy of Bethany Bowman's journal from his glove box.

But instead of reading it, his thoughts drifted to how he could get Israel Cobb to open up. They'd got nothing out of him the first time and, according to Nightingale, the detectives she'd sent to confirm his alibi for the night of Cornelius Green's murder had got short shrift too. Perhaps he had gone in too hard last time. Bradshaw had told him his toes smelled bad. He'd called him a hobo-Jesus.

The trick this time would be to stay calm.

Chapter 85

'I know you're in, Mr Cobb,' Poe yelled, hammering on the door. 'I've just watched you lurch back from the pub.'

He listened for movement. Nothing. Cobb was either already asleep or he was hiding behind the door. Poe's money was on the latter – Cobb was the kind of man who wouldn't be caged by the landlord's timetable; he would want to drink until the small hours.

Poe banged on the door again. 'I have nothing better to do, Mr Cobb; I can keep this up all night.'

This time he heard shuffling.

'You and the constabulary appear to be having communication problems, Sergeant Poe,' Cobb said from behind the door. 'I didn't kill Cornelius Green; my alibi checked out. Ask Detective Sergeant Rigg. He was the chap who interviewed me and the landlord of the Dog and Gun.'

'I'm not here about that.'

'Then what are you here for? Because a third visit is bordering on persecution. From now on, if you want to make an appointment, please go through my solicitor. He's called—'

'I'm here because we believe you're in danger, Mr Cobb. I am required by law to deliver an Osman warning.'

Poe had delivered Osman warnings many times, usually to people who already knew they were in danger. Reactions varied. Some demanded around-the-clock protection, others told him to piss off. Cobb seemed to be nearer the 'piss off' end of the scale.

'Consider me warned,' Cobb said. 'Now, please leave me alone.'

'I also want to talk about your tattoos,' Poe said.

The silence that followed was absolute. Even the night creatures seemed to recognise this was a bell that couldn't be un-rung. Poe had gone all in. Eventually a hooting owl broke the spell.

'What tattoos?' Cobb said eventually.

'We know what they mean,' Poe said, ignoring the question. 'And we know what we're going to find when we exhume the graves.'

More silence. Then, 'I don't know what you're talking about, Sergeant Poe.'

'Then let me refresh your memory. Cornelius Green had six alphanumeric tattoos on his lower torso and upper thighs; tattoos he penned himself. These tattoos are the locations of graves, and because of a badger with a wonky sense of direction, we already know one of those graves contained an extra body.'

Cobb didn't rise to the bait. Poe wondered why. If the flash of black he'd glimpsed last time *had* been one of Cornelius's alphanumeric tattoos, rather than a random Bible verse or the name of a long-dead loved one, Poe's words should have rocked Cobb's world. They should have elicited a response. A resigned denial, the spluttering threat of legal action.

But all Poe got was a sombre, 'I have nothing to say.'

'Someone's going to prison, Mr Cobb, and with Cornelius dead, you're now the only one without a chair after the music's stopped.'

Still nothing.

Poe rubbed his eyes and ran his fingers through his hair. He needed a different approach. The proverb, 'You catch more flies with honey than with vinegar' might literally be the best way to bait a flytrap, but as a way of getting people to do things they didn't want to do, it was inherently flawed. People only ever did what was in their own best interest. They responded to politeness and threats in exactly the same way – what's in it for me?

But Poe had tried and failed with the implicit threat of the tattoos, and he had nothing he could offer Cobb. Keeping quiet cost Cobb nothing. Talking could potentially cost him everything.

Not that Cobb had a lot. He had no real possessions and other than his nights in the local, he had little to do with the human condition. Which gave Poe an idea. Maybe there wasn't anything he could give Cobb. But there was certainly something he could take away.

'If you don't let me in, here's what's going to happen, Mr Cobb,' he said. 'Because I think you know more about Cornelius Green's murder than you're letting on, I'm officially changing your status from witness to person of interest.'

Poe paused a beat to let that sink in.

'And the first thing I'm going to do with your newfound status is drive into the village and drag the pub landlord out of bed and take him down to the station for an interview under caution,' he continued. 'He provided you with an alibi and I'm going to make him wish he hadn't. I'm going to sweat him and I'm going to hold him for the full twenty-four hours. By the time I've finished you'll be *persona non grata* at the Dog and Gun. I'll then move on to the locals. One by one I'll drag them down to the station too. And I'm not going to tell them what it's in connection with. I'll let them decide why the village oddball has come to the attention of the National Crime Agency, an agency that now includes CEOP.'

'I don't know what CEOP—'

'Child Exploitation and Online Protection Command, Mr Cobb,' Poe said. 'The paedophile hunters.'

'But you're with that other lot. The serial killer unit.'

'The NCA is only really known for two things: arresting gangsters and arresting child sex offenders. Now, you know your neighbours better than I do, Mr Cobb, but when the mums and dads in the village google what it is the NCA does, what conclusion do you think they'll leap to? That the weirdo hermit who lives at the end of the lane is an organised crime boss, feared throughout Europe, or he's the type of person who parks a van full of puppies outside the local school? How long before you have a mob with torches and pitchforks outside your house? A day? Two? Certainly not more than three.'

Poe waited to see if that had hit home. Eventually the door opened an inch.

'You'd better come in,' Cobb said.

Chapter 86

'Cornelius put these tattoos on me, Sergeant Poe,' Cobb said. 'I have no idea what they represent.'

Which was predictable. It was the only explanation Cobb could give that wouldn't immediately land him in jail. After he'd let Poe into his living room, Cobb disappeared into the kitchen to get a beaker. After he'd filled it with neat vodka, he stripped down to his underwear, a pair of stained, white Y-fronts, and showed him the six alphanumeric tattoos on his scrawny frame.

Poe took photographs and emailed them to Bradshaw. He didn't need her to tell him they were the same as Cornelius Green's – he was seeing them in his sleep. Bradshaw would confirm it later, but the shape and slant of the letters and numbers seemed to match the tattoos on Cornelius Green and Nathan Rose. Poe was certain Cobb was telling the truth about that at least: Cornelius Green *had* tattooed him.

'Really?' Poe said. 'And you didn't think to ask what they meant? You just let him tattoo you without asking a single question? Why do I find that implausible?'

Cobb sighed. 'Bluster and unpleasant threats aside, I'm going to assume you're not a complete imbecile, Sergeant Poe; if you say my tattoos are the locations of graves then I'm taking that as a fact.'

Poe rolled his eyes. 'That's very generous of you.'

'I'm also taking as a fact there are bodies in those graves, bodies that shouldn't be there.'

'The SIO is applying for exhumation orders as we speak,' Poe said. 'It's why I'm here on my own.'

'That sounds like a lengthy process.'

Poe shrugged. Exhumations were notoriously complex. It wasn't a case of simply getting the nod from the coroner. It was a traumatic event for the deceased's next of kin, so they had to be informed before an application could be approved, and in some cases they had to grant permission. The site had to be evaluated, as reopening graves was a high-risk health-and-safety activity. It was dangerous. Microorganisms in bodily fluids, blood and contaminated soil could be highly infectious. The risk of airborne diseases being released was real. The graves could collapse. And at all times respect had to be shown to the deceased, which, given what they expected to find, was going to be a challenge.

'It might take some time,' Poe admitted. 'But we know where the graves are and the bodies under the coffins aren't going anywhere. The superintendent has already put police officers in each graveyard to make sure no one is tempted to go and do some housekeeping. Maybe remove what shouldn't have been there in the first place.'

'What's your point?'

'My point is, we will exhume those bodies, Mr Cobb. And when we do, we're going to science the shit out of them. There will be some loss of forensic evidence because of the timescale, but that loss won't be absolute. If you were involved in this, we *will* find out.'

'So, what? This is my chance to come clean?'

'I'll start you off, shall I?' Poe said. 'The burial dates of the graves all coincide with off-the-books courses run by Cornelius Green, courses that appeared to stop after you had your big falling-out. When I asked Nathan Rose what had happened on *his* course, he killed himself rather than answer our questions.'

Cobb blinked rapidly for a moment. His rounded shoulders slumped even more. He seemed disorientated. That had hit home. 'Nathan's dead?' he said. 'When?'

'Recently.'

For a moment Poe thought Cobb was going to burst into tears. His breathing became shallow and it was a full minute before he got it under control. He put his hands in his lap and stared at them.

'There's no one left then,' he whispered.

'What does that mean, Mr Cobb?'

Cobb looked up. 'Can I pour you a vodka, Sergeant Poe?' he said.

'No, I don't want a bloody vodka. I want—'

'Have a vodka, Sergeant Poe.'

'Why?'

'Because I have a story and I don't want to be drinking alone when I tell it.'

Chapter 87

'I don't know who killed Cornelius, Sergeant Poe,' Cobb said. 'I don't expect you to believe me, but it's the truth.'

'You wanted to tell me something,' Poe said.

He was perched on the arm of the sofa. Cobb had put his clothes back on. He was in his armchair. The back and the cushion were both patched with masking tape. Poe took a sip of his drink. He tried not to wince. He didn't like vodka. Never had. And neat, room temperature vodka in a stained coffee mug was gag inducing. Cobb was drinking it like a thirsty man. He was shaking now, but Poe didn't think it was the booze. He seemed scared.

'Tell me about the courses,' Poe said.

'What do you know?'

'I think you are befuddled, Mr Cobb. We're not friends. We're not two mates having a chat after the pub has shut. I'm a cop and you're a suspect, and that means I ask the questions; you *answer* the questions. If you lie about something I already know, you're going to prison for perverting the course of justice. Is our relationship clearer now?'

Cobb drained his vodka and wiped his lips. He reached for the bottle, but Poe stopped him. 'After,' he said.

'You know about the conversion therapy courses we used to run?'

Which was technically another question, but Poe let it slide. He nodded. 'They still do.'

'We didn't run many, but when we did they were always over-subscribed. Some of the people who find solace in the Children of Job have unshakable beliefs when it comes to homosexuality, Sergeant Poe. Even when it has no impact on them in the slightest, they can't abide that it happens. To them the Same Sex Couples Act is nothing short of appeasement. Part of a plot to ban Christianity altogether.'

'I've been to the compound,' Poe said. 'I've met the kind of people you're talking about.'

'Then imagine these same people find out they have a gay son. What do you think their reaction might be?'

'Extreme?'

Cobb shook his head. 'Panic,' he said. 'These people aren't evil, Sergeant Poe. They love their children, but having a gay son isn't an option. Consider what they might do to help him?' Cobb wrapped 'help' with air quotes.

'Nothing positive,' Poe said.

'And now imagine there's a charismatic guy who says he can cure homosexuality. He tells them their son isn't gay; he's just confused. That by attending intensive prayer and therapy sessions he can be put back on God's path. For a fee, of course.'

'Cornelius was a grifter?'

'Absolutely not. He genuinely believed in what he did. And you must remember things were different back then. Conversion therapy hadn't been universally condemned. Little was known about it, so if you searched online you would find what appeared to be balanced arguments from both sides of the efficacy debate. And if homosexuality was abhorrent to you, if you genuinely believed your son was condemning himself to hell, wouldn't you roll the dice on a two-day course?'

'And that's all they were? Prayer and therapy?'

'For the most part.'

'But not the six courses you have tattooed on your back?'

Cobb reached for the vodka bottle again. This time Poe let him refill his beaker.

'I've said Cornelius Green was a charismatic man, Sergeant Poe,' Cobb said. 'The kind of man who turned everyone else into background, dominated every room he was in by sheer force of presence. But looking back, he was also the most manipulative man I've ever had the misfortune to meet. He had a terrible . . . well, instinct I suppose you'd call it, for uncovering people's fears and hopes and prejudices and then exploiting them.'

Poe put his mug of vodka on a scarred table. He leaned closer to Cobb. 'Explain,' he said.

'He knew when parents were absolutely at the end of their tether. He knew when to push and he knew when to sit back and let them approach him. And he knew which kids were mentally suited to his special courses.'

'Why weren't they recorded anywhere?'

Cobb took a long drink before pressing the beaker to his forehead and closing his eyes. 'Because by any definition what he . . . sorry, what *we* did was illegal.'

'You as well?'

'I told you, Sergeant Poe; Cornelius Green was an expert at exploiting prejudices and I was a different person then. I took the Old Testament literally. I believed life starts at conception; that being gay was a fast track to an eternity in hell. All the rest of the things religious extremists get into a tizzy about. At the time, I thought Cornelius was a kindred spirit. The firebrand activist to my more measured conservatism. We complemented each other. Or at least that's what he made me believe. He said I was his éminence grise, the powerful adviser operating behind the scenes. The reality was he couldn't run these extra courses on his own. And the more I think about it, the more I realise he needed a witness he could bend to his will; someone who could corroborate his version of reality.'

'What did you do to those kids, Mr Cobb?'

Cobb drained his beaker. He wiped his chin and said, 'Terrible, terrible things, Sergeant Poe.'

Chapter 88

'Now Nathan is dead, there is no one else to corroborate what I'm about to tell you, Sergeant Poe,' Cobb said. 'Nothing we did was written down. If it goes further than the inside of my house, all you'll have is the ramblings of a drunk. I'll deny it the second the police doctor declares me sober enough to be interviewed.'

Poe didn't think Cobb was drunk. Not any more. Poe thought Cobb was probably the soberest he'd been for years.

'Knowing this, are you sure you want me to continue, Sergeant Poe?' Cobb asked. 'You can walk out of here now without understanding what happened. Think carefully before you answer because this isn't something you can *un*-know.'

Poe didn't hesitate. 'Tell me everything,' he said.

'Very well.' Cobb filled his beaker again. His hands, shaky before, were now as steady as a surgeon's. 'I'm not excusing my role in this,' he said, 'but at the time I genuinely thought I was helping those young boys. That I was literally saving them from hell.'

Poe believed him. Even if Cobb had been just another of Cornelius's followers back then, he'd definitely been a zealot.

'The first thing you need to know is these courses took place in the old school basement,' Cobb continued. 'In shadows and in secret. The student was locked in there at night and at no point was he allowed to mingle with anyone else on campus. At all times either Cornelius or I were present. We were there to offer support and to continue the therapy, but also to make sure they didn't leave before it ended.'

Cobb took a drink. Shut his eyes as the vodka burned his throat.

'The first thing we did was read and discuss carefully curated passages of the Bible,' he continued. 'This wasn't just a soft lead into what was to come; it was important the student was clear about why he was there. Why what followed was necessary.'

'And what did follow, Mr Cobb?'

'Do you understand standard aversion therapy, Sergeant Poe?'

'Just the basics,' Poe replied. 'It involves pairing unwanted behaviour with discomfort. Putting a bitter-tasting chemical on the fingernails to discourage nail-chewing could be classed as aversion therapy.'

'That's right,' Cobb confirmed. 'Like a dog being squirted with water every time it barks, the subject learns to associate the unwanted behaviour with an unpleasant experience. Eventually the unwanted behaviour is quelled. It's a tried and tested psychological treatment.'

Poe didn't think Edgar would learn anything from being repeatedly squirted in the face with cold water. He, however, would definitely learn how many bandages a dog bite to the hand required.

'Have you seen *A Clockwork Orange*?' Cobb asked.

Poe nodded. 'I have.'

'Alex, the head "droog", undergoes aversion therapy to cure his "ultra-violence". He's strapped to a chair with his eyes clamped open. He's then injected with drugs and forced to watch films depicting sex and violence while listening to Beethoven, his favourite composer. Later, while in the house of a previous victim of his violence, Alex hears Beethoven's Ninth and the pain is so terrible he tries to kill himself.'

'Who are you, Barry Norman?' Poe said. 'I said I'd seen *A Clockwork*—'

'Our chair had straps too, Sergeant Poe,' Cobb cut in quietly.

Chapter 89

Poe said nothing. He tried to hold Cobb's gaze, but Cornelius Green's éminence grise had his eyes fixed on the grubby carpet.

'It was called the mercy chair,' Cobb continued. 'Cornelius had it shipped from the States. He said it had once been used to execute criminals on death row and I believed him. It still had the leg and arm restraints, and you could see where the head clamps had been fitted.'

The time has come for me to sit on the mercy chair. That's what Nathan Rose's suicide note had said. Despite the muggy heat, Poe suddenly felt cold. 'It was used to restrain the boys?' he asked, already knowing the answer would be yes.

Cobb nodded but didn't make eye contact. 'Although each course was tailored to the individual boy,' he said, 'they had two common phases. The first, the intensive Bible study at the beginning, I've already told you about. Cornelius and I decided how to proceed based on how each boy responded to phase one. If he needed more time to pray, he was allowed it. If we felt more Bible lessons would be beneficial, then we catered to this too.'

'What was the second common element, Mr Cobb?' Poe asked. 'How did the course end?'

Cobb started to tremble. A single tear fell to the carpet. Poe watched it sink into the thin weave. It left a small dark mark, one among many.

'In the chair,' Cobb whispered. 'It ended in the mercy chair.' He seemed to have aged a decade in a few minutes. 'I still hear them beg, Sergeant Poe. I still hear their cries and their screams and their threats. I remember their struggles against the restraints as if it was yesterday. The panic in their eyes when they realised it wasn't an elaborate bluff. That it was really going to happen.'

Poe leaned forwards. 'What did you do?' he urged.

For the first time since he'd started talking, Cobb looked Poe in the eye. His stare was unwavering, manic even. 'We tortured them,' he said.

Chapter 90

'Define torture,' Poe said. 'Do you mean watching *The Jeremy Kyle Show*, or the kind of torture that lands you in The Hague?'

'The boys were strapped into the mercy chair,' Cobb replied. 'Their shoes and socks were removed. And while I showed them photographs of naked men, Cornelius whipped the soles of their feet with a length of hosepipe filled with sand. That kind of torture, Sergeant Poe.'

'The second kind then,' Poe said.

'That's it? That's all you have to say?'

'No. I'm buying myself some time so I can process my thoughts and come up with a more measured response than you're an evil bastard.'

'We were in the business of saving souls, Sergeant Poe. There wasn't anything we wouldn't do for those boys.'

Poe stood. In three strides he had reached Cobb's armchair. Cobb tried to rise to meet him, but Poe jabbed a finger into his bony chest and forced him back down.

'You don't get to excuse this,' he hissed. 'You don't get to talk yourself out of torturing children. I don't care that there are no more living witnesses – you're going to prison for at least fifteen years.'

'May I stand, please?'

Poe stepped back.

Cobb struggled out of the sagging armchair. He faced Poe and held out his arms. 'You want to arrest me?' he said. 'Then arrest me.'

'Not me,' Poe said.

'Why not?'

'I don't know the right words.'

'You don't know—'

'We're going to sit here like adults, Mr Cobb, and you're going to answer every question I ask. You're not going to ask for a solicitor and you're not going to drink any more vodka. And when we've finished, I'll call Superintendent Nightingale and she can send someone to arrest you. Deny it, don't deny it; it makes no difference to me. I'll prove it in the end, I don't care how long it takes.'

Cobb slumped into his armchair. Poe returned to the arm of the sofa.

'Did any of these boys die, Mr Cobb?' Poe said. 'Is that who we're going to find in these graves?'

Cobb shook his head. 'Every one of those students walked out alive and well.'

'I doubt that.'

'Alive then.'

Poe mulled it over. Cobb had admitted to GBH with intent, but unless he was going to repeat what he'd said sober, under caution and in the presence of a solicitor, his confession was meaningless. And given he could argue that he'd thought he had the boys' explicit consent, Nightingale might not even get GBH to stick.

Something else was bothering Poe. The torture certainly helped explain Nathan Rose's suicide. And although Cobb had said there was no one left, if a surviving relative of one of the boys had decided to take revenge, it might even explain Cornelius Green's murder. But the torture didn't explain the bodies hidden in the graves. That still didn't make sense.

'If it's not students in those graves, then who?' Poe asked.

Cobb shrugged. 'I don't know.'

'Yet you have the same tattoos as Cornelius Green.'

'If you say. Cornelius didn't tell me what they meant and when I persisted he got aggressive. I'm not a brave man, Sergeant Poe.'

'OK, here's something you might know: why did these secret courses stop?'

'Because of Aaron Bowman,' Israel Cobb said.

Chapter 91

'Aaron Bowman was fifteen years old, Sergeant Poe,' Cobb said, 'but he could easily have passed for twelve. He was gentle and sweet and he was petrified from the moment he arrived. He didn't understand why he was there and for some reason Cornelius was treating him more harshly than anyone else we'd worked with so—'

'No one knows I'm here, Mr Cobb!' Poe snapped. 'If you describe torturing children as "work" one more time your body will never be found. Are we fucking clear?'

Cobb swallowed hard and nodded once. 'That's fair,' he said.

'I need to know everything you did to him.'

'I'm not sure I can, Sergeant Poe. The memory of it is . . . too painful.'

'I don't care. I need to know.'

'We tortured him!' he yelled. 'Are you happy now? He was fifteen years old and we tortured him just like we tortured the others. He cried and he screamed and he begged us to stop and we wouldn't. We wouldn't stop hurting him and he wouldn't stop screaming.'

'I need details, Mr Cobb.'

'Why?!'

'Because after the course he had a blazing row with his younger sister, Bethany,' Poe said. 'I now think they were arguing about how she had failed to protect him from what you had put him through. *This* is why she ran away from home that night.'

Cobb winced.

'And it's why she returned five years later to slaughter her parents,' Poe continued. 'She'd wanted revenge for what they did to Aaron, but at the time she was only fourteen and wasn't physically strong enough. Or maybe she'd simply had time to mull it over. Decided that her parents didn't deserve to live any longer.'

'I remember from the newspapers that the constabulary believe Aaron's murder was accidental. That the murderer hadn't meant to kill him.'

'Murderer?' Poe said.

'Aaron spoke warmly of Bethany. He said she was a wonderful person and the best sister a brother could ever have. From what he told me, if Bethany had accidentally killed him, she'd have been overcome with grief. She certainly wouldn't have hidden what she'd done. She would have waited beside his body until the police arrived.'

Which was exactly what Alice Symonds had said, Poe thought. 'You don't think Bethany Bowman killed her parents, do you?'

Cobb shrugged. 'I never met the girl. I suppose the more important question is what do *you* think, Sergeant Poe?'

Poe paused a beat. 'I think I want you to start from the beginning.'

'But I've already told—'

'From the beginning,' Poe said.

So Cobb told his story again.

He told Poe about the mental and physical abuse of six young men and boys. He told Poe about the pornographic pictures he had held in front of their faces while Cornelius whipped the soles of their feet with a hosepipe. He said the area between the ball and the heel was particularly pain sensitive but remarkably resistant to injury, even bruising. He explained how when the courses were over he would bathe the boys' feet and apply a cooling balm. It was at this stage that Cornelius would tattoo everyone involved. He said it was a reminder of what they'd all been through. Poe asked again why the tattoos were the locations of graves, but Cobb insisted he hadn't known they were until that evening.

Cobb said he and Cornelius would meet with the concerned parents after each course had finished. They were anxious to discover if it had worked and what follow-up therapy would be required. Poe asked if the parents had known what the courses entailed, and Cobb confirmed they had. Poe made a note of this and under-lined it three times. With nothing recorded anywhere, he doubted Superintendent Nightingale would have enough to arrest the parents for conspiracy to commit grievous bodily harm with intent, but he knew she'd give it a go.

Cobb eventually got to the end of his monstrous tale. Poe asked a few follow-ups but it was clear he'd been told everything. He reviewed his notes and saw he'd filled sixteen pages.

Poe had one last question.

'Why aren't you dead, Mr Cobb?' he said.

'I may have a drink problem, Sergeant Poe, but I can assure you I'm still a man of reasonable health.'

'That's not what I meant and you know it. I want to know why we haven't found you stoned to death as well. It doesn't matter if it was Bethany or someone we don't yet know about who killed Cornelius Green, he was almost certainly killed for what he did to those boys. And even if you've massively exaggerated your own role, you're clearly as culpable as your former partner in crime. So I'll ask again – why aren't you dead?'

Cobb sighed. 'Despite what I've just told you, I doubt this was a case of *post hoc ergo propter hoc*, Sergeant Poe.'

Bradshaw occasionally used this Latin phrase. It meant, 'After this, therefore because of this.' Or, if event B follows event A, event B must have been *caused* by event A.

'You don't think there's a causality between what Cornelius did and what happened to him?' Poe said. 'No cause and effect between the torture he inflicted and his own murder?'

'I've already told you he was a manipulative man with terrible instincts; he collected enemies the way other people might collect bottle tops. I assume he was also involved in things he didn't need my help with.'

'He was killed for something else he'd done?'

'There will be many people who had cause to see him dead, Sergeant Poe, but I don't think the boys were ever one of their number. They were never angry with him. Not really, not when they saw what he was trying to achieve. Even if it didn't work, it came from a position of faith. As a result, no, I don't think I'm in any danger.'

Poe believed that Cobb believed that. While he was distraught at what he'd revealed, he didn't seem concerned about his own safety. Poe knew it was time to wrap up. Cumbria CID would have to follow up on this. They would push Cobb hard, but if he went 'No comment' during interview they wouldn't be able to charge him. He was right; there were no more living witnesses.

There was just one last thing to do. Poe reached into his pocket and pulled out the age-progressed photo printout of Bethany Bowman.

'If you go "no comment" on all this after you're arrested, you'll probably get bail,' Poe said. 'Despite what you believe, I think you need to take your Osman warning seriously. If you see this woman, you run away as fast as you can. You're a weedy runt of a man and she's got a stun gun. So you run and you don't stop until you get to a police station.'

He handed the printout to Cobb.

'Who's this?' he asked.

'That's Bethany Bowman, Mr Cobb.'

'But . . . no one has seen Bethany since she ran away from home. No one knows what she looks like now.'

'Wrong,' Poe said. 'We *didn't* know what Bethany looked like now, but then again, no one had asked Tilly to develop an age-progression program with a ninety-eight per cent accuracy rate. Eve gave me some old photographs of Bethany and Tilly put them through her program. She handed me this not thirty minutes before I came to see you. By tomorrow evening, Bethany's going to be the most famous thirty-year-old in the country. So, do me a favour and sleep with one eye open from now on. I would hate to think she might get to you before your trial.'

Cobb scrabbled around on the coffee table until he found a pair of reading glasses. The lenses were greasy and he wiped them on his shirt. Poe wasn't sure that would make them cleaner. Cobb stared in disbelief at Bradshaw's age-progressed image of Bethany Bowman. He flinched. What little colour he had drained from his face. His mouth formed a perfect 'O', and he began blinking wildly. He looked like a condemned man. His hands started to shake so much it was as if the photograph was rattling.

'You've seen her, haven't you?' Poe said. 'Where? I need to know where and I need to know when, Mr Cobb. What was she wearing, what was she doing? Have you talked to her?'

'Nooooo!' Cobb cried out, shaking his head and baring his teeth.

'Are you OK?' Poe asked, standing up, aware the sudden change in Cobb's demeanour was similar to the change that had come over Nathan Rose. Right before he'd jumped through a loft hatch with a tow rope around his neck. If Cobb was about to do something stupid as well, Poe was ready to stop him. No way was he taking the easy way out.

'Tell me where she is!' Poe urged.

Cobb shut his eyes and took deep, measured breaths. He did this for almost a minute. Poe didn't interrupt. After a while his manic expression faded into one of serenity, like he'd been meditating. His eyes opened.

'Bethany Bowman didn't kill Cornelius Green, Sergeant Poe,' he said. 'And if you circulate that image you'll look extremely foolish.'

'You seem very sure.'

'I am.'

'Why?'

'Because Bethany Bowman is dead,' Cobb said.

'And how could you possibly know that?'

'Because I'm the person who killed her.'

Chapter 92

'Israel Cobb *killed* Bethany?' Doctor Lang asked, astonished. 'But ... but ... why?'

'If you're looking for something more sophisticated than he and Cornelius were extremely vile, vile men, I'm not sure I have anything,' Poe said. 'Nothing that makes sense anyway.'

'I don't understa—'

'They tortured vulnerable boys, Doctor Lang,' Poe said, snipping her protest. 'They took in boys who were gay, or confused about their sexuality and, while they were tied to a chair, Israel showed them pictures of naked men and Cornelius whipped their feet with a hosepipe.'

'You've already said that.'

'I have,' Poe agreed. 'You're an experienced therapist; you'll understand the theory underpinning aversion therapy.'

'It's a recognised technique,' she said. 'I rarely use it, but then again I rarely treat patients with addictive behaviour.'

'Fair point,' Poe conceded. 'But, from what I've described, just how successful would they be at putting these boys back on the path to heaven?'

Doctor Lang considered the point carefully.

'Trying to change someone's sexuality doesn't work,' she said after a short pause. 'This is a scientific fact. At best you've wasted your time; at worst you've caused untold psychological damage. And what Cornelius and Israel were doing wasn't only ineffective; it was crude and cruel. Nathan Rose committed suicide when you challenged him about the course he'd attended. I think *post hoc ergo propter hoc* probably did apply there. It sounds as though he killed himself because your visit brought back these terrible memories,

memories I imagine he had successfully repressed. The brain's like that; it will do its best to protect itself from traumatic events.'

Poe gave Doctor Lang a grim nod. 'That much I know,' he said.

'Are you suggesting Bethany Bowman committed suicide as well? That she killed herself because of what happened to her brother? Israel felt responsible for her death, but he didn't *literally* kill her?'

'That's not what happened.'

'It isn't?'

'No,' Poe said. 'And Nathan Rose didn't kill himself because I reminded him about what he'd been through.'

'How can you possibly know?'

Poe held Doctor Lang's stare.

'Nathan Rose killed himself because of what he'd *done*,' he said.

Chapter 93

'I was telling the truth when I said we strapped those boys to the mercy chair, Sergeant Poe,' Israel Cobb said. 'And I was telling the truth when I said I showed them pictures of naked men while Cornelius whipped the soles of their feet.'

'But what were you lying about, Mr Cobb?' Poe said.

'I haven't lied. But I have sinned against you.'

'How?'

'The sin of omission, Sergeant Poe,' Cobb said. 'I told you that although each course was tailored to the individual boy, they all shared two common elements.'

'You did. Bible readings at the start, a good old feet whipping at the end.'

'The course didn't conclude with the boys being tortured in the mercy chair, Sergeant Poe. That wasn't the big set piece, the finale, the thing that put them back on the straight and narrow.'

'Other than you and Cornelius Green being a pair of sadists, what was the point of it then?'

'We called it essential conditioning,' Cobb said.

'What the hell does that mean? Essential conditioning for what?'

'For what came next.' Cobb stopped looking at Poe and cast his eyes to the floor. 'You want to know who the people in those graves are?' he said, his voice barely above a whisper.

'I do.'

'They were nobodies, Sergeant Poe. Worse than nobodies. Abominations. Unrepentant sinners. People who had been given the gift of life and spat it back in God's face. According to Cornelius anyway.'

'Who were they?'

'Men, Sergeant Poe. *Gay* men. Cornelius would go to Manchester or Newcastle or Glasgow and scour the streets for the homeless and the drug addicts and the rent boys until he found the ones no one would miss. He offered them salvation, a roof over their heads, a warm meal, but really he was—'

'Delivering damnation,' Poe finished.

'They weren't even people to him,' Cobb continued. 'He wouldn't let us use their names. If we had to refer to one at all, we called him "it". "Strap it to the mercy chair, Israel," Cornelius would say. "It's screaming too much, Israel; put a gag in its mouth."'

'"It" seems to be a popular word at the Children of Job,' Poe said, remembering Bethany's diary and how her parents had referred to her as 'it' as well. 'And what happened to these men?'

'I think you already know,' Cobb said.

'You forced those boys to kill these men?'

'We did.'

'How?'

'You know how.'

Poe thought about the injuries found on the boy the badger had dug up. 'They were stoned to death.'

Cobb nodded. 'It was how they graduated. The purpose of the essential conditioning was so, at that moment in time at least, the boys hated gay men. *Hated* them. We made them believe that gay men had caused all their pain and humiliation. Gay men were why they were going to hell. And then we gave them a target for their hate. A chance to take their revenge. And to purge themselves of that terrible affliction.'

'They took it?'

'They all threw at least one stone.'

'It was that easy? None of them resisted?'

'Some did. The more devout ones couldn't bring themselves to break the Ten Commandments. Murder is one of the great mortal sins.'

'But they threw a stone anyway?'

'They were all vulnerable and Cornelius was one of the most forceful men you could ever meet. Some needed the threat of the hosepipe again, but in the end they all did what was expected of them.'

'You turned them into murderers,' Poe said.

'Christian soldiers. That's what Cornelius called them. But as it happens, there is only so much essential conditioning you can do. In the end, only two of the six boys killed anyone. Nathan Rose did, but he was an easy case; he just wanted to please everyone. Didn't matter if it was his parents, his friends or Cornelius. When we told him to stone his victim, he did exactly that. He didn't need to be asked twice. The second boy to kill his victim was probably the only one of the six who believed what Cornelius was selling: that stoning the man in the mercy chair would put him back on God's path.'

'And the others?'

'The rest all threw stones, but none of them did it with any real venom. Most didn't even aim for the body. In my darkest days I like to think the four boys who resisted Cornelius as best they could, proved themselves before the eyes of God. That they were tested and not found wanting.' Cobb reached for his vodka but the bottle was empty. Poe still had some in his stained coffee mug. Wordlessly, he passed it over. 'What we did was evil,' Cobb continued. 'I understand that now. I think I understood it then, of course, but Cornelius was persuasive and he spent a lot of time dehumanising the men we killed. I felt nothing for them. It was as if we were putting them down.'

He put the dirty coffee mug to his crusty lips and drained the vodka in two noisy gulps. He squeezed his eyes shut for a few seconds.

Poe took the time to sort through his most burning questions. 'The tattoos?' he said eventually. 'Why put such incriminating evidence on your bodies?'

'It was Cornelius's idea,' Cobb said. 'He had contacts in churches all over the county and he knew when graves were going to be dug. Over one hundred people a week die in Cumbria, so he wasn't tight for choice. It was my job to take the dead men to these isolated, rural graveyards. A man, it was always a man, would meet me there and together we would wrap the body in plastic sheeting and put it into what was an extra-deep grave. We would shovel fresh earth on top of the victim and tamp it down so he wouldn't be seen on the day of the funeral. Cornelius tattooed the grave's location on the people involved in each murder. I have six, as does Cornelius. The boys only had the murders they were involved with.'

'As a reminder?'

'As a warning,' Cobb said. 'Cornelius knew people grew consciences. This was his way of warning them they had been willing participants.'

Poe had heard enough. It was time to call in Nightingale. Cobb had rights and Poe was probably abusing them. And so far, all he had was a story. It fitted the facts as they knew them, but it was still just a story. It was time for Nightingale to match it against the evidence. He reached for his phone but stopped. He wanted to ask one last question.

'And this is why you and Cornelius fell out, is it?' he said. 'In 2007, after Aaron Bowman was forced to go through this, you'd had enough. You said you'd threatened to expose him.'

'I did.'

'Why?'

'I've already told you, Aaron Bowman was a fragile—'

'They were *all* fragile, Mr Cobb. They were all under duress. What was so different about Aaron? And why did you say you'd murdered Bethany? We know she and Aaron rowed about something when he got back from that course. That she ran away the same night.'

Cobb didn't answer.

'But I don't think that's what happened now,' Poe said. 'I think Aaron and Bethany were so close that even though you'd sworn him to secrecy, he told her anyway. I think she took the pragmatic, and in my opinion accurate, view that a fifteen-year-old boy wasn't culpable for what he'd done. Not under those circumstances. I think she told Aaron that if he wouldn't go to the police, she would.'

Still Cobb kept quiet.

'So, when you say you murdered her, I think you did exactly that,' Poe said. 'I think Noah and Grace Bowman, who, for reasons we'll probably never understand, hated their youngest daughter – they found out what she was planning to do and told you or Cornelius. She was murdered to keep your secret. A story was invented about her running away from home and everyone involved kept it. She'd run away before so no one looked too hard this time.'

'That's what you think, is it?'

Poe shrugged. 'Tell me I'm wrong,' he said. 'Tell me you didn't involve Aaron in a murder just to "cure" his gayness. Tell me Aaron didn't tell Bethany what he'd been forced to do.'

Instead of answering, Cobb got to his feet. He limped to his old-fashioned television and opened the cabinet it was sitting on. He had a video recorder rather than a DVD player. To the side of it was a pile of videocassettes. Six, all in plain cardboard boxes. Each box had a handwritten label, although Poe wasn't close enough to read them.

'What are they?' he asked.

'The *other* reason Cornelius and I fell out.'

Poe felt a jolt of nerves, like he'd touched an electric fence. He had a terrible feeling about this. He reached for his phone.

'I need you to see something first, Sergeant Poe,' Cobb said, watching him carefully. He removed the top cassette from its box and pressed it into the slot. It clunked its way into the guts of the machine. Cobb turned on the television. It was already on the video channel. He pressed play then spent a few seconds adjusting the tracking.

When he turned to face Poe, tears were already running down his face.

'Aaron Bowman wasn't gay, Sergeant Poe,' he said.

Chapter 94

'Were the videos what I think they were?' Doctor Lang asked. 'Were they the murders of those men? The ones Cornelius Green had lured from the streets of Manchester and Newcastle?'

'And Glasgow,' Poe nodded. 'Israel had stolen the tapes before he left the Children of Job. He made copies and hid them carefully as an insurance policy. He kept the originals at home.'

'And you watched them?'

'I did.'

'All of them?'

Poe nodded again.

'Why?'

'It was my job to watch them,' he said.

'I'm sorry, Washington, but that shouldn't be your job,' Doctor Lang said. 'That shouldn't be *anyone's* job.'

'If not me, then who?'

'You can't keep putting yourself into situations like this and expect nothing to happen. There's a cumulative as well as an immediate psychological impact with traumatic events, Washington. At some point, you have to take a step back and let someone else shoulder the burden. Occasionally you have to put yourself first. Your nightmares are a warning shot; I doubt you'll get another.'

Poe didn't respond. He knew she was right. At some point, the bill became due.

'I don't think you should tell me what you saw on those videos, Washington,' she said. 'I don't want to be responsible for you having a psychotic episode.'

Poe paused for several moments. Eventually he said, 'You say there's a cumulative psychological impact to everything I've seen, everything I've done. And maybe you're right—'

'I *am* right.'

'But if there was an *immediate* impact on my mental health with this case, watching those videos wasn't it.'

Doctor Lang looked sceptical.

'You don't look convinced,' he said.

'You haven't convinced me.'

'Watching those videos was an appalling experience. I'm certainly not trying to downplay what I saw. They were horrific and I will never forget them.'

'But?'

'But there was worse to come.'

Chapter 95

'Worse?' Doctor Lang said. 'Worse than watching an execution by stoning?'

Poe held up his hands. Kept four fingers down on his left. '*Six* executions,' he said. 'And only two of them were death by stoning. Israel was right when he said four of the boys couldn't be compelled to murder, even under the threat of more torture.'

'How did the men die then? Cornelius couldn't have let them go.'

'I'll get to that.'

'Do you want to talk about what you saw?'

'No, but I will. It's important you understand. Without the context of what was on those videos, you won't truly understand the horror of what happened afterwards.'

'Shall I call for more tea first?' she said. 'I don't know what the time is, but we must have been talking for a good couple of hours.'

'A cup of tea would be nice,' Poe said. 'You stay there; I'll go and find someone. I could do with stretching my legs.'

Ten minutes later they were drinking lukewarm tea again. At least the orderly had brought a plate of biscuits this time. Poe grabbed a handful. He waited until he had finished eating before he spoke. He was about to describe people being murdered; it didn't seem right to do that while he was dunking a custard cream.

'Israel Cobb told me that Cornelius had trawled the streets of Manchester and Newcastle and Glasgow searching for the homeless, the drug addicts,' Poe said. 'He was looking for people who wouldn't be missed. Israel claimed he'd only ever picked up gay men, but I thought, given what was about to happen to them, Cornelius probably just focused on the weak and the vulnerable. Ignored their sexuality.'

Poe took a swig of tea. It was already cold.

'I put this to Israel and he recoiled in horror,' he continued. 'He said, "Cornelius would never do that." Apparently Cornelius genuinely believed they were doing God's work; taking shortcuts would have damned them all to hell.'

Doctor Lang snorted in derision.

'Obscene, isn't it?' Poe said. 'Anyway, Israel played the videos in chronological order. The first was recorded in 2001, the second in 2003. I suspect they waited a couple of years between one and two to make sure they were going to get away with it. They then ran one course a year until Aaron Bowman's in 2007. Six in total.'

'You don't need to tell me about them, Washington,' she said. 'Not if you don't want to.'

'To understand what I'm going through now, you have to understand what I went through *then*,' he said. 'I think I need to tell you.'

Doctor Lang finished her tea and took a biscuit: a Jammie Dodger that had been hiding under a stale digestive.

'OK, Washington,' she said, taking a bite and catching the crumbs in her cupped hand. 'Like I said earlier, this is your story. You tell it the way that makes most sense to you. This isn't a case review – I'm here for you, and you alone. What's said in this room, stays in this room.'

'This isn't pleasant,' Poe warned. 'What about *your* mental health?'

She shrugged. 'The difference is you'll be describing a memory; I'm just a conduit, little more than a voyeur. You remembering what happened without *reliving* what happened is how you get better, Washington. And you need to do that in a safe environment.' She gestured at their surroundings and smiled. 'I think this is about as safe as you can get.'

So Poe talked.

Chapter 96

'The mercy chair was kept in the basement of the old school at the Children of Job compound,' Poe said to Doctor Lang. 'Israel told me that he and Cornelius had sectioned off one end of the basement with plywood. Made a whole other room. The door to this room was padlocked at all times; from the outside when the sectioned-off area wasn't in use, from the inside when it was.'

'How did they explain what the room was for?'

'Cornelius just told everyone to stay away from it. And when there was a course running no one was allowed in the basement at all.'

'And nobody got curious?' Doctor Lang asked. 'It must have been like Bluebeard's secret chamber; the one his wives were banned from entering.'

'The hold Cornelius had over them all was ironclad. His word was law and if he told his followers not to do something, they didn't do it. That's how Israel Cobb described it and I've heard nothing since to suggest he wasn't telling the truth.'

'And did the chair look like it might have been an old electric chair, like Israel claimed?'

'Possibly,' Poe admitted. 'It was definitely old and sturdy enough. The leather restraints looked like they were original. It certainly could have been used to electrocute death-row prisoners.'

'But?'

'But really, how can you tell?' Poe admitted. 'Superintendent Nightingale has detectives in the States still trying to track down where it came from. I hope she finds the seller to be honest; I would hate to think someone in the UK had made it to order.'

They lapsed into a strange silence, almost as if they were putting off what was coming up next.

Doctor Lang broke it. 'You said Israel had shown you the videos in chronological order?'

Poe nodded. 'What he *hadn't* said though, was how young their victims were. The way he told it, Cornelius had abducted – because that's what it was – grown men, but the guys on the videos were barely older than the boys attending the courses.' He paused a couple of ticks. 'I guess the longer you live on the street, the more wary you become of too-good-to-be-true offers such as the one Cornelius was peddling.'

Doctor Lang nodded. 'I see a lot of street kids. Some have had to grow up so fast it breaks your heart.'

'Cornelius didn't start recording until the victims were securely strapped into the mercy chair,' Poe continued. 'I have no idea if they struggled while they were being restrained. They looked sedated, so maybe not. The first victim, the one from 2001, looked to be around eighteen years old, but he could have been much younger. Living on the street prematurely ages you.'

'Were they scared?'

'More nervous, I think. At least until they understood what was happening.'

'Which was when?'

'When Cornelius brought the boy in,' Poe said. 'And at this stage it was clear the boy didn't know what was happening either. The shock on both their faces was genuine when Cornelius explained what was about to happen.'

'How soon after the boys' feet had been whipped did this take place?' Doctor Lang asked.

'Not long. Israel told me they were tortured then taken some-where to get cleaned up. When they were brought back into the part of the basement with the mercy chair, the victim was waiting for them.'

'And what they'd endured was enough for the boys to at least go through the motions of stoning the victims?'

'No. Not at first. With the exception of Nathan Rose and one other boy there was pushback. But Israel hadn't been exaggerat-ing when he said Cornelius Green was a charismatic man. The way he bent the boys to his will was extraordinary. He raged and he screamed and he fell to his knees in prayer, spittle and foam at the corners of his mouth. He would get up and pace back and forth, all the time urging the boy to do what was right, what was *just*. He was like one of those fire and brimstone revivalist preachers, the kind Stephen King writes about. All that was missing was the rattlesnakes.'

'He didn't try to hide from the video?'

'No,' Poe said. 'He owned what he did. Israel too. The camera must have been on a tripod, as it didn't move. It was trained on the man in the mercy chair, but they were all in view. Cornelius was apoplectic, Israel was measured and focused, and the boy and the victim were both crying and begging. The victim for his life; the boy because of what he was being told to do.'

Poe took a silent moment as it all became a bit too raw. He had to explain, however, had to make her understand what had happened. He closed his eyes and shuddered at the memory. He opened them, clenched his jaw, and continued.

'"Look how weak it is!" That's the type of thing Cornelius would shout at the boys. "See how it begs for its worthless life," or, "It's an abomination; the kindest thing you can do is put it out of its misery."'

'Subtle,' Doctor Lang said.

'But effective,' Poe countered. 'You could see the boys' resistance crumbling in real time. While Israel fixed a hessian hood over the victim's head, Cornelius told the boys, "This is your only way out." He turned them so they were facing the young man in the mercy chair, handed them a baseball-sized stone, and screamed, "Throw it!"'

'And they did?'

'Yes,' Poe confirmed. 'Every one of them flung the stone at the man in the mercy chair. Some screamed as they did, others, like Nathan Rose, were eerily calm. And after they had thrown it, Cornelius encouraged and praised them. Told them they were stepping back on the path of righteousness. Only two of the boys, Nathan Rose and the one who actually believed in what he was doing, repeatedly hit the victims on the head. The others either intentionally missed or lobbed them like grenades, nowhere near hard enough to kill. Whatever the boys did though, it didn't seem to matter to Cornelius. Israel offered them all another rock, but neither he nor Cornelius seemed concerned if they refused.'

Poe shut his eyes again.

'It's a sound no one should have to hear,' he said. He opened his eyes and blinked in surprise, almost as if he hadn't known he'd closed them. 'When it was obvious the boy on the course had given everything he had to give, they would all shake hands and pray together. This sometimes went on for no more than a minute, sometimes it was half an hour. And after they'd finished, Cornelius told Israel it was time for the boy to graduate.'

'And what did *that* mean?'

'It meant Israel taking a Stanley knife from his pocket, lifting up the man's hessian hood and, if he wasn't already dead, slitting his throat from ear to ear.'

Chapter 97

'Do you want to continue?' Doctor Lang asked. 'Watching those videos must have been horrific. Just talking about them will be deeply traumatic for you.'

Poe nodded, but not convincingly. He had tried turning off that particular spigot, but it was stubborn. The screams of the victims, the terror on the faces of the boys hurling the rocks – they were memories that weren't easily forgotten.

'Why did you watch all six?' she asked.

'Excuse me?'

'Israel Cobb made you watch the first video, right?'

Poe nodded.

'It was basically a snuff movie,' she continued. 'You watched a man being murdered.'

'I did.'

'And you described it as horrific.'

'The worst thing I'd ever seen,' Poe agreed.

'I'll ask you again then: after you'd watched the first video, why did you watch the next five? Why didn't you arrest Israel Cobb and let better-equipped people take it from there? This was Superintendent Nightingale's case, not yours – why not spread the pain around a little? Why try to carry this burden alone? Look what it's done to you.'

'You think I *wanted* to watch them all?' Poe said. 'The people strapped to the chair were terrified and they died in agony. The boys throwing the stones were going through a kind of hell I can't even begin to imagine. You think I wanted to watch that more than once?'

'So why did you?'

'Because he made me!' Poe half-yelled. He closed his eyes again and tried to control his breathing. Doctor Lang didn't press him to expand so Poe said, 'Cobb told me that if I didn't watch them all in the order he wanted to show them, I wouldn't be able to see the bigger picture. I wouldn't have the context for what happened later.'

'And you believed him? The man was obviously a sadist.'

'No, I didn't believe him and, yes, I have no doubt he was a sadist,' Poe said. 'But he said if I didn't watch all the videos, he wouldn't tell me where he'd buried Bethany Bowman.'

'He blackmailed you?'

'I suppose he did.'

'And you capitulated. Why?'

'I needed to know where Bethany was. I felt I owed her.'

'Was he telling the truth when he said watching all the videos would help you see the bigger picture?'

Poe nodded grimly. 'He was.'

'OK, before we get to what you saw, I need you to understand something, Washington,' Doctor Lang said.

'What's that?'

'I don't know what you're about to tell me, but it's OK *not* to be OK. Watching six men die like that can change someone.' She thought about what she had just said. 'Scratch that; watching six men die like that *should* change someone.'

'That's the thing, Doctor Lang,' Poe said. 'I *didn't* watch six men die.'

'You didn't?'

Poe shook his head.

'My apologies,' she said. 'I thought you said you'd watched them all.'

'I did.'

'Then—'

'I haven't told you about the sixth video yet,' Poe said. 'I haven't told you what happened when it was Aaron Bowman's turn.'

Chapter 98

Israel Cobb ejected the fifth video from his top-loading machine, a forty-year-old JVC. He put the cassette back in its cardboard sleeve and handed it to Poe.

Poe didn't want to touch it. He hadn't wanted to touch any of them, didn't think there would be enough soap in the world to scrub his hands clean. Nevertheless, he took the video and placed it into one of the evidence bags he'd brought in from his car. Just as he had done the previous four times.

So far, each video had been horrifically and gut-wrenchingly similar. The camera had started rolling when the victim was already strapped into the mercy chair. Four were hooded, one hadn't been. Cobb said they were given a choice. Poe wondered what he would have done if it had been him. Was it better to see it coming, to watch the rock all the way home? Or was it better to close your eyes and hope the first one turned your brain into mush? He hoped he would have had the courage to look his killer in the eye, scream 'Fuck you!' as the first one was hurled, but he suspected he'd have taken the hood.

The boys were brought in and there was a moment of shock while Cornelius Green explained what he wanted them to do. Although most of them pushed back, none of them were able to stand up to Cornelius when he turned into full-on foam-flecked ranting man. Like bending a dry twig, they could only bear so much before they snapped. Poe had little trouble believing Cornelius held the same control over the Children of Job members. No doubt they had been terrified and enthralled in equal measure.

So Cornelius had ranted and panted and sprayed spittle everywhere and eventually each boy had taken the rock he offered them.

Some threw them hard and fast, no doubt hoping to get it over with. Nathan Rose and the other boy aimed to kill from the first rock. Others were less sure. Maybe they hadn't played sport at school and weren't as confident with their throwing; maybe they just didn't want to hurt someone that day.

It was the gesture, a commitment to their cure that counted though.

If the boys threw one stone or ten, it didn't matter. Not to Cornelius. When the boy refused to take the next stone he was offered, *really* refused, Cornelius hugged him and cried with him. And after Israel Cobb had used his Stanley knife to finish off the man in the mercy chair, the three of them ignored the pooling blood and dropped to their knees to pray together.

Nathan Rose's victim was in his teens and couldn't have weighed more than eight stone. He had long, stringy hair and it sharply contrasted against Nathan's short back and sides with the neatly combed parting. He had refused the hood, the first one to do so, and as soon as he'd understood what was about to happen, he hurled venom at Cornelius, Israel and Nathan. Some of his words must have hit home as Cornelius threw Israel a roll of duct tape and told him to gag the boy. The tape was thick and adhesive, the kind Poe had called 'black nasty' when he was in the army. He didn't know whether that was just army slang or whether it was the tape's actual name.

Nathan threw ten stones and aimed for the victim's head each time, but it was obvious he didn't believe in what he was doing. Nathan Rose was the type of man who'd married a woman he wasn't attracted to simply so he would be accepted. Poe had little doubt he stoned a man to death for the same weak reasons.

In that moment, Poe hated him for it, and he was glad he had jumped through his loft hatch with a tow rope around his neck. Poe had carried the burden of thinking he had dredged up unpleasant memories. Now he knew Nathan Rose had ended his life so he wouldn't have to deal with what was coming.

What a fucking coward. Poe didn't care that he was dead.

***

291

Cobb reached for the sixth and final video, Aaron Bowman's video, but Poe said, 'New pair of gloves first, please.'

Poe had no control over the prints that were already on the video-cassettes, but he could damn well make sure no more were added. As far as Poe was concerned, every single person who had watched these videos was going to prison and that meant giving forensic services the fairest possible crack of the whip. If Cobb was insisting they watched these videos before he'd tell him what had happened to Bethany Bowman, they were both going to wear rubber gloves while they handled them.

Poe wasn't sure if he'd believed Cobb when he said Bethany was dead. It could simply be a ruse to make Poe suffer the same way Cobb had no doubt suffered over the years. Poe didn't care who you were; having images such as these playing on a loop in the memory bank would turn even the sanest person crazy.

This could be Cobb's last act of spite.

But if Bethany Bowman *was* buried in a shallow grave, they needed to know. Not just because her body would have to be recovered, but also because she was Superintendent Nightingale's one and only suspect in Cornelius Green's murder. If Bethany Bowman was dead, not only had she not killed Cornelius, she hadn't slaughtered her family either.

Poe couldn't risk Cobb clamming up after taking legal advice. So, even though he knew these videos would undoubtedly cause untold psychological scars to manage in the not-too-distant future, he told Cobb to play the final tape.

It was time to watch the Aaron Bowman video.

Chapter 99

Cobb removed the forensic gloves he was wearing and passed them to Poe. Poe sealed them in an evidence bag. He passed Cobb a fresh pair and watched him struggle into them. After Cobb had made a meal out of what was essentially a simple task, he held up his hands to show Poe.

'Happy?' he asked.

'We'll watch the Aaron Bowman video,' Poe replied, 'but then you're telling me what happened to his sister. And if this was only a ruse to make me watch this sick shit, you won't make it back to the station.'

Cobb shook the last video out of its sleeve and pushed it into the machine. He pressed down on the spring-loaded mechanism until it locked. The JVC didn't have a remote and Cobb didn't press play.

'What are we waiting for?' Poe said.

As he had done with the previous five films, Poe had his phone held up so he could document what came up on the screen. At least if the machine chewed the tape – a not unlikely possibility given how old Cobb's technology was – Poe would have a record of what was on the cassette.

'This is the last time Cornelius and I did this, Sergeant Poe,' Cobb said. 'In a moment you'll understand why.'

Up until then, if Poe had been asked what he was feeling he would have said 50 per cent rage/50 per cent revulsion. Rage at what Cornelius Green and Israel Cobb had forced those boys to do. Revulsion at the sickening way the victims had died. He thought both emotions were a rational response to what he had witnessed.

But right now all he felt was unease. He suppressed a shiver. Despite the night's lazy warmth, goosebumps popped up like hives.

The murders Cobb had filmed were as nightmarish as anything Poe had ever seen. Any one of them would attract life without the possibility of parole and Cobb was admitting to six. What was Cobb about to show him? What was a step too far for a man like this?

'What did you do, Israel?' Poe said, his voice thick with fear. 'What was different about Aaron Bowman?'

Cobb cleared his throat.

And told Poe a horror story.

Chapter 100

'The first thing you need to know, Sergeant Poe,' Cobb said, 'is that Aaron Bowman wasn't gay. He wasn't in a relationship with another boy. He wasn't exploring his sexuality that way.'

'He was heterosexual?' Poe asked.

'If he was anything.'

'Then why the hell did his parents put him through conversion therapy?' Poe said. 'I mean, I get from the way they treated Bethany that they had a cruel streak, but why put themselves at risk like that? You said the parents all knew what was going to happen.'

Cobb shrugged. 'It was implied before they signed up and it was made implicit afterwards. They were shown the video of what their sons had done. This was to show they hadn't been ripped off, but also to ensure their silence.'

'What was in it for Noah and Grace Bowman then?' Poe said. 'Because as far as I can tell, it was a lose–lose situation. They risked going to prison for the rest of their lives and they psychologically screwed up their only son for no reason at all. Why would they do that? I get that they were stupid and they were bigoted and they were sadistic, but the way they hid their abuse of Bethany meant they did at least have some animal cunning.'

'You're still not seeing the bigger picture, Sergeant Poe.'

'You keep saying that, Mr Cobb; that these videos provide the missing context. Fine, show me then. Press play and let's see this big picture of yours.'

The VCR had a mechanical button, and the force needed to press play turned the end of Cobb's finger white.

The familiar scene of the sectioned-off area of the old school basement flickered on to Cobb's old-fashioned television, a cathode-ray tube set. The bulky things that looked like they had an arse. Cobb had more problems with the tracking this time, as if the film had been viewed more often than the others. He fiddled with a button Poe couldn't see and the picture stopped jumping.

Poe noticed the difference immediately. The previous five videos had started with the victim already strapped into the mercy chair. This time it was empty.

Cobb pointed at the small boy on the right of the screen.

'You can only see the back of his head,' he said, 'but trust me, that's Aaron Bowman.'

'Why's the chair empty?'

Cobb ignored him. Instead, he paused the video and said, 'Do you notice anything different about Cornelius?'

Poe got down on his hands and knees and shunted towards the television. He put on his reading glasses and leaned into the screen. Cornelius Green was holding Aaron, talking quietly into his ear. Aaron was shaking, probably crying, but Cornelius looked . . . ecstatic. There was no other word for it. He couldn't have looked any happier if Jesus himself had just walked into the room wearing an 'I love Cornelius Green' T-shirt.

'He's not usually this excited,' Poe said.

'No, he is not,' Cobb confirmed. 'Do you want to know *why* he was so happy?'

Poe wasn't sure he did. He nodded anyway.

Cobb pressed play.

There was another minute of Cornelius talking to Aaron.

'Where were you at this point, Mr . . . ?' Poe asked.

He didn't finish. Cobb had walked onscreen.

And he wasn't alone.

He was pushing someone in front of him. Jabbing them in the back to keep them moving forwards. Someone small, smaller even than Aaron and he was tiny. He stumbled and fell. Cobb hauled him to his feet and forced him into the mercy chair. There was a brief struggle, but Cobb was a grown man and he was wrestling a child. He grabbed the boy's right arm and wrapped a leather strap around it. He pulled it tight and buckled it closed. He did the same with the left arm. With the arms done, he bent down to secure the ankles.

And for the first time Poe could see who was being restrained. He gasped. Whether it was out loud he didn't know. He tried to swallow but couldn't.

He understood the context now.

He saw Cobb's bigger picture.

'That's . . .' Poe whispered. He couldn't finish.

Cobb knew what he was going to say though. It was the only thing he *could* say.

'Yes, Sergeant Poe,' he said. 'The person in the mercy chair is Bethany Bowman.'

Chapter 101

'Aaron Bowman killed his own sister?' Doctor Lang said, stunned.

'As good as,' Poe confirmed.

'But . . . but why? What possible reason could there be? Let's not kid ourselves, murdering gay men to cure homosexuality is as abhorrent a thing as I've ever heard, but, if you view the world through Cornelius Green's bile-tinted glasses, to him at least, it *did* make a sick kind of sense. In his world the gay man is going to hell anyway, why not sacrifice him to save the soul of a believer? But asking a fifteen-year-old boy to stone his fourteen-year-old sister to death makes no sense whatsoever. Not from an extreme religious dogma point of view, and not from a common bloody sense point of view. Tell me why Bethany had to die, Washington?'

Poe's expression was a faraway one, like he was listening to music only he could hear. He tapped a beat on the desk. After a moment, his jaw hardened. Life came back to his eyes.

'I'll try to explain this as best I can,' he said. 'The way I think it happened.'

'The way you *think* it happened?'

'Call it an informed guess. Noah and Grace Bowman were by any standards unconventional parents. Yes, they hated their youngest daughter, but it went far deeper than that. And while Bethany clearly bore the brunt of their craziness, Aaron and Eve suffered too. Eve told me none of them were allowed friends and Bethany's journal confirmed this. Eve and Aaron were allowed to mingle with the other kids when they were at church, or the Children of Job compound, but other than that Noah and Grace kept them isolated.'

'That's probably why the bond between Aaron and Bethany was so strong. Younger siblings often cling to each other in abusive childhoods.'

'Funny you should mention that,' Poe said.

'Why?'

'Have you read *Flowers in the Attic* by Virginia Andrews?'

Doctor Lang frowned. 'Wasn't there a film adaption?'

'There was,' Poe confirmed.

'I think I saw it when I was younger.'

'You understand the basic premise: a woman trying to win back her father's approval after she'd married her half-brother, locks up her children in the attic of the family's ancestral home? After a year or so of confinement, the two elder children develop a physical attraction to each other.'

He let his words hang. It didn't take long for Doctor Lang to understand what he was saying.

'Bethany and Aaron were in a sexual relationship?' she asked.

Poe shook his head. 'According to Israel Cobb it never got that far. He also said it was a one-way thing. That Aaron became attracted to Bethany when he was going through puberty but she rebuffed him. I think she thought he was being silly.'

'Which isn't as uncommon as you might think,' Doctor Lang said. 'Once you put teenage hormones and insular childhoods in the melting pot of puberty, anything can happen. A brother developing a crush on his sister is surprisingly common. It rarely leads to anything, but it does happen. Was there a catalyst?'

'Aaron was caught with Bethany's underwear under his pillow. More than once, I think. That was what had got him in so much trouble on the night Bethany described in her journal.'

Poe stopped to trace a circle in some spilled tea.

'Grace spoke to Cornelius about it and Cornelius said he would cure Aaron the same way he cured homosexuality. Israel only became aware of what Cornelius had been planning when Aaron turned up with an overnight bag. By then Bethany was already sedated and secured somewhere in the compound.'

Doctor Lang shook her head in dismay. 'They sacrificed their youngest daughter to cure something a first-year psychologist wouldn't break a sweat on?'

'The more we delved into this case, the more we came to realise just how expendable Bethany was to Noah and Grace. It wasn't that they didn't care about her; it was more that they actively hated her. Cornelius knew about their feelings towards their daughter and, when he explained what they needed to do to cure Aaron, they jumped at the chance. Probably wished they'd thought of it sooner.'

'They were monsters,' she said.

'They were.'

'And you watched this video?'

'I did,' Poe said.

Chapter 102

'You've got to understand how small Aaron Bowman was,' Poe said to Doctor Lang. 'I mean, he was tiny. We had the video cleaned up later, of course, but even on the rough cut Israel Cobb showed me, Aaron could easily have passed for eleven or twelve years old.'

'You don't have to tell me this, Washington,' Doctor Lang said. 'Not if you don't want to.'

Poe continued, as if he hadn't heard her. 'He was terrified,' he said. 'So was Bethany, of course, although she also had a resigned look. Almost as if she'd expected something like this to happen to her. But, out of all the videos I watched, Aaron kicked back the most. He resisted to the point I thought Cornelius might actually give up.'

'But he didn't?'

'No, he was enjoying himself too much to stop. I have no idea what Bethany could have done to make so many people hate her, but Cornelius was definitely one of them. In fact, the only person in her life who *didn't* seem to hate her, was the person throwing rocks at her.'

'Cornelius convinced Aaron in the end?'

'Convinced isn't the word I'd use. It took almost an hour of in-his-face ranting, but in the end, yes, Aaron surrendered to the inevitable.'

Poe closed his eyes as he recalled the final moments of Bethany Bowman's life.

'Aaron could barely lift the first rock Cornelius handed him,' he said. 'He had to throw it underhand, like he was playing French cricket. It bounced harmlessly off Bethany's shoulder. I doubt it even bruised her.'

'And the second?'

'There was a break between the first and second.'

'What happened?'

'Cornelius and Israel had a blazing row. Israel was begging him to let Bethany wear the hood and Cornelius was refusing.'

'She wasn't offered a hood?'

'No, for some reason Cornelius was being particularly vindictive with her. He'd instigated the murder of five men before Bethany, but he hadn't taken any pleasure from their deaths. Like I said, he referred to them as "it" if he referred to them at all. They were just things to him, of no more importance than the toy from a Christmas cracker. But when Israel was begging him to let Bethany wear a hood he seemed genuinely happy. As if Israel's distress was equally as important as Bethany's terror.'

'Like he was punishing Israel as well.'

'That's *exactly* what it was like,' Poe agreed. 'I asked Israel why Cornelius had acted this way and he swore he didn't know.'

'Bethany was never offered the hood?'

Poe shook his head. 'No,' he said. 'And to be honest, I'm not sure she'd have accepted it anyway. You should have seen her, Doctor Lang. She was as fierce as a mongoose. When the argument was over and Aaron was ready to throw his second rock – a more manageable one this time – Bethany started taunting Cornelius. This fourteen-year-old girl, strapped to a chair and knowing she was about to die, began calling him names. Admittedly she didn't seem to know any good swear words, so it was mainly "sinner" and the old Bowman family favourite, "bad biscuit", but that simple act of defiance is the bravest thing I've ever seen. I honestly don't think I've admired anyone as much as I admired Bethany Bowman.'

'But she died anyway?'

Tears stung the back of Poe's eyes. One rolled down his cheek. It wasn't the first he'd shed over Bethany Bowman, and it wouldn't be the last. He'd wept over the five dead men too, of course, but none of them had hit him as hard as Bethany. Right up until the end, her raw, untameable spirit had remained unquenched.

Doctor Lang passed him the box of tissues and took one for

herself. She wasn't crying, but liquid was brimming at the bottom of her eyelids. Poe dried his face and answered her question.

'Cornelius made Aaron carry on throwing rocks until he was too weak to lift them,' he said. 'I counted seven in total.'

'Did he kill her?'

'No. I don't think Aaron had the upper body strength to do more than bruise her.'

'But you saw her die?'

'I did.'

'Was it Cornelius?'

'It wasn't.'

'What happened?'

'Israel and Cornelius had their second row of the night,' Poe replied. 'It was short and it was vicious, but when it was over, Israel Cobb, as he had previously, walked over to the mercy chair, pulled out his Stanley knife and slit Bethany Bowman's throat.'

Chapter 103

'You arrested him after that?' Doctor Lang said.

'Who, Israel Cobb?' Poe said. 'I read him his rights as soon as I'd watched the first video.'

'You took him to the station?'

'I called Superintendent Nightingale and told her what Cobb had told me. What he'd *shown* me. She sent someone straight over, but as he lived in the middle of nowhere we still had some time and I didn't want to waste it. Not while he was so chatty. He still wanted to talk and I still wanted to hear what he had to say.'

'What did you discuss?'

'First of all, I wanted as much detail as I could get about the five men he and Cornelius had killed. I had other questions, of course, but this seemed to be the most pressing. I took the names of the boys who'd attended the courses, the four we didn't know about. The names of the parents too. I asked him why we wouldn't find Bethany's body in the sixth grave. He said they'd used five of the graves to dispose of the dead men, but even though Cornelius had arranged a sixth for Bethany, Cobb didn't use it. It's another of the things that Israel and Cornelius had their falling out over. He didn't tell Cornelius he had made his own arrangements for Bethany's burial until the following day.'

'Where was her body?'

'Cobb wouldn't say,' Poe said. 'He said that, rather than hiding her underneath someone else's coffin, he'd found somewhere, in his words, "peaceful, on a sunny hill with a nice view". He didn't want her disturbed, not by us, not by Cornelius.'

'Did you ask him the obvious?'

'I did.'

'You asked him why he'd told you any of this? He was sentencing himself to life in prison. Why would he do that?'

'I thought long and hard about his motivations,' Poe admitted. 'At first I thought he'd panicked when he discovered we knew what his tattoos signified. Probably thought he'd have to cop to something and he knew he'd get away with whipping the boys' feet. Although there *is* a limit to consent when it comes to causing physical harm, when I told him Nathan Rose was dead, he knew there were no living witnesses left to contradict him. Admitting some culpability was more believable than a flat-out denial, and a lie is best hidden among truths. The tattoos were all in Cornelius's handwriting, so I guess it might have fooled a particularly stupid jury.'

'So why did—?'

'Why did he decide to show me those videos? Why admit to murders he didn't have to?'

Doctor Lang nodded.

'He had his reasons,' Poe said.

Chapter 104

'I need you to go home, Poe,' Superintendent Nightingale said.

'I'm fine.'

'Don't give me that macho shit. You're *not* fine. Anyone with half a brain can see you're not fine. How could you be? You've just watched six snuff movies while sitting next to one of the men responsible. I'd be worried if you were fine. I only watched a bit of the first one and I wanted to go home and hug my kids.'

It was quarter to four in the morning and they were in the back of Nightingale's car. Poe had met her in a layby, a mile from the Children of Job compound. Nightingale's uniformed cops had arrived at Cobb's and arrested him again. He was now safely tucked away in a police cell. And because Nathan Rose had chosen a short drop with a sudden stop, rather than face up to what he'd been involved in, Poe had made sure Cobb was put on suicide watch. He still had questions to answer.

CSI had turned up fifteen minutes after uniform and seized the videos. The team would stay in Cobb's house and process it with everything they had. Poe wasn't sure they would find anything else, but not doing it would be irresponsible.

Nightingale hadn't driven to Cobb's as Poe had expected. Instead, she had called and asked his opinion on the veracity of the videos. Poe had replied, 'Trust, but verify, ma'am.' He thought they were real, but Bradshaw had told him there was now some bullshit called 'deep fakes', where perverts put celebrities' faces on to porn stars. Apparently it looked very realistic. Poe didn't think that was the case here – the tapes looked as old as Cobb claimed they were – but until someone who knew about this stuff had checked, 'trust but verify' was as certain as he was prepared to be.

Nightingale had thanked him, got a crusty old magistrate out of bed and demanded he sign a warrant to search the Children of Job compound. She told him she had six snuff movies he could watch if he didn't believe she had reasonable grounds. The magistrate had signed without comment.

The time on the warrant was 4 a.m. so there was a short delay before they could execute it. Nightingale's car was the last in a long line of police vehicles. Dogs, specialist search teams, CSI vans, the works.

At the stroke of four they would go in mob-handed.

'OK, I'm *not* fine,' Poe admitted. 'But I don't think going back to an empty cottage is the best thing for me right now. I need to be among the living for a bit longer.'

'Estelle is—'

'—in London, ma'am,' Poe cut in. 'On her way to Brussels.'

'If I can finish?'

'Sorry.'

'I was about to say that Estelle is getting on the first flight out of Heathrow,' Nightingale said. 'She lands in Newcastle in a few hours.'

'But how . . . ?'

'How did she find out? How do you think?'

'Tilly told her,' Poe said. 'I really wish she hadn't.'

'Face it, Poe; you have people who care about you now. You're no longer a weirdo loner. So go home. You've done enough; let us handle it from here. And don't forget, I'm a superintendent and you're a ten-a-penny sergeant. If I need to, I'll order you. Even have uniform follow you with their blues and twos on.'

Poe scowled. He knew Nightingale was right, knew that relationships were a two-way street, and Estelle being worried about him wasn't something he could brush off. But until he'd established, in his own mind at least, that the videos had been filmed in the old school basement, he wouldn't be able to sleep anyway.

'You up for a compromise, ma'am?'

'No. Go home.'

'It won't take long to confirm the films were shot here,' Poe said regardless. 'The amount of blood on those videos was considerable. Even if they used bleach on the floor, some of it will have soaked into the concrete. And if we find blood then it's safe to assume the murders weren't staged. As soon as we've established that, there's really nothing more for me to do. I'll gladly go home and wait for Estelle.'

'Fine,' Nightingale said, throwing up her arms in capitulation. 'You can stay until we've found blood. But, as we have a specialist cadaver dog with us, I imagine that will be two minutes after we're through the front door.'

Poe scowled again, realising he'd been played, but also recognising that Nightingale was operating from a good place.

She checked her watch. 'Ten minutes,' she said. 'Will they be expecting us?'

'Doubt it,' Poe replied, thinking about Joshua Meade. 'I kind of got the impression Cornelius had become a bit of an embarrassment to the newer members. Some might even have been relieved by his death. That it would allow Joshua and the more media-savvy bigots to press the reset button. The country's becoming less interested in organised religion every year, and he knows that while screaming into the void might have worked for them in the past, it won't now. But with Cornelius Green dead, Joshua can concentrate on reshaping the Children of Job into a lobby group.'

'Out with the old cult, in with the new?'

Poe nodded. 'I think if Joshua had known there were skeletons this smelly in the cupboard he'd have distanced himself from them a long time ago. People like him have an agenda, one they relentlessly pursue, and they can't afford scandal.'

'Which leads me to my next question: now we know Bethany Bowman didn't murder Cornelius, who the hell did? I was going to ask if Joshua Meade was worth a pull, but I guess you'd say no?'

'Anything's possible, but Joshua doesn't make sense,' Poe said, shrugging. 'I think it's Aaron we need to be looking for now. I'm convinced that when he was old enough and big enough, he took his revenge on the parents who arranged for his baby sister to be murdered. It explains why it was only Noah and Grace's bodies that were recovered.'

Nightingale twisted in her seat to face him. 'He faked his death?'

'It fits every fact we have. He kills his parents and leaves behind evidence that it was his dead sister who did it. He probably still had some of her stuff. Maybe he even blamed her for what he'd been through.'

'And the row between him and Bethany?'

'Never happened,' Poe said. '*Can't* have happened – Bethany was already dead. But Noah and Grace needed to explain away her absence to both Eve and the school. They make up a row between Bethany and Aaron. Eve wouldn't have believed Bethany had run away after yet another argument with her parents – she was in almost permanent conflict with them by then – but running away after a row with her beloved Aaron? I imagine that was something Eve *would* believe.'

'And it was in Aaron's interests to go along with it.'

'It was,' Poe nodded. 'He'd just seen what his parents were capable of. And he had just been involved in his sister's murder.'

'And Cornelius's murder?' Nightingale said. 'Do you think Aaron killed him as well?'

'Hard to think anything else. If he's alive, he has every motive.'

'Why wait all these years though?'

'No idea. Maybe he tried to forgive Cornelius but couldn't. Or maybe something triggered him.'

They lapsed into silence as they worked out the kink in the new theory.

'Badgers,' Nightingale said eventually.

Poe blew out a whoosh of relief. The gap between the murders must have been bothering him more than he'd thought.

'It was all over the news,' Nightingale continued. 'It was even on CNN and Al Jazeera.'

'I remember. Sky News tried to interview me about it.'

'That's right,' Nightingale laughed. 'Sophy Ridge had to bleep out your response. But anyway, if Aaron had seen this on TV and understood the significance, it could have elicited something, a primal response he'd managed to keep in a bottle until then.'

'Or maybe he just didn't want Cornelius talking,' Poe said. 'He knew the badger would start an investigation, one that might lead to him. And he'd have known that somewhere there was a tape of his sister's murder.'

'So why not kill Israel Cobb as well?' Nightingale said. 'He'd already killed his parents and he's now killed the man who engineered the whole thing; why not go for the set? Why not kill the man who slit his sister's throat?'

'We only found Israel because we put Tilly on it,' Poe replied. 'Alice hadn't been able to find him, and she'd been looking for over fifteen years.' He paused. 'Or maybe there's something we don't yet know.'

Nightingale snorted. 'In this case? I'd be surprised if there wasn't. And you have no idea why Cobb showed you those videos? He must know he'll spend the rest of his life in prison.'

'I don't think he gives a shit. Which is weird, as he certainly gave a shit when I first got there. Couldn't get his tattoo cover story in quick enough. Soon as he realised we'd linked them to the extra bodies in the graves he immediately blamed Cornelius. Said he had no idea what the alphanumeric strings meant. I don't doubt that what he and Cornelius had done had eaten away at him over the years – hell, I cried all the way over here and I've only lived with it for an hour – but something happened tonight that moved him from keeping his role covered up to full disclosure. At first, I thought it was something to do with Bethany; he certainly had a visceral reaction to Tilly's age-progression photo, but that doesn't make sense. She's dead, but so were the other five on the videos.'

'Perhaps seeing her as the woman she would have become pushed him over the edge?' Nightingale said. 'Like you said, there's only so much guilt you can suppress before it starts leaking. If the badgers triggered Aaron, maybe the age-progressed image of Bethany triggered Cobb?'

She checked her watch again.

'We'll have to revisit this, Poe,' she said. 'As far as I'm concerned it's four a.m. and I have a warrant to execute. Let's get these idiots out of bed.'

Chapter 105

Nightingale had said the cadaver dog, a black Labrador called Pat, would sniff out the blood in two minutes. Pat didn't. In fact, Pat didn't find any blood at all, not in the amount the videos had suggested he would.

Nightingale and her crew had woken Joshua Meade along with the rest of the Children of Job's live-in members. He had objected and issued threats of religious persecution lawsuits, but it was water off a superintendent's back to Nightingale. It was what happened when search warrants were executed and she'd heard it all before. Anyway, it was hard to take Joshua seriously. Puce-faced with rage, he was wearing an eighteenth-century nightgown, the kind worn by upper-class Victorians and out-of-touch Tories. If he'd been wearing a bedcap Poe would have assumed the man had an undisclosed Scrooge fetish.

Poe glared at Joshua, convinced he must have known something about what had gone on prior to his tenure at the Children of Job. Israel Cobb said no one else had been involved, but surely someone must have heard the screaming. Seen the bodies being taken out. Heard a rumour.

Joshua bristled under Poe's naked hostility. 'Who do you think you are, Poe?' he barked.

'I'm the Ghost of the Children of Job Are Finished, you sinister motherfucker,' Poe barked back. 'When this is all over, I'm making you the most famous cult in the world. By the time me and Tilly have finished, not even the Westboro Baptist Church will return your calls.'

'How dare you! The Children of Job is *not* a cult, it's a—'

'That's enough!' Nightingale snapped. 'Poe, if you can't be civil,

I'll have you removed. And Mr Meade, I would advise you to tread carefully. *Very* carefully. We are way beyond Cornelius Green's murder now.'

While Nightingale performed the legal niceties of explaining what they were looking for and what the search warrant allowed them to seize, a team secured the old school basement.

Pat the cadaver dog went in first. He didn't bark or otherwise indicate there was anything there.

By the time Nightingale had finished with Joshua, Pat was back outside and CSI were inside, chipping away at the concrete floor, taking samples to the mobile lab they'd brought with them. They split the basement into one-metre grids and took a sample from each one.

Still nothing.

Poe didn't like the basement. Didn't like to think he was loitering in the same place Bethany and the other victims had died. Instead, he removed his forensic barrier clothing and sat in the main hall with the guys not actively involved in processing the basement. The seats and tables that had been set up for the graduation ceremony had gone, replaced with pews arranged in a herringbone pattern. A pulpit centred the stage. Poe sat on one of the pews and stared into space for fifteen minutes, trying to figure out what the lack of blood meant. He was convinced they were in the right place. That it was the school basement on those videos. But if the dogs or the CSI team couldn't find blood, it meant the videos had been staged, and that made no sense at all. Poe doubted anyone at the Children of Job would have had the technical skills to pull off something so sophisticated, and even if they had, the bodies being pulled out of those graves were very real. Nightingale had taken a call earlier confirming that a corpse had been secreted under the coffin in another exhumed grave. Including the badger-exhumed grave, that was three for three now.

Nightingale wasn't about to give up after an hour. Poe knew that even if she had to dig right down to the school's foundations, she would find corroborating evidence. She'd seen one of the videos as well. Motivation like that didn't wane easily.

Poe glanced at the huge crucifix hanging above the stage, the one the Christian rock band had been rehearsing under, in what seemed like a lifetime ago. In the harsh CSI lights, the crucifix seemed even bigger than he remembered. None of the cops or techs or support staff were paying the crucifix the slightest bit of attention, which once again reminded Poe of the closing scenes in *The Life of Brian*. He started humming 'Always Look on the Bright Side of Life' then stopped. He didn't feel like looking on the bright side of life right now. He wanted to brood.

Nightingale came up from the basement entrance to the left of the stage. She caught his eye, pulled down her mask and flashed him a what-you-gonna-do? grimace. She grabbed two coffees from the urn that someone had set up and sat down beside him. Poe shuffled along to give her room. She passed him a Styrofoam cup. It was full to the brim with black coffee. 'It tastes foul, but it's as hot as a volcano and loaded with caffeine,' she said.

Poe took a sip. She was right; it was foul. He drank some more anyway. 'Anything?' he asked, knowing there wasn't. If there had been she'd have led with it.

'There's nothing down there,' she said.

'There has to be. The brickwork, the floor, the height of the walls, it all matches what was in the videos.'

'It does,' she agreed. 'And don't get me wrong; we're not giving up. I'm just telling you it doesn't look good.'

They sat in silence and finished their coffees. Nightingale got to her feet and said, 'I'm going back down.' She faced Poe. He hoped he didn't look as tired as she did. 'Do yourself a favour, Poe – go home. Have a long, hot shower. Try to scrub the stench off your soul. Believe me, you don't want to live with this any longer than you need to. Trust us to do our jobs.'

Poe nodded. It wasn't the worst advice he'd been given. And a shower did sound good right now. Maybe a long walk with Doyle and Edgar. 'I'll give it another half hour then I think I'll do exactly that, ma'am.'

'Go now,' she said. 'I promise you, yours will be the first number I call if we make a breakthrough.'

'I can't.'
'Why not?'
Poe pointed at the door.
'That's why,' he said.

Chapter 106

'Is it true?' Alice Symonds shrieked, running into the main hall.

A uniformed constable tried to stop her but he was too old and Alice was too nimble. She dodged around him and skidded to a halt in front of Poe.

'Is it true?' she asked again, louder this time.

Joshua Meade had followed her in. He was wearing a suit. Poe could see confusion etched on his face. Alice had discarded 'Mad Alice' like a snake sheds its skin. She was just Alice now.

'I don't know what you know, Alice,' Poe said gently. He suspected he *did* know what she knew, but until she'd confirmed it he wasn't going to admit anything.

'I've been told Bethany's dead,' she said.

'Who told you that?'

She didn't answer.

'Now isn't the time, Alice,' Poe said.

'I don't care; tell me!'

'Not until you've told me who told you.'

'I've been trying to find out what happened to Bethany for years,' she said. 'I didn't limit myself to this place when it came to gathering information.'

'You have a source inside the police.' Poe didn't phrase it as a question. Of *course* she'd cultivated someone inside the police. It's what he'd have done.

'I've been told there are videos.'

Poe sighed. He didn't want to break this news to her. He also knew he was the only one who could.

'I think we'd better sit down,' he said.

***

'Aaron killed Bethany?' Alice said it like she was testing some unfamiliar words.

'Technically I doubt he did more than give her some nasty bruises,' Poe said. 'It was Israel Cobb who actually killed her.'

'But she's definitely dead?'

'He slit her throat,' Poe confirmed.

'Did you *see* this happen, or did Israel Cobb simply tell you that it happened?'

'I saw it. She's dead.'

Alice slumped on the pew they were sharing. Poe didn't think he'd ever seen anyone look so defeated.

'But you should have seen her,' he said. 'She fought them every step of the way; didn't give an inch. I'm not saying this just to offer comfort, but it was the bravest thing I've ever seen.'

Alice nodded. 'That sounds like Bethany,' she sniffed. Her eyes widened as the ramifications occurred to her. 'She didn't kill Grace and Noah then.'

'She couldn't have.'

'It must have been Aaron.'

'That's what we think,' Poe said. 'We assume he faked his death and left Bethany's clasp knife for the police to find. Cops jumped to the only conclusion they could.'

'I'm glad Grace and Noah are dead then. And I'm glad Cornelius Green died in agony.'

Poe looked over his shoulder, checked he couldn't be overheard. 'I am too,' he said quietly.

'Does Eve know yet?'

'Not yet. I'll drop in on my way home. Better it comes from someone she knows.'

'This will devastate her,' Alice said.

'It will,' Poe agreed. 'She could probably use a friend from the old days if you're ever in the area.'

'I'll call in this week. Make sure she's OK.'

Poe spent ten more minutes with her. Alice wanted to talk about Bethany and he was saddened to hear she was now referring to her in the past tense.

'You going to be OK?' Poe asked.

'I should ask you the same thing.'

'I'm not sure that I am,' he replied honestly.

'Do you need to talk to someone about it?'

Poe looked up. 'I doubt I'll have a choice,' he said.

Bradshaw had just entered the old school gymnasium.

Chapter 107

Poe left Alice to her memories and gestured for Bradshaw and Linus to join him on the stage. The three of them were perched on the edge, facing the busy gymnasium, legs dangling. Bradshaw's eyes were red, like she'd touched them after chopping chillies, and her face was pale and pinched. She knew what he'd seen, and even though he'd tried to downplay the horror of the videos, there wasn't really any nice way of saying you'd watched six young lives being snuffed out. Linus looked even worse. The young spook didn't seem to have enjoyed his first experience of a murder investigation. In fact, the more Poe thought about it, he realised they *both* had pale, pinched faces.

'You've watched the videos, haven't you?' he said.

Bradshaw sniffed and nodded. 'Only one.'

'Even though I explicitly told you not to?'

She faced him, her expression defiant. 'It's not only *your* job to watch these things, Poe. Cumbria's high-tech crime unit have a backlog, and even if they didn't have, none of them know how to verify the authenticity of an old VHS tape. And also, DI Stephanie Flynn is my line manager, not you. You don't have the authority to stop me.'

Poe sighed. He *did* have the authority. They both knew that. He was a sergeant and Bradshaw wasn't. He'd explained many, many times how a command and control organisation worked, but as she'd only ever had him as a role model it had always been a case of monkey see/monkey do. He'd previously taken advantage of her newfound rebellious nature; he could hardly complain about it now. So, instead of getting cross, he said, 'Is the video authentic?'

'While I have no way of telling if the murder was staged, I can say with absolute certainty that the video has not been tampered with or edited in any way. It is a genuine recording.'

'Why hasn't the cadaver dog found anything in the basement then?'

'I don't know, Poe. But it was definitely filmed down there. I've compared the photos I took when Joshua Meade gave us a tour of the basement. The colour, shape and texture of the brickwork is distinctive.'

'Did you watch the video, Snoopy?'

'I did,' Linus said. 'I wish I hadn't.'

'So why did you?'

'I'm here to observe.'

'That's a stupid answer,' Poe said. 'Like Tilly said, it's our job to swim in this shit. And we do it so people like you can sit in your nice London offices and post things like "Defund the police" on Twitter. And that's OK; that's how it's supposed to be. This isn't a participation sport but you've gone out of your way to join in. Why?'

'I told you, there's an ongoing audit—'

'Oh fuck off,' Poe said. He turned his back on Linus. He wasn't in the mood to be lied to. Not right now.

'You must be hungry, Poe,' Bradshaw said, rummaging in her bag. 'We stopped off at an all-night supermarket on the way and got you something to eat.'

'Did this "something" once have bones?'

'Of course not.'

'I don't want it then,' he said.

Bradshaw handed over a tub of pre-prepared food.

'What's this?' he said, eyeing the contents suspiciously.

'Don't be so ungrateful, Poe.'

He pointed at some brown things sitting on top of what looked like tomatoes, carrots and weeds. They were the shape and colour of small onion bhajis, but he doubted he'd be that lucky. 'What are those things?'

'Falafels, Poe. They're made from ground chickpeas. They're an excellent source of fibre.'

He opened the lid and sniffed the tub's contents. 'They look like dog balls.' He picked one up and nibbled on it. 'Next,' he said, passing the tub to Linus.

'Oh, give it here,' Bradshaw said, her face splitting into a grin. 'That's not really what I bought you.' She reached into her bag again and pulled out a brown paper bag. It had the most gorgeous-looking grease stains. She passed it across. 'I had to get Linus to buy this, Poe. The smell at the hot food counter was making me feel ill.'

Poe peered into the bag and breathed out in relief. It was an honest-to-goodness, no-frills butcher's pork pie. Chopped pork, salty jelly and thick, crunchy pastry. He took a bite and sighed in satisfaction. He hadn't realised just how hungry he was.

'You do realise that every pork pie you eat takes scientifically measurable time off your expected life span, Poe?' Bradshaw said.

Poe looked at the CSI investigators, the detectives, the rest of the cops in the gymnasium. Decided he didn't like what he saw. 'Is there any way to speed up the process?' he said.

Bradshaw didn't answer. She was munching on her weird salad and checking her emails. She looked OK, better than he felt. He wished she hadn't had to watch a single second of those videos, but now that she had he at least knew the tapes were genuine. If she said they hadn't been tampered with, they hadn't been tampered with.

Poe jumped down from the stage. The basement was beneath his feet and he didn't want to be near it any more. The night was still warm, the main hall was getting stuffy and he needed some fresh air. Eating a pork pie under the last of the night's stars might lift his spirits. In fact, even the *thought* of eating a pie under the stars lifted his spirits. He started singing 'Always Look on the Bright Side of Life' on his way out, loud enough that if Joshua was nearby he'd be sure to hear.

He reached the gymnasium exit just as he got to the part about life seeming jolly rotten. He stopped and looked at his feet. He muttered to himself then turned around and marched back down the hall. When he got to the crucifix on the stage, ignoring the open-mouthed Bradshaw and Linus, he turned round and started singing again, to himself this time, as he walked back out. He reached the exit at the jolly rotten bit again.

'That's weird,' he said.

Chapter 108

'I'm not convinced, Poe,' Nightingale said. 'If I do what you're asking on the basis of a Monty Python song I'm going to end up as a cautionary tale on the National Investigators' Exam.'

'I'm telling you, ma'am,' Poe insisted, 'when I walked the length of the main hall I got to the jolly rotten bit of "Always Look on the Bright Side of Life". When I was in the basement with Joshua, I only got to the line about life's gristle. I know it's not a scientific way of measuring distance—'

'What, really?'

'But I'm telling you – even taking the stage into account, the basement is at least ten feet shorter in length than the gymnasium.'

'It could have been built that way.'

Instead of responding, Poe pressed his hand against the basement wall. The mortar was smooth and the bricks were cherry-red. Not the pale red of bricks that had been weathered by time, these were the same colour they'd have been on the day they were baked. The question was: when had they been laid – at the same time as the three other walls in the basement, or was this wall newer? Poe thought a different brickie had laid these ones, but he was wise enough to know that could be confirmation bias.

Nightingale ran her hands through her hair, damp with sweat, her resolve weakening. 'We'd need to measure it properly,' she said.

'Of course.'

'And we'll need a structural engineer to do an assessment before we can remove so much as one brick.'

'That's very sensible.'

'Which will take at least three days.'

'Maybe even longer,' Poe said.

Nightingale turned on her heels and said to the men and women in the basement, 'OK, everyone out. Get some fresh air while I make a couple of phone calls.' She followed her staff but turned at the bottom of the stairs. She gave Poe a look. It was only fleeting, but it was the look he'd been expecting.

As soon as she'd left, Poe grabbed one of the sledgehammers the CSI techs had used to break up the concrete floor.

'Whatever are you doing, Poe?' Bradshaw asked.

'What's it look like I'm doing, Tilly?'

'It looks like you're about to knock down that wall. But I know that can't be true as Superintendent Nightingale has just left to make sure we have permission.'

'That's one way of looking at it,' Poe said. It had been a while since he had held a sledgehammer and it took him a moment to get used to the unfamiliar weight.

'I don't think there *is* another way of looking at it, Poe.'

'Superintendent Nightingale and I shared a glance before she left.'

'Excuse me?'

'She passed on an unspoken message. She wants me to buy her seventy-two hours. That's how long it'll take to get the permission she needs.'

'That's because if it isn't a false wall, it might be a *load-bearing* wall,' Linus said.

'But what if it *isn't* a load-bearing wall, Snoopy?'

'What if it isn't . . . ?!' Linus spluttered. 'That's not how risk assessments work!'

'The only thing a risk assessment will achieve is delay. Some health-and-safety cube dweller will insist we can't go ahead until a natterjack toad survey has been carried out and the ceiling is shored up with props and jacks.'

'Linus is right, Poe,' Bradshaw said. 'Doing this is dangerous.'

'Thank you, Tilly,' Linus said. 'Someone has to be responsible for thinking about—'

'You'll need safety goggles,' Bradshaw nipped in, passing Poe a pair of Perspex glasses.

'Oh my God, you two are bloody nuts!'

'Feel free to leave,' Poe said.

'Well, we're certainly not standing around waiting for the roof to come down on our heads. We'll see you outside. Come on, Tilly.'

'I'm staying here, Linus.'

'And I'm going to insist you come with me.'

After Poe and Bradshaw had stopped laughing, Poe said, 'Piss off, Snoopy.'

Linus burned bright red before turning on his heels and stomping out of the basement. Bradshaw watched him disappear up the basement steps. 'He's an idiot, isn't he, Poe?'

'He is, Tilly. But that doesn't mean he's wrong. Perhaps you'd better wait upstairs too.'

'No, Poe.'

'This isn't one of those times when we both have to be in danger, Tilly. It's OK for one of us to be safe.'

'That's not why I'm staying, Poe.'

'It isn't?'

She shook her head. 'I don't think you can see it yet, but this case has taken a huge toll on you.'

'Oh, I *can* see it. I don't understand why that means you have to stand under a collapsing roof.'

'If this *is* a false wall, you shouldn't be on your own when you see what's behind it.'

Poe rested the sledgehammer on his foot, winced as he remembered he wasn't wearing steel-toe-capped boots. 'You're a good friend, Tilly,' he said. He then grasped the handle, lifted it into position and widened his stance so his feet were shoulder-width apart. He aimed at a spot on the wall about four feet from the ground and smashed the sledgehammer against it as hard as he could.

Chapter 109

The basement wall was sturdy and well made, but it was no match for Poe as he poured his rage into every swing of the sledgehammer. The first crunching blow sent a piece of brick shrapnel humming towards his head. He swerved out of the way, but it nicked his ear. He felt the warm blood on his neck.

'Maybe you'd better stand back a bit, Tilly,' Poe said.

There were no references to his authority this time. Bradshaw stepped to the side and made sure her safety glasses were snug.

Poe lifted the sledgehammer again and sent it crashing against the wall.

He did it again.

And again.

As Bradshaw watched in silence, Poe hit the wall until the sweat had plastered his hair to his forehead. He hit it until his eyes were stinging. He hit it until he could no longer lift the sledgehammer. And when that happened he ignored the blood and the pain and used his hands to tear out the remaining loose bricks until he had made a hole big enough to fit his head through. He stepped back, panting, grabbed a CSI lamp and dragged it across the floor. He aimed it through the hole but the air behind the gap was thick with brick dust and visibility was down to zero.

He couldn't tell if it was a walled-up room or just a wall cavity.

Poe spent the extra time widening the hole. It wasn't long until he could fit his head and torso through. While he waited for the dust to settle, he rooted among the search team's gear until he found a heavy-duty torch. It was twelve inches long with a black, vulcanised rubber handle. He headed back to the hole and forced his upper body through. He switched on the torch. In the dark basement the beam was an almost physical thing. A solid white tube, like one of the lightsabers Bradshaw waved around at Halloween.

The gap behind the wall was almost fifteen feet deep, far too big for a cavity wall. Poe aimed the torch straight ahead and picked out the wall on the other side. The *original* wall. He was right; this end of the basement had been sectioned off. The wall he'd knocked through was a false wall.

The beam of light picked out something among the gloom and the dust. Something angular, a shape even a child could recognise.

'Oh no,' he whispered.

Waves of nausea threatened to overwhelm Poe. He jerked his head out of the hole in the wall and raced up the basement stairs, Bradshaw hot on his heels. He grabbed an empty evidence bag from the CSI table and, as his stomach heaved, got it to his mouth and vomited noisily.

When he'd finished, Bradshaw passed him a moist towelette and he cleaned his mouth and chin. He threw it into the bag and sat on one of the pews, head in his hands. Bradshaw passed him another towelette, took a seat beside him and hugged him tight. He pressed the damp cloth against his face and the back of his neck.

'What did you see, Poe?' Bradshaw asked.

A crowd of cops had begun to gather around him. One of them was Nightingale. Joshua Meade was hovering over her shoulder. Poe struggled to his feet and shouldered his way through the crowd. The gymnasium descended into a charged silence. Joshua shrank back.

'Did you know?' Poe said, quiet, menacing.

'Know what?' Joshua said, backing away.

Nightingale nodded at two uniformed cops and they blocked Poe's path. They didn't put a finger on him, but the message was clear: they would if he tried to push past them.

'That Cornelius Green and Israel Cobb were murdering people as part of their conversion therapy!'

'What *are* you talking about?'

Joshua's righteous indignation had returned now he was no longer in physical danger.

'Cornelius Green was abducting gay men from the streets and he was forcing those poor boys to murder them. Right under where we're standing now, he was strapping them into something he called the mercy chair and making the boys stone them to death. So, I'm asking you: did you know?'

Poe took another step forward. One of the cops held up an arm. Poe would now have to go around him or through him.

Joshua considered what Poe had said. The cops watching Poe aside, all eyes were now on the Children of Job's most senior member. It didn't look as though anyone had any sympathy for him. The mood had darkened.

'Like I told you, I wasn't here then.'

'This is still on you!' Poe snapped. 'People like Cornelius Green can't exist in a vacuum. They need their enablers, their snivelling politicians. They need people like you to justify their actions.'

'That's enough, Poe,' Nightingale said.

'You think the Nazis had the skills to manufacture their gas chambers, ma'am?' He jabbed his finger in Joshua's direction. 'No, they needed their lickspittles, people too scared to dirty their hands but fanatical about the cause nonetheless.'

Joshua said nothing.

'Or maybe I'm wrong,' Poe continued. 'Tell me you condemn what Cornelius did. Say it now. Loud enough so the rest of your obscene cult can hear.'

'I'll do no such thi—'

'Say it!'

Joshua looked round for support. Got nothing from the massed ranks of Nightingale's cops, technicians and ancillary staff. They didn't know everything, but they knew enough. For a moment, Poe thought Joshua was going to capitulate. But an excited chatter at the far end of the hall caught his attention. Some Children of Job members had entered, no doubt drawn to the shouting. They were standing around aimlessly, like there had been a badly organised fire drill.

Poe saw Joshua's resolve harden.

'If what you say is true, that's unfortunate,' he said. 'But—'

'That's it?' Poe said. 'That's all you have to—'

'*But* homosexuality *is* a sin, Sergeant Poe.'

Nightingale joined her two cops. She turned her back on Joshua and said, 'Go home, Poe.'

'I'm not going any—'

'I won't ask again. Go home. Spend some time with Estelle. We can take it from here, and rest assured if this man does know something, we'll find out.'

Bradshaw placed a hand on his shoulder. 'Come on, Poe,' she said. 'I'll drive you home and stay with you until Estelle gets back.'

Poe slumped in defeat. 'We can't let them . . . how did he put it last time we were here? . . . "redirect the narrative", Tilly. Not this time. This time the world has to know what their hate led to.'

'They will, Poe. I'll help you.'

Joshua offered a sad smile. It didn't reach his eyes. He doesn't care, Poe thought. Worse than that, he *approves*. He knows the timelines make him bulletproof.

'And what about Bethany Bowman?' Poe said, his voice steady. 'Was she a sinner too?'

'I don't know who that is.'

'She's the fourteen-year-old girl Cornelius Green and Israel Cobb murdered. She wasn't gay, she was just a schoolgirl whose parents didn't like her. Cornelius put her in the chair anyway. Had her brother throw rocks at her head. And when that didn't kill her, Israel Cobb slit her throat.'

The mood in the hall changed again. This was news to almost every cop in the room. Even the cult members at the back of the gymnasium looked uneasy.

'Learn her fucking name, Joshua,' Poe said. 'She's about to make you famous.'

Joshua cleared his throat nervously, aware that every eye in the room was on him now and not Poe. 'Well, yes, that does seem to have been a regrettable lapse of judgement,' he said.

'A regrettable lapse . . .'

'I'll pray for her.'

Poe lunged.

Chapter 110

'You hit him?' Doctor Lang asked.

Poe shook his head. 'Superintendent Nightingale's cops stopped me.'

'And if they hadn't been there, or if you'd managed to break free?'

'I don't know. Probably not.'

'Do you think you were fully in control?'

'I do.'

She picked up her plastic cup and studied his face as she finished the last of her cold tea.

'So when you lunged at Joshua Meade it was all for show?' she asked kindly, aware he'd walked into her trap, but not wanting to dwell on it.

'OK, maybe I *wasn't* fully in control.'

'And by this time people were starting to realise you weren't coping. Superintendent Nightingale had told you to go home several times. Tilly was so worried about you she'd called Estelle back from London. She refused to leave your side when you broke down that wall.'

'I was upset,' Poe admitted. 'And yes, I would have assaulted Joshua if I hadn't been held back, but I'm not sure that was what led to my nightmares.'

'No?'

'No. There was still worse to come.'

'And we'll get to that, no doubt. But right now I need you to describe what you saw when you stuck your head through the false wall in the basement, Washington. I need you to be able to remember it without being transported back there. I know you think it was a single, traumatic event that led to the PTSD you're undoubtedly struggling with, but I think in your case it is more likely a cumulative effect. In other words, it doesn't matter which straw it was, it's the combined weight that broke the camel's back.'

Which made sense to Poe. How much was too much? If you asked one hundred cops what the worst thing was about the job, they'd all tell you it was that there were never any good days. Being a cop was like having sewage drip-fed onto your psyche for thirty years. The only ones it didn't affect were the sociopaths.

'Cornelius must have erected the wall after Israel Cobb had been booted out of the Children of Job,' Poe said. 'Everything Cobb told me, everything he *showed* me, was accurate. If he'd known about the false wall, he'd have said.'

Doctor Lang leaned forwards and planted her elbows on the desk. She steepled her fingers and rested her chin on the bridge. 'What was behind the wall, Washington?' she asked softly.

Poe didn't answer. For a moment he was lost in his memories, the sledgehammer on the floor where he'd thrown it, his fingers torn and bloodied from the rough, dry bricks he'd pulled out by hand. Bradshaw at his side, shining her iPhone torch through the gap he'd made, adding to the light of his torch.

'What did you see?' she asked again.

Poe shook his head. Tried to get back to the present. Found his mouth was dry. He picked up his empty cup and sucked the last dregs of tea. Licked the rim.

'The chair,' he said, his voice breaking. 'I saw the mercy chair.'

Chapter 111

'The mercy chair was still there?' Doctor Lang asked incredulously.

'It was,' Poe replied. 'I knew it would be, of course, although I was kind of hoping it wasn't, you know? That it had all been an elaborately staged piece of anti-LGBT propaganda.'

'Why hadn't Cornelius destroyed it?'

'I doubt he wanted to. The more I came to know about the man, the more I understood that he genuinely didn't think he'd been doing anything wrong. Israel Cobb had stolen the videos, so he'd been blackmailed into stopping his courses, but I honestly believe Cornelius thought he'd be able to start them again one day. Maybe when Israel died and he was sure the tapes weren't going to turn up at a police station.'

'Was the chair intact?'

'It wasn't the type of thing you could take apart with a screwdriver, Doctor Lang. It had been built using dovetail and tenon joints. Dowels instead of screws. Other than some rivets to secure the straps, there was no metal on it whatsoever. Which, if it *had* been designed as an electric chair, isn't surprising. Wood isn't conductive; metal is.'

Doctor Lang smiled.

'Sorry, that was what Tilly calls mansplaining,' Poe said. 'But my point is, you couldn't take that chair apart. Not without destroying it.'

'What did it look like?'

'Exactly like it did on the videos. About what you'd expect from a hundred-year-old chair. Simple design. Not a single curve on it, just a series of right angles. Looked like a medieval throne. Leather restraints on the arms and the legs, designed in such a way that even if the prisoner managed to get a hand free, it would have been difficult to free the other. Removable panel on the seat in case the prisoner needed the toilet. The oak was dull with the oil they'd used to maintain it. I wasn't there when forensics took it apart, but I'm told the wood was stained with blood. They collected DNA and linked it to Bethany and five other mispers—'

'Mispers?'

'Missing people. There were two from Newcastle, one from Manchester and two from Glasgow. Bethany was the only Cumbrian.'

'And it was seeing this chair that made you rush upstairs to vomit?'

'It was.'

'Because when you saw it, you knew everything in those videos was true.'

'Not just that.'

'Oh?'

'I say this knowing full well I'm in a secure hospital talking to a therapist.'

'What is it, Washington?'

'I saw her, Doctor Lang,' Poe said, wringing his hands, his voice barely above a whisper.

'Who?'

'Bethany Bowman. I mean, I know she wasn't actually there, but I swear for a moment she was. I could see the terrified fourteen-year-old as clearly as if I'd been standing next to her when she died.'

'You had a visual hallucination?'

'If that's what it's called.'

'It's trauma-based memory,' she said. 'Almost certainly the first external manifestation of your PTSD. It also explains why you had such a strong reaction to Joshua Meade's "regrettable" comment. At that point, I doubt you were even aware of your actions. Luckily Superintendent Nightingale recognised this and took precautions.'

'I know that now.'

Doctor Lang nodded. 'Because if those police officers hadn't been there, I think you might have killed Joshua Meade.'

'He dismissed Bethany's murder as nothing more than bad PR,' Poe said. 'Something he'd have to manage. And he didn't care at all about the five gay men Cornelius had abducted and killed.'

'I need you not to dwell on this. Not now, not ever. Life is full of regrets for things we *have* done, Washington. Worrying about things we might have done, but didn't, is a first-class ticket to this place.'

'That's easier said than done.'

'It is. It's also why you're here talking to me instead of sitting under a viaduct with a bottle of turps.' She smiled. 'What happened next?'

'Superintendent Nightingale escorted me outside. Ordered me to go home.'

'And did you?'

'I did not,' Poe said. 'I went to see Eve. I went to tell her we'd got it the wrong way round. That Bethany hadn't killed her brother; it was her brother who had killed Bethany.'

'What time was it?'

'About six in the morning. It was just getting light and I knew Eve rose early to do her yoga.'

'Was that a wise thing to do?'

'I felt I owed it to Bethany,' Poe explained. 'And it wouldn't have been long before the press got hold of it. At the end of the day, Eve didn't deserve to get ambushed. But, given what happened next, I'd have to say all things considered, it was *not* a wise thing to do.'

Chapter 112

Poe's phone rang five minutes after he had joined the M6. Bradshaw had wanted to drive him home but he assured her he was fine. He squinted at the car's onboard display. It was Superintendent Nightingale. He wondered if Joshua had already made a complaint. He considered ignoring it, but he had too much respect for her to hide away from bad news. He accepted the call just as the sun crested the skyline. Visibility immediately went from full to zero as the low sun beamed into the car like the 'punter blinders', the harsh lights a band aim at the crowd during a rock concert. All he could see was a filthy windscreen, smeared with grime and welded with bug entrails. He reached for his sunglasses but dropped them in the footwell.

'Damn,' he said.

'Excuse me?'

'Not you, ma'am. Just been blinded by the sun. Give me a second.'

He fumbled around his feet until he found them. Visibility improved, but not by much. He moved into the left-hand lane, tucked himself behind a Tesco wagon and took advantage of the shade.

'Sorry about that,' he said.

'Poe, we have a problem.'

'Joshua Meade? I know he used to be a solicitor, but that was quick.'

'It's not Josh—'

'And obviously I'll take full responsibility. One of the bonuses of me not being a Cumbrian cop.'

'Poe, will you shut up a second,' she said. 'This isn't about Joshua Meade.'

'Oh. What is it?'

She told him.

'Shit,' he said.

'An understatement.'

'How is that even possible?'

She told him.

'Shit,' he said again.

'I'm telling you this as a courtesy,' she said. 'For obvious reasons, I don't want it getting out.'

'My lips are sealed.'

'Are you nearly home?' she asked, changing direction.

'I'm popping in to see Eve Bowman first, ma'am. I know I messed up with Joshua Meade, but Eve needs to be warned before the press get hold of her.'

'She does, but you need sleep, Poe. Let uniform do it.'

'It should be someone she knows, ma'am.'

'It's early, Poe.'

'She gets up early,' he said. 'Does yoga every morning before she starts work. But if the lights aren't on, I'll wait.'

'Fine,' she sighed. 'But I want you to call me the moment you're done.'

'Of course.'

'And do me a favour while you're there: get some photographs of Aaron Bowman. The one we have on file is an old photocopy. Tilly wants something better to put through her age-progression program. As soon as we've done that, we can start flushing him out.'

'I'll get as many as I can, ma'am,' Poe confirmed.

'Thanks, Poe. And try not to worry about that other thing. If it wasn't today, it would have been tomorrow. People like that always find a way.'

'I'm sorry, ma'am.'

'About what?'

'I know it's an awful thing.'

'But?'

'But I just don't care.'

Chapter 113

It seemed Eve Bowman was sticking to her early morning, pre-work yoga routine. Poe was impressed. Even when he was in the army he'd hated exercise for exercise's sake. Couldn't believe there were people living in Cumbria who drove to the gym to sit on an exercise bike for an hour instead of cycling up and down the fells. These days he exercised by walking Edgar, sometimes for hours at a time, and by chopping logs for his wood burner. He liked cutting his own fuel; for one thing, he got warm twice.

As she had the first time he'd visited, Eve opened the door before he'd had a chance to knock.

'Three times in a week, Sergeant Poe,' she said. 'If we're not careful people might think we're having an affair.'

'Sorry, Eve. I'd have called first and made an appointment, but I live nearby and I don't actually have your number.'

'That's OK,' she said. She peered at him. 'Have you been up all night? You look exhausted.'

'It's been a long shift,' he admitted. 'And it's kind of why I'm here.'

'Oh? You'd better come in then. The coffee's on and the kitchen's still nice and cool.'

She led him to the back of the house. She was right; the kitchen was beautifully cool. It was south facing, so hadn't yet been touched by the morning sun. Eve poured him a mug of coffee and he sniffed it appreciatively. It was nectar compared to the slop in a Styrofoam cup Nightingale had handed him only a couple of hours earlier.

'Before I forget,' Eve said, 'you mustn't leave here without some of my jam. Thomas has it all labelled and ready for the pantry. You have to take some of the raspberry; it's to die for.'

'I will,' Poe said. And he meant it. He didn't ordinarily like sweet stuff, but he'd make an exception for homemade raspberry jam.

'Now, what can I do for you, Sergeant Poe?'

'There's something I need to tell you and it isn't going to be pleasant to hear. Has your husband left for work yet?'

'No, he's working from home today.'

'I think he needs to hear this as well.'

'You're scaring me, Sergeant Poe,' Eve said. 'What is it?'

'Can you call Thomas, please?'

She moved to the stairs and shouted for her husband.

'He'll be down soon. He enjoys a lie-in when he works from home, but he was awake and reading when I came down for my yoga.'

Thomas took the seat next to his wife and picked up the coffee she'd poured him. He was wearing pyjamas and a loosely tied paisley dressing gown. Poe watched as he put three spoons of sugar in his coffee.

'What brings you all the way here, Sergeant Poe?' he asked.

'He has something to tell us,' Eve said.

'He does?'

'I do,' Poe said. 'Things have moved quickly in the last few hours, and I wanted to let you know what I can. You'll appreciate some of it needs to stay under wraps for now.'

He spent five minutes taking them on an evolutionary journey that began with Cornelius Green's murder and ended with him sitting in Israel Cobb's living room.

'What does all this mean, Sergeant Poe?' Eve asked. 'While it does sound absolutely dreadful, I'm not sure it warranted you driving all the way here.'

'Bethany didn't kill your parents, Eve,' Poe said, like he was ripping off a plaster.

Eve's eyes widened then went blank. Her mug stopped halfway to her lips. Thomas put his arm around her and pulled her close.

'Sergeant Poe, I'm going to assume you're not a stupid man,' Thomas said. 'So if you say Bethany didn't kill my wife's parents it's because you know with absolute certainty that she didn't.'

'I do.'

'Then I think you'd better explain.'

'No!' Eve shouted. She slammed down her mug; didn't glance at the spilled coffee. 'Bethany killed Aaron and she killed my mum and dad! I'm not having that bitch wriggling out of it! I don't care what you think you've found, Sergeant Poe; there's not an alibi she can provide that I'll believe. She killed my baby brother and nothing you can say will change my mind!'

'Perhaps we should listen to what Sergeant Poe has to say, darling,' Thomas said.

Eve wriggled out from underneath his arm. 'No! This is just like her. She didn't take responsibility for her actions then and she's not taking responsibility now.'

'Bethany didn't kill your parents and she didn't kill your brother, Eve,' Poe said. 'And the reason I can say this with the absolute certainty Thomas has mentioned, is that by the time Noah and Grace were murdered, Bethany had been dead five years.'

'Dead?' Thomas said. 'What do you mean "dead"?'

'She was murdered in 2007. And this isn't up for debate; her death was videoed.'

'*Videoed?*'

Poe nodded. 'I watched it yesterday evening. She was murdered in the old school basement at the Children of Job's compound. She was one of six people who were killed while strapped to something they called the mercy chair. That's where I've come from. We've found the murder site hidden behind a false wall.'

'But who would do such a thing?'

'I'm afraid that's the other thing I'm here to tell you,' Poe said. 'She was murdered by three people, Eve. And one of them was your brother, Aaron.'

Chapter 114

As Poe led Eve and Thomas through the events of the last twenty-four hours, their resistance weakened and their resolve hardened.

'That little bastard!' Eve hissed after Poe had given them the PG-rated version of Bethany's murder. He spared them the details he hadn't been able to spare himself. No one needed to be inside his head right now.

'Steady, Eve,' Thomas said. 'Sergeant Poe said Aaron was under duress and it sounds like he didn't have a choice. And he *was* a child.'

'He had a choice about stealing her underwear though!' she snapped. 'And don't give me that "he was a child" crap; Aaron knew Mum and Dad hated Bethany. He should have known they'd completely overreact.'

'If it wasn't Bethany who killed Eve's family, Sergeant Poe, who was it?' Thomas asked.

'We now think it was Aaron,' Poe said. 'We think he waited until Eve was out of the house and he killed them for what they had forced him to do. Our working theory is that he faked his own death after leaving behind evidence suggesting it was Bethany the police should be looking for.'

'Her clasp knife?'

Poe nodded. 'The police had it on record that she had run away five years earlier and the only people who knew otherwise had a vested interest in keeping quiet.'

'I never actually saw Aaron and Bethany rowing after he returned from that course,' Eve admitted. 'Mum and Dad told me it had happened and there was no reason for me not to believe them.'

'The police got it the wrong way round?' Thomas said. 'They put their resources into looking for the dead person they thought was alive and didn't consider the living person they thought was dead?'

'That's about the long and short of it,' Poe said. 'And although I wasn't involved in the case back then, I know I'd have reached the same conclusion.'

'And Cornelius Green?' Eve said, her eyes red and fierce. 'Did my darling brother kill him too?'

'We think so.'

'At least he did something right then.'

Poe said nothing.

'Why did he wait so long?' Thomas asked.

'We're in conjecture territory here, obviously,' Poe said, 'but we believe it's possible that an event in a Shap graveyard a few months ago triggered this second bout of violence. A badger dug up a body that shouldn't have been there and it was news all over the world.'

'I remember seeing that,' Eve said. 'Sky News tried to interview the police officer who'd found the body. He gave them short shrift.'

'Yes, indeed,' Poe said, reddening slightly. 'Anyway, the extra body was one of Cornelius Green and Israel Cobb's victims. It's how they disposed of the bodies of the men they had killed. They used pre-dug graves as deposition sites.'

'Bethany is in one of these graves too?' Thomas asked, shocked. 'I assume you're exhuming them? I think Eve and I would like to give her a proper burial.'

Eve wiped away a tear and nodded. 'That would be nice,' she said.

'I'm afraid that won't be possible,' Poe said. 'Not yet anyway.'

'Why ever not? I understand there'll be some police things you have to do first, but surely her body will be released to her family?'

'For reasons we don't yet understand, Israel Cobb hid Bethany's body. He refused to use the grave Cornelius Green had earmarked for her.'

'And he wouldn't say where?'

Poe shook his head. 'Point-blank refused. The most he would say was that it was on the side of a sunny hill, somewhere peaceful with a nice view.'

'But surely it's not for him to make that decision?'

'He made it anyway,' Poe said softly. He finished his coffee, stood and reached for his wallet. He picked out a tattered business card and placed it on the table, careful to avoid the coffee Eve had spilled. 'You'll be assigned a family liaison officer later today, but if you ever feel that you're being left out of the loop, please, don't hesitate to give me a call.'

'Do you think Aaron poses a risk to Eve?' Thomas asked, getting to his feet as well.

'I don't,' Poe replied. 'I think Aaron killed Noah and Grace because of what they forced him to do to his little sister, and he came back for Cornelius, almost certainly because that grave in Shap was disturbed. I can see no reason at all why Aaron would hold Eve responsible for anything.'

'Why did he leave Israel Cobb alive though? Surely, in Aaron's eyes, he deserves to die as well.'

'Undoubtedly,' Poe agreed. 'But we think Aaron ran into the same problem everyone else has had.'

'Which was?'

'He couldn't find him. Israel wasn't exactly hiding, but he wasn't on any publicly available databases. Alice Symonds had looked for over fifteen years without success. That said, Superintendent Nightingale won't be taking any risks – the FLO she assigns will stay on site until Aaron has been arrested.'

'Thank you, Sergeant Poe,' Eve sniffed. 'That's reassuring.'

Poe shook their hands. He was about to leave when he remembered Nightingale's request. 'Before I go, could you let me have a photograph of Aaron, please?'

Eve's eyes narrowed. 'Why?'

'It's for my colleague's age-progression software. Unless he's had extensive cosmetic surgery, we have the ability to get an incredibly accurate likeness of what Aaron will now look like. We'll make this age-progressed picture public and, in the words of Superintendent Nightingale, start flushing him out.'

Eve and Thomas exchanged a glance.

'Is there a problem?' Poe asked.

Eve hesitated before answering. 'I don't know if I want Aaron caught, Sergeant Poe.'

Which wasn't what Poe had expected at all. 'Oh,' he said.

'He's my baby brother,' she explained. 'And yes, he did something awful, but as Thomas said, he was a child and you made it sound like he had no choice whatsoever. It seems my parents deserved everything they got, and I will not shed a single tear for Cornelius Green.'

'We still need that photograph, Eve,' Poe said gently. He cast his eyes over the frames on the kitchen shelf but they were all of Eve and Thomas. Some of her parents. None of Bethany, which was understandable; up until twenty minutes ago Eve believed Bethany had murdered her entire family. She'd kept Bethany's photographs in the farmhouse basement. But why weren't there any photographs of her little brother?

Eve saw him frown. She glanced at Thomas and shrugged.

'Have it your way, Sergeant Poe,' she sighed. 'If you follow me into the basement you can root through the filing cabinet and take what you need.'

'Thank you.'

Unlike the Children of Job's, Eve's basement was a high-ceilinged room. It had four posts to support the floor above. They reminded Poe of the posts First World War deserters were staked to before being shot at dawn. The basement was warm, like a proving oven. It was being used the way families in modern homes use their lofts: as a place to store junk, unsightly but valuable furniture and Christmas decorations. Shelves with boxes, some labelled, some not. The camping equipment Thomas was checking the last time Poe had been there was neatly laid out on a foldout table.

'Which part of the Lakes are you and Thomas heading to?' Poe asked.

Eve walked over to the table and picked up the tent-peg mallet. It looked like a smaller, wooden version of Mjölnir, Thor's war hammer. Sometimes Poe missed the pre-Bradshaw days, when he hadn't known useless shit like that. Eve turned the mallet in her hands, as though she was examining it for woodworm.

'Weekend in Buttermere,' she replied. She leaned against the table and studied Poe carefully. 'But that's not important right now.'

'It isn't?'

She shook her head.

'What's going on, Eve?' Poe said, rubbing the back of his neck. It felt clammy.

'Nothing's going on, Sergeant Poe.'

'Then why are we really down here? Is there something you want to tell me, something you don't want Thomas to hear?'

Eve said nothing.

'I asked you a question, Eve.'

'You really are the most bothersome man, Sergeant Poe,' she said before taking three steps forward and smashing the mallet into the side of his head.

Chapter 115

Poe began sensing pain rather than regaining consciousness.

Years ago, when he'd taken more of an interest in popular culture, he had watched *Casino*, a film about how the Chicago mob had moved into Las Vegas and changed Sin City for good. It was a violent film, even by Scorsese's standards. And in one stomach-churning scene, made worse as it was based on real events, a mob enforcer put someone's head in a vice and turned the handle until an eye popped out.

That's how Poe felt now. Like his head was in a vice.

The pain was hot and hard, as if he'd been drinking cheap whisky in a bad mood. Everything felt heavy, from the top of his head to the tips of his toes. His ears were ringing, his mouth tasted briny, and the rhythmic throb of blood pounded into his skull. His left temple felt swollen and numb. He went to touch it but couldn't – his hands were fastened tight behind his back, the binding thin and vicious.

Poe tried opening his eyes, but even the dim light of the basement was too harsh. He ignored the searing pain and opened them anyway. He was almost blind in one eye and his vision in the other was blurred and narrow, as if he was looking through an unfocused telescope. He could see crazy zigzag colours. The basement began to spin wildly. Poe had seen enough head injuries to know he was badly concussed. He tried blinking his eyes into focus, the way he sometimes tried with an ill-fitting contact lens, but realised something was wrong with his eye socket. The bone moved under his skin and his eye felt loose. He hoped it wasn't about to fall out.

Poe held the grogginess at bay long enough to take stock of his predicament. He was still in Eve's basement. He had been secured in a sitting position to one of the supporting posts, his legs stretched out in front of him like shotgun barrels. He regretted the 'shot at dawn' internal narration earlier. Now it was all he could think about.

'You really shouldn't have asked for a photograph of Aaron, Sergeant Poe,' Eve said from somewhere behind him.

Poe twisted his head to see where she was, but immediately regretted it as the pain in his skull flared. He slowly, gingerly faced forward again. He felt vulnerable with his back to Eve, but really, what did it matter? He was completely at her mercy. Being able to see her wasn't going to make any difference.

'Where's Thomas?' he asked, his voice thick and slurred.

'Upstairs. He'll join us soon.'

'Why didn't you want me seeing a photograph of Aaron, Eve?'

'I'm not bothered if you *see* one, Sergeant Poe,' she said. 'You've just watched him on a video. I *know* you know what Aaron looked like.'

'Then what?'

One moment Eve was behind him, the next she was at his side. She was still holding the mallet, but not aggressively, more like she'd forgotten to put it down.

'Promise it'll stay between us?' she said, smiling.

'I'd cross my heart if I could,' Poe replied. The way she was smiling frightened him.

'I couldn't risk a photograph of Aaron being put through your colleague's age-progression software, Sergeant Poe,' she replied.

'I know he's your baby brother, but we'll catch him eventually, with or without your help.'

Even as he skirted around the edges of unconsciousness, as his vision began to swim and fade in and out of focus, he knew he was missing something. Eve's actions didn't make sense. The thick fog in his brain meant it was hard to make connections, but taking a police officer hostage was a staggering overreaction to a simple request. And Eve seemed too calculating for that. She had reasons for doing what she was doing, reasons that, to her at least, made sense.

A noise from the basement stairs made them both look up. It was Thomas. He joined his wife. If he was surprised to see Poe tied

344

up and with a serious head injury, he didn't show it. He put his arm around Eve and she leaned in to him. She rested her head on his shoulder and nuzzled into his neck. Thomas gently lifted Eve's face until it was level with his. They kissed deeply.

Public displays of affection made Poe uncomfortable at the best of times, but something else was happening here. It was as if Eve and Thomas were putting on a display. His own private peep show. After they had finished kissing, Eve tilted her head and eyed Poe coyly. Her face was flushed and her breathing was so fast and shallow she was almost panting.

'He wants to know why we can't risk a picture of Aaron being put through their age-progression software,' she said in a girly, sing-song voice.

'What did you tell him?'

'Nothing.'

'Has he worked it out yet?'

'I don't think so,' Eve said. 'He doesn't seem very bright.'

She smiled sweetly. Poe turned away from her and faced Thomas instead. He didn't have his wife's confidence. Eve was almost hanging off him, but Poe got the impression Thomas was very much the beta to her alpha.

What was it he hadn't worked out yet? He instinctively knew it was something to do with Thomas. He looked nervous whereas Eve was enjoying herself. Poe had hunted and caught husband-and-wife tag teams before. Couples who killed for pleasure or profit, sometimes for both. He didn't think that was the case here. This was something he hadn't seen before.

He cast his mind back. Way before Cornelius Green's murder had brought him into their orbit. He visualised the Bowman massacre file. Was the answer in there somewhere? He thought it might be.

For some reason, what Aaron had looked like when he was a child was important. No, that wasn't right. Eve had said it was making sure Bradshaw didn't get hold of a photograph of a young Aaron that was important. So important that she and Thomas had embarked on a course of action that could only end with them murdering a police officer.

Something in Poe's muddled brain clicked and, like a spotlight had been turned on, everything became clear. The moment he separated the photograph from the boy, he was able to see what Eve was determined to protect. It had been in front of him all this time, but up so close he hadn't been able to bring it into focus.

The isolated house.

The husband who wouldn't take a job locally.

The boy who couldn't be put through an age-progression program.

Poe locked eyes with Eve's husband.

'Hello, Aaron,' he said.

Chapter 116

'You're a good liar, Eve,' Poe said. 'One of the best I've ever met.'

Poe hadn't meant it as a compliment, but she took it as one all the same.

'Thank you,' she said. 'When you're in a relationship with your brother, your whole life is a lie. It's the tent we live under. Lying becomes second nature.'

They were alone in the basement again. Eve had asked Thomas to make sure there was nothing incriminating in Poe's car. He suspected it was so he and Eve could talk, although it could just as easily have been so Thomas didn't have to watch Poe die. Eve wore the killer's trousers in their family, not him. She picked up the mallet and this time Poe knew he wouldn't wake up.

'For what it's worth, this isn't personal,' she said.

Poe didn't think it was worth anything, but he kept quiet. He was about to die. He knew that now. No one was going to rescue him. Nightingale knew where he was, but she wouldn't be expecting his call for an hour. By the time someone thought to check up on him, his body would be cold. In a shallow grave or at the bottom of the Irish Sea with a chain wrapped around his ankles. A less stubborn man might have begged for his life. Made implausible promises about not telling anyone if he were allowed to live. Instead, he said, 'You've already killed to protect your secret.'

She angled her head and gave him a small smile. 'You know this how?' she said.

'Bethany's dead, so it wasn't her who killed your parents. And although Aaron faked his own death the night they died, I don't see him as a stone-cold killer. You on the other hand . . .'

Eve shrugged. 'We got tired of sneaking around,' she said. 'I was twenty-one by then; Aaron was twenty. And you know what they put him through when he was fifteen. What they did to Bethany. Our parents were monsters and I was glad to do it. So yes, we arranged for me to attend Bible study at that dreadful place to make sure I had an alibi for that night. Aaron picked me up in our parents' car at three in the morning and drove me home. I opened their throats with Bethany's old clasp knife and we watched them gurgle to death. And I cut Aaron's arm so it looked like he had been killed too. We bundled their bodies into the Range Rover and Aaron drove to St Bees, dropping me back at the Children of Job on the way. I'd been gone for less than an hour. No one had missed me; I had my alibi. Aaron dumped Mum and Dad in the Irish Sea and, while I was finishing off my Bible study group, he made his way to Wales. Started living as Thomas Gruffud. I joined him a suitable time later.'

'You let Bethany take the blame.'

'She was dead, Sergeant Poe. There was nothing either of us could do about that. And despite what he was forced to do to her, she loved Aaron. I don't think she'd have minded taking the blame for Mum and Dad's murders. After all, she hated them the most.'

There was a certain twisted logic to this. Poe thought Bethany probably *would* have enjoyed people thinking she had killed her tormentors.

'I assume Aaron has one of Cornelius's tattoos?' Poe said.

'On the sole of his right foot.'

Poe nodded then wished he hadn't. 'People know I'm here, Eve,' he said. He ignored the biting pain and twisted his wrists as far as he could. Tried to force some give in his bindings. They moved slightly but nowhere near enough to get a hand free. 'I'm not going to insult your intelligence by telling you I won't immediately arrest you if you let me go, but you're about to move from killer to cop killer. That isn't a badge you wear lightly.'

'They'll know where you *were*, Sergeant Poe.'

'They'll come with dogs and search teams and they'll never *ever* drop it.'

'I won't deny that you came to see us, Sergeant Poe. Why would I

348

deny something so easily proved? No, you called, got what you came for and left. That's all Thomas and I know.'

'You mean that's all you and *Aaron* know.'

She smiled. 'It's a lovely name, isn't it? I do so wish I could use it when we are out in public.' She shook the thought away. 'Anyway, by the time they arrive, you and your car will be long gone. You came here to warn us about the risk Aaron posed. Your colleagues will assume you stumbled into that very risk yourself.'

'You're going to blame Aaron?' Poe said.

'Of course.'

It would work too, he thought. They would think Poe had come off worse in an altercation with Aaron. What else *could* they think? He thought about Bradshaw and what his disappearance would do to her. He wasn't sure she would be able to cope. Doyle too. The pair of them would never stop looking. It would ruin what was left of their lives. Flynn would be more pragmatic, as would Superintendent Nightingale, but it would crush Bradshaw and Doyle.

'Why didn't you just tell me you don't have any photographs of Aaron?' he said. 'Why risk all this?'

'It would have been delaying the inevitable, Sergeant Poe. Sooner or later you, or someone like you, would have started wondering *why* I didn't have any photographs of him. No, better to nip this in the bud now. A stitch in time and all that.'

'How *will* you explain not having photographs of him?' Poe asked. 'Yes, people will get distracted looking for me, but there's still an ongoing murder investigation and Aaron is the police's number-one suspect. Sooner or later someone *is* going to ask you for a photograph.'

'I won't have to explain not having any photographs of Aaron,' she replied. 'I'll simply say that you took them all with you.'

'And what if they don't believe you, Eve? What if someone wants to look a bit deeper into my visit here?'

'Like you said, Sergeant Poe: I'm a good liar. I'll *make* them believe me.'

'You have it all worked out, don't you?'

'There's nothing I won't do to protect the life we have, Sergeant Poe. Nothing.' She picked up the mallet and stood in front of him.

'Now, unless there's anything else, I think we should do this now. I promise you, I'll make it as humane as possible.'

'Cornelius Green,' Poe said.

'What about him?'

'Why did you kill him?'

Eve frowned.

'You got away with murdering your parents,' Poe continued. 'You moved back to Cumbria with your brother. He's now a thirty-one-year-old man and doesn't look anything like the scared twenty-year-old he was on the night you killed your parents. And, just to be careful, you move to the middle of nowhere and he keeps himself to himself. Doesn't even take a job locally. So why kill Cornelius? Why risk all this attention? You must have known we'd end up on your doorstep eventually.'

Eve picked up the mallet. 'We didn't kill Cornelius Green, Sergeant Poe.'

'You didn't?' Poe said, puzzled. 'But you must have. It's the only thing that makes sense.'

'It wasn't us.'

'Then who?'

'I don't know,' she said. 'And I don't care.'

She raised the mallet. Poe wondered how long it would hurt. He hoped it would be quick.

The doorbell rang.

Eve paused; the mallet poised to strike.

'Can you get rid of whoever that is, darling?' she called up to Aaron. She lowered the mallet, put her hand in her pocket and pulled out an embroidered handkerchief. She forced it into Poe's mouth. 'Shush, my sweet,' she said. 'It'll soon be over.'

Poe heard Aaron answer the door. There was a muffled conversation then the door shut. Poe had hoped it would take longer. For an ever-too-brief moment he'd even hoped it might be Nightingale's family liaison officer.

Eve raised the mallet, waiting for the all-clear from her brother. They both heard his footsteps as he walked down the basement stairs, slow and methodical, like a metronome.

When he reached the bottom of the stairs, he would give the all-clear and Eve would kill Poe. No ifs, no buts, no more questions. Poe braced himself.

'Who was it, darling?' Eve asked, her eyes fixed on Poe's.

No answer.

Poe craned his neck and peered over Eve's shoulder. His good eye widened.

'What?' Eve said.

Poe said nothing, dumbstruck, staring in horror at the person walking down the basement steps. He blinked, and then he blinked again. For a moment he thought it was a symptom of his concussion. What he was seeing wasn't possible. Yet he knew he wasn't hallucinating. This *was* happening, right in front of him.

Eve noticed she no longer had his full and undivided attention. She turned to see what was more important than her mallet. Her expression collapsed so suddenly it was as if her face muscles had been cut. It went from mild irritation to out-and-out shock so fast it was like she was having a stroke. She gasped. The mallet fell to the floor. She bent at the waist, put her hands to her face and screamed through them. 'Nooooooo!' A pause. Then, 'This isn't happening!'

Time froze as the figure approached Eve, the stun gun used on Cornelius Green held casually and confidently at their side. Poe watched as it was raised then held against Eve's chest. He counted ten Mississippis. He saw the crackling blue arc of pulsing electricity, smelled the burning flesh. He saw Eve collapse to the floor, convulsing.

The figure stood over her.

'Hello, sis,' Bethany Bowman said.

Chapter 117

Bethany grunted as she dragged her unconscious brother down the basement steps. She pulled him by the legs and didn't seem to care that his head bounced off every concrete step. He'd been unconscious longer than Eve, but Bethany clearly viewed her sister as the bigger threat. Eve was already tied to the post next to Poe. The drool leaking from the corner of her mouth had formed a pool on the floor.

Aaron was a deadweight, and although Bethany's expression was as fierce as it had been in the video Poe had just watched, she wasn't a heavy-set woman. It took her five minutes to secure Aaron to the post on Poe's right. Poe was now in the middle, literally and figuratively, of what had to be the sickest family squabble since Richard III had locked his nephews in the Tower of London.

Bethany had barely glanced at Poe, but with her brother and sister secured she finally had time to address the elephant in the room. She reached out and turned Poe's head to the side, examined the damage Eve's mallet had made. She wasn't rough, but she wasn't gentle either. Bethany wore her hair long. Despite the oppressive heat, a light scarf was tied around her neck.

She removed the gag Eve had put in his mouth. 'You don't look as though you're having a good day, Mr Wrong-Place-at-the-Wrong-Time,' she said.

'I've had better,' Poe admitted, wincing. If he got out of this, he'd have to congratulate Bradshaw on her program. The likeness she'd generated for Bethany was uncanny.

She touched his fractured eye socket. 'Eve did this?'

'With the mallet at your feet.'

'Why?'

'I asked her for a picture of Aaron. We were going to put it through some fancy age-progression software.'

'That would do it,' Bethany nodded. 'I suppose you'd better tell me who you are.'

Poe did. Explained what he'd been doing and why. How he'd ended up tied to a post in her brother and sister's basement. When he said it out loud, he realised just how foolish he'd been.

'Do you know who *I* am?'

'You're Bethany Bowman.'

'Yet you seem surprised to see me,' she said.

'You're not wrong,' Poe replied. 'I watched you die.'

'Please explain.'

Poe did. Told her that until the previous night she'd been the main suspect in the murder of Cornelius Green, her parents and her brother. He talked her through his meeting with Mad Alice and how that had started him down a path that ended with him being whacked on the head with a tent-peg mallet.

'They filmed what they did to me?' Bethany asked.

'Not just you. They filmed them all.'

'I saw the camera, but I didn't think for a second there was film in it. Why on earth would they film themselves committing murder?'

'Leverage,' Poe said. 'As long as those tapes existed, no one could claim they weren't there. The tapes proved *everyone* was complicit.'

'Well, it seems that rumours of my death, yada yada yada.'

'I wouldn't be doing my job if I didn't ask what happened that night.'

Bethany said, 'Not yet,' and zapped him with the stun gun.

Chapter 118

'Bethany was alive all this time?' Doctor Lang asked in bewilderment.

'She was.'

'But you saw Israel slit her throat.'

'I did.'

'They staged the whole thing then?'

'They didn't,' Poe said. 'Those rocks were real. That Stanley knife was real. The blood gushing from Bethany's throat was real.'

'Then why—?'

'Why wasn't she dead? Why wasn't she in a grave on the side of a sunny hill like Israel claimed?'

Doctor Lang nodded. She looked bewildered.

'Because the case still had one more arrow in its quiver,' Poe said. 'And in the end, it all came down to why Noah and Grace had hated their daughter . . .'

Chapter 119

Poe came to first. He hadn't been zapped for as long as Eve or the man he now knew was Aaron, but it was the second time in an hour he'd been knocked unconscious and he was starting to feel punch drunk. His head felt like it had been pumped with too much blood and his chest burned where he'd been zapped. He was almost glad he was still tied to the basement's supporting post; he doubted he could have sat up straight without assistance.

Almost glad.

Bethany was nowhere to be seen, although Poe thought he could hear noises coming from the kitchen. Five minutes later, Aaron woke.

'Where am I?' he said groggily. Poe waited for his brain to catch up with his mouth. 'Why would Eve tie me up; it's you we have to kill?'

'That's the spirit,' Poe said. He wasn't surprised at Aaron's conclusion. He knew better than most what Eve was capable of. He must have lived through the last decade with a niggling doubt at the back of his mind, wondering what Eve would do if she ever tired of him.

'You're a policeman,' he said to Poe.

'So?'

'Do something!'

'Like what?'

'I don't know. Call for assistance. If you say it was all Eve's fault, I'll give you some money.'

'How much?'

'Three . . . no, *five* thousand pounds!'

'As tempting as the offer of a month's wages is, I'm going to have to decline, I'm afraid,' Poe said.

'Why?'

'I'm not leaning against this post so I can look cool when I smoke my last cigarette, you fucking dickhead. I'm tied up as well.' Poe thought about what he'd just said. 'In fact, why am I telling you this?' he added. 'You *know* I'm tied up. And it wasn't Eve who did this to you.'

'Of course it was,' Aaron said. 'She's a psychopath.'

'No argument from me there, Aaron. But if you look to your left, you'll see *why* it wasn't your older sister.'

Aaron did as Poe suggested. He frowned. 'Why would Eve tie herself up?'

'I don't know, Aaron; why *would* Eve tie herself up?' Poe said. 'It's almost as if you've put no thought at all into that question.'

'What's happening then?'

'Have you heard the phrase, "Your chickens have come home to roost"?'

'Of course.'

'Well, in your case it's not so much "chickens" as it is your sister, Bethany, and it's not so much "coming home to roost" as coming home to kill you and Eve.' Poe grimaced as a fresh stabbing pain hit him right behind his eyes. He closed them for a moment. 'Then again, I could be mistaken,' he added. 'I *have* just been hit on the head with a mallet.'

'Bethany's dead,' Aaron said. He looked round as if there were clues to be found in the basement. 'Someone else is doing this. Whoever it was at the door when I answered it.'

'Bethany *isn't* dead, Aaron,' Poe said. 'I was just speaking to her.'

'You know that's not true, Sergeant Poe. You saw what Israel did to her. I was there, don't forget.'

'Nevertheless.'

'This is absolutely unacceptable!' Aaron shouted suddenly. 'Whoever's doing this to me, you're in big trouble!'

'Sergeant Poe's right, Aaron,' Eve said. 'Bethany *is* alive. I saw her with my own eyes.'

Poe hadn't noticed Eve come round. He wondered if she'd been awake to hear Aaron call her a psychopath. He doubted it mattered now.

'What is this?' Aaron said. 'Why are you and Sergeant Poe trying to trick me?'

Poe sighed. 'Has he always been this stupid?' he asked Eve.

'He's frightened,' she said.

'We're *all* frightened.'

'Why are you frightened?' Eve said. 'She's your guardian fucking angel. You'll walk away from this a hero.'

Which was when Bethany came back down into the basement. She was holding the mallet.

Aaron started to cry.

Chapter 120

'How do you plead, brother mine?' Bethany asked.

Aaron, the man formerly known as Thomas, was too terrified to answer. Poe didn't think he'd ever seen anyone so scared. His trousers were wet and steaming at the crotch. He was trembling so fast it looked like he was vibrating. He started blubbering like a toddler who'd dropped his ice cream the second he'd seen Bethany and he hadn't stopped since. Tears streamed down his face; snot bubbles popped from his nostrils.

'Will you stop that, Aaron!' Eve snapped. 'Be a man for once in your life.'

'But-but she's going to kill us,' Aaron snivelled.

'Don't be so stupid. Of course she isn't going to kill us.'

'She-she-she isn't?'

'Why would she? We're family, the only family she has left.'

Which Poe thought was a bold statement. Family can be murder, burst unbidden into his mind. He thought Bethany *was* going to kill her brother and sister. In her mind, they deserved to die. And then she would kill him too. He doubted Bethany wanted to add 'cop killer' to her CV, but he also knew it would come down to a straight choice between walking away with the world still believing she was dead or being hunted for the rest of her life. That didn't seem much of a choice, not even to Poe.

'But she's tied us up,' Aaron whined.

'She's just trying to frighten us,' Eve said. 'You know, like we were trying to frighten Sergeant Poe.'

'But we were going to kill—'

'Shut up!'

'He *really* isn't that bright, is he?' Poe said.

Bethany watched the exchange with apparent amusement. She had been leaning against the camping equipment table, but she pushed herself away and walked over to Aaron.

'I asked you a question.'

'I'm sorry, Bethany,' Aaron sniffed. 'They made me do it. You *know* they made me do it.'

'I won't ask you again,' she said, raising the mallet. 'How do you plead?'

'Not guilty! Not guilty!'

'What a surprise.' Bethany turned to Eve. 'And how about you, sis? Are you a revisionist as well?'

'Bethany Bowman!' Eve snapped. 'You let me go this instance. This charade has gone on long enough, even for a freak like you!'

'Not guilty as well then,' Bethany said. She rolled her eyes and tutted. 'Family,' she said to Poe.

Poe thought he'd better try to intervene. 'Where have you been all this time, Bethany?' he asked. 'How did you survive the mercy chair?'

'Are you trying to save everyone, Sergeant Poe?' she replied. 'What's the plan? Buy some time. Keep me talking until your colleagues arrive.'

'No one's arriving,' Poe said. 'I said I'd pop in on my way home to tell Eve and the person I knew as Thomas what we'd found in the Children of Job's basement.'

'I know. I checked your phone when I was upstairs.'

'Then you know I'm not trying to trick you. I just want to know what happened.'

Bethany checked her watch. 'OK, why not?' she said. 'What do you already know?'

'Only what was in your journal,' Poe said. 'A bit of what Eve told me, although I should probably take everything she said with a pinch of salt.'

'Noah and Grace had always hated me, Sergeant Poe, but it wasn't until after I'd sat in the mercy chair that I understood why . . .'

Chapter 121

'Have you any idea what it was like to grow up in that family?' Bethany asked Poe. 'Noah and Grace were insane. I understand that now. The punishments, isolating the three of us from children our own age, the constant need for approval from Cornelius and his acolytes, none of that was normal. But back then I thought it was. I knew they favoured Eve and Aaron over me, of course. They didn't try to hide it and, apart from during the final few months, Eve and Aaron did everything they could, bearing in mind they were children as well, to mitigate the worst of Noah and Grace's excesses. They brought me food, they warned me when they heard something bad was going to happen. Gave me enough time to get out of the house.'

'That's why you kept running away?' Poe asked.

'Noah and Grace were always arguing about me, usually over who hated me the most. Sometimes one of them would get so incensed with me that Eve would fear for my life. When that happened she would smuggle me through her bedroom window. Cover for me as much as she could.'

'But you kept returning.'

'They might have been certifiable, but they also lived in a country with laws. They couldn't just cancel me like I'd never happened. I was on databases and school systems. There were birth records. In other words, despite them wishing otherwise, I *existed*.'

'And people would look for you if you suddenly stopped going to school. They'd start asking questions.'

'Exactly. So Eve, sometimes Aaron, would get me out of the house. Keep me safe from their rage. We'd wait until they had calmed down. I'd return then.'

'Why bother?' Poe said. 'You had an awful life. Why keep returning to it?'

Bethany gave him a side-smile. 'Because of him,' she said, flicking her thumb in Aaron's direction. 'He was a delicate child and without me he wouldn't have survived school.'

'Alice said the same.'

'She was a good friend and it was her I turned to when I had nowhere else to go.'

'She never stopped looking for you.'

'You've said. I like to think we could have been more than friends in a different life.'

'How did we get to this?' Poe asked. 'You three seem to have had each other's backs. What went wrong?'

Bethany nudged Eve with her foot. Not gently. Not hard enough to cause an injury, but with enough force to bruise the skin.

'Her,' she said.

'Me?' Eve protested. 'What did I do?'

Bethany smiled at her sister then turned back to Poe. 'Teenage hormones,' she said. 'That's what went wrong, Sergeant Poe. Teenage hormones that parents like Noah and Grace were singularly ill-equipped to deal with.'

'I'm not following you?'

'Aaron and I were close. Always had been. Eve was the eldest and, because Aaron was immature for his age, they didn't really have anything in common. It inflated the age gap between them. Aaron and I were much closer in age, and we became friends as well as siblings. When Eve went through sexual maturation, she no longer saw me as her little sister.'

'What did she see you as?'

'A rival,' Bethany said. 'She was a fast developer sexually, the first to have "naughty hair", as Grace called it. When it became apparent that Noah and Grace were more likely to eat a weasel than let her have a boyfriend, she turned her eyes to her own brother. Aaron was the only male available to her, but Aaron and me were close. Far too close for her.'

'You and Aaron were never sexually active though,' Poe said.

That's what Israel Cobb had told him. He'd said that Aaron had become infatuated with his younger sister, but it had been unrequited.

Bethany vehemently shook her head. 'Never. Our relationship was as it should have been. We were siblings, nothing more.'

'But he *did* steal your underwear,' Poe said. 'It was why you ended up in the mercy chair. Your parents sacrificed you to rid Aaron of his obsession.'

'Aaron?' Bethany said. 'Feel free to chip in here.'

'Bethany and me never did anything,' Aaron confirmed, his eyes still wide with terror.

'I don't under—'

'It was all Eve, Sergeant Poe,' Bethany said. 'She was the bad biscuit who kept hiding my underwear in Aaron's room. She knew Noah and Grace would come down hard on him, but she also knew they would ultimately blame me. You say my parents sacrificed me to rid Aaron of his obsession, and you're right, they did. They were insane and that's what insane people do. But the thimble rigger was my cold and calculating big sister. She manipulated Noah and Grace like a master chess player. Sacrificed me like a pawn to get me out of her way. She didn't know about the mercy chair, of course. I think she was just hoping they would kick me out. Leave her alone with Aaron. Without me there, she could bend him to her will. And, as a few years later they're living as husband and wife, I'd say she got exactly what she wanted.'

'And when Aaron told Eve what had happened at the Children of Job, what had *really* happened – that you hadn't run away, you'd been murdered – she had the perfect patsy for the murder of your parents a few years later.'

'Oh, this is too much, Bethany,' Eve sneered. 'You know as well as I do that the moment you'd grown a pair of tits you'd have been panting after Aaron as well. What choice did I have? I'm sorry for what you went through, obviously—'

'You're sorry?' Bethany deadpanned.

'Yes, believe it or not, I *am* sorry. I cried when Aaron told me what had happened.'

'Oh. You *cried*. Everything's OK then.'

'Yes, it is! And then Mum and Dad said you'd run away after arguing with Aaron. I knew it wasn't true, but I had to keep it secret anyway. We were just as much victims in this as you were.'

'I told you she'd try to rewrite history, Sergeant Poe,' Bethany said.

'Oh, cut it out, Bethany,' Eve said, her voice like a fingernail down a blackboard. 'We both know you're not going to kill us. Untie us and disappear back to whatever rock you've been hiding under all these years. We'll get rid of Sergeant Poe, and we can all go back to our lives.'

'Thanks,' Poe said.

'I'm curious, Eve; why do you think I won't kill you?' Bethany asked.

'Because I'm your fucking sister!'

'Actually,' Bethany said, smiling sweetly, 'you're not.'

She turned to Poe. Found his eyes in the gloom and held them.

'*Now* do you understand?' she said.

Chapter 122

And finally Poe *did* understand.

He could see the thread that connected it all. One thing after another tumbled into place. He knew why Noah and Grace Bowman had hated their daughter. He knew why she had survived the mercy chair. He even knew why Cornelius Green had revelled in her torture. Life's harsh reality had taught Poe that genuine altruism was so rare that, as Bradshaw had once put it, it was statistically irrelevant, but Israel Cobb, insane as he was, had been an outlier. When he'd shown Poe the video of Bethany's death his only motivation was to protect her. He'd admitted to her murder, to *all* the murders, so the police would stop looking for her.

'You're Eve's *half*-sister,' Poe said. 'Israel Cobb is your father.'

Bethany smiled. It looked like an act of self-harm.

'They had an affair,' she said. 'My chaste, butter-wouldn't-melt mother had an affair with Israel. When she told Noah she was going to the Children of Job for spiritual guidance, she was visiting Israel in his room. And because Grace believed birth control was a sin, the inevitable happened.'

'You.'

'Me. I found out later that Noah and Grace had drifted into a sexless marriage, and when my mother missed her period Noah put two and two together and came up with being a cuckold.'

'An abortion would have been out of the question,' Poe said.

'Their only option was the charade of me being a planned and welcome addition to the family. In public, I was their cheeky scamp. Rebellious, yes, but loved all the more for it.'

'But in private they hated you?'

Bethany nodded. 'To Noah I was an ever-present reminder of

Grace's infidelity. To Grace I was God's punishment for breaking the Seventh Commandment. So yes, they hated me. I remember coming home early from school one day because I'd vomited during PE. That night I heard them praying it was cancer.'

'I saw the entry in your journal,' Poe said. 'Things like that made it easy for us to believe it was you who had murdered your parents.'

Neither Eve nor Aaron had spoken since Bethany had told them about her true parentage, but it was clear neither of them had known. Aaron started blubbering again; Eve was staring at Bethany with undisguised hostility.

'You should be thanking me then, Bethany,' she said, her voice strained and brittle. 'Instead of making idle threats, you should be on your knees grovelling for what I did.'

'And what did you do, Eve?'

'I killed Noah and Grace for you.'

Bethany swung the mallet at Eve's head. It sounded like steak being hit with a meat tenderiser. Poe winced and Eve went limp. Bethany turned to Aaron. 'Is that true?' she asked as if nothing had happened. '*Did* our sister kill Noah and Grace to avenge me?'

Aaron stared in horror at the mallet. He shook his head manically. 'It was so we could be together,' he sobbed.

'In other words, it wasn't about me, it was about her.'

Bethany raised the mallet again.

'Wait!' Poe said.

She gave him a reverse head nod. 'What is it? As you can see, I'm busy.'

'Israel Cobb being your biological father explains why he wanted you to survive the mercy chair,' Poe said, 'but it doesn't explain *how*. I saw him slash your throat, Bethany. He didn't fake that. He *couldn't* fake that, not while Cornelius was watching.'

She lowered the mallet. 'Tell me what you saw,' she said.

'Israel Cobb ran that blade across your neck like he was scouring pork. Your skin sprang apart like it was elastic. There was blood. Lots of it. That couldn't be faked.'

Bethany faced him. She untied her scarf and leaned in to Poe, close enough for him to see her neck. 'No,' she said, 'it couldn't.'

'But . . . how?'

Her scar was white and glossy and thin, like there was a fishbone under her skin. It started just under her left ear and stretched to her right. It was neat, as if a surgeon had cut her. Poe knew that, fully extended, Stanley knife blades were an inch long. An injury like that wasn't survivable.

If the blade had been fully extended . . .

'Israel retracted the blade, didn't he?' Poe said.

Bethany nodded. 'He told me he was panicking by then,' she said. 'He'd meant to save me by having me wear a doctored hood. He'd stuffed it with wire wool and metal padding. He thought that would be enough to absorb the worst of the rocks. He'd then tell Cornelius that the stones had killed me.'

'But because Cornelius had refused to let you wear a hood, he had to improvise.'

'Cornelius knew I was Israel's daughter. Don't ask me how. I suspect Grace confessed to him. She probably asked him for advice. Israel breaking one of the Ten Commandments had enraged Cornelius. He had believed my biological father to be as devout as he was: pure and untainted and unconcerned with worldly possessions and desires. By having an affair, Israel had betrayed him.'

'Which is why Cornelius wanted Israel to see your face.'

'It was. Watching his daughter die was his punishment. And because Aaron was unable to land any serious blows with the rocks he was throwing, Cornelius ordered Israel to finish me off. He had taken a perverse delight in that.'

'He went to plan B,' Poe said. 'Tried to kill you without killing you.'

'He left the tip protruding, enough to pierce the thin skin on my neck, but retracted the rest of the blade. And because he'd jerked my head back before he did it, it looked more violent than it actually was. He didn't know if it would work, but he was out of options by then. He had to cut me deep enough for it to look real, but he wasn't a doctor; he had no way of gauging what a safe depth was. The man who later patched me up told me that if the blade had been protruding even one more millimetre it would likely have been a fatal cut.'

Poe nodded. It had been a desperate move. Wouldn't have worked nine times out of ten. Bethany would have bled out or screamed in pain. 'A cut like that would have been like a head wound,' he said. 'Lots of blood, but ultimately superficial. And luckily Cornelius didn't check.'

'It wouldn't have occurred to him, Sergeant Poe. To check would be to admit he wasn't confident his orders were being carried out.'

Poe thought that sounded about right. Cornelius Green was the Children of Job's founding member, their magnetic leader. His word was infallible.

'Did you know Cornelius had a grave earmarked for you?' Poe asked.

'Yes. Israel told me.'

'Where did he take you instead? Your scar isn't raised or lumpy so I assume you had medical attention that same night.'

'Before the Children of Job, like Cornelius, my father had been active in what he called the fight to preserve the sanctity of life. But whereas Cornelius's background was in direct action, such as firebombing abortion clinics in the States, Israel had been one of a select few who sought out the underground networks. Northern Ireland was a fertile battleground in those days as abortion was illegal in all but a few circumstances. A lot of girls were smuggled across to the mainland to give birth or to have their pregnancy terminated. My father tried to stop the doctors secretly performing abortions over here. The transport arrangements. The families who looked after these young, often terrified girls, while their parents thought they were away on a school trip. The ones who made sure that when they returned to their communities no one was any the wiser. He sniffed them out like a bloodhound.'

'To stop them?'

'A prevented abortion is a soul saved, he told me. He sought them out. Exposed them when he could. Disrupted them when he couldn't.'

'He knew doctors then,' Poe said. 'Doctors who wouldn't ask too many questions?'

'Yes, Daddy was quite the hypocrite. He begged help from those he'd previously tried to destroy.'

'He had you patched up?'

'And spirited abroad to recuperate. As well as families who would see girls through their secret abortions, there was also a well-established network of families who would take on the babies of the girls who couldn't go through with, or just plain refused to have, an abortion. Some of these families were abroad. The family I ended up with were good people. They showed me the love I'd never had before and that's all I'll say on this matter.'

'You got better.'

'And I made a life for myself.'

'But sixteen years later you came back to murder Cornelius Green. Why put yourself through all this again?'

'Some things can never be forgiven, Sergeant Poe.'

'I get that,' Poe said. 'I really do. But why now?'

Bethany frowned. 'I don't . . . I can't be sure. I remember seeing something on the news, something that reminded me of what Cornelius had planned to do with me. That he wanted to bury me underneath someone else's coffin. I think I must have snapped. To be honest, Sergeant Poe, it's all been a bit of a blur. I can't remember parts of the last sixteen years. I imagine I've found a way to block out the worst memories.'

'But the news article brought it all back?'

She nodded. 'I returned to Cumbria and sent a note to Cornelius saying I was a mother who needed advice about her gay son. I asked if we could meet at an out of the way place.'

'The Lightning Tree?'

She nodded again. 'I used to go there with Alice. She would pinch a can of her dad's cider and we would pretend we were drunk.' She smiled at the memory. 'Cornelius couldn't resist that, of course. He didn't recognise me, even when I stunned him and tied him to the tree. It wasn't until I showed him the scar on my neck that he realised the peril he was in.'

'You stoned him to death.'

'As he had wanted Aaron to do to me. Except I didn't beg for mercy. He did. He cried for his "momma" at the end. Kept crying for her right up until I crushed his skull with a rock the size of a melon.'

Poe resisted saying *Good for you*. Instead, he said, 'And you spared Israel because he'd saved your life sixteen years earlier?'

'Oh no,' she said, smiling grimly. 'I'll be making time for dear Papa. He might think he's found redemption, but I have a long memory and a short temper. He'll get out of prison eventually and when he does, I'll be waiting for him.'

'Israel Cobb will never be released,' Poe said quietly.

'I think you underestimate his knack for self-preservation, Sergeant Poe. He'll have information on some of these extremists. He ran with them in his activist days, and some will still be making a nuisance of themselves. He's bound to know something the authorities will find useful. He'll do a deal and get a much-reduced sentence.'

'Israel Cobb will never be released,' Poe said again.

'How can you be so—'

'Because he's dead, Bethany.'

Chapter 123

'I don't understand,' Bethany said. 'You said you'd just been with him. Was that a lie to get me talking?' She picked up the mallet. 'Because if it was, that makes you a bad biscuit and now is *not* the time to be a bad biscuit, Sergeant Poe!'

She screamed the last part. Poe felt her warm breath on his face, her spittle on his cheek.

But Poe wasn't lying. It was what Superintendent Nightingale had called about. Despite being classed as an exceptional risk of suicide, Israel Cobb had found a way to make sure he wasn't forced or tricked into revealing anything about his daughter. If he hadn't been such an evil bastard, his self-sacrifice might have been heroic.

'He killed himself a couple of hours ago, Bethany. If you check my call log, you'll see it happened when I was on my way here.'

'But how? You said Nathan Rose had hanged himself in front of you. Surely the police should have been expecting something like this?'

How do you explain the impossibility of keeping someone alive when they are determined to be dead, Poe thought. If you don't care how you do it, anything can be used to attack your own body. Soap becomes poison, mattress springs become blades. A shirt is a noose and a wall is a blunt object.

And in Israel Cobb's case, eleven pieces of toilet paper stuffed down the back of his throat became death by suffocation. Nightingale told Poe that because the toilet areas in police cells must be pixelated, it was a full minute before anyone realised what he was doing. Cobb had been declared dead by the force medical examiner thirty minutes later.

'My father is dead?' she said after Poe had finished explaining what had happened.

'I'm sorry.'

'I would have liked him to know I haven't forgiven him. That I hated him most of all.'

'He knew, Bethany. Trust me, he knew.'

'What if he didn't?'

'Then take comfort from the fact that he died alone in a rank police cell with toilet paper stuffed down his throat. Take comfort from the fact that everyone will know what he did to you.'

Eve moaned. Her eyes fluttered open. 'What's happening?' she said, her voice a hoarse whisper.

Bethany caught Poe's eye and winked. Despite the heat, he shivered so hard it was like a spasm.

'You don't have to do this, Bethany,' Poe said. 'By any modern measure, an eye-for-an-eye is barbaric. And while I get Cornelius Green deserved everything he got, please don't forget that Eve is right. She and Aaron *were* victims of Noah and Grace. Yes, they betrayed you, and yes, they murdered and lied. But they deserve prison, not death. And if you let them go, I'll make sure that happens.'

'An eye-for-an-eye doesn't mean revenge, Sergeant Poe,' she said. 'It means reciprocal justice. It's about limiting compensation. The Old Testament is very clear: a life *must* be paid for with a life.'

'But you're no longer dead.'

'And I no longer believe in God's justice.'

She turned her back to Poe and pushed the mallet under Eve's chin, lifting up her face. She gently kissed her half-sister on the lips.

'Goodbye, Eve,' Bethany said. 'I'll try to make this quick.'

'No!' Poe screamed.

But it was too late. The first blow had already removed Eve's jaw.

Chapter 124

Eve was dead.

Even with a sluggish, concussed brain, Poe knew she had to be. He had clamped his eyes shut after Bethany's first blow, but he hadn't been able to block out the sound. Bethany had started slowly and methodically, but after half-a-dozen blows, it had transformed into a rage-fuelled attack.

After two minutes, she stopped. The only sounds Poe could hear were Bethany panting, Aaron crying and the pitter-patter of blood on the basement floor.

He risked opening his eyes and then wished he hadn't.

Eve's injuries were catastrophic and unsurvivable. Her jaw was hanging, pendulum-like, by a thin flap of skin. She was missing an ear. Her skull was misshapen and flattened, like a lump of dropped clay.

Poe hoped Eve had lost consciousness after the first blow. She hadn't deserved Bethany's mercy, but no one should die like that. He glanced at Aaron; he was in shock. His skin was pale and clammy; his lips tinged with blue. Dilated pupils and shallow, rapid breathing. He had been staring in horror at his dead sister, but when Bethany eventually caught her breath, he turned to her.

Later, much later, when Poe was asked about Bethany's state of mind in the moments after Eve's murder, he would answer 'Calm.' She was still holding the mallet – its striking face wet and stained – but only because she had forgotten to drop it. Her arms and face were spattered red, as if she'd been bobbing for apples in a bucket of blood. But, despite her outwards appearance, it looked like she had found some inner peace. A serene smile danced across her lips and her eyes were still and tranquil.

Aaron burst into tears again, a high-pitched mewl that snapped Bethany out of whatever Zen-like trance she had been swimming in. She blinked twice and looked at the mallet. She seemed surprised to see there was blood on her hands. Cat-like, she licked them. She held them up to one of the bare bulbs hanging from the ceiling and, satisfied they were clean, she turned to her brother.

'Let me give you the choice I never had, brother mine,' she said. She moved to the table with the camping equipment and picked up a canvas bag of tent pegs. She upended it and they watched the pegs fall out. They landed in a pile, like she was setting up a game of Mikado.

'Do you need the hood, Aaron?'

Aaron turned away from Bethany. 'Do something!' he yelled at Poe.

'You tied me up, mate,' Poe replied.

'That was Eve! She's the bad biscuit, not me!' A cunning look stole over him. He turned to Bethany. 'And it was Eve who kept putting your underpants in my bedroom,' he whined.

'Is that so?' Bethany said.

'Yes! And it was Eve who made me keep quiet about what happened when you were in the mercy chair. I wanted to tell a teacher!'

Aaron clearly thought blaming Eve was a seam worth mining. And why not? Blaming a dead sister had worked for him before.

'She even killed Mum and Dad. She made me go and live in Wales on my own. I didn't know anyone and people picked on me for being English.'

'Sounds awful.' Bethany looked at Poe and winked again.

'It *was* awful actually,' Aaron insisted. 'I've never been strong like you, or nasty like Eve. I was a weak child and, I'll be the first to admit, I'm a weak man. When she sent me away I cried myself to sleep every night.'

'Poor lamb.'

Aaron nodded enthusiastically, misinterpreting Bethany's responses.

'You're blameless then?' Bethany said.

'I am, yes! And I won't tell anyone about this, honest. And

neither will Sergeant Poe. That's right, isn't it, Sergeant Poe? You won't tell anyone if Bethany lets us go?'

'I'd better untie you then,' Bethany said.

'And just so you know, if you *don't* want to let Sergeant Poe go, I won't mind. I'll even help you hide his body.'

'Aw, that's so kind of you,' Poe said.

'You keep out of this!' Aaron snapped. 'This is a family matter! Eve and me were going to take him to St Bees and weigh him down in the sea, Bethany. We were going to make it look like you'd done it. But now everyone thinks you're dead, they'll think it's someone else entirely.'

'Why don't we do that then, Aaron?'

'And you were there, Bethany – you know I didn't want to throw those rocks at you. I was only a little boy; I had no choice.'

Bethany stroked the side of his face. 'I know, Aaron. I don't blame you for that. I never have.'

Aaron blew out a sigh of relief.

'No,' she continued, 'I blame you for not saying anything when Noah and Grace thought I was trying to seduce you.'

'But Eve told me not to say anything!'

'And because you helped cover up her lie, I was tied to a chair and had rocks thrown at my head. Because of you I had my throat slashed from ear to ear.'

Aaron averted his eyes, cast them down at the bloodstained floor. 'I didn't want Eve to shout at me,' he mumbled.

'All the times I stuck up for you at school, all the bullies I faced down. And the one time I needed something in return, you said nothing. I expected it from Eve; she was always self-absorbed, but I thought you might have found the courage to stand up for me.'

Aaron didn't respond.

'So, I'll ask you again,' she said. 'Do you want the hood?'

Aaron started to gasp. He writhed against his bonds, but they were tight and held fast.

'Suit yourself,' Bethany said. She raised the mallet again.

And this time Poe didn't close his eyes.

Chapter 125

Aaron was dead too. Bethany hadn't dispatched him with the same kind of frenzy as she had Eve. Her eyes hadn't burned with rage. She had remained calm and methodical. She had ignored Aaron begging for his life and hit him as hard as she could on his temple. The crunching sound, like the first bite of a crisp apple, was loud and decisive. Poe knew if it hadn't killed Aaron outright, it would have knocked him insensible. Bethany hit Aaron again. And again. Blow after blow, forehand, backhand, like she was playing herself at Swingball. After what seemed like an age, but was probably no more than thirty seconds, she stopped. She reached over and checked her half-brother's pulse.

'It's done,' she said to Poe, her face wet with tears. They had made tracks in Eve's dried blood.

Poe said nothing. He didn't think there was anything he *could* say. It might have been after the sixth blow, it might have been after the seventh, but at some point an arc of blood had spilled far and wide. It felt warm on the side of Poe's face. He could taste it. He could smell it. He could feel it clotting in his hair.

He didn't know if it was the distress of what he'd just witnessed or his ongoing head trauma, but Poe was hanging on to consciousness by a thread. If he hadn't been tied to the basement post he'd have collapsed. The vision in his remaining eye was cloudy and the ringing in his ears had grown steadily louder. His head slumped to his chest. He vomited but made no move to avoid it. It splattered down his shirt and pooled on his groin. *I'll have to throw away my belt*, he thought. For some reason this bothered him. And then it made him giggle. He started to cry. Not the great wracking sobs of Aaron, but the gentle weeping of someone who'd had enough.

Bethany looked on in pity.

'You seem like a decent man, Sergeant Poe,' she said. 'Which makes what I'm about to do even harder.'

She picked up the tent-peg bag.

'I'm not giving you the option of refusing,' she said. 'I don't want you feeling shame for choosing it. Wearing the hood is my choice, not yours.'

Poe grunted. From the moment Bethany had zapped Aaron, he'd known there was no chance he would walk out of the basement. He'd known that for Bethany to stay dead, he would have to die. Superintendent Nightingale and Bradshaw and Estelle and Flynn would think he'd stumbled upon Aaron Bowman tidying up loose ends. They'd assume Poe had been, as Bethany had put it earlier, Mr Wrong-Place-at-the-Wrong-Time. That his luck had finally run out. With Bethany being officially dead, the police would reach the only conclusion available to them – that Aaron had returned to kill Cornelius Green, and then, for reasons known only to him, he'd also murdered his sister Eve and her husband Thomas. And when Bethany murdered Poe, there would be no one left alive to explain that Thomas and Aaron were one and the same.

Poe's case would never be closed, but it would quickly grow cold. With nothing for his friends to do but get over it.

'I'll wear your hood,' he said. 'But do me a favour?'

'If I can.'

'Go far away from here. Find some peace and live your life. Forget about what was done to you and forget about what you had to do. Make my death mean something.'

'I will,' she nodded. 'Are you ready?'

'I am.'

She placed the canvas bag over Poe's head and pulled the draw-string tight. It was rough and smelled of wood and earth. It was pitch black but he closed his eyes anyway.

'I'm so sorry,' Bethany said, her voice muffled.

Nothing happened.

No pain. No sudden white light. No . . . eternal nothing.

Instead there was a new voice in the basement. A woman's voice.

'No, Bethany! This is wrong! He's a police officer!'

Poe jerked his head up. Turned to face where he thought the new voice had come from. 'Alice, is that you?'

No reply.

'Alice, if it *is* you, get out of here!' Poe screamed, thrashing and writhing, straining with every ounce of strength, testing his restraints until his bones ached and his sinews stretched. They didn't budge. 'She was your friend, Bethany; please don't hurt her! Alice, run!'

'Why would I hurt her?' Bethany said.

And then things *did* go blank.

Chapter 126

'I woke up in hospital,' Poe said to Doctor Lang. 'I was in what the doctor called a "minimally conscious state" when they found me. There was significant swelling on my brain and I spent a week in an induced coma.'

'So the file says,' Doctor Lang said. 'Alice obviously managed to persuade Bethany not to kill you?'

'I have no idea what happened after I passed out. All I know is that when I didn't turn up for breakfast, Estelle called Tilly to see where I was. A missing cop sets off all sorts of alarm bells and it wasn't long before Superintendent Nightingale dispatched a team to Eve Bowman's house.'

'Where they found you?'

'My car was still in the drive. When there was no answer, they broke down the door. They found me lying on the floor in between the cooling bodies of Eve and Aaron Bowman.'

'Alice had untied you?'

'Bethany had.'

'I take it she was long gone?'

'No. She was sitting on the floor beside me. I'm told she was in some sort of fugue state.'

'Dissociative fugue,' Doctor Lang said automatically. 'The terminology has changed.'

'Yeah, that sounds right. Anyway, she didn't seem to know where she was, or what had happened.'

'Was Alice waiting with her?'

'Bethany was alone,' Poe said.

'The police officers arrested her?'

'She was in court a few months ago charged with the murders of

Cornelius Green, Aaron Bowman and Eve Bowman.'

'How did she plead?'

'After considering three psychiatric reports, which all concluded there was an abnormality of mental function, the Crown Prosecution Service accepted a plea of manslaughter by reason of diminished responsibility. The judge sentenced Bethany to life imprisonment combined with a Section 45A Hospital and Limitation Direction Order.'

'That isn't one I'm familiar with.'

'They're sometimes called hybrid orders,' Poe explained. 'It means she'll stay in a secure hospital until she no longer requires treatment. At that point, she'll be transferred to prison where she'll see out the remainder of her sentence.'

'That seems . . . harsh?'

'Actually, the judge was remarkably understanding,' Poe said. 'He was sympathetic to what Bethany had been through and he sentenced her accordingly. He had to protect the public, obviously, but he only put an eight-year tariff on the manslaughter charges. That means if Bethany can get well, she can apply for parole before she's forty.'

'And if she *doesn't* get well?'

'She'll spend the rest of her life in hospital.'

'That poor girl,' Doctor Lang said. She closed Poe's file. 'We'll leave it there for now, Washington, but this has been a productive session. You've suffered enormously, but you've been extremely honest about it. I've had police officers as patients before and they rarely open up, and because of that they rarely get better.'

'Am I going to be OK?'

'You'll be fine,' she smiled. 'Now, this is a bit cheeky, but can I ask two more questions? They're just to satisfy my own curiosity, so please don't feel you need to answer.'

'Ask away, Doctor Lang.'

'What happened to the Children of Job?'

'Folded,' Poe said. 'Joshua stuck to his guns and refused to denounce Cornelius's actions, but with the press camped outside for a month, members drifted away. The senior members all became tabloid hit pieces. In the end, Joshua was left all alone. No members, no income. I think a hotel chain picked up the estate for pennies on the pound.'

'I'm glad,' Doctor Lang said.

'I am as well,' Poe said. 'You said you had *two* questions?'

'Did you ever find out what Linus Jorgensen was up to?'

Poe held up his scarred hands and scowled.

Chapter 127

One week after Eve Bowman's basement

Poe woke confused, exhausted and weak, like he'd been swimming in treacle. His mouth was drier than cat litter and he had a hangover-like headache. When he finally gathered his wits, a bright-eyed nurse offered him a cup of tea and sat with him while he drank it. She explained he had been in a medically induced coma until the intracranial pressure had reduced to a safe level, but his consultant had recently stopped administering the barbiturates that had kept him unconscious for a week. After a battery of cognitive, reflex and vision tests, she and an orderly wheeled him out of intensive care to a private ward. Flynn, Doyle and Bradshaw were waiting for him.

Despite Poe protesting that all her patients were dead, Doyle went into full doctor mode. She asked his consultant about something called electroencephalography and seemed pleased by his answers. 'It seems you have some brain activity left, Poe,' she said before dragging the bewildered consultant from the ward for a grilling.

While Doyle was busy finding out how long Poe would be a drooling idiot, Flynn and Bradshaw filled him in on what had happened during the week he'd lost after Eve's basement. Bethany was in custody, but she hadn't said a word since her arrest. Flynn wasn't sure she ever would. He asked if Alice was OK after what she'd seen in Eve's basement. Said he wanted to thank her for saving his life.

Flynn's answer stunned him.

He asked questions but Flynn didn't yet have all the facts. 'We're getting almost hourly updates, Poe,' she said.

'I could have sworn . . .'

Flynn shrugged. 'It was a bit of a shock,' she admitted. 'Just as well though.'

Poe nodded. It *was* just as well.

'How are you feeling, Poe?' Bradshaw asked. 'You've had major reconstructive surgery on your fractured eye socket. Is it sore?'

It wasn't, but he suspected that was the barbiturates talking. He carefully touched his eye socket, but it was heavily bandaged and his fingers came away damp with iodine.

'Who's paying for this room?' he asked.

'I do wish you'd occasionally read the terms of your employment, Poe,' Flynn replied, sighing. 'All NCA employees have private medical insurance. And even if we hadn't, every doctor in Europe seems to owe Estelle a favour. The surgeon who operated on your eye socket flew in from Austria.'

Poe wasn't sure how he felt about that. The ward was on the ground floor and he had views across the hospital's landscaped grounds. The walls were painted a soothing, non-institutional cream and were scrupulously clean. The bedsheets were crisp, the pillows starched. Poe was hooked up to a bunch of shiny monitors and machines. Some blipped and beeped, others observed. The occasional chairs looked comfortable and the television on the wall looked new. The instructions by Poe's bed said he had access to Sky, Netflix, Disney+, Amazon Prime and Apple TV. He'd heard of Netflix, but the others could have been porn channels for all he knew. Probably not Disney, he thought. Not unless they'd recently rebranded. Other than that, a private ward seemed to be the same as an NHS ward.

'This is all a bit . . . privileged, isn't it?' he said eventually.

'You needed urgent medical attention, Poe,' Flynn replied. 'And because Superintendent Nightingale told Estelle what had happened, she raced over to Eve Bowman's house and helped stabilise you before you were put in the ambulance. By the time you got to hospital, her surgeon friend was already on his way to the airport. Every single person involved in your care is the best in their field and none of them are taking a fee.'

'What are you saying?'

'I'm saying that you being in a small room in the private wing of an NHS hospital is just the tip of your privilege iceberg. You have plenty of things to feel uncomfortable about, Poe; this isn't one of them.'

'Fair enough. How's Superintendent Nightingale getting on?'

'Busy. She has two more murders to go with Cornelius Green's now. She also has Nathan Rose's suicide and a death in police custody inquiry to be getting on with.'

'The exhumations?'

'All done. Not including the grave the badger dug up, there were four extra bodies in the remaining five. Like Israel Cobb said, only the grave earmarked for Bethany was empty.'

'There's no one left alive to charge with those murders.'

Flynn shook her head. 'Superintendent Nightingale tried tracking down the remaining boys in the videos, the ones Cornelius forced to do the stonings, but it was a dead end.'

'Can't find them?'

'No, it was a *literal* dead end. Cobb hadn't been lying when he said Nathan Rose and Aaron Bowman were the only ones who had survived into adulthood. Three, or four if you include Nathan, committed suicide, and the other died of a drug overdose. Superintendent Nightingale told me this is the most complex case anyone in Cumbria has ever been involved with.'

'Tell me something I don't know,' Poe replied.

'St John's Wood is the only London Underground station to not share any letters with "mackerel",' Bradshaw said without hesitation.

'No, Tilly, that doesn't mean . . . what, really?'

Bradshaw nodded. 'It only works because on the tube map, "Saint" is shortened to "St". It's nonsense really.'

'Speaking of nonsense,' Poe said, 'did we ever find out what Snoopy was up to?'

Flynn didn't answer. Doyle re-entered the ward. Poe's consultant wasn't with her.

'Have you moved your bowels, Poe?' Bradshaw said, starting to go red. 'The doctor said that moving your bowels is a sign you're getting better.'

'You shouldn't ask people things like that.'

'But I'm your friend; you can tell me anything.'

Poe turned to Flynn. 'Boss, tell her.'

'Answer the question, Poe,' Flynn said.

Poe raised an eyebrow, wincing as he did. Bradshaw could always be relied upon to misread social situations, but right now her Tillyness was dialled up to eleven. Something was up. Her voice was a little too bright, a little too cheerful, as if she was overcompensating for something. All Flynn did in response was shrug. Poe turned back to Bradshaw. Her face was burning like a brake light, and this was the woman with no embarrassment threshold. Either she was lying, which was unlikely, or there was something she hadn't been allowed to tell him. It certainly wasn't about the health of his bowels; a team of whipped vegans couldn't have stopped her talking about that.

'What was Snoopy up to, Tilly?' Poe asked again.

'Later, Poe,' Doyle said. 'Right now you need to rest.'

'Why later?'

'Estelle said we'll talk about it later, Poe,' Flynn said. 'And we will.'

Poe said, 'If someone doesn't tell me what's going on right now, I'm getting out of bed and I'm discharging myself.'

Doyle sighed. 'You're a stubborn, stubborn man, Poe,' she said. Then to Flynn, 'You'd better tell him.'

Bradshaw sniffed. Unshed tears shone in her eyes.

Flynn approached the bed. 'They're disbanding the unit, Poe,' she said.

Chapter 128

Something stirred in Poe, something he hadn't felt in a long time. It wasn't fear. Fear was useful. The powerful, primitive emotion elicited a biochemical response that flooded the body with chemicals such as adrenaline. Poe *embraced* fear. Kept it in check until he was ready to use it. But what he was feeling wasn't fear, it was dread. You couldn't use dread. Dread gave nothing back; all it did was take.

'What the hell are you talking about?' he said, struggling into a sitting position, stifling a yelp as the too-sudden movement sent shock waves coursing through his body. 'MI5 can't simply disband a whole unit of the National Crime Agency. They don't have the authority.'

'No, they can't,' Flynn confirmed. 'But they *can* put pressure on certain people. Make sure the detective sergeant and the detective inspector roles are redesignated as civilian posts.'

'But why bother going to all that trouble? There must be easier ways to stop me annoying the wrong people.'

Flynn shook her head. 'We got it all wrong, Poe,' she said. 'This wasn't about you. This was *never* about you.'

'Who was it about then?'

'Tilly.'

'Tilly? I don't understand.'

'MI5 wanted her. They wanted her and we had her.'

'This entire bullshit exercise was just a smokescreen to get Tilly out of SCAS?'

'And into their clutches,' Flynn confirmed.

'It's not fair!' Bradshaw wailed.

'It was a heist,' Poe snapped. 'It was a heist and Snoopy was their fucking safecracker.' His head started to throb. He pinched the bridge of his nose to stem the pain. Doyle sat up straight but he waved away her concern. 'I'm fine,' he said. 'That's what Snoopy was doing? Finding a reason to break up the unit – one that our top brass would find palatable.'

'Seems so.'

'Van Zyl will never go for it,' Poe said.

Edward van Zyl was the director of intelligence. He was protective of SCAS, saw it as the jewel in his crown despite everyone else telling him it was the turd in his swimming pool.

'This was decided at ministerial level, Poe. There was nothing he or anyone else in the NCA could do. They said SCAS has done remarkable work, but as a resource it is an unjustified expense while extremism remains the country's dominant threat. That type of shit.'

'I'll bloody kill him. I don't care which office in Thames House the snivelling little shit's cowering in, I'll find Snoopy, and I'll bloody—'

'Jolly good, Poe,' Doyle nipped in. 'Maybe wait until your arse isn't hanging out of a surgical gown though? And while murdering a member of the security services would undoubtedly improve your current predicament, Stephanie tells me that Linus wasn't the problem in the end.'

'He wasn't?'

'No,' Flynn conceded. 'He met with me and Van Zyl and explained that, while any dirt he was able to dig up would undoubtedly be useful in achieving their objective, his primary reason was to undertake a field evaluation of Tilly's capabilities.'

'Which she passed, of course?'

'It was deciphering Cornelius Green's tattoos that clinched it. He said he'd never seen anything like it. Hadn't even *heard* of anything like it. The security services can't move for codebreakers, but because of the work we've done together over the last few years, Tilly can now adapt mathematical theorems to real-world applications. They don't have anyone who can think like that.'

'I didn't know I was being tested!' Bradshaw protested. 'How could I?'

'It's not your fault, Tilly,' Poe said. 'We should have seen this coming. You hacked an MoD laptop in under two minutes a few years ago; of course they were casting envious eyes in your direction.'

'That *was* mentioned,' Flynn said.

'What did Snoopy do after Tilly passed his field evaluation?'

'He wrote his report, and while it said that in moments of extreme national security Tilly should be seconded to the security services, the best use of her talents right now is with SCAS. He recommended no further action be taken. It seems you won him over.'

'I imagine that was mainly Tilly,' Poe said. 'I was occasionally abrupt with him.'

'Oh pur-lease!' Bradshaw said. 'You were rude to him every single day, Poe! If you weren't calling him Snoopy you were calling him your intern. And you left him in Keswick when he went to get us some hot drinks.'

'No, he liked Poe too, Tilly,' Flynn said. 'He told me he's never seen anyone so focused on getting to the truth. He said Poe has a knack for provoking a reaction, and if more of their agents were like him, the security level would never get above moderate.'

'What happened then?' Poe said. 'If Snoop . . . if *Linus* recommended no further action be taken, why is the unit being disbanded?'

'It seems the decision had already been made,' Flynn said. 'He was only there to justify it.'

'What am I missing?' Poe said. 'This isn't Soviet-era East Germany and MI5 aren't the Stasi. National security or not, Tilly can't be compelled to work for them.'

'That's what *I* said!' Bradshaw said. 'I didn't want to work for them. I *don't* want to work for them. I think they're slippery fish and I told them to go and boil an egg.'

'I assume they made a counter offer?'

Bradshaw flushed red again. Twice in one lifetime, Poe thought. Things must be bad.

Flynn answered for her. 'They used Tilly's loyalty against her,' she said.

Chapter 129

'Mrs Rose made a formal complaint,' Flynn explained. 'She blames you for the death of her husband.'

'But he hanged himself.'

'She alleges that by dredging up Nathan's past, you committed a criminal offence. By forcing her husband to relive his time as a gay man you goaded him into suicide.'

'*I* committed a criminal offence? He tried to cure his homosexuality by stoning someone to death.'

'Nevertheless, she wanted you prosecuted under section two of the Suicide Act 1961. She said you should have completed a risk assessment before you visited her husband.'

'Section two?' Poe said. 'I'm not familiar . . .'

'Encouraging or assisting suicide, Poe!' Bradshaw burst out, her frustration boiling over. 'You could have been sent to prison for *fourteen* years!'

'That's ridiculous,' Poe said.

'It is. And Professional Standards would ultimately have dismissed it out of hand.'

'What's the problem then?'

'The problem, Poe, is that elements of her complaint *did* have merit.'

'How?'

'They found that by ridiculing Mrs Rose's religious beliefs, you *had* broken the NCA code of conduct.'

Poe put his head in his hands and groaned. 'The Björn Borg joke?' he said.

'The Björn Borg joke,' Flynn confirmed.

'But she wasn't supposed to hear that.'

'It doesn't matter. She did. And what do you think she'll find more palatable? That her husband was hounded to his death because of his religious beliefs, or he hanged himself because he was about to be arrested for murder. Which version of events allows her to hold her head high in church on Sunday?'

'What do you mean, "did"?' Poe said.

'Excuse me?'

'You said, "elements of her complaint *did* have merit". "Did" implies they don't have merit any more.'

'That's where they tested just how loyal Tilly was.'

Poe glanced at Bradshaw. Her head was low and her shoulders were shaking uncontrollably. He looked away. She wouldn't want him to see her crying like that. Realisation dawned. He slowed his speech and took care with his response. 'They blackmailed her, didn't they?' he said, anger creeping into his voice anyway. 'They told her that if she did what they asked they'd see to it that the complaint disappeared.'

'As good as,' Flynn confirmed. 'They said that although they couldn't make it go away, they would make sure you kept your job and your rank.'

Bradshaw looked up. Her eyes were red and brimming. 'If I didn't do what they wanted, they said you couldn't be a police officer any more, Poe.'

'As soon as Tilly agreed to work for them, Professional Standards decided the legitimate element of Mrs Rose's complaint could be dealt with by management action. I've spoken to Van Zyl and he will explain that your behaviour fell short of the expectations set out in the NCA code.'

'That's it? No other sanction?'

'You also have to attend counselling.'

Poe swallowed a string of profanities. 'I don't need counselling,' he said irritably. Bradshaw and Flynn exchanged a look. 'But fine, I'll do what I'm told,' he added before it could escalate. 'Have we been reassigned yet?'

'We have.'

'Bad?'

Flynn nodded. 'Until you have a clean bill of health, you've been posted to the training unit.'

'And you?'

'I've been made Acting-Detective Chief Inspector, reassigned to MSHTU.'

'The Modern Slavery Human Trafficking Unit?'

'It's not too bad. Interesting work and I'll be closer to home.'

'What about you, Tilly?' Poe asked. 'Do you know what you'll be doing?'

Bradshaw nodded sadly. 'I do, Poe.'

'And?'

'I'm not allowed to tell you. I'd be breaking the Official Secrets Act if I did.'

Poe didn't think he'd ever seen anyone so dejected. 'We're always going to be friends, Tilly,' he said. 'You know that, right?'

'It won't be the same though,' she sniffed.

'No, it won't,' Poe admitted.

'You'll *hate* the training unit and I don't want to go back to . . . a desk job.'

'I won't hate the training unit, Tilly. It'll be a welcome change of pace.'

'What a load of hooey. Seventeen months and two weeks ago, you said new police officers were as much use as a sponge leg in a muddy swamp.'

'Ah, but that's because I hadn't trained them,' Poe said. 'I'll lick those . . .' A wave of nausea overwhelmed him. He reached for the cardboard bowl by the side of his bed and held it under his chin as his mouth flooded with saliva. One of the machines he was hard-wired to started beeping.

Doyle, who had been keeping quiet, bent down and pressed a couple of buttons. A whirr was followed by a two-inch-wide printout exiting a hidden slot. It curled up, like a till receipt. Doyle examined it and said, 'This is why this news should have waited.' She made a few adjustments to the machine.

Poe's urge to vomit subsided. 'Are you qualified to do that?' he said.

Doyle ignored him. 'Come on, everyone out,' she said. 'Poe needs rest and he isn't going to get it with you two doom merchants talking end of days. It's a job, not a cancer diagnosis.'

Bradshaw scowled.

'That means you too, Tilly,' Doyle added gently. 'You can visit Poe again tomorrow. He isn't going anywhere.'

After Flynn and Bradshaw had reluctantly left the ward, Doyle dragged a chair over to his bed. She put his hand in hers and said, 'Are you going to be OK? Tilly's right: you'll hate the training unit.'

'It won't be for long,' he replied. 'The plan is obvious: I'll tell Sigmund Freud what he wants to hear and get myself declared sane. I'll be back on the street in no time.'

'That's the spirit, Poe,' Doyle said, rolling her eyes.

'And as soon as I am, I can start fixing this. They've benched us, Estelle, that's all that's happened. Who are they going to turn to when the next ghoul crawls out from underneath the bed? Me and Tilly and the boss, that's who.'

Doyle patted his hand but said nothing. After a while Poe's eyes closed. His breathing slowed. Doyle stood and checked the machines he was hooked up to. Satisfied his vital levels were stable, she slipped out of the room, gently closing the door behind her.

The moment the door had clicked shut Poe's eyes snapped open. His breathing quickened. He reached for his phone and thumbed a quick email to Superintendent Nightingale to let her know he was OK. He fired another one off to Alice Symonds. Letting her know the same. He considered sending one to Van Zyl, asking if there was any wriggle room on attending counselling. He decided against it. Counselling was a stupid idea but telling that to the person who had just decided it was necessary probably wasn't politic right now. He turned off his phone and threw it on to the seat Doyle had vacated.

He was about to turn on the TV when his eyes were drawn to the oak tree outside his window. It was old and grand and looked as if it had been there for centuries. It dappled the low evening sun streaming into his room. Made the shadows on the wall dance. It looked like the Lightning Tree might have done before three hundred million volts had passed through it.

A crow landed on one of its upper branches. It ruffled its inky feathers. Another crow joined it. And then another. It must be their roost, Poe thought. He shuddered but didn't know why. More joined them. Pretty soon there were dozens, black and ominous, silhouetted against the fading light. Watching, waiting, emotionless, like Bosch's owls.

Poe usually liked crows. They didn't care about jobs and they didn't need therapy. Crows just . . . were. But for some reason their presence tonight was unsettling, threatening even.

He remembered the body dug up by the badgers all those months ago, the body that had started it all. The body had a name now. His parents had been told. He remembered how the crows had fed on it, picking the bones clean. He remembered their feathers, wet with bodily fluids. It was the kind of memory that would reform later as a nightmare.

So Poe turned his back on the crows.

And after a while he started to weep.

Chapter 130

'If only I hadn't crammed all those pickled onions into my mouth,' Poe said to Doctor Lang. 'If I hadn't, Tilly wouldn't have solved that stupid maths problem. And if she hadn't solved the maths problem, she wouldn't have been invited to America to receive that big prize.' He thought it through to its logical conclusion. 'And if Tilly and Estelle had still been in the country, I wouldn't have been in the pub when the badgers dug up that corpse. It could have been someone else sitting here today.'

'Do you really think the cause and effect is that clear?' Doctor Lang replied.

'I suppose not,' Poe admitted.

'And having lunch in that pub was a coincidence, Washington. Nothing more.'

'But—'

'But nothing. Answer me this: if you *hadn't* been in the pub that day, would you still have investigated Cornelius Green's murder?'

Poe nodded. 'The link between Cornelius and the corpse the badgers dug up wasn't established until *after* Tilly had solved the tattoo riddle.'

'Exactly. And Tilly being a maths genius would not have been news to the security services. She undertook research at Oxford. She'd worked with them before. The bio DI Flynn provided states they had already tried to recruit her.'

'Twice, apparently.'

'And didn't you say she'd hacked an MoD laptop in under two minutes a few years ago?'

Poe shrugged.

'I'd imagine they'd had their beady eyes on her for a while,'

Doctor Lang continued.

'I guess.'

'It was probably only a matter of time before they made a move.'

'There's a point to this?'

'My point, Washington, is you don't need my qualifications to know that crows aren't the cause of your nightmares.'

'They're not?'

'No. All the crows did was bookend a horrific experience. They're not the harbingers of doom your subconscious thinks they are.'

'What are they?'

'You're a fighter, Washington. It's what you do. What you've *always* done, I suspect. The truth is your North Star. It's what guides you and it's what makes you keep on fighting against injustice.' She tapped the file on the table. 'And because you're a fighter, it's how you chose to deal with what you've been through. Your subconscious needed a fight and it chose crows as the battleground.'

'I hardly think—'

She held up her hand to stop him. 'We've already established your involvement in the case would have happened regardless of you being present when the first victim was discovered. And I think we've agreed that the security services had almost certainly been after Tilly for a while.'

Poe nodded. He didn't know why. Being analysed so easily was an unsettling experience. Anger had always been the fuel that burned his engine, but having that stripped down to its component parts was unnerving.

'In your mind, beating the crows means beating your PTSD,' Doctor Lang continued. 'Nathan Rose committing suicide in front of you. Being forced to watch the tapes of those young men being stoned and murdered. Discovering the awful truth about the Bowman family. Being there when Bethany murdered Eve and Aaron. Almost being murdered yourself. In your mind, the crows represent it all.'

'OK, how do I fight . . . how do I *manage* this?'

'Together,' she said. 'We manage this together. It isn't a black hole: it won't pull you in, not unless you let it. The mind is resilient, yours more than most, I suspect, and, with a bit of help, it won't be long before you can remember what happened without *reliving* what happened. When that happens, the nightmares will stop.'

'When do we start?' Poe asked.

She smiled without showing her teeth. 'We already have.'

'Oh . . . that's good then.'

'I'd like to see you again in a fortnight, Washington. Will the training unit let you have the time off?'

'I'm not with the training unit any more. I had a . . . disagreement with one of the other instructors. As soon as I recovered from my injuries, he found a reason to move me on.'

'What are you doing now?'

'Officially? I help tackle the threat of drugs before they reach the UK.'

'And unofficially?'

'I work with some misfits from the Border Force on the stupidest pilot scheme in the history of law enforcement. We go out to sea on the smallest, leakiest tug in the Royal Navy fleet and do intelligence-led stop and searches of fishing vessels. We board the boats and me and this bloke called Amer root through their catch to see if they're smuggling drugs.' He held up his hands. 'It's why my hands are so badly scratched – the fins and teeth on some of those fish are razor sharp. And it's why, no matter how long I shower, or how hard I scrub myself, I always smell of halibut.'

'That seems a . . . waste of your talents.'

'I suspect Tilly's new employers would prefer it if I quit,' Poe said. 'Wasting my time and talents is probably the point.'

'And Tilly? How is she coping?'

Poe shrugged. 'I think she must be somewhere she's not allowed her phone; there are huge blocks of time when I don't hear from her at all. I rarely speak to her; I see her even less.'

'And you have no idea what it is she does?'

'She won't tell me. Won't even tell me where she's based.'

'Is she happy?'

'No,' Poe said. 'I don't think she is. I thinks she misses her friends and I think she misses the work we did.'

'And Alice? How is she coping?'

'She's doing OK,' Poe said. 'We keep in touch.'

'It must have been a shock for her to realise her best friend was alive after all. And that she'd just murdered her brother and sister and was about to murder a police officer.'

Poe said nothing.

'It was just as well she turned up when she did,' Doctor Lang continued. 'I doubt we'd be having this discussion if she hadn't.'

'It wasn't Alice who stopped Bethany from murdering me, Doctor Lang,' Poe said quietly.

'It wasn't? But you said it was.'

'No. I said I *thought* it was Alice. But I was concussed, and Bethany had made me wear that hood. Alice was still at the Children of Job compound, forty miles away. She was nowhere near that basement.'

'Who stopped Bethany, Washington? Tell me who saved your life.'

Poe's eyes flattened. His expression hardened.

'You did,' he said.

Chapter 131

Doctor Lang folded her arms and examined Poe carefully, her eyes radiated an intense, uncompromising intelligence. She didn't look surprised at what he had said; resigned, maybe. Eventually she sighed and said, 'I was afraid something like this might happen.'

'Something like what?' Poe said.

'You're a fighter, Washington. We've already established that. But we haven't yet discussed the other part of you. The part of you that wants to hunt, that *needs* to hunt. It's what makes you the detective your friends and colleagues say you are. But it also makes you vulnerable during periods of inactivity.' She paused a couple of ticks then added, 'Periods of inactivity like, how did you put it, going out to sea on the "smallest, leakiest tug in the Royal Navy fleet"? Rooting around in fish guts instead of hunting the men and women who would hunt us.'

'You think hunting serial killers is my seven per cent solution?' Poe said, referencing Sherlock Holmes's famous battle against cocaine addiction.

'Do you not?'

Poe shrugged. 'I've never thought about it that way,' he admitted.

'And without it, you're lost, Washington. You say it was me who stopped Bethany killing you, *I* say you're in the middle of a psychotic episode.'

Poe didn't respond.

'Do you know what a non-bizarre delusion is, Washington?'

'I don't.'

'It's the misinterpretation of an experience or perception that, while untrue, *isn't* out of the realms of possibility. I suspect there's an imbalance of neurotransmitters in your brain, almost certainly caused by your concussion. It's nothing to worry about, but it will need medical intervention. I'll speak to your GP and see if we can't get you on the right neuroleptics.'

'I'm not ill, Doctor Lang,' Poe said.

'You *are* ill, Washington. Your subconscious has invented a scenario where the case isn't closed yet. It means that, in your mind at least, you aren't "benched", as you called it earlier; you're still on an active case. You're still chasing leads, you're still talking to suspects, you're still *hunting*.'

'I'm not ill,' Poe repeated.

'What seems most plausible to you, Washington? Someone you met for the first time today is secretly involved in a case that you say yourself ended months ago, or the combination of your head injury, the trauma you have been through and the grief of losing the job you loved has caused you to suffer delusions? You're an intelligent man, Washington. Tell me what you think is most likely.'

'This isn't the first time we've met, Doctor Lang.'

'You have me at a disadvantage then,' she said gently, 'because I don't remember you at all. This is all part of your delusion, Washington. You must see that.'

Poe said nothing.

'OK, I'll play along for now. Tell me where we met for the first time.'

Poe gestured around the doctor's office they were sitting in. 'I first *saw* Doctor Clara Lang in here,' he said.

'In here?' she replied woodenly.

'Yes,' Poe said. 'This isn't the first time we've done this.'

Chapter 132

Doctor Lang studied Poe with unwavering attention, her eyes locked on his like a magnet. She stayed like that for thirty seconds. No one likes being put under the microscope and he squirmed in his seat accordingly.

'How long have you felt this way?' she said eventually.

'You don't believe me,' Poe said.

'That's because it's not *believable*, Washington. It isn't real; it's just a figment of your imagination.' She sighed, then added, 'Look, this isn't a sectionable delusion, Washington, as I don't believe you present a danger to yourself or others. But you *are* very ill. I'm going to recommend you take some time off, and when you return to work I think your employers need to find a more suitable role for a man of your talents and . . . disposition.'

Poe nodded as if he had expected her to say this. 'Look around,' he said. 'Does any of this look right to you?'

Doctor Lang frowned a little. 'What do you mean? I don't understand.'

'Have you ever seen a doctor's office like this?'

'I told you, it's not mine,' she replied. She glanced around, humouring him. 'Like I said earlier, it's being refurbished; hence it's a bit barer than it would normally be. Other than that, it looks perfectly normal.'

'Does it?' Poe asked.

'It does.'

'There's a massive table between us, Doctor Lang. You're an experienced therapist; is it considered good practice to have a table this size between you and the patient?'

'Of course not, but as I've told you, this isn't my off—'

'In fact, another word for this desk might be "barrier".'

Doctor Lang's brow furrowed.

'I'm sure there's a—'

'And have you noticed how heavy these chairs are? They're not bolted down, but I know I'm not strong enough to pick one up and throw it.'

'This is a psychiatric hospital, Washington,' she said, on surer footing. 'Occasionally patients get upset. Heavy furniture, the big desk, this is all about staff and patient safety.'

'And I'm sure that's exactly what they have on the secure wards,' Poe said. 'Except, according to you, we're *not* on a secure ward, we're on an administrative wing.'

She frowned a bit more. 'I'm sure there's an explanation. Perhaps it's occasionally used to treat patients.'

Poe nodded. 'OK then,' he said. 'Think about this: in the four hours we've been here, tea and biscuits have been brought in three times.'

'We *have* been doing a lot of talking.'

'But did you notice that the tea has always been lukewarm? Warm enough to drink, but nowhere near hot enough to scald if thrown.'

'That's absurd.'

'The drinks came in disposable cups and the biscuits were served on a paper plate. Sugar lumps, so we didn't need a spoon. Hell, even your file's treasury clips are made of plastic, not metal.'

Doctor Lang didn't respond.

'And now consider me,' Poe continued.

'You?'

'When I first sat down, you said you didn't have a pen. You asked to borrow mine and I told you I'd forgotten to bring one. You asked if it was unusual for a police officer to be without a pen. And I said I'm—'

'—An unusual police officer,' she cut in. 'It was only a couple of hours ago, Washington.'

'Thing is, Doctor Lang, I wasn't *allowed* to bring in a pen. I don't have a pen, you don't have a pen, and when you looked in the desk drawers to borrow a pen, what did you find?'

'There weren't any,' she mumbled.

'Are you allowed to carry pens on the high-security wards, Doctor Lang?'

'No.'

'And why not?'

'Because they can be used as weapons.'

'Because they can be used as weapons,' Poe agreed. 'As can spectacles, which is why I don't have my reading glasses with me. I have no keys, not even my wallet.'

'Your wallet . . . ?'

'Sharpened credit cards, Doctor Lang. In fact, if you look around this room you'll see there's nothing that could potentially be used as a weapon.'

'That still doesn't mean—'

Poe knew people would be gathering on the other side of the door, ready to rush in if needed. 'One final question before we move on,' he said. 'You've worked on secure wards for years?'

'I have.'

'Then you'll know what the number-one cause of non-natural inpatient deaths is.'

'Suicide,' she said automatically.

'Now, tell me what you're wearing.'

'What *I'm* wearing?'

'Yes.'

'It's a dress.'

'Describe it, please.'

'I really don't see where this is going, Washington.'

'Humour me,' Poe said.

She looked down at her green dress. It was sleeveless, sturdily quilted and made of Cordura, a material ten times stronger than denim. It was tear-proof, fire-proof and so thick it couldn't be folded or rolled into cords. The blood drained from her face as she understood the relevance.

'Yes, that *is* a noose-proof anti-suicide smock, Doctor Lang,' Poe said gently. 'Now do you understand?'

Tears welled up in her eyes. She wiped them away with the back of her hand and nodded. 'I'm not a therapist here, am I?' she said, her voice no more than a whisper.

'No, Doctor Lang, you're not,' Poe said. 'You're a patient.'

Chapter 133

'I don't understand,' Doctor Lang said. 'Until I read your file I'd never even *heard* of Bethany Bowman. Yet you seem to think I was the one who stopped her from killing you.'

'You did.'

'Are you saying I've blocked it all out?'

'What do you remember of your childhood, Doctor Lang?'

She shrugged. 'It was nothing special. My parents are English, but I grew up in Mindelheim. It's about sixty miles west of Munich.'

'In Bavaria?'

'Yes. You've been?'

'Not there. But I spent time in Germany when I was in the army.'

'It's a beautiful town,' she said. 'Lots of tourists, a bit like your Lake District. They're both a curse and a blessing. Can't live with them, can't survive without them.'

'You don't have a German accent though.'

'Like I said, my parents are both English. They're both teachers.'

'But you grew up around Germans. You went to school with German children. Surely you should have a bit of an accent?'

'I'm bilingual,' she said. 'My German accent is flawless, I'm told.'

Poe nodded as if that explained it. 'Tell me about your childhood,' he said.

'I studied psychology at the Ludwig Maximilian University of Munich then went on to specialise in psychotraumatology. Unlike CBT, psychotraumatology isn't covered by German mandatory healthcare insurance. As a result, patients there can have trouble accessing good-quality care.'

'No, Doctor Lang. That's what you did in your late teens and early twenties. I want to hear about your *childhood*.'

'But . . . I've just told you. I grew up in Mindelheim.'

'Describe a specific childhood memory.'

'Drinking rum and hot chocolate with my friends after we'd been skiing.'

'That sounds like a teenage memory. Tell me about your tenth birthday party. That's always a big thing for a child. I bet your parents made a fuss.'

'They did,' she nodded.

'What type of birthday cake did you have? Was it chocolate? I bet it was. The Germans make a good chocolate cake.'

Doctor Lang frowned. 'I . . . I can't remember,' she said after a minute.

'Did you have a party? You must be able to remember that.'

'I can't,' she said, her voice low and uncertain. She bit her lip and clenched her jaw. She began balling and unballing her fists. 'Why can't I remember my childhood, Washington? What's happening to me?'

'You can't remember your childhood, Doctor Lang, because something terrible happened. Something so horrific you weren't safe in your own head. So your mind used an extraordinary, but entirely normal, coping strategy to survive: it completely blocked out the first fifteen years of your life.'

'I was Bethany's friend when I was younger? Is that why I turned up in Eve's basement?'

'No.'

'What are you saying?'

'You know what I'm saying, Doctor Lang.'

'Tell me anyway,' she said, her voice hollow and empty.

'You didn't know Bethany Bowman,' Poe said. 'You *are* Bethany Bowman.'

Chapter 134

'I take it you know what dissociative identity disorder is?' Poe said.

'It's a formally recognised psychiatric diagnosis,' Doctor Lang said mechanically. 'The patient must show at least two identities, which routinely take control of the individual's behaviour. Almost without exception, patients have had significant attachment-based trauma, usually occurring in their child . . .'

She didn't finish.

'Yes, Doctor Lang,' Poe said. 'I'm told most DID has its genesis in childhood, and although everyone has a unique experience, it often manifests as competing and conflicting identities.'

She shook her head. Poe wasn't sure if she was denying what he'd said, or just clearing her mind. 'This doesn't make sense,' she said.

'Doesn't it?' Poe replied. 'Because it makes perfect sense to me. Your parents hated you, then they sacrificed you. Your sister betrayed you and your brother tried to stone you to death. Your biological father slit your throat. I'd say taking a break from being Bethany was an entirely rational choice, wouldn't you?'

'But DID isn't how it's portrayed in the movies,' she protested. 'It's never the case that one personality is evil while the other is kind and gentle. The characteristics of the separate personalities already have to exist.'

'No one is suggesting Bethany is evil, Doctor Lang.'

'But she murdered people. She *tortured* people.'

'Bethany's a survivor. She's fierce and protective and she loves you very much. In times of great stress or danger, dissociation is triggered. Doctor Clara Lang disappears and Bethany Bowman the survivor takes control. We think up until recently you were, as you've said, living a peaceful life in Germany. You were practising as a trauma therapist and you had put Bethany's experiences behind you. You were happy. But something happened. Something happened and it was on the news. You must have seen it in Germany and, for reasons you probably didn't understand, it made you anxious. Scared even. And when you're scared or anxious your dissociation is triggered. And Bethany doesn't feel scared, Bethany *acts*. She does what she has to do to keep Clara safe. We've spoken to the people you believed to be your parents and they told us that you simply disappeared one day. The German police have been able to track your movements though. They know the trains you took and they know the shop where you legally purchased your stun gun. They know the ferry you took at Rotterdam. We were able to track you from Hull to Cumbria. When Superintendent Nightingale's police officers turned up at Eve's house, they didn't find Bethany in the basement, they found Doctor Clara Lang. The danger had passed; there was no one left to punish. You had dissociated back.'

She eyed him suspiciously but offered no commentary.

'I had thought there were two people arguing about what to do with me in Eve's basement, but I was wrong; there was just the one. One person, *two* identities. And for a while your two identities had argued about what to do with me. Bethany thought killing me was the best way to protect you, but Doctor Clara Lang is too good a person to allow that to happen. Eventually she wrested back control from Bethany, which is why it was Doctor Lang the police officers found when they arrived.'

'And I'm sure you believe—'

'And where we are now,' Poe continued, waving his arms around, 'this is so Doctor Lang can feel safe. Not just this office, the whole corridor. Because when you don't feel safe, well, that's when bad things happen.'

'Bad things?' she asked, her voice hoarse.

'Four months ago, Doctor Clara Lang was eating her lunch. She was, as she always did, keeping herself to herself. Not bothering anyone. A woman called Jeanie didn't like that. She took your pudding.'

'What happened?'

'Bethany took Jeanie's eyes. She grabbed her by the hair and jammed her thumbs into her eye sockets. Pushed them all the way up to the knuckle. A minute later Doctor Lang was back. I've seen the CCTV footage; she seemed confused by all the commotion. She had no idea what had just happened. You've been on multi-professional continuous observation ever since – that's when you are kept within eyesight of at least two staff members at all times, and one of them must be within arm's length – and you're no longer allowed to mix with other patients.'

There was a long delay before she responded.

'There must be another explanation,' she said. 'I accept I must not be well, but if I was the one the police found, how do you know Bethany hadn't disappeared somewhere? How can you be sure *I'm* Bethany? Even if you've matched my fingerprints to the clasp knife Eve framed Bethany with, I could have known the Bowmans. Who's to say I hadn't touched the knife at some point?'

'You remember me saying Tilly had put a photograph of four-teen-year-old Bethany through her age progression program?'

She nodded.

'And when Israel Cobb, your father, saw this likeness, he imme-diately came clean about the mercy chair? Tried to convince us you had died in it?'

She nodded again.

'May I?' Poe said, pointing to the file on the table.

'Be my guest.'

He started flipping through the documents. What he was look-ing for was at the back.

'I thought you hadn't seen what was inside?' she asked.

'Actually, I said I didn't need to see what was inside, not that I *hadn't*. This is the sixth time I've sat down with the most dangerous patient in this hospital, and I know what's in the file because I wrote most of it.' Poe found what he was looking for. He unfastened the plastic treasury clips and detached it. He slid it across the table. 'Does this look like anyone you know, Doctor Lang?'

She picked up the age-progressed image of Bethany Bowman

and studied it. A flush started in the nape of her neck and travelled up to her face.

'This isn't proof,' she said. 'These programs are open to interpretation.'

'They are,' he nodded. 'Tilly's, not so much, but I take your point.' He reached into his pocket and removed a rolled-up piece of paper. He held it in the air so the people observing the session through the covert CCTV cameras could see. 'I haven't told you about this,' he said loudly. 'But I want to use it.'

'What is it?' a voice said through an equally covert speaker.

'A mirror.'

'A mirror, absolutely not! Move away from the patient please, Sergeant Poe.'

Poe didn't budge. 'It's safe,' he called out.

A pause, then, 'How?'

'It's just a reflective sheet. A flexible one with an adhesive back. I've fixed it to some A4 paper I took from the work printer.' Poe didn't wait for permission. He unrolled his makeshift mirror and passed it to Doctor Lang. 'You want proof,' he said. 'Here's your proof.'

'I don't understand,' she said. 'I know what I look like.'

'Do you?'

'Of course I do.'

'Have a look then.'

She did. 'I agree, there *is* a likeness to the image Tilly produced,' she said eventually. 'But this isn't proof. If we walked down the high street we'd see half-a-dozen people who look like this.'

'Possibly,' Poe said. 'But I don't want you to look at your face.'

'You don't?'

'No. I want you to look at your neck.'

Confused, she angled the mirror down.

And saw the scar that ran from ear to ear.

Chapter 135

'That's the scar Israel Cobb gave you,' Poe said. 'From the cut that convinced Cornelius Green you were dead.'

Doctor Lang stared at the mirror in horror. Poe had seen the scar eight times now – seven times in this office and once in Eve's basement – and he still marvelled at the fact she had survived. They had spoken to the doctor who had saved her life and he'd confirmed what Bethany had told him in the basement; that if the blade on Israel Cobb's Stanley knife had protruded just one more millimetre the wound would have been fatal.

'You *are* Bethany, Doctor Lang,' Poe said softly. 'But that's OK, as it's Bethany I want to speak to now. Would that be possible?'

Doctor Lang ignored his question. Still glued to the mirror, she said, 'All this has been a game? You faked PTSD to win my trust?'

'I'm not that good an actor,' Poe said. 'My PTSD is real; my nightmares are real. What we go through together is *real*. Director of Intelligence Edward van Zyl did order me to have counselling. But you've got a flavour of me now and you'll probably agree that if I'm told to do something, I'll kick back against it. Even when it's against my own interests.'

'So why . . . ?'

'My brilliant fiancée, actually. She knew I'd either refuse to go to counselling, or I would mess about. She suggested this.'

'And what's this?'

'You were a superb trauma therapist, Doctor Lang,' Poe said. 'And who knows, maybe you can be again. And because you would only speak to your doctors and nurses as Doctor Lang, they had to pretend to be your patient. But you're far too experienced for that and you saw through what they were doing every time. Your therapy wasn't working. So Estelle said that if Doctor Lang wanted a patient, why not give her a real one? Consequently, once a month, in this carefully managed room, I tell you my story, and because it's also *your* story, we talk and we sit here and we remember together.'

'But I *don't* remember, Washington.'

'You will,' Poe said. 'And now I'd like to speak to Bethany, please.'

'My name is Doctor Clara Lang. I'm thirty years old and my parents are Philip and Gwen Lang. I live in Germany.'

'No. Your name is Bethany Bowman, illegitimate child of Grace Bowman and Israel Cobb. Half-sister to Eve Bowman and half-sister to Aaron Bowman. You lived in Keswick until you were fourteen and after you had survived the mercy chair you were spirited away to Germany and placed with a family there.'

'No!'

'Yes,' Poe insisted.

'Please, I want you to stop.'

'Not until I speak to Bethany.'

'But I don't know anyone called Bethany!' Doctor Lang cried.

'Yes, you do,' Poe said. 'And I want to speak to her.'

'You can't!'

'I must.'

Her eyes glazed over. Only for a second, but Poe had been watching out for it. He braced himself.

'You-you-you . . .' she stuttered.

'You what, Doctor Lang?'

'You BAD BISCUIT!'

Chapter 136

Bethany Bowman lunged across the table, hands outstretched, aiming for Poe's eyes. He didn't move a muscle. He had the first time. The first time Bethany had gone for him he'd flinched so sharply he'd hurt his neck. This time he was expecting it.

The tether around Bethany's waist, considered bad practice in psychiatric care, but the only way the hospital could get insurance for Poe's sessions, held fast. Bethany jerked backwards like she'd pulled a parachute ripcord. She bounced back into her seat. Immediately got up and tried to attack him again, hands out in front as if she was reaching for the sun.

'Bethany, sit down!' Poe said. 'If you don't, they'll come for you.'

But she was too far gone. Doctor Lang had disappeared completely and Poe knew she would have no recollection of this. Wouldn't remember the session they'd had, wouldn't remember dissociating to Bethany. All that was left now was rage. Snarling, spitting, rage. Poe stood so the orderlies could pump her full of rapid tranquilisation. Take her, drooling and semi-conscious, back to her room.

When she woke she would be Doctor Lang again.

A group of burly orderlies entered the room. They weren't scared but they were definitely wary. With well-rehearsed moves they controlled the screaming, thrashing woman and removed the tether. Once she was out of the chair they got her ready for the doctor, an orderly on each limb, another controlling her head.

Poe sighed. He'd hoped they'd make a breakthrough today. Previous attacks had happened much earlier in the session. The doctor entered the room. He was called Richard Gray and he was holding a pre-prepared syringe. Poe knew it was full of lorazepam and it would knock out Bethany in seconds. This would be the sixth time he'd seen Doctor Gray use it. He pushed aside her anti-suicide smock and readied the needle.

'Wait!' Bethany cried out. She struggled against the orderlies and managed to twist her face free so she was facing Poe. 'There's something I have to know!'

'Who am I speaking to?' he said.

'Doctor Clara Lang, of course.'

There was a stunned silence. This was the fastest Bethany had ever dissociated back to Doctor Lang. It usually took hours. Doctor Gray lowered his needle.

'What is it, Doctor Lang?' Poe asked.

'Did Tilly ever go to tea with Bugger Rumble?'

Poe smiled. 'Ah well, that's a whole other story. Maybe we can talk about that next time?'

Chapter 137

'You did well in there, Poe,' Doyle said.

'That was exceptional,' Doctor Gray said, nodding in agreement. 'Genuine progress. That was the first time Doctor Lang's been able to remember anything about your sessions after dissociating back from Bethany.'

'I'll tell Bugger he's been helping in her therapy,' Poe said. 'He'll be pleased.'

'The two identities are finally starting to bleed into each other,' Doctor Gray continued. 'If this carries on we should be able to draw them both out in a safe environment.'

'Is she getting better?' a small voice asked.

Poe turned. 'I'm sorry, Alice, I didn't see you there. Were you in the observation room?'

Alice nodded.

Of course she was, Poe thought. Alice came to every session and she spoke to Bethany's doctors every week. She was Bethany's designated advocate and she had moved house to be closer to the hospital. These things convinced Poe that Bethany would eventually get better.

'Certainly, today was a step in the right direction,' Doctor Gray said.

'Will she ever get out?'

'If she's well enough. It might not be for years, but yes, I think she will be discharged to prison at some point. After that it'll be up to the parole board.'

'Good,' Alice said. She turned to Poe. 'And you'll keep coming, won't you, Sergeant Poe?'

'For as long as it takes, Alice,' he replied. 'Too many people have let Bethany down. I won't be one of them.'

'Thank you. And how are your nightmares?'

'Not great,' Poe said. He looked at Doyle. 'But I have a good support network. I'll be fine.'

'I'm glad.'

Alice said her goodbyes and trundled off down the corridor. She stopped at the secure doors and waited to be buzzed through.

'Anything from Tilly while I was in there?' Poe asked Doyle.

'Sorry, Poe. I sent her a text reminding her there was another session today, but she hasn't replied yet. Stephanie called to see how it went. She'll ring you tonight.'

'Tilly's probably busy,' he said, trying not to sound too miserable. He missed Bradshaw terribly but was trying to put on a brave face. It didn't fool Doyle for a second, but he thought she appreciated the effort.

He glanced down the hospital corridor, to the fob-controlled navy double doors. Bethany's room was on the other side. She'd be sleeping now but would wake soon. The bravest woman he'd ever met. She had survived hell and had come out the other side punching and kicking.

Maybe he would always see crows when he closed his eyes, but however bad his nightmares got, Poe knew one thing: they could never be as bad as the things Bethany Bowman saw when the shadows lengthened. If she could survive the mercy chair, Poe could damn well cope with missing his friend and having a crappy job.

He linked his arm through Doyle's, smiled and said, 'Let's go home, Estelle.'

Acknowledgements

The Mercy Chair is arguably the darkest book in the Poe and Tilly series to date. And when I submitted an early draft to my agent, David Headley, it was a whole lot darker. Like *really* dark. Usually when I send David the new Poe, I just want it submitted to my editor. But this time I wanted, and *needed*, his editorial input. He helped me find the balance. And this book had to be balanced. The light and the dark had to cancel each other out. So the first person I'm thanking is my friend, David Headley.

My wife, Joanne, who reads the first draft and the last draft and makes suggestions I listen to. And yes, I know, listening to your suggestions is not the same as acting on those suggestions, but I'm trying . . . Thank you for putting up with me.

I need to thank my long-suffering beta readers next – Roger Lytollis, Simon Cowdroy and Angie Morrison (I've listed them in descending order of how many horses they own). As always, your input was irrelevant, unasked for and unappreciated . . .

Thank you to my editor, Krystyna Green (I can't believe they're still letting us do this, Krystyna), my line editor, Martin Edwards, my copy-editor, Howard Watson, my desk editors, Amanda Keats and Rebecca Sheppard, and my proofreader, Joan Deitch. Each one of you takes credit for making the book incrementally better.

Sean Garrehy gets a special mention for consistently raising the bar when it comes to the Poe and Tilly covers. The way you listen to my suggestions then sensibly ignore them is probably why the series is doing as well as it is.

Beth Wright and Brionee Fenlon, because who has the bandwidth to remember the difference between publicity and marketing, have made sure the books have been visible since *The Puppet Show*.

There is no doubt in my mind that so many people read about Poe and Tilly's ridiculous adventures because of the work you do. Thank you.

Thanks to everyone at Little, Brown. It's a privilege being published by you guys.

And finally, thank you to all the readers, booksellers, librarians, reviewers and bloggers – a book isn't a book until it leaves my desk and hits yours. You guys rock.

Let's do this again sometime.

Mike

Author Q&A:
M.W. Craven on Poe and Tilly

What are the origins of Poe and Tilly? How did they come into being?

When I signed with my agent in 2015, he asked me to write a new series but to keep it set in Cumbria. I took the bare bones of what would have been the plot for the third DI Avison Fluke book and reimagined it as the first in a new series. This would eventually become *The Puppet Show*. All the way through the early drafts of *The Puppet Show* (or *Welcome to the Puppet Show* as it was called then) I had PLACEHOLDER NAME for the main character as I hadn't thought of his name yet. And Tilly Bradshaw (who was initially called Tilly Dowbakin) was far more streetwise than she is now. It wasn't until I laughed at something in the *Washington Post* that inspiration struck. This person, who has asked to remain nameless, asked me what I was laughing at and when I told them, they said, 'What's the Washington *Poe*?' Like a bolt of lightning, I had a name I loved and one I thought could carry a series. The problem I had was that Poe was Cumbrian and I needed to explain away his name's provenance. To resolve this, I ended up rewriting *The Puppet Show* and giving Poe a horrific backstory. The character became a lot darker than I'd initially written him. To counterbalance that I made Tilly a lot lighter. Her naivety juxtaposed against his cynicism perfectly. And the result was a *lot* of fun to write.

How do you break up an average working day when you are writing? Is there a structure or detailed plan to everything?

I've been a full-time author since 2015, so I've become disciplined when it comes to ensuring I can get my contracted novels to my agent then on to my editor by the deadline given. I start thinking about the next book while I'm writing the current one. This is handy as it means I can seed in things that might be needed in the following year's. I kind of plan the next novel by opening a Word doc and doing three sections. The first is what the crime is. Who did it and why. The *why* is important. The second section is where I drop Poe and Tilly into the mix and jot down notes on how they might solve it. The third – and most important – section is a series of bullet points in which I list the key events in the order I want to write them. I keep adding and taking away from this live document until I'm ready to start. I then highlight each bullet point as the scene is written. Of course, as Mike Tyson once said, everyone has a plan until they're punched in the face – and I'm no different. Where I think the book might go is rarely where it does, but it's somewhere to start . . .

As for my day, if it's a usual one-book-a-year year, I will work Monday to Friday and try to get down at least 1000 words. I used to start the new book on 1 December and knew that I would then be ready to submit late summer/early autumn the following year. Because I had to spend time crafting the two books in the Koenig series the timescales have shifted and I now start the new book on 1 May.

Do you have a favourite book in the series – and why?

That's a tough one to answer. I used to say it was *Black Summer* because it had *that* opening chapter (still the one that elicits the most visceral feedback), but I think my favourite is now *The Mercy Chair.* My writing is better than it was in 2018, it deals with real-world issues. I also think the major twists are well-hidden and one of the characters was so much fun to write that she'll be a series regular going forwards. Also, my agent had to go for a walk after he'd finished reading, something he's never had to do before . . .

Outside of Poe and Tilly, *Night Watch* by Terry Pratchett is my favourite book by my favourite author. It's perfect. I love all Terry's books, but I particularly enjoy the City Watch series, of which *Night Watch* is the sixth. It's funny and moving with an incredible cast of characters. Satire at its finest. Readers of Terry may recognise certain attributes that Sam Vimes and Washington Poe share. A healthy disregard for authority. A loyal team. A fondness for food that might not be that healthy . . .

My favourite childhood book is *Watership Down* by Richard Adams. There's something magical about the world-building and the rabbit mythology that Adams created. It's very special and, like *Night Watch*, is one of the few books I try to reread every year.

In *The Mercy Chair* we are shown a more vulnerable side to Poe, as he speaks with his psychiatrist. Was it hard to write in this different facet into his character?

Poe does show vulnerability in *The Mercy Chair* – although Poe being Poe, he initially tries to deal with it using sarcasm and humour – but Doctor Lang quickly calls him to task. It was tricky as he'd never really shown this side before, but I thought it was important for him to have a very human, very emotional response to the events he'd been through. For him to have shrugged it off as if nothing had happened wouldn't have been fair to readers of the series. Showing him struggle made him seem more real to me. The events of *The Mercy Chair* change Poe for ever.

***The Third Light*, which publishes in 2025, will be the seventh book in this series. Going forwards, do you have any big surprises in store for the reader?**

Because of the events of *The Mercy Chair*, the unit Poe and Tilly worked for has been all but disbanded. Poe is still seeing Doctor Lang, he still has PTSD and he still has the punishment job he was given at the end of *The Mercy Chair*. But, when a sniper starts killing people at random, Poe, Tilly and Flynn are called upon once more . . . I'm describing *The Third Light* as the transition book and although I'm not saying why yet, it *will* usher in a new direction for the series. Oh, and if that doesn't tempt you, there's the will Poe/ won't Poe get married to Estelle issue to address (which includes Tilly's best man speech at the rehearsal dinner), the introduction of a major character from another series, as well as Poe being tricked into dressing up like *Doctor Who* . . .

CRIME AND THRILLER FAN?

CHECK OUT **THECRIMEVAULT.COM**

The online home of exceptional crime fiction

KEEP YOURSELF
IN SUSPENSE

Sign up to our newsletter for regular recommendations,
competitions and exclusives at **www.thecrimevault.com/connect**

Follow us

 @TheCrimeVault

 /TheCrimeVault

for all the latest news